Alison Roberts has been lucky enough to
live in the South of France for several years
recently, but is now back in her home country of
New Zealand. She is also lucky enough to write
for the Mills & Boon Medical line. A primary
school teacher in a former life, she later became
a qualified paramedic. She loves to travel and
dance, drink champagne and spend time with her
daughter and her friends. Alison is the author of
over one hundred books!

Also by Alison Roberts

One Weekend in Prague
The Doctor's Christmas Homecoming
Fling with the Doc Next Door
Healed by a Mistletoe Kiss

Morgan Family Medics miniseries

Secret Son to Change His Life
How to Rescue the Heart Doctor

Paramedics and Pups miniseries

The Italian, His Pup and Me

Discover more at millsandboon.co.uk.

FORBIDDEN NIGHTS WITH THE PARAMEDIC

ALISON ROBERTS

REBEL DOCTOR'S BABY SURPRISE

ALISON ROBERTS

MILLS & BOON

First published in Great Britain 2024
by Mills & Boon, an imprint of HarperCollins*Publishers* Ltd,
1 London Bridge Street, London, SE1 9GF

www.harpercollins.co.uk

HarperCollins*Publishers* Macken House, 39/40 Mayor Street Upper,
Dublin 1, D01 C9W8, Ireland

ISBN: 978-0-263-32152-4

03/24

FORBIDDEN NIGHTS WITH THE PARAMEDIC

ALISON ROBERTS

MILLS & BOON

PROLOGUE

THEY STOOD, shoulder to shoulder, in matching tuxedos at the front of the church.

Three men.

Three brothers.

Born thirty-two years ago, within minutes of each other, there'd never been any doubt that they would be together in such a significant moment in all their lives when the first of them, Michael, had decided to break their pact to remain bachelors for as long as possible.

Edward had come all the way from Australia, meeting James in London, where they'd both caught a train up to Aberdeen. It wasn't the town they'd grown up in but it was where their older sister, Ella, had chosen to make her life with the man she loved and that was close enough to a home base for three brothers who had never been ready to settle anywhere. Or with any*one*.

Until now.

Mick turned his head again, hoping to catch a glimpse of his bride, Juliana, preparing to walk down the aisle. His brothers instinctively turned as well, but the vestibule was still clearly empty. Instead, they shared a smile with Ella, who was sitting in the front pew, holding her husband Logan's hand.

Turning back to face the front, Eddie and James shared a glance that was brief but still spoke volumes.

They weren't completely comfortable being here. Sure, Mick was madly in love, but deciding to get married felt like a decision that had been rushed. A shotgun wedding?

What had happened to that pact they'd made after they'd lost both their parents when they were only teenagers—that life was too short and that they had to make the most of it—so, alongside an exciting career, they needed to cram in as many adventures and beautiful women as they could find? Just because this particular gorgeous girlfriend, whom Mick had met in Brazil on one of his recent deployments with *Médecins Sans Frontières,* was pregnant, it didn't mean they had to instantly commit to being together for the rest of their lives, did it?

Something didn't feel quite right.

And it seemed as if the brothers' disquiet was spreading throughout the small congregation in this church that was divided into a section with Michael's friends and family on one side and a few young Brazilian people on the other. Ella glanced at her watch and then whispered something to Logan. More than one of the guests on the bride's side of the church were turning their heads in the direction of the vestibule and one of them got up to walk outside, texting on his phone as he went.

The woman playing an organ began another rendition of Beethoven's 'Moonlight Sonata' and Mick's body language advertised an increasing tension.

'Brides love to be late,' Eddie reassured him quietly. 'It makes people even happier to see them walk down the aisle.'

Someone did appear but it wasn't the bride. It was the

minister, who came through a side door close to where the brothers were standing. He smiled at Mick.

'Could you come with me for a moment, Michael?'

'What's wrong? Oh, my God…has something happened to Juliana?'

The minister's smile looked frozen now. 'Come to the vestry so we can talk in private.'

Eddie and James shared another glance. Privacy was not an option. Something was going on and they were not going to leave their brother without support. Ella and Logan were already on their feet, also ready to follow the minister and Mick.

The young Brazilian man who'd left the church a few minutes earlier was in the vestry.

'I am Juliana's brother, Lucas,' he told them. 'I'm sorry, but she cannot be here, after all.'

'Is she all right?' Mick had gone very pale.

'She is good,' her brother replied. 'Not unwell in any way.'

'So why isn't she here?'

Eddie and James moved closer on either side of Mick. Close enough for their shoulders to be touching.

It was the minister who broke a rather awkward silence by clearing his throat. 'It appears that there is someone else involved who arrived from Brazil this morning. The father of the baby Juliana is carrying.'

'*I'm* the father.' Mick sounded bewildered. 'She told me.'

Lucas shook his head. 'No. She was pregnant before she went to the medical centre where she met you. To José. He did not want to acknowledge the baby but now he has changed his mind. And Juliana is still in love with him. They are on their way to the airport to return to Brazil.'

Ella and Logan looked at each other. Then they looked at Mick.

'Stay here,' Ella said gently. 'Eddie and Jimmy will stay with you until we've sorted everything and sent people home.'

An hour later the church was empty and the reception venue cancelled. Two hours after that, the brothers were in a hotel room and the first bottle of Scotch they'd ordered had just run dry.

'I'm calling room service,' Mick declared. 'We need another one of those.'

'Let's order dinner,' James suggested. 'Maybe some wine.'

'Champagne,' Mick muttered. His laughter held no amusement. 'Let's celebrate the fact I'm still single.'

'Hey, mate…' Eddie put his hand on Mick's shoulder. 'I know it hurts right now but you'll get past this. She wasn't the one for you.'

'Yeah…' James shook his head. 'Reckon you dodged a bullet there, bro. She was just using you to make her boyfriend jealous.'

'First and last time I'm getting married.' Mick shook his head. 'What was I thinking? We all know that life's too short and we need to live hard.' He raised his almost empty glass to his brothers. 'Take this as a warning and don't even go there.' He downed the last of his drink and grinned at them. 'Why settle down when there's a whole world to explore? And why buy a book when there's a whole library to enjoy?'

Eddie and James clinked glasses with him.

'Life *is* short.' Eddie nodded. 'Sometimes it's awesome and sometimes it sucks.' He draped his arms over each of his brother's shoulders. 'At least we've got each other. We can celebrate the awesome stuff and be there for each other for any of the bad stuff.'

The moment's silence following his words was verging on misty and Mick's voice was not much more than a whisper when he spoke.

'That's all we need,' he said.

CHAPTER ONE

Four years later...

'I'M NOT GOING BACK.' Edward Grisham shook his head slowly to underline his resolution. 'I can't.'

The man standing beside him in the hospital corridor was staring at him. Horrified.

'But you can't *not* go back,' he said. 'You've been here ever since the accident. Day and night. For *weeks*.'

'Exactly. That's why I can't go back.'

'So what am I supposed to tell your brother when he wakes up and you've just walked away?'

'I'm not leaving *Mick*, you idiot.' Eddie couldn't believe he'd been so misunderstood. 'I'm talking about not going back to *Australia*.'

'*Och*...' James Grisham tipped his head back as he blew out a breath that sounded relieved. 'Sorry...colour me sleep-deprived.' He threw a weary smile at Eddie. 'I've only had a couple of hours of shut-eye since a crazy busy night shift in Emergency last night. Let's go and get a coffee and you can fill me in properly.'

The route from the high dependency, acute section of this specialist spinal injury centre that was attached to Glasgow's Central Infirmary was all too familiar now but, on the plus side, they had discovered a small private courtyard not far from the cafeteria and, for a change, it was fine enough to get outside for a bit of fresh air. They ordered their coffee in takeaway paper cups and headed for a wooden bench that faced a small water feature in the courtyard garden.

'So…' James took another appreciative sip of the strongest coffee that had been on offer. 'You're going to leave your dream job with Air Rescue Australia?'

'Yep. Already have. I've got someone packing up my stuff to ship home as we speak.' He glanced at his watch. 'Or she will be when she wakes up and gets my message.'

'*She…?*' James raised an eyebrow. 'You leaving a girlfriend behind as well as your job?'

'Nah…that relationship was over a long time ago. Kylie and I are just friends now.'

'Keeping the pact, huh?'

Ah…that pact. The one that meant you never let a relationship get serious enough to interfere with what you wanted to do in your own life or worse, that would leave you in broken pieces when it crashed and burned—like Mick had been after he'd waited at the altar for a bride who was never going to arrive.

Not that any of the Grisham brothers had ever been disrespectful to women in any way. They'd always made it clear they weren't looking for anything serious. They made sure the chosen woman had as much fun as possible while they were enjoying their friendship with benefits and they almost always managed to leave before anyone got hurt and a continuing friendship—without the benefits—became unlikely.

The very idea of that pact, and the lifestyle that had fostered it, was becoming increasingly distasteful.

Eddie shrugged. 'I guess…'

'You don't sound too sure.'

Eddie rubbed his forehead with the pad of his middle finger. 'It's kind of changed everything, don't you think?'

'What? Mick's accident?'

'Yeah...'

'It's certainly changed everything for Mick.' James had to clear his throat as his voice roughened. 'What do you think the odds are that he'll be able to walk again?'

'You're the doctor, man. I'm only a paramedic. What do *you* think?'

The silence spoke volumes. Neither of them wanted to discuss a worst-case scenario. They'd approached this journey as a family, one step at a time, ever since they'd first heard the awful news of Mick's serious accident when he was hang-gliding from the rugged slopes of Ben Nevis in the Highlands of Scotland. Mick had been flown by helicopter to this hospital and specialist spinal unit for his initial assessment and treatment and the family had gathered. James had been closest, currently working in an Edinburgh hospital, and he'd been waiting at the unit when Mick had arrived. It had taken Eddie thirty-nine hours to get here from Sydney, Australia, but he hadn't left since—thanks to the accommodation provided for close family members on the grounds of this centre.

That had been six weeks ago.

'He's due for some luck,' James said quietly. 'He's had just about every complication available so far, hasn't he?'

'I thought the worst was going to be seeing him in ICU on a ventilator when I came straight from the airport. Nobody warned me that I needed to buckle up for the rollercoaster that we've been on since then.'

'I know. Two rounds of surgery. Spinal shock, those cardiac complications of arrhythmias and, I don't know about you, but I found the levels of hypotension scarier than I wanted to admit. And then there was the paralytic ileus, pneumonia, unmanageable pain…'

Eddie's smile was wry. 'And I'd been so relieved to hear that the injury was incomplete. That it was at a thoracic level so he hadn't lost any sensation or function in his arms or hands. That there was a possibility he might walk again.'

'It might not feel like it but it's still early days.' James took a last mouthful of coffee. 'It could be weeks before he completely recovers from the spinal shock and who knows how much residual inflammation is there from both the injury and the surgery. At least he's stable enough to be able to be moved to a rehab centre in Aberdeen. At least Ella and Logan won't have that long drive so they can visit more often. Mick adores Ella.'

Eddie could hear a new level of concern in his voice now.

'I'm worried about how flat he's been in the last couple of weeks,' James added quietly. 'He's hardly eating. And I think all this sleeping might be a way of avoiding talking to us.'

'I've thought that too,' Eddie agreed. 'It wouldn't be surprising to have a clinical depression setting in after the initial fight to stay alive is done and dusted.'

'He's certainly showing some symptoms of depression.'

Eddie sucked in a breath. 'If anyone can help, it'll be Ella.'

Ella was the older sister of the triplet brothers. A second mother to them when they were growing up who'd married the love of her life a few years ago and was living and working in Aberdeenshire. She was the obvious anchor point for the brother who was going to need so much support from his family for the foreseeable future so it had been an easy choice to pick a centre in Aberdeen for the next stage of Mick's recovery and rehabilitation.

'And you're going to be a whole lot closer too?' James crumpled his cup. 'That's...' He gave Eddie a soft punch on his upper arm. 'That's awesome news, bro. Will you go and stay with Ella? Will you look for work around Aberdeen?'

'Don't need to.' Eddie took a deep breath. 'It seems that the universe was waiting for me to get back home. I've got a job lined up with the Aberdeen Air Ambulance—Triple A as they apparently like to call it—not to be confused with an abdominal aortic aneurysm.' He smiled at James. 'I can even take over the lease of an apartment from the medic I'm replacing.'

'Sounds perfect.'

'Yeah...' Eddie got to his feet. 'Hope so...'

James followed him back inside, his frown advertising concern. 'You still don't sound too sure.'

Eddie shrugged. 'Like I said...everything's changed. It's like we've just been playing at being grown-ups until now. Going wherever we wanted in the world, doing the jobs that excited us the most.' He gave his brother a sideways glance that felt almost embarrassed. 'Making sure we stayed single so we could play the field like a bunch of irresponsible celebrities?' His sigh was heartfelt. 'Well... life got real the moment Mick fell out of the sky, didn't it?'

They walked back to Mick's room in silence but Eddie couldn't help thinking that he'd played a part in this whole catastrophe. He'd gone along with that pact that the three of them would live life to the fullest. That they'd avoid getting caught by a relationship or family responsibilities for as long as possible. That they'd grab every adventure they could in every part of their lives—their careers, their love lives and their hobbies.

Okay, Mick had taken it to a slightly higher level, but who could blame him after getting jilted like that and having to find a way through his heartbreak? It wasn't as if he or James had done anything to try and persuade him to tone it down. They'd listened to his stories about his work in dangerous places with *Médecins Sans Frontières*, and his narrow escapes with his extreme sports like scuba diving and hang-gliding, and…and they'd been happy that he was loving life again.

But then it had all come crashing down. For Mick most of all, of course, but it was affecting every sibling of this close-knit family.

Everything had changed for them all and Eddie knew that their carefree, playboy, adventurous approach to life was most definitely one of the biggest changes.

Life *was* short, but that didn't mean you should give up caring about actually staying alive. Or the effect that pushing the limits might have on the people who loved you the most. Right now, it felt like their priorities had been off centre and the most important one—that family bond—hadn't been given the importance it deserved.

It felt like it might be time to grow up properly.

Jodie Sinclair had arrived at Aberdeen's Air Ambulance base, located at the far end of one of the runways of the city's main airport, even earlier than usual this morning and it wasn't just because that new coffee machine in the staffroom was so good.

Was it because she was feeling a wee bit nervous?

No… She shook her head at the ridiculous notion as the discreet side door to the base buildings clicked open in response to the pin she could only enter after her fingerprint was recognised by the biometric lock. Getting nervous was on the list of negative emotional responses that she'd learned long ago to dismiss before they had any chance to affect her—professionally or personally.

Jodie took a moment to look around the space inside this vast hangar because this was what it was all about, wasn't it? Right in front of her, with its skids sitting on a large wooden platform, was one of the sleek black H145 helicopters her crew would be using today. The wheels on the platform were on a length of railway line that went beneath the roller door that ran the whole width of the hangar and out to the helipad. With just the press of buttons, the door could be raised and the helicopter moved outside, ready to take off at a moment's notice. That the destination was still unknown and the emergency they were being sent to was still a mystery was part of what Jodie loved the most about this job.

She climbed a steel staircase that took her up the wall of the hangar on the opposite side to the winch training simulator that was the hull of a helicopter fixed to a platform just beneath the roof. It was part of the background that was more than a second home for Jodie—it was the setting for what was, without doubt, the most important part of her life.

Just arriving at work was enough for her to be focused. To feel that kind of anticipation that, for some people, might be close to excitement but, for Jodie, it was simply the space she needed to be in to do this job to the very best of her ability. She didn't need other people to tell her that she was at the top of her game. She didn't want them to, in fact, because there was always room to improve.

Unless something held her back.

Like a new crew partner who was a total stranger?

Someone who'd been working on the other side of the world. An Australian who might be trained as a paramedic and qualified to work on helicopters but could also be some kind of a cowboy who regarded protocols as merely guidelines. She'd seen those Crocodile Dundee movies with that laid-back hero with the lazy accent and the ridiculously large knife he carried around. If her new crew partner displayed the slightest hint of being a maverick like that, he was going to be in for some serious readjustment if he wanted to fit in to her crew.

The internal door from the hangar led directly into the staff area and, beyond, to the offices of the people who managed service operations, communications, maintenance and many other aspects of what it took to run a busy air rescue service. Jodie had been working here long enough to know everybody. Dion, the head of service operations who managed the day-to-day running of the base, was making a coffee for himself as Jodie went into the staffroom. Angus, one of their pilots, was sitting at a long table with a plate of toast and coffee in front of him. Alex, the crewman and co-pilot for their watch, was near the floor-to-ceiling windows of this space that was a great place to watch planes landing and taking off on the main runways of the airport.

'You ask him, Jodie,' Angus said. 'He won't tell me.'

'Ask him what, Gus?'

'Why he's still drinking that instant muck when he could be getting a really decent coffee from that new machine.'

'I know what I like,' Dion muttered. 'Why does everything have to keep changing?'

'I hear you.' Jodie grinned. 'But hey…it's only coffee. I've got to work with a new crewmate today and I haven't even met the guy.'

'You'll like him.' Dion opened the fridge to get a carton of milk. 'He flew through his orientation. I even rang the head of the base he worked at in Australia and they're gutted to be losing him. Told me we could count ourselves lucky he's decided to come back home to Scotland.'

'Back home? I thought he was an Aussie.' Jodie picked up a pod to slide into the coffee maker.

'He's as Scottish as the rest of us. Born and raised in Dundee, I believe. He's got a sister who's an obstetrician at Queen's, here in Aberdeen. Couple of brothers as well who are both doctors. High-flying medical family by the sound of it.'

'High-flying?' Angus spoke around a mouthful of toast. 'Pun intended?'

Jodie was watching the coffee trickle into her mug. 'We'll see,' she said. 'If I'd known you were going to appoint someone while I was away on holiday, I wouldn't have gone away.'

Dion's huff of laughter dismissed her claim. 'You're saying you would have given up your dream holiday of paragliding off Mont Blanc that you'd been planning for at least a year? I don't think so…'

Jodie grinned at him again. 'You do have a point.'

One of the lessons she'd learned long ago when the life she'd assumed she was embarking on had been ripped away from her, was that if you wanted life to mean anything at all you needed a goal to work towards. Preferably a big one. One that would take time and effort to reach.

Even better, you'd have another one in place before the previous goal had been successfully dispatched. Not only bucket list holiday destinations for adventurous people but career goals as well.

Before leaving on her trip to the French Alps, Jodie had started putting plans in place to take her training to an even higher level that would take her to a Pre-Hospital Consultant Practitioner—a qualification that usually required the background of working as a doctor, not a paramedic. She was going to start by doing a PhD in paramedic science and already had topics under consideration with the appropriate academic committee. It might take a few years to get there but that made it possibly the best goal yet and...there wasn't anything else she wanted to do with her life, was there?

Alex turned away from the view and broke into her thoughts as the machine finished adding frothy milk to the espresso in her mug.

'So how was it?' he asked. 'That dream holiday of yours that would be most people's nightmare?'

'Unbelievable.' Jodie had been about to take her first sip of coffee but paused as the memory of that first jump filled her mind and sent a tingle throughout her body. She could feel, even more than hear, the exhilaration that coated her next words. 'You really haven't lived until you've tried jumping off a mountain like Mont Blanc. When you get the wind lifting your sail and then you turn and run and jump into nothingness, with nothing more than a nylon sail to keep you from falling thousands of feet onto the rocks. When you can sail over crevasses deep enough to hide a city as big as Aberdeen and close enough to glaciers to feel like you could reach out and touch them. It's the closest thing to flying that you could ever experience.' Jodie let her words fade into a sigh of happiness. 'It's the best feeling ever...'

She was turning as she spoke and she suddenly caught her breath, embarrassed by what must have sounded like an impassioned advertisement for the sport of paragliding to someone who didn't know her and probably wasn't the least bit interested in her recent holiday.

Someone like the man standing on the other side of the room, by the top of the staircase that came up from Reception? He was staring at Jodie as if she had been talking about something that wasn't simply over the top but possibly highly offensive.

A tall stranger who was dressed in the same uniform she was wearing herself. Heavy boots. Black trousers with a tee shirt tucked into them. A black tee shirt with the logo of the Aberdeen Air Ambulance service beneath one shoulder and a small blue and white Scottish flag on one sleeve. Hair as dark as his clothing and facial features that were defined and eye-catching.

He was good-looking, there was no question about that, but that wasn't what was making this first impression of this man something completely out of the ordinary. There was a presence about him. A sense of calm, perhaps, that suggested he was totally in command of both himself and what was happening around him. For someone who preferred to remain in complete control herself, it was actually a little disturbing—as if a large rock was about to be thrown into the relatively calm pool of Jodie Sinclair's life.

So she stared back as if she could deflect anything that was potentially unwelcome. There might have been just a hint of defiance in her look that could well have contributed to the awkward silence that became apparent as the echoes of Jodie's enthusiastic response to the question of how her holiday had been evaporated. It was Dion who broke the silence.

'Eddie...come in.' He was smiling at the newcomer. 'Come and meet your crew partner and your pilot. Jodie, this is Edward Grisham. Eddie, this is Jodie, our chief paramedic.'

The stranger covered the gap between them with long, easy strides. It would have been rude to look away from him at this point but the steady gaze from a pair of eyes as dark as his hair seemed to be assessing her and, for some peculiar reason, Jodie felt her heart skip a beat—as if it mattered rather too much what he might be thinking of her? That was also disturbing...

'Good to meet you, Jodie,' he said, holding out his hand. 'I'm looking forward to working with you.'

His eyes advertised intelligence at this close range and that smile suggested he found it easy to make friends. Jodie, however, found it easy to ignore that kind of superficial charm and she was still a little rattled by her first impressions of her new partner, so it might have taken a beat too long for her to put her mug of coffee down on the table before taking his hand to shake it.

'Good to meet you too, Edward.' Her smile was one of genuine welcome but she wasn't about to offer the same assurance of looking forward to working with him. That would depend entirely on how good he was at his job— in real life, not according to a CV or hearsay or what he might think of his own abilities.

'Eddie, please...' He was still smiling at her. 'Or Ed. Only officers from Revenue and Customs tend to call me Edward these days.'

Jodie simply nodded. What she ended up calling her

new colleague might also depend on how she felt about working with him but, in the meantime, it was quite nice to have a choice.

'Is there anything you'd like to go over before we start our shift? Any equipment you're not so familiar with, or protocols that are different to what you're used to?'

His gaze was level. 'I think I'm good, thanks. I might need to be reminded where things are for a day or two but I'm a quick learner.'

Jodie held his gaze and it felt like a challenge. 'Coffee's over there,' she said, tilting her head towards the bench. 'There's a pod machine or some very average instant. Milk's in the fridge. You've got plenty of time to grab a cup before our team briefing starts in the meeting room at six forty-five, but I'll be doing the drug check and re-stock for the shift in about five minutes. You might want to join me in the storeroom?'

She turned away to pick up her own coffee mug again and found Dion watching her, one eyebrow raised. Had she been rude, not offering to make coffee for their new team member?

Maybe. But guilt was another one of those emotions she had learned to control. She'd be more than happy to make a cup a coffee for Edward Grisham at some point.

He just had to earn that privilege first.

She wasn't tall. Five foot five at the most, given that the top of her head would barely reach Eddie's shoulder. And there was no getting away from noticing that she was se-riously...*cute*.

Oh, man... Honed over the last couple of decades, Eddie had a skill that had become so automatic he was barely aware of his ability to absorb every detail about the appearance of a woman within the first few seconds of meeting her. He noted Jodie's height and the way her crew tee shirt hugged her curves. How the short style for her dark auburn hair suited her round face and that she had freckles she hadn't bothered to disguise scattered all over her nose and the top of her cheeks.

Her physical appearance was only the background impression Eddie was getting, however. There was something else about her that he could feel like a punch in his gut. Something almost compelling.

Did Jodie Sinclair have this effect on everybody?

Did that explain the slightly odd conversation he had had with the station manager, Dion, during his recent orientation days?

'You'll be working with Jodie Sinclair,' he'd told Eddie. 'Outstanding paramedic who's about your age.' An eyebrow had been raised. 'A female partner's not likely to be a problem for you, is it?'

Eddie had blinked in surprise. 'Why on earth would it be?'

Dion had looked a little embarrassed. 'It's just a bit of a sensitive issue around here. We had a crew on another watch that, shall we say, imploded due to a relationship that was going on between crew members. A patient's care was put at risk while they were having some...ah... personal issues.' He'd given Eddie a stern look. 'That's never allowed to happen again. Not on my watch.'

Eddie had assured Dion that he had nothing to worry about and he'd meant every word he'd said. Besides, there were more important things to be aware of in this first meeting with Jodie than any physical attributes. Maybe it was something professional about his new partner that he was finding so compelling? Like the impression of intelligence and that gleam in Jodie's eyes that told him she liked being in charge. And that he was being assessed just as rapidly as he was assessing her.

Fair enough.

Eddie had found an article online last night about this rescue base that contained profiles of the team members and Jodie's skills and achievements had been described in glowing terms. As an advanced practitioner in critical care, she had done extensive postgraduate training in pre-hospital medicine, completed a master's degree in paramedic science and gained high level qualifications in therapeutic procedures and drug administration. She might be a couple of years younger than Eddie but she was very definitely his senior as far as rank was concerned.

He had no trouble respecting that authority. He was quite prepared to earn any respect he might be given in return and he was more than happy to forgo a cup of coffee to be in the storeroom with her to go through the medication packs, which was just as well because he knew damn well that that had been an instruction rather than an invitation.

What Eddie was having a little difficulty with as he started this first day on his new job was what he'd overheard her saying as he'd arrived, when she'd been talking about hurling herself off one of Europe's most prominent mountains. Or, rather, it was the way she'd been talking about it, her tone dismissing any dangers inherent in the activity because of the pleasure it provided.

Just the way Mick used to talk about every new extreme sport he'd thrown himself into in the last few years. She must have seen the life-shattering consequences of bodies being badly broken or people losing their lives even when they weren't flirting with the dangers for plea-sure. Eddie had to hope that it was just bravado that was making her sound so blasé about it. Or that he was overly sensitive on the subject right now because of Mick.

He had to work with this woman. In a profession that relied heavily on following safety procedures to the letter. Eddie was all too aware of how quickly the conditions in a mission could change. Given her seniority to him, his own life could depend on the decisions that Jodie would have the final say on and it wasn't the best start to have a warning light flashing in the back of his mind.

He was quite prepared to trust her. But trust had to be earned.

CHAPTER TWO

BY THE TIME he was halfway through his first shift with
Aberdeen Air Ambulance's Blue Watch, Edward Grisham
was confident that his new crew could well turn out to be
up there with the best people he had ever worked with.
Gus, the pilot, and their crewman, Alex, were both obviously highly experienced and competent in their roles and
were disguising any wariness about the new boy at school
with a friendliness that was very welcome. He could understand their curiosity about him and was quite happy
to answer their questions about his time in Australia and
his background when they stopped for a meal break.

'So you grew up in Dundee?'

'I did. With my older sister, Ella, and my two brothers.'

'Older or younger brothers?'

'Well, technically, they're both older than me but only
by a few minutes. We're triplets.'

'No way...' Even Jodie had been startled by that information and the curiosity in her eyes as she glanced
up from her paperwork made Eddie notice their colour
properly for the first time. Her eyes were brown but a
much lighter shade than his own. A kind of milk chocolate sort of brown. The same warm colour of those freckles, in fact.

Nice...

'So you got cloned before you were even born.' Alex looked impressed.

'We're not identical. Ella's dad died when she was a baby and our mum got married again when Ella was about six years old. She and Dad wanted a baby of their own but nothing was happening so they tried IVF. Didn't work the first time with two eggs so they talked their doctor into chucking another one in on the next round for luck.'

'And they got three of you?' Gus was grinning. 'Your poor mother.'

'Ella was eight by then so she was like a second mum to us.' He made a face. 'I think it might have put her off ever having her own kids.'

'What was it like?' Jodie sounded still curious. 'I had friends at school who were twins and I always thought that was special. You're the first triplet I've ever met.'

Eddie rather liked the way she was looking at him as if *he* could possibly be something special himself. He wanted Jodie to like him, he realised. So he held her gaze for a heartbeat longer as he gave her the smile that he had every reason to believe made women melt at least a little.

'We were a pretty wild little pack by all accounts. Ella loves telling the story of how we nicked Mum's nail scissors and gave each other haircuts when we were about three years old. She says we thought the whole escapade was even more hilarious when she told us it looked like someone had run over our heads with a lawnmower.'

Jodie didn't return the smile. 'At least you didn't come back from Australia with a mullet.'

She went back to her paperwork, having dismissed his childhood reminiscence. It was definitely time Eddie stopped talking about himself and it was clearly far too soon to expect to hear any snippets of his senior paramedic partner's early years.

She wasn't being unfriendly despite not smiling back. And he hadn't found anything to account for that niggling disquiet about her during their work together so far today.

Jodie Sinclair was just as competent as Gus and Alex. She was focused, quick but efficient, and seemed to be following protocols to the letter so automatically that it was easy to work with her. Not that they'd faced any particularly challenging missions so far—two interhospital transfers, a man with an evolving myocardial infarct who needed urgent treatment that a rural clinic couldn't provide and a car accident that had ended up not needing the skills of the air rescue crew for the minor to moderate injuries involved.

Not that Eddie had any concerns about how this crew would respond to a serious event. Not at all. He was looking forward to being part of such a call-out, in fact. It was just that...

...that something was still bothering him. Nothing he could put his finger on, exactly, but it was there at the back of his mind. An unknown. Perhaps it was because of a natural wariness on both sides as to how this crew would gel when they were tested with more than simply routine work. Or maybe it was a leftover antipathy from early this morning to the way he'd heard her talking about hurling herself off mountains. She might be winning some trust on a professional level but, personally—despite that curiosity about his own upbringing as a triplet, she was still a stranger.

Maybe his disquiet was due to the fact that what was bothering him felt like a warning of some kind.

One that went up a notch, for some reason, when the

call he'd been hoping for came through just after their lunch break.

'It's near Fort William,' Dion told them, coming into the staffroom as their pagers were sounding. 'Closer to Glasgow than us, but currently we're the only chopper available. A mountain rescue team has been activated but it's going to take them some time to get to the scene. Sounds like the access is going to be a wee bit gnarly.'

The crew were already moving—heading for the staircase that led down to the hangar, their boots clattering on the steel treads.

'Mountain biker,' Alex relayed, managing to read a screen as he kept moving. 'Hit a log on a downhill run and went headfirst over the handlebars.'

'Head, neck and chest injuries.' Jodie was first into the cabin of the helicopter and clicking her harness into place as Eddie climbed in after her.

'Have we got a GCS?' he asked.

'Apparently fifteen,' Jodie responded. 'Conscious and alert. The other rider with her is making sure she's not moving but she's in a lot of pain.' She fastened the strap of her helmet. 'Gus? What's our ETA?'

'Twenty minutes flight time or thereabouts.' Their pilot's voice was loud and clear in the helmet's inbuilt headphones. 'But we can't know your ETA to the patient until we have a look at what the access is like. I've been in the area before and winching you in might not be an option, given the tree cover and the wind gusts we're getting today.'

Twenty minutes was more than enough time to remind himself of everything important Eddie had learned or dealt with when it came to potential head, chest and neck injuries. He knew they would have to check carefully for any major trauma and that anything compromising the airway or circulation took precedence over a potential spinal injury. He knew the whole raft of interventions and drugs that could be used to stabilise the patient enough to move them to the nearest major trauma unit in a tertiary hospital. He knew how to ensure the patient was appropriately immobilised, positioned and protected from any secondary injuries for that transport.

But this felt completely different to any other call he'd had to an accident like this.

Because of Mick.

Because he now had personal experience of just how life-changing an accident like this could be. Eddie had always been aware of the weight of responsibility that came with the job he did. Aware of the power he had to change the course of the rest of someone's life. Or even save that life. But this was the first possible spinal injury he would be assessing since Mick's accident and that awareness was so acute, his adrenaline levels were high enough to be making his heart speed up and his mouth feel dry.

As if he was nervous?

It didn't help that the glance Jodie gave him suggested that she'd picked up on the tension he was feeling. Eddie knew she would be assessing every action of his along with her assessment of the scene and their patient. Nobody wanted a nervous crew partner. It also didn't help that, as they circled the GPS co-ordinates they'd been given, it became apparent that Gus had been correct. There was no obvious place to land close to the scene and the tree cover on the steep hill was so dense it took some time to even catch a glimpse of the high vis vests the mountain bikers were wearing. A winch operation was well out of any safety boundaries.

'There's a clearing beside that hut on the summit,' Gus pointed out. 'I can land us there but you're going to have to carry your gear down the track from there.'

'The mountain rescue team are already on the track heading uphill,' Alex added. 'They're carrying a basket stretcher which will make it easier to carry her back up.'

The on-board portable stretcher was one less thing the crew needed to carry downhill, but they were approaching a patient who'd had a significant mechanism of injury and whose condition could well have deteriorated since their last update. They had to carry a life pack and oxygen, equipment to deal with any serious airway or breathing issues from an intubation kit to a suction device and a portable ventilation unit, as well as many other items, including IV gear, drugs, tourniquets, splints and dressings. Gus would be staying with the helicopter but there were packs for each of the others to carry and it didn't escape Eddie's notice that Jodie reached to pick up the largest one.

'I can take that,' he said.

Her quick glance told him the offer was neither needed nor welcome. She slipped her arms through the straps and had clipped the belt buckle into place by the time Eddie and Alex had gathered the rest of the gear and then led the way towards the track opening from the clearing, with a quick look over her shoulder to make sure the men were keeping up with her.

Eddie lengthened his stride.

The real test had just begun, hadn't it?

Jodie was watching her new colleague carefully but not overtly, with a sideways glance here and a look over her shoulder there when he might not expect it. Something had been bothering her ever since she'd noticed how tense he was on their flight to this scene, thanks to that bunched muscle in his jaw that told her he was gritting his teeth and the way his hand clenched into a fist when he wasn't using his fingers to scroll through the information coming in on their tablets. She hadn't considered him to be showing any nerves so far today, so what was so different about this job? Given his track record, he had to be experienced enough in being dispatched to a trauma case of unknown severity for it not to be a problem. Was his current level of tension because this was the first case that might demonstrate to his new colleagues just how good he really was at his job?

If so, and he did have anything to worry about, Jodie wanted to know exactly what it was.

After a sometimes slippery and unpleasantly steep descent on a few parts of this mountain biking trail, they had arrived at the scene of the accident and Jodie deliberately held back to let Eddie approach their patient first.

The young woman was lying on her back amongst rocks on the side of the trail, covered with a coat and with a woollen jumper folded and tucked under her head. A young man wearing only a tee shirt was holding the helmet she was still wearing, to keep her head still. Eddie nodded at him but crouched low so that the woman could see his face.

'Hey…' The tone of his voice was as reassuring as a smile. 'You're Caitlin, yes?'

'Y-yes…'

'Sorry we took so long, sweetheart.'

Ohh… Beneath that Crocodile Dundee casualness, as if they were just a bit late for a coffee date or something, Jodie could actually *feel* his sincerity. If he was acting, he'd nailed it well enough to win an Oscar. If she was in Caitlin's position hearing those words and seeing his face that close to her own, she would feel as if she was the only person who mattered in the world in this moment.

And what better way to feel when you were in pain and frightened and had no idea what was about to happen to you? Even if that was the only contribution Eddie was about to make to the management of this patient, making her feel that she was about to taken care of by someone who cared this much was priceless.

'I'm Eddie,' he was saying now. 'And I've got Jodie and Alex with me. We're going to look after you, okay?'

'O-okay...' Caitlin was shivering, despite the extra coat over her shoulders. And then she started crying. 'It hurts...'

'What's hurting the most for you?'

But Caitlin was dragging in a breath following a sob and couldn't get any words out. Jodie could see that Eddie was doing a rapid assessment. He shone his pen torch across both eyes to check pupil size and reaction and moved the jacket covering Caitlin, gently unzipping the one she was wearing underneath, so he could watch the way her chest was moving as she breathed. He put his fingers on her wrist, checking for a pulse, and Jodie knew he was taking in her colour and heart rate, and an idea of how low her blood pressure might be at the same time as scanning the surrounding rocks for any evidence of blood loss.

Jodie was doing the same thing as she was opening their packs and getting gear out. She nodded approvingly at Alex, who had also taken in the first impressions and was ripping open the package for a foil blanket. They *had* taken a while to get here and hypothermia was a risk factor. He had the vacuum mattress kit on the ground beside him as well, which was their best bit of equipment for moving a patient with suspected spinal injuries.

'It's her neck.' It was Caitlin's companion who answered for her when she just groaned again. 'And I think she's hurt her ribs because she said it hurt her to breathe and…and she's going to be okay, isn't she?' His face was ashen. 'She was going so fast when she hit that log and she landed on her head and just flipped over like a pancake and landed on these rocks. I've been too scared to let her move and…and it's taken so long for you guys to get here.'

'I know… I'm sorry. What's your name, mate?'

'Ian.'

'Good job keeping her warm and still, Ian. And getting help on the way. Was Caitlin knocked out by the fall?'

'She was a bit out of it, but not really unconscious. Just groaning and stuff.'

'You're a friend of Caitlin's?'

'We're getting married next year.'

'Hey…' Eddie was smiling again. 'Congratulations. Caitlin? Can you hear me?'

'Mmm…' The sound was a stifled groan.

'Can you squeeze my hand?'

Eddie's gaze flicked up to meet Jodie's but she could see there was no movement at all in Caitlin's hand as it lay completely limp inside his.

But Eddie gave hers a squeeze. 'That's great,' he said. 'I'm going to get your helmet off now, very carefully, and we're going to put a collar around your neck. I'm going to take care of your head so nothing moves that shouldn't, but we do need to shift you a wee bit to get you off these rocks and onto something more comfortable while we find out properly what's going on.'

'*No...*' Caitlin had tears rolling down her cheeks. 'Please don't move me... It hurts...'

'We're going to take care of that pain for you right now, sweetheart. Are you allergic to anything that you know of?'

'No...'

'Are you on any medications at the moment or have any medical conditions we should know about?'

'No...'

Eddie got to his feet again. 'Ian, I'm going to take your spot at Caitlin's head there so I can look after her neck, but we're going to need your help when we lift her off these rocks, okay?'

'Okay.'

'You go down by her feet so you can be ready to help lift in a minute or two. Jodie, can we get some pain relief on board for Caitlin, please? And, Alex, could you come and hold her head steady while I get this helmet off? Throw me a collar too, thanks.'

Jodie slipped a cannula into a vein on Caitlin's arm. If her blood pressure was as low as was indicated by how hard it was to feel her radial pulse, their patient was going to need more than IV pain relief. She would need fluids and drugs to maintain enough blood pressure to keep her spinal cord perfused.

It was automatic to warn about the sharp scratch of the needle but her heart sank when it was obvious how little sensation Caitlin had in her upper limbs. It meant that her spinal injury was at a high level and, while it was impossible to know what the prognosis was when these signs could be due to something temporary like spinal shock, it was an ominous sign. It also meant they needed to keep a sharp eye on her breathing and it was an indication that intubation might well be necessary to look after her airway and keep her still enough during transport to avoid any additional damage when they couldn't know how unstable a spinal fracture might be.

Eddie had to be thinking about the same things, judging by how serious his face was as he directed everybody's hand positions and issued instructions for how and when they moved, while he took responsibility for keeping her cervical spine in line with the rest of her spinal column as they did a log roll to get Caitlin onto the vacuum mattress that Alex had pumped air out of to make it a stiff board.

'Up on the count of three,' Eddie ordered. 'One, two…*three*…' He had his hands splayed on either side of Caitlin's head to make sure her neck bones stayed in line with the rest of her spine as she was turned.

Caitlin cried out in pain but, in her position controlling the shoulders, it was possible for Jodie to steady her body against her legs as she ran her fingers down her spine to check for any obvious deformities or painful areas. There was no bleeding that she could see. With Ian's assistance they tucked the stiff mattress behind Caitlin and then it was time to turn her back again.

'Down on the count of three.' Eddie's face was so focused it looked almost grim now. 'One, two…*three.*'

They could slide the mattress onto flat ground now, away from solid objects like smaller rocks that could cause problems. They let air back into the mattress so it could conform to her body shape and then took enough out for it to shrink and provide immobilisation support while they did a rapid but thorough primary survey, assessing breath sounds and chest movement more accurately and attaching monitoring equipment to get baseline measurements of blood pressure, oxygen saturation and heart rhythm.

With that done, and the timely arrival of the mountain rescue team with their carrying power and expertise in navigating difficult terrain for an extrication, they were ready to take the remaining air out of the mattress and secure the straps which would provide the safest immobilisation and meant that Caitlin could be easily lifted into the basket stretcher the mountain rescue team was carrying. The high sides of the plastic basket and all the handholds were designed to help carry someone up steep terrain like this and having Caitlin cocooned in the vacuum mattress would make the switch to the helicopter's stretcher seamless.

Eddie bent the top of the air mattress closer to Caitlin's head as it shrank to provide the same kind of support that sandbags or blocks could offer, but Jodie suddenly signalled Alex to stop pumping.

'Wait...' She glanced at the monitor where an alarm was beeping and then at Caitlin's chest. Her breathing rate had increased but it was still shallow and her oxygen saturation was falling, despite having oxygen running into the mask she was wearing.

'I don't want her head secured yet,' Jodie said quietly. 'I'm not happy with her respiratory effort.'

'Caitlin?' Eddie leaned down, close to her ear. 'Can you open your eyes for me?'

There was no more than a flicker of her eyelashes. Caitlin had been drowsy since they'd administered powerful drugs to control her pain but this was a deeper level of unresponsiveness.

'Blood pressure's down to eighty-five over fifty.'

'SpO2's under ninety.'

'She's tachycardic.'

'Respirations well over thirty.'

Eddie caught Jodie's gaze. 'You want to intubate?'

She gave a single nod, which he mirrored. It was obvious to both of them that getting control of her airway before they packed up their gear and started what could be a slow and difficult climb up the hill was a no-brainer. She needed another fluid bolus and medication to try and bring her blood pressure up as well. Alex was already getting the airway pack open and the laryngoscope was visible, along with its blades and the plastic tubes that would secure an airway. The small portable ventilator unit they had carried down with them was waiting to one side as well.

The mountain rescue team were looking after Ian. He had his warm coat back on and someone had provided a hot drink. They were also supporting him as it became obvious that his fiancée's condition was more serious than he might have realised.

Eddie was already at their patient's head, in the perfect position to do the intubation.

'I'll stabilise her neck from underneath,' Jodie said. 'You happy to do the intubation?' It wasn't really a question. She was already in position to assist rather than take the lead in this procedure. She was leaning in, ready to steady her elbows on Caitlin's chest and put her hands around her jaw bones to keep her head steady when Eddie's response made her stop in her tracks.

'No,' he said.

Jodie blinked. 'What?'

She was actually confused for a split second. Had her

new *junior* crew partner just refused to do what she'd requested? In a tone that had been flat enough to suggest he had no intention of changing his mind or even discussing it? He had been looking down at Caitlin's face between his hands as he spoke and he still hadn't raised his glance so he couldn't see Jodie's incredulous expression.

'I'm not moving until we've got her secured,' he said. 'You can work around me to remove the collar and then intubate, yes?'

Jodie could feel Alex's startled glance but didn't look in their crewman's direction. This wasn't the time to comment on not only Eddie's refusal to follow her directions but telling her what to do. That would most certainly come later, but right now there were far more important things to focus on and yes…she could work around and through the position of his arms.

It did mean, however, that she had to crouch close enough beside Eddie for her hip to be pressing against his leg and her arms to be repeatedly touching his and she wasn't that comfortable being close to someone that she clearly couldn't trust to work with her the way she was entitled to expect, but this was also not the time to even think about that. They had work to do and they needed to do it swiftly.

The first task was to carefully undo the straps holding the cervical collar closed because it would make it impossible to open the mouth far enough for the procedure. With her arm leaning on his to steady herself, Jodie could feel how rigidly Eddie was holding Caitlin's head still as she worked. Alex was busy drawing up the drugs needed to anaesthetise and paralyse their patient.

The intensity of Eddie's focus as he provided just enough tilt, and not a millimetre more, to let her insert the laryngoscope blade and then stylet and the plastic tube was, quite literally, palpable. It might have influenced the way Jodie also concentrated, completing the procedure smoothly and swiftly and then securing the tube, attaching oxygen and setting up the ventilator. It was only after the air mattress was flattened onto either side of Caitlin's head that he finally moved his hands. And it was only then that he looked up to make eye contact with Jodie.

And he looked…angry?

Jodie stared back for a heartbeat. What was going on here? She was the one who should be angry because he'd flatly refused to comply with her request as the senior paramedic on scene. It was insupportable and she was going to have a chat with Dion when she got back to base because she wasn't at all sure she wanted to work with this newcomer.

One member of the volunteer mountain rescue team was going to take Ian—and the two bicycles—down the track and get him back to his own vehicle so that he had transport to get to the hospital.

'Where are you going to take Caitlin?' he asked.

'The closest major trauma centre will be Glasgow, and that will be the very best place she can go because there's a specialist spinal unit attached to the hospital. We'll be able to let you know before you get back to your car.'

The only communication made on the trip back up the track between everybody involved was information being shared, from monitoring Caitlin's condition, radio communication to arrange their destination and give Gus a heads-up that they would be taking off soon and directions from the mountain rescue team as they passed the stretcher from hand to hand to get it over narrow gaps

between large boulders and muddy slopes that could have
been dangerously slippery.

Jodie was the one who was angry now but, like any
negative emotion, she had it completely under control,
well in the background, and it was easy to keep it completely private by avoiding direct eye contact with Eddie
and focusing absolutely on their patient. By the time they
landed on Glasgow's Central Infirmary's roof helipad,
however, the issue simmering at the back of her mind
had led to a decision.

Edward Grisham might not have come back from Australia with a mullet hairstyle but he'd picked up an attitude that was unacceptably arrogant.

Or maybe he'd always been like that?

Whatever. He was a cowboy. A maverick. Someone
who was going to do what *he* wanted to do, no matter
what anyone else had decided was the best course of action. And maybe it hadn't done any harm in this instance
but, as far as Jodie was concerned, it meant their partnership was not going to work and she had every intention of marching into Dion's office the moment they got
back on base and asking him to arrange to swap Eddie
onto a different watch.

It was Jodie who gave a detailed handover to the emergency department consultant and the specialist orthopaedic surgeon from the spinal unit who was amongst the
team waiting for them. They were complimented on their
management of Caitlin so far and as the emergency department staff handed back their vacuum mattress and
were busy setting up their own monitors, Jodie turned
away, reaching to start pushing their stretcher from the
trauma resuscitation area, satisfied that they had done
their best for this patient.

And then she froze.

The surgeon was stepping towards Eddie. Shaking his hand.

'I thought I'd seen the last of you, Ed,' he said.

'Me too, Andrew.'

Jodie could feel her eyes widening. Her new colleague was on first name terms with a Glaswegian specialist orthopaedic surgeon? More than that, there was a feeling that they shared something that was significant to both of them. What was going on?

'First day on my new job in Aberdeen,' Eddie added with a wry smile. 'Guess I can't keep away from this place.'

The surgeon was returning the smile but his frown advertised concern. 'How's Mick?'

The shadow crossing Eddie's face was noticeable. 'Ah…you know. Still settling in. It's…not easy…'

'I know. Keep in touch, won't you? Let me know if I can help in any way.'

'Will do, thanks.'

Eddie didn't look at Jodie as they took the stretcher to the nearest lift to get back to the roof, where Gus and Alex were waiting to take them back to base. She was at the back of the stretcher and she found herself staring at Eddie's back as he pressed the button to take them up. The silence in the lift as the doors closed felt heavy and Jodie took a deep breath. She knew perfectly well that she might be crossing a boundary between professional and personal but this felt important.

'Who's Mick?' she asked.

Eddie didn't turn around. 'My brother.'

Another silence fell that lasted as the lift slowed to stop at another floor. When the waiting nurses saw that it was already filled with a stretcher and two people, they stood back and the doors slid shut again.

'Mick's just spent a couple of months in the spinal unit here,' Eddie said quietly. 'He had a hang-gliding accident up in the Highlands.'

It took only a second for several things to fall into place.

The way Eddie had been looking at her when he'd arrived this morning, when she'd been raving about how life-affirming it was to be jumping off mountains. The tension he'd been showing on that flight to their last patient. That fierce determination that nothing was going to interfere with his protection of her neck so that her potential injury was not exacerbated in any way.

In the same instant, Jodie could see herself the way Eddie must have been seeing her. As someone with little respect for the sanctity of life. Possibly with less respect than she actually felt for protecting the life of a patient in her care. She could even hear an echo of the sharp tone in her voice when she'd responded to his refusal to move his hands from Caitlin's head.

Thinking that they weren't actually suited to be working together was probably not one-sided and…and she couldn't really blame Eddie if he might be wondering if he'd made a mistake coming to work at Triple A.

Worse, she didn't like the glimpse she was getting of herself through his eyes.

Eddie cleared his throat. 'His injury's not as high as Caitlin's but it's still going to be a long road back to recovery.' The lift was slowing again as it reached their destination. 'That's why I've moved back from Australia. And why I've taken the job in Aberdeen. Mick's just been transferred to a rehabilitation centre there.'

It was in that instant that Jodie realised he hadn't been acting in that sincerity he'd displayed with Caitlin. If the bond that had to be there with his brother was enough for Eddie to have overturned his whole life in order to be close enough to support him for as long as he was needed, then he was more than capable of caring as much as he'd appeared to for a patient.

There was a single word that she could hear in the back of her head right now.

Sweetheart...

Nobody had ever called Jodie 'sweetheart'. Not even Joel. But they'd practically grown up together, dating since high school, and their endearments were more likely to be cheeky than cheesy. He'd called her 'short stuff'. Or 'spot', because of her freckles. But it hadn't mattered because their love was rock solid. They were going to be together for life.

Until they weren't...

The lift shuddered to a halt and there was that tiny bit of time before the doors opened that might be the last private moment Jodie had with Eddie before they were sucked back into the noise and busyness of the rest of their shift. She needed to say something, but Jodie's thoughts were very uncharacteristically tangled.

Those memories of Joel certainly hadn't helped, but she'd already been messed up with a level of emotion she would never normally allow to happen.

Ever.

She wasn't about to let it happen for a moment longer either. Because, if it did, it would take her even further back, to a space she had fought so hard to get away from, a very long time ago. The time when her life had been intact.

As perfect as she'd ever hoped it would be.

'I'm sorry,' was all she said as the door slid open onto the roof.

It was more of a mutter, really. Maybe because Jodie wasn't exactly sure what it was she was apologising for.

The devastating accident that one of his brothers had experienced?

For coming across as being...what...flippant, perhaps?

For not being able to express, or even feel, the level of emotion that Eddie was obviously capable of?

For having decided that she was going to make a request to not have to work with him any longer?

No...

The apology was for all of those things, but it was also because she had misjudged him. And, if she was really honest with herself, was it because she was sorry she wasn't more like him herself? Someone who had attributes on a personal rather than a professional level that were admirable. Attractive, even...?

It would be all too easy to resent someone who'd held up a mirror to show her something that she didn't like about herself, but Jodie wasn't going to allow herself to do that. She could work with this man and not let anything personal affect their professional relationship.

When they settled in to working together they could, in fact, make a great team with the way they could complement each other's skills, which was a much more positive way to view what had happened. It wasn't as if his refusal to follow her direction on their last case had compromised the care of their patient in any way. It could even be argued that she was partly to blame herself when she had, after all, phrased her request by asking if he was happy to do the procedure. He'd had good reason to say he wasn't, so she should just let it go.

As long as it didn't happen again.

Jodie ducked her head as they pushed the stretcher towards where Alex was waiting to help them stow their gear beneath the rotors on the helicopter that were already gaining speed.

'We've got another call to make on the way home,' Alex told them. 'A paediatric transfer from a medical centre in Laurencekirk. Respiratory distress probably due to bronchiolitis, but there are concerns about whether the kid's stable enough to send by road.'

Jodie felt something very like relief as she heard the stretcher wheels lock into position and she could sit down and strap herself in for the flight. It was one of the best things about this job—there was always something just around the corner that could completely distract you from dwelling on anything remotely personal.

CHAPTER THREE

HE WASN'T GOING to let it bother him.

That less than sympathetic apology from Jodie Sinclair when he'd told her about Mick's accident. Or the carefully professional distance she'd been keeping from him ever since.

What had he expected? Some real interest in his personal life? Some genuine concern for the difficulties his brother—and therefore his whole family—were facing? Perhaps he'd hoped that telling her might break the ice in getting to know each other better.

'It's not that she's not friendly,' he told his brothers when he visited Mick after his shift had ended. 'I'm just not sure she likes me much.'

It was a new experience for Edward Grisham. People tended to like him instantly. Especially women...

Was it that Jodie didn't like anyone much? That she was one of those rare women who were lone wolves?

He'd certainly got that impression with the look she'd given him when he'd refused to let go of Caitlin's head in order to perform the intubation. He would have been happy to discuss it with her as a debrief when the mission had been completed, but he'd ended up working with Alex to clean and restock the gear in the helicopter cabin while Jodie disappeared into the secure storeroom to check and replenish the drug and airway kits.

He'd found her sitting at the table in the staffroom as their shift ended, completing the patient treatment report, but when he'd started speaking she'd held up a hand in an unmistakable gesture to stop him saying anything.

'Just give me another few minutes? I don't want to get any of these drug dosages or times incorrect.'

'No worries,' Eddie had said. 'It can wait. I need to head off, anyway. My brother James has come up from Edinburgh to visit Mick and I said I'd try and get to the rehabilitation centre to catch up with them both.'

Jodie had clearly stopped focusing on inputting her data, her fingers poised above her tablet keyboard. 'Of course. Go.' Her glance slid across his. 'See you tomorrow.'

Remembering the smile she had given him at that point was enough to make Eddie wonder now if he was overreacting. It had, after all, been his first day working with Jodie and perhaps he'd misinterpreted both that look and the lack of sincerity in that apology?

Judging by the amused sound from his brother James, he wasn't the only one who thought his impression might have been incorrect.

'Maybe she fancies you,' he offered. 'You know, like the girls at primary school that could be mean because they didn't want you to know they liked you that much in case you didn't like them back?'

'I *don't* like her back. Not like that, anyway. When I said I wanted to get to know her better, I wasn't talking about jumping into bed with her.'

James lifted an eyebrow. 'Because she's part of your crew? I get it. If she wanted more than something casual, it could get a bit awkward in a confined space like a helicopter cabin. At least I've got a whole emergency department to use if I want to create some distance.'

Had James not been listening the other day when Eddie had said how he felt as if everything had changed since Mick's accident? That what was important in life suddenly seemed to be something a lot deeper than skating through life in a completely self-centred way, working hard, focusing entirely on having an exciting career during work time and playing just as hard out of work hours, with as many gorgeous women as possible?

'You must have noticed how cute she is,' James added. 'Stunning, even. I was showing Mick that online article about her when I got here this afternoon. The one with the photograph of her standing beside the chopper with her helmet under her arm? Is she single?'

'I've got no idea. And I'm not about to ask.' Eddie shook his head slowly. 'And it's not just that there are some strict rules in place for not messing around with your crewmates. Don't you ever think that it's a bit… shallow—wondering if every beautiful woman you meet might be up for a bit of fun? That you might be hurting people even if they don't make it obvious? Or wasting time when you could be making a real connection with someone?'

James blinked. 'Not if they know you're not interested in anything more than a bit of fun. There's plenty of girls out there who are more than happy to play—as you well know.'

Eddie did know. And he didn't like that he knew.

'What's the point of making a "real" connection, anyway?' Mick's tone was bitter. 'That just means that *you're* the one that's going to end up getting hurt.'

It was always there, wasn't it? The memory of that awful time at the wedding, when it became obvious that Mick's bride wasn't going to be making an appearance. Mick's devastation had been contagious and the bond between the three brothers had never felt so strong.

It felt like that again now. Eddie could sense how desperate James was to change the subject he'd been responsible for introducing.

'It wasn't just the photo,' he said. 'Sounds like your Jodie is a smart cookie. She seems to be set on becoming the highest qualified paramedic in Scotland. We were both impressed, weren't we, Mick?'

'Aye...'

But Mick didn't sound particularly impressed. Or interested. He was lying flat on his bed in his private room, with the wide doors that led out to a wheelchair accessible garden, staring at the ceiling—as he had been ever since Eddie had arrived. Mick's wheelchair was parked in the corner of the room, near the door to the ensuite bathroom.

'I'm sorry you're having to work with someone you don't like much,' Mick muttered. 'Or who doesn't like you.' He closed his eyes. 'You didn't have to leave the job you *did* like so much, you know. I never asked you to move back to hang around for me.'

'I know.' Eddie tried to sound offhand, but he was kicking himself mentally for giving Mick the idea that he might be less than happy with his major life decision. 'I did it because I wanted to. It was time I came home again—I hadn't realised how much I missed Scotland. All this lovely rain...' He found a smile. 'I kind of missed you guys too, believe it or not.'

'Not.' But James was also smiling as he glanced at his

watch. 'I'll have to hit the road before too long, if I'm going to get back in time to start my night shift. How 'bout we get you out of that bed and you give us a guided tour of this place, Mick? From what I saw on the way in, it looks pretty flash.'

'Great idea,' Eddie agreed, relieved that his new job—and his new partner—were no longer the focus of their conversation. 'I'd like to see the gymnasium and the pool and the games room. Is there a pool table in there?'

Mick shrugged, his eyes still closed. 'Wouldn't know. Haven't been able to sit in the chair long enough to go anywhere. They're still juggling my pain meds.'

'Have you got your timetable for all the therapy sessions?' Eddie asked. 'They told us they'd be giving you a thorough assessment after you'd had time to settle in and then the whole team would be meeting to draw up a plan for your individualised programme.'

Mick opened his eyes, which only made his expression bleaker. 'Apparently you lose a lot of muscle strength by lying around for too long. Who knew? My arms are like strings of spaghetti. I can't even turn the wheels of that chair.'

'You'll get there.'

'Get where, exactly? It's not like I can go back to a clinic in Ethiopia or be on standby for a natural disaster somewhere, is it?'

The silence between the brothers acknowledged how much had changed and Eddie's tone was gentle.

'Hang in there, mate. And don't even think about giving up hope yet. None of us know how much function you're going to get back. And, knowing what you're like, you're going to smash this challenge like everything else you've ever done in your life.'

'I'll get back up on my next proper day off,' James told Mick. 'But I'll give you a video call before then.' He picked up his leather jacket and motorcycle helmet. 'I'm keeping an eye out for a locum position up here too. Logan tells me the Emergency Department at Queen's is a good place to work. Hey... I could move into your apartment with you, Eddie. That'd be fun.'

Eddie shook his head. 'It's only got one bedroom,' he said. 'We might have shared a womb once, mate, but I'm not sharing my bed with you.'

Mick didn't join in the burst of laughter but at least he was smiling for the first time during this visit.

'Maybe he's saving that side of the bed for his cute crew partner. It's not as if you haven't broken a few rules in your time.'

'I think that's my cue to head off as well.' Eddie shook his head. 'Before you two come up with any more ridiculous ideas.' He got to his feet. 'And, just for the record, I'm not planning to share my bed with anyone for the foreseeable future. I've got more than enough going on in my life right now.'

'That makes two of us.' Mick had his eyes closed again. 'Get lost, you two. I'm tired.'

Eddie glanced over his shoulder as he left the room, more worried about his brother now than he had been when he'd arrived. Sure enough, Mick had a hand on his forehead, shading his eyes. From a non-existent bright light? Or was he disguising the fact that he was shedding a tear?

The prickle behind Eddie's own eyes could be blinked away easily enough but the sadness in his heart seemed to be getting bigger. And trying to settle in a little deeper.

* * *

It was no wonder an echo of Mick's voice haunted Eddie's sleep that night, but it was something James had said that was foremost in his mind when he arrived at the base the next day to find Jodie with Gus and Alex as they were preparing to move the helicopter out of the hangar and he could hear her laughing at something Gus had said.

He'd seen her smile but this was the first time he'd heard her laugh and he found the corners of his own mouth instantly curving upwards in response—as if he'd heard the joke himself and it had been a particularly good one. It was the first time he'd seen the way genuine mirth could light up Jodie's face as well, and he realised that James had been spot-on.

She really was quite stunning.

It wasn't just her looks. There was an aura about her that was undeniably attractive. She was the kind of person that everybody would gravitate towards at a party— men and women—and it was not necessarily anything to do with sexual attraction.

Her laughter hadn't quite faded when she noticed Eddie approaching so that was another first, to see the way that her eyes could dance when she found something funny. Did they do that when she was happy too? It would be impossible not to feel happy yourself if you were lucky enough to be close enough to see that.

Eddie was feeling better than he had moments ago, that was for sure. He was still smiling as he headed for the staircase.

'G'day,' he called.

'G'day, mate,' Alex called back, exaggerating an Australian accent.

Gus raised his hand and Jodie nodded in response to

his greeting but, if she'd said anything, it was lost in the sound of the giant roller door starting to rattle as it rose to open the hangar and signal the start of a new shift.

A shift that included a mission that took them up the coastline to a beach north of Aberdeen and the view Eddie had from his window was spectacular. The wild surf of the North Sea, dramatic cliffs with occasional ruins of ancient stone castles to be seen and stretches of golden sand between rocky outcrops. A fisherman had slipped on rocks like that and was in trouble with a chest injury that was bad enough for a local ambulance crew, who had reached the injured man via the beach by using a quad bike from a nearby farm, to call for the assistance of the air rescue service. The man had suffered multiple rib fractures and was experiencing increasing respiratory difficulties.

Eddie had two thoughts running through his head as he took a moment to soak in the scenery floating past beneath them. The first was that if Jodie asked him to intubate this patient he'd have to have a very good reason to say no or he might as well kiss goodbye to ever having the kind of relationship he'd want to have with someone he had to work with this closely. He'd seen the look in Jodie's eyes when he'd refused to move and risk losing that protection of their patient's spinal alignment yesterday. Incredulity, that was what it had been. Followed by a sharp dismissal of something that could distract her from doing what needed to be done. She'd avoided direct eye contact after that, which told him she was less than happy, but that had changed when she'd seen him talking to the neurosurgeon in the emergency department in Glasgow.

When he'd told her who Mick was.

The other thought that came from nowhere was something he'd said to his brothers yesterday—that he hadn't realised how much he'd missed his homeland of Scotland. He could feel that bond very strongly right now, with the wildness of the land beneath them. He could almost imagine a lone piper standing on the walls of one of those ruined castles, in the teeth of a freezing wind from the North Sea, perhaps, with the mournful wail of the bagpipes hinting at a breed of stoic people who could face any kind of challenge head-on.

They had their own challenge before they even landed on scene. The fishermen had gone down a cliff track. The local ambulance crew had used a farm bike to travel a considerable distance along the beach. The only way the helicopter could get close, without it taking too long, was to land on the sand between the cliffs and the breaking waves.

'Good thing the tide's still out far enough,' Gus said. 'We've got some nice firm sand to land on. It's on the way in, though, so let's make this as quick as we can.'

Eddie knew not to offer to carry anything Jodie chose to pick up, but he didn't have time, anyway. She had a pack on her back and was out of the aircraft as soon as Alex had opened the door.

By the time they reached the huddle of people at the end of the beach where the sand finished and the rocks began, it was obvious that if they'd taken any longer to get here it would have been too late. The man was struggling to breathe, despite oxygen running at a high flow through the mask he was wearing. They could hear his rasping, dry cough and, even through the plastic of the mask, they could see the blueish tint to his lips. His breathing was too rapid and the monitor the local paramedics had attached was showing a heart rate that was dangerously fast. What was even more concerning was that it was clear that this man's level of consciousness was dropping fast and he knew how much trouble he was in. He looked absolutely terrified.

Jodie crouched beside him. 'We're going to do something to help your breathing and give you something a bit stronger for that pain,' she told him. 'And we're going to take good care of you, okay?'

Eddie could see some of that fear drain from the man's eyes but Jodie might not have noticed because she had her gaze on the disc of her stethoscope as she listened briefly to each side of his chest.

'Breath sounds absent left side,' she said, looking up seconds later. 'There's obvious tracheal deviation and jugular vein distention. Ed, can you draw up some lignocaine and ketamine, please?'

'On it.' He had the drug roll open and reached for the ampoules and a syringe. The paramedics on scene had already gained IV access and had fluids running so it would take very little time to provide the sedation and anaesthetic required to perform the lifesaving procedure of creating an opening in the side of the chest that would save this man's life.

Eddie had seen a finger thoracostomy done many times. He'd done them himself and knew just how careful you had to be with the pressure when you used forceps to open the space between the cut on the skin and the outside of the lung. Not going far enough wouldn't release the air and blood that was caught in the pleural space and creating a lethal pressure that could stop both the lungs and the heart from functioning. Going too far could do damage to the lung or the diaphragm.

He could see how fierce Jodie's concentration was and

he was watching her closely enough to see the moment she felt the 'give' of the outer layer of the pleura that was attached to the chest wall. She took the forceps out then, and inserted her finger to do a sweep to ensure that access was enough to release the accumulated air and blood— very carefully, because there was a high risk of injury due to coming into contact with fractured ribs.

Eddie had never seen this procedure done quite this swiftly and effectively but the only indication of satisfaction in a job very well done from Jodie was a single nod. 'I can feel the lung inflating,' she said. 'Can you open a dressing for me, thanks, Ed?'

He already had one in his hand. Alex had the stretcher ready for their patient with the monitoring equipment they would need already switched on and waiting for electrodes, blood pressure cuff and a pulse oximeter to be put in place. They would be ready to take off within a matter of only minutes, so Eddie began packing up their gear as soon as he'd held out the opened package for Jodie to extract the sterile dressing.

She was watching the changes in vital signs that were confirming the success of the procedure. The heart and breathing rates were dropping and the level of circulating oxygen was rising.

But, for a split second, Eddie wasn't looking at anything but Jodie.

It definitely wasn't simply her looks that were stunning.

It wasn't even that aura she had of being more alive than anyone he'd ever met.

Watching her put her skills into action like he'd just witnessed had to be the sexiest thing he'd ever seen.

And okay...nothing was going to happen between

them. Not just because of having been warned off by Dion before he'd even met her. Or that Eddie still thought that Jodie didn't like him that much. No…there was something else that was off-putting. He didn't really know what it was, to be honest, but it felt as if something was missing? A small piece of the human jigsaw puzzle that made up Jodie Sinclair but probably not one that mattered, given that getting really close was out of the question. It wasn't something that would stop him being able to be a good colleague with this woman. A friend even, if she'd let him get at least a little closer.

And, oddly, it also didn't seem to be stopping him feeling as if he'd just fallen a little bit in love with her, but it was easy to persuade himself that a first impression could often be a little over the top.

It would wear off soon enough if he ignored it.

There was a punching ball suspended from a rafter in the far corner of the garage of the small house Jodie had inherited from her father. It hadn't been used for a long time, because she preferred to get her exercise by going for a run and using hand weights for a bit of resistance training.

But it was being used tonight and it was remarkably satisfying to be punching it as hard as she could with the protection of her dad's old boxing gloves covering her hands.

It was frustration rather than anger that she needed to deal with.

She wasn't even sure why she was feeling like this, but perhaps that was why the emotion had accumulated to this level over the last couple of weeks that she'd been working with her new partner.

Edward Grisham.

Ed.

Eddie?

No, that felt too familiar. Too...friendly.

Did she want to be friends with Ed?

No.

Yes.

Jodie punched the bag harder and faster. Left, right, left, left right... She could feel perspiration trickling down her spine.

Of course she wanted to be friends with him. Just like she was friends with Gus and Alex and Dion and lots of other people on the air rescue base who were more than just workmates, they were her family.

But there was something different about Edward Grisham.

It wasn't that she didn't trust him. On a professional level she couldn't fault either his skills or his sincerity in the way he cared about his patients. He had a passion for his work and Jodie had worked with enough people in the pre-hospital setting to know that there was something special about Eddie.

That first serious case they'd worked on together, in rescuing that unfortunate mountain biker, was a great example of that. Jodie had rung the spinal unit in Glasgow today to get an update on Caitlin and she'd been delighted to be able to share the good news with the rest of her crew. Caitlin had had successful surgery to stabilise her C5, C6 incomplete fracture and the spinal shock was wearing off to the extent that she had feeling and some movement back in all her limbs. Her consultants were cautiously predicting a much better than expected outcome for her. She might even be able to walk down the aisle unaided for her wedding next year.

Jodie had been watching Eddie when she'd delivered that news. She would have understood completely if his reaction was mixed. Happy for his patient but possibly even a little resentful that his brother hadn't been so lucky? But she hadn't detected anything other than a genuine delight in hearing how well Caitlin was doing.

And who knew how much of that was down to the way Eddie had been so determined to take responsibility for her spinal stability? Ensuring that an incomplete injury didn't become complete due to a secondary injury from an avoidable movement. Not that he was about to take any credit for the part he'd played. Eddie was a team player, wasn't he?

A nice guy.

A nice, highly skilled, intelligent, good-looking guy.

Really, *really* good-looking, with that mop of dark hair and eyes that would be even darker if it wasn't for that glint of whatever it was in them. Amusement? Mischief? *Joie de vivre?*

Jodie hit the punching bag so hard she felt a painful twinge shoot up her arm as far as her shoulder which made her stop. She needed to catch her breath, anyway. She didn't really need to crouch on the floor and press the squashy boxing gloves against her eyes but that was what she did.

To stop herself crying.

Because that was why she couldn't be friends with Eddie.

That attitude to making the most of life in combination with being so *nice*.

It was what she'd loved so much about Joel, wasn't it?

What had attracted her to him in the first place. What had come so close, in the end, to utterly destroying her life.

No...

No, no, no...

She wasn't going to get sucked back into that space and she'd had years of practice with how to make sure it didn't happen. Lesson number one: move your body. Not that it was easy to push herself to her feet and get started but that was what Jodie did. And then she ripped off her gloves and kept moving. Straight out of her garage to head for her favourite running route bordering the River Dee through the woodlands towards and around the Inchgarth Reservoir.

The calming hypnosis of her feet drumming on the pathways and being near water and grass and trees was exactly what she needed to ground herself. Lesson number two: be in the now.

She wasn't going to think about anything to do with the past, like Joel. Like their gap year, when they'd impulsively decided to get married on a tropical island beach. Like their actual wedding day when Joel had been dragged out to sea in a rip. Like that endless, agonising wait for his body to be found and brought back for her to cradle.

She wasn't going to think about the future either. Because, no matter how disturbing it might be, that included Eddie and there was something about him that was dangerous, no matter how solid her belief was that she was never going to get as close to anyone as she had been to Joel.

She would never risk going through a life-destroying loss like that ever again, but Jodie was confident she could maintain the safety barriers she had built so painfully and slowly, piece by piece, putting one foot in front of the other as she tried—and finally succeeded—to move forward and rebuild her life.

Lesson number three: take one day at a time.

CHAPTER FOUR

IT SHOULD HAVE worn off by now.

That attraction that Eddie had been ignoring so effectively that he was quite confident nobody would have guessed that he was so aware of his new crew partner.

Well…not so new, now. How long had he been working at Triple A?

Nearly a month.

Long enough for them to have found a way of working together that was making the reconfiguration of Blue Watch a tight team. The best ever, even, if only that annoying hyperawareness of Jodie would quietly evaporate and he didn't keep finding himself captivated by something like the sound of her voice for the first time that day, or sunlight catching a thread in her hair and making it glow like fire. Even the deft movements of her hands when she was doing something as simple as snapping the head off a drug ampoule and drawing the contents into a syringe could be enough to make it difficult not to let his focus get hijacked.

It was also long enough to wonder whether the medication Mick had been prescribed was actually going to kick in and help him get past this concerning low point in his recovery journey, but that was something else that wasn't yet going quite the way Eddie had been hoping it would. It wasn't helping that it had been a quiet day on base so far, without a single call and far too much time to think. And read.

Eddie clicked out of the medical journal article he'd been reading online because it also wasn't helping to learn that spinal cord injury patients had almost a doubled risk of developing mental health issues, such as depression and anxiety and, not unexpectedly, living with chronic pain was a major factor. Was there something more he could be doing to support Mick? It was all very well to keep telling him to 'hang in there' and that 'things will get better' but, right now, Eddie was beginning to feel like his words were simply platitudes.

He'd had a heart-to-heart with his big sister and brother-in-law about this only a day or two ago when he'd gone out to their gorgeous barn conversion in the countryside just out of Aberdeen. It had been warm enough to sit outside for a barbecue and watch the ducks floating calmly on the pond at the bottom of the garden, which had been a balm all on its own. Ella and Logan's advice had been exactly what he'd needed, as well—which was to look at this period as a stage of grief for everybody involved as they came to terms with and accepted the inevitable changes and losses that Mick would need to adapt to.

'Sometimes,' Logan had told Eddie, 'all you can do is be there for someone and that's all they need you to do. It's their journey and they have to do it at their own pace.'

Ella had stood on tiptoes to fold Eddie into a hug when he was heading home. 'The Mick we all know and love is still in there, I promise. We'll see him back again before too long, I'm sure of it.'

So maybe Eddie was the one who needed to 'hang in

there' and give things in his new, rather upside-down, life time to settle properly.

Right now, Eddie was alone in the staffroom. Dion and other admin staff were all occupied in a meeting with city councillors and other officials about an upcoming fundraising event for the air rescue base. Deciding that a breath of fresh air would be a good idea, Eddie took the stairs down into the hangar. He could hear Alex and Jodie, who were busy with some kind of stocktaking in the storeroom and, when he got outside, he found Gus was still pottering around with maintenance chores on his beloved helicopter. Currently he was hosing off the windows and bubble with a spray setting.

'Need some help, Gus?'

'I'm just getting rid of any dust specks so I don't scratch the glass when I'm washing it properly. I'm sure you've got something more interesting to do than cleaning windows.'

'I'm waiting for Dion to finish his meeting. It might be a good time, while it's quiet, to catch him and talk about the boat winch training session he mentioned the other day.'

'Aye… I'd like to talk about that too. But now that you've mentioned the "Q" word, it probably won't happen.' Gus shook his head. 'Grab one of those microfibre cloths and get it wet in that bucket of soapy water and you can help finish this before we get the inevitable call in less than ten minutes. Vertical strokes only, okay?'

'No problem.'

'What are the others up to?'

'Checking expiry dates on some stock. I offered to help but I was told it was a two-person job.' Eddie was leaving a trail of soap bubbles as he pushed the cloth over the windows.

'Gets a bit cosy in that storeroom with more than two people anyway.'

'Yeah…' Eddie gave a huff of sound that was meant to convey relief that he'd dodged a potentially awkward situation but…dammit…there it was again. That prickle of awareness that ran over his skin like a soft breeze at the thought of getting up close and cosy in a restricted space with Jodie Sinclair.

It was a good thing that he was outside with another member of his crew. That the base building was right behind him and behind one of those upper storey windows was Dion's office. What better way to deal with that uncomfortable awareness than to remind himself of the warning he'd been given before he'd even started work here?

'I expect there's a rule or two about that kind of cosy.' He threw a sideways glance at Gus. 'What exactly happened that made Dion warn me that no shenanigans between crew members were going to be tolerated under his watch?'

Gus was still holding the hose, ready to rinse off the soapsuds Eddie was leaving on the acrylic glass.

'That was a couple of years ago. On Red Watch. Mark was the crewman and Zoe was one of the paramedics. They fell for each other and nobody minded but it ended badly. Apparently, Mark cheated on her and they broke up but still had to work together for the rest of that roster and the air was tense enough to cut with a knife. When Mark walked off just before they had to deal with an asthmatic patient who crashed it could have been a disaster. Fortunately, the patient survived but Mark got fired and

Zoe resigned because she didn't want to work here even with him gone. It was chaos around here while we covered shifts until we filled the gaps.'

Eddie whistled silently, stooping to get his cloth rinsed and then soapy again. 'That explains a lot. Fair call from Dion, I'd say.'

'At least you don't have any potential shenanigans to worry about, working with Jodie.'

Eddie shook his head, feigning disappointment. 'And there I was, thinking she was starting to like me.'

Gus laughed. 'I'm sure she does. She just likes her job a whole lot better. Lives and breathes it. I reckon she'd convert one of the offices upstairs into a bedroom and live on base if she could get away with it.'

'Really?' Eddie moved onto the bubble at the front of the helicopter, stretching to reach as high as he could. 'Might be a bit of a downer as far as a social life goes.'

'Don't think Jodie's got one,' Gus said. 'Or wants one. I've yet to see her go out with anyone more than once or twice. She was married very young, I believe, and it didn't last long. "Been there, done that," she told me. "Never doing it again." She's happily single and intends to stay that way.'

How intriguing… It seemed like Jodie Sinclair might be a female version of the person that Eddie had been for so many years. The version of himself that he wasn't that impressed with any longer. Maybe she'd had a more valid reason to avoid commitment after a disastrous marriage and Eddie might be moving on to a more settled lifestyle but his memories of so many good times could still make him smile.

'She's a girl after my own heart,' he said.

'Just as well Dion told you the score then.' Gus turned

the hose back on and Eddie stood back, dropping his cloth into the bucket. 'Crew members are off-limits.'

'No worries,' Eddie assured him. Then he grinned. 'You're quite safe, mate.'

He had to duck as a spray of water came in his direction. They were both still laughing as their pagers went off but then Gus shook his head.

'How long was that? Eight minutes?'

''Bout that.' But Eddie was still smiling. He knew Gus was just as happy as he was to get the callout. This was what they were all here for. Stocktaking and washing helicopters was just marking time between the opportunities to provide the best possible care for sick and injured people in that vital space of time before they could get to the emergency department of a well-equipped hospital.

It was only a short flight this time.

A thirty-four-year-old farmer, Dylan McKenzie, in an area only fifteen minutes' flight time north of Aberdeen, had apparently been gored and trampled by one of his Highland cattle. Local first responders and the police were in attendance, currently working on controlling an arterial bleed.

The cattle, and their calves, had been cleared from the field and there was plenty of room for Gus to bring the helicopter down not far from where a police vehicle was parked on the grass. They had arrived before the ambulance that had been dispatched from the nearest station by road.

The first responders were doing their best but the dressing over a wound they were applying pressure to was blood soaked and the young farmer's skin was a nasty shade of grey that Eddie knew was an ominous sign of potential haemorrhagic shock from massive blood loss. He was also agitated, which was another sign that his brain wasn't receiving enough oxygen.

'Someone needs to look after my wife…' was the first thing he said, between gasps of pain, as Jodie crouched beside him. '… Debbie… She's pregnant…'

Eddie had already noticed the young woman who looked to be in the late stages of pregnancy. She was standing beside the police car and had a small boy who was clutching her legs and sobbing. A policewoman had her arm around the young mother's shoulders.

'She's being taken care of,' Jodie calmly assured Dylan. 'It's my job to take care of you and I've got Eddie and Alex with me. I'm just going to put a mask over your face so we can give you some oxygen, is that okay?'

But Dylan was shaking his head. 'They didn't mean to hurt me,' he said. 'It's because…they were trying to protect their calves. *Oh*…help me…please…'

He sounded in extreme pain and increasingly short of breath. Eddie opened a pouch on the side of the defibrillator and took out the SpO2 monitor. He put it on Dylan's finger and then nodded at the first responder, a middle-aged man wearing overalls that advertised his job as a mechanic with a local garage.

'You've done a good job, mate,' he said. 'Can I take over from you there?'

'Please…'

Eddie lifted the dressing to find an ongoing pulsatile blood loss. He folded a gauze square and used it, with his finger, to apply a very direct pressure to the bleeding vessel because the pressure that had been put on so far had been too diffuse to allow a clot to form and block the damaged artery.

Alex was cutting the thick woollen jumper and shirt underneath to expose Dylan's chest and Jodie was watching the chest wall movements as she fitted her stethoscope to her ears and then put the disc onto skin as she listened to his breath sounds. Eddie had seen the severe bruising already appearing on one side of the chest which told him that they could probably add fractured ribs to the list of injuries.

There was so much that needed to be done in the shortest possible time to try and stabilise this patient before they could move him.

'Alex, can you grab a CAT tourniquet for me, please?'

'Sure.'

'And I need a non-rebreather mask and the oxygen cylinder, thanks, Alex.' Jodie glanced up at Eddie. 'Breath sounds equal. Respiratory rate thirty-six. Heart rate around one forty.'

Eddie acknowledged the information with a nod. The higher-than-normal vital signs for heart and breathing rates fitted the picture of haemorrhagic shock and if they were going to save this patient they had to try and stop any further blood loss and replace volume. He slipped the strap of the Combat Application Tourniquet through the buckle and pulled it tight before fastening it. Then he twisted the plastic rod until the bleeding from the gash in his arm was finally stopped.

Jodie was on the side of Dylan's uninjured arm, holding his wrist, but the quick shake of her head told Eddie that there was no palpable radial pulse. Trying to gain peripheral IV access was only going to waste time and it was imperative that it happened quickly. It wasn't just to provide pain relief, replace fluid volume and infuse the blood products they carried in the helicopter that

Alex had just been sent to fetch. There were also drugs that needed IV administration, like TXA that could help stop the bleeding by influencing the clotting process and others that could cause constriction of veins to help keep blood volume in vital organs or help the heart pump harder to move what blood remained through the body.

'I'm going to cannulate the external jugular,' Jodie told Eddie. 'And we might get a second line in via an intraosseous access.'

An ambulance pulled into the field as Eddie was doing a body sweep to make sure they weren't missing any other obvious injuries that were contributing to blood loss and someone else, possibly a relative, arrived to take the small boy away from the scene. Eddie ran his hands down Dylan's side, into the gap beneath his lower spine and down each leg, but there was no blood to be seen on his gloves. What he did find, however, made his heart sink.

The cry of pain from Dylan when he'd touched his hips and lower back made him gently palpate both iliac crests above each hip.

'Pelvic instability,' he informed Jodie quietly.

She glanced up for a split second, from where she was unrolling a kit that contained everything she needed to insert a wide bore cannula into the large vein on the side of Dylan's neck. The eye contact was so brief it almost didn't happen, but it still conveyed how much of a challenge they were up against. If Dylan was losing blood internally due to a serious pelvic fracture on top of the amount he'd already lost from an external arterial bleed, they could well be fighting a losing battle.

If anything, that knowledge only made them fight harder. This was a young farmer. A husband. A father. His distraught wife was watching the efforts to save

Dylan but probably couldn't see very much with another ambulance crew and more emergency responders crowded around and trying to assist by holding up bags of IV fluid and blood, supplying equipment, drawing up drugs and finding blankets to try and keep Dylan warm. It was probably just as well she couldn't see too much as Dylan slipped into unconsciousness and then cardiac arrest but Eddie liked that Jodie was using one of the extra medics to keep his wife informed at every step about what was being done to try and save her husband.

Her skill in leading a large team of people was something he hadn't seen before and Jodie was as capable in this tense scenario as in everything else she did, but, sadly, in the end there was nothing more they could do. Dylan was still losing blood faster than they could replace it and so, when he went into cardiac arrest, there was simply not enough blood volume for the heart to be able to pump. As lead medic, it was Jodie's call to stop the resuscitation attempt and it was impossible not to notice how calm her voice was when she made the decision.

'I'm calling it,' she said. She glanced at her watch. 'Time of death fifteen forty-three hours.'

Her face was expressionless as she got to her feet, turned away from the patient they'd been working on so desperately hard for what seemed like for ever but had probably been no more than about forty-five minutes, and walked towards where Dylan's wife, Debbie, was still standing beside a police car. He couldn't look away as he watched the two women—Jodie standing so upright but Debbie crumpling as she received the news, despite knowing it was coming. He saw Jodie reach out but there were other people closer who could catch the devastated woman and care for her.

Perhaps it was only Eddie who saw that Jodie's fingers clenched into a tight ball as she turned away. That her face was so rigid it was obvious that she was struggling to keep her composure. Then, she seemed to take a deeper breath and regain control. By the time she noticed Eddie watching her she was close enough for him to see that she was focused on what needed to happen next.

And, of course, she knew exactly what the protocols were for a situation like this.

'There's a standardised post-resuscitation procedure for all unexpected adult deaths in the community, that you might not have caught up with yet?'

'No, sorry. I haven't seen that yet.'

'The main thing we need to be aware of is that when attempts have been made to resuscitate the patient and the death has been confirmed at the scene, we need to leave everything in place—the ET tube, cannulas, ECG electrodes et cetera. It's up to the police and the SFIU—the Scottish Fatalities Investigation Unit to organise the next steps and remove the body because this now becomes an investigation of a sudden death in the community. Could you explain that to the relatives, please, Ed? The wife might be a bit shocked to have us just pack up and disappear.'

'Of course.'

Eddie was still watching Jodie like a hawk but he couldn't detect any other signs that she wasn't totally in control. He could, in fact, almost *feel* the barriers that had gone up with the distance being created by a man with a name suddenly becoming 'the body' and the distraught mother of his children, who had to be about the same age as Jodie, becoming simply 'the wife'.

But Eddie had seen behind the mask, hadn't he?

Just for a blink of time, but it had been long enough to realise what it was that had been niggling at the back of his mind. What that 'something' was that had felt as if it was missing.

Empathy?

An emotional connection with her patients?

It wasn't that it wasn't there. It was that Jodie chose not to let it show. Or maybe she didn't even want to acknowledge it herself.

And Eddie wanted to know why.

She didn't want to.

She tried not to.

But Jodie couldn't stop that glance from the window as the helicopter rose straight up from the scene until they were high enough for Gus to turn them towards home. She knew what she would see. All unnecessary people had been cleared from the area as police tape was put up to secure the scene. The wash from the helicopter rotors was blowing some of the debris of packaging away from the still figure of the young father but that was evidence as well and someone else would be responsible for cleaning it up at a later point.

They had protected Dylan's dignity as much as possible, leaving a pillow under his head and covering him with a blanket. His wife was the only person near him as the air rescue crew finally departed. She was kneeling and leaning over Dylan as best she could with her pregnant belly, and maybe it was Jodie's imagination but, even at this height, she thought she could see Debbie's shoulders shaking with her agonised sobbing.

The way she'd knelt over Joel's body that day…? Would Debbie also try and hold her husband the way she'd held

Joel—as if her own body warmth could somehow breathe life back into him?

Ohh... That pain didn't often surface these days, but when it did, it was still more than sharp enough to cause real pain.

Jodie shifted her gaze, being careful not to look in Eddie's direction or say anything that might spark conversation between any of the crew. She flipped over her tablet in its almost bombproof casing and tapped it into life. Paperwork for any patient could be detailed but for a case like this, that would automatically be part of a wider investigation, the reporting had to be immaculate. She didn't want the distraction of anyone talking to her. Or even looking at her.

Especially Eddie.

Because Jodie had the horrible feeling that he'd noticed the way she'd had to hang on to her control a little more tightly than usual, after having to remove any last shred of hope that she knew Debbie would have been clinging on to that they were going to be able to save her husband and the father of her child and unborn baby. She also knew what Debbie was about to face and how hard it was going to be to survive that tsunami of grief.

The sooner this job was over and done with, the better. It was a good thing that by the time they'd sorted out the mess their gear was in and restocked depleted kits it would be past the end of their shift and she could go home. And then she could run and run and run, until the ground—and the foundations of her life—felt completely stable again.

Alex and Gus focused on what needed to be done inside the helicopter when they were back on base. Eddie and Jodie opened their kits on the floor of the storeroom and found everything they needed to replenish supplies. The drug roll was the last task to be done. Gus and Alex had already brought the helicopter back into the hangar. They poked their heads into the storeroom.

'Need a hand?' Alex asked.

'No, we're all good,' Eddie told them. 'We'll be done soon.'

'We're heading into the Pig and Thistle for a quick beer before we go home,' Gus said as he turned away. 'Maybe you'd like to join us?'

Eddie was already familiar with the nearest pub to the base, which also happened to be very close to the apartment he'd taken over from the paramedic whose position he'd filled. He was also a big fan of having an informal debrief to tackle the emotional aftermath of a case like they'd just had, but this time he shook his head regretfully.

'I'm visiting my brother,' he told them. 'I promised I'd arrive with some fish and chips for his dinner. It was always his favourite Friday night takeaway when we were kids.'

Not that Mick was likely to do more than taste it, but Eddie wasn't about to break his promise.

'Next time, then,' Alex excused him. 'Jodie?'

'I'll see how I go when I'm done with the paperwork.'

'Okay…no pressure…'

It took another fifteen minutes to go through the raft of drugs they'd used in Dylan's attempted resuscitation and everything had to be recorded and signed for by both of them in the drug register.

'I've got the last one.' Eddie held up two glass ampoules. 'Tranexamic acid, five hundred milligrams in five mils, solution for injection.' He held out the ampoules for Jodie to double check. 'Expiry date next year.'

He slotted the ampoules into the drug kit while Jodie was recording the details. She signed the column and then held out the pen.

'Your turn.'

Eddie scribbled his signature and then closed the book. 'So…you heading to the pub with the others, then?'

'I don't think so.' Jodie took the book and slotted it back on a shelf.

'How come?'

The query slipped out before Eddie had given it any thought. He knew instantly that he'd made a mistake as Jodie turned and gave him a glance sharp enough to cut paper. Her tone was just as cutting.

'Maybe I don't want to. Does it matter? Is it actually any of your business?'

Whoa…

Eddie held her gaze. He could take this the wrong way and back off, but he knew that if he took the easy way out of this suddenly intense moment he'd never get the chance to find out why Jodie was so good at hiding.

Which was what she was doing now. Hiding from his question. Hiding from him. Hiding from the other people she had worked with long enough for them to know not to put any pressure on personal boundaries.

Eddie got it.

And perhaps he got rather more than Jodie might think he got. Because he'd had the wake-up call of a family crisis and could look back on the way he'd been living his life as a way of hiding from the stuff that really mattered. Like committing to relationships in a way that actually meant something.

He wasn't about to put any pressure on her either, but he wanted Jodie to know that if he had seen behind her mask she could trust him not to use it against her or even mention it.

That she could trust *him*.

Maybe his lips curved just a little, but it was Eddie's eyes doing most of the smiling and Jodie caught her bottom lip between her teeth.

'Sorry,' she muttered. 'I didn't mean that to sound so…erm…'

'I know.'

Eddie was still holding her gaze. Or maybe Jodie was holding his. Maybe it didn't matter because something bigger was holding them both. The air in this small room, with its shelves so tightly packed with medical supplies and the heavy security door firmly closed, seemed to be getting heavier. Pressing down on them.

Pushing them closer together.

Neither of them said a word. They didn't seem to need to. By whatever means, whether it was body language or telepathy, apparently the desire was expressed, permission sought—and granted.

Jodie slowly came up onto her tiptoes. Eddie bent his head just as slowly, turning it in the last moments, just before he closed his eyes and finally broke that contact, so that his lips were at the perfect angle to cover Jodie's with a soft, lingering touch.

When he lifted his head, he found Jodie's eyes were open before his. Maybe she hadn't closed them at all? Because of their soft, chocolate brown colour, he could also see that her pupils were getting bigger fast enough to tell him that she had liked that kiss as much as he did. That quick intake of her breath suggested that she wanted more.

Eddie had played this game often enough to be an expert. He knew there was an easy way to find out...

This time, the kiss wasn't nearly as soft and her lips parted beneath his, her tongue meeting his almost instantly.

Oh, yeah...

She wanted more.

So did Eddie. But not here. Not now. Not just because they'd be breaking all sorts of rules and it was a bad idea, anyway. No...he had a promise to keep to someone else and Edward Grisham never broke a promise.

He broke the kiss, instead.

'I have to go,' he said.

Jodie's gaze slid away from his. 'Me too. We're done here.'

But Eddie was smiling as he turned away. He spoke softly but he knew that Jodie would be able to hear him perfectly well.

'I'm not so sure about that,' he said.

CHAPTER FIVE

IT WAS STILL THERE.

The memory of that kiss.

How long had it been since Jodie had experienced a kiss that had the ability to make time stop like that? One that even an echo of it, in the form of a memory, was guaranteed to generate that kind of delicious sensation, like the anticipation of experiencing something you wanted more than anything else in the world, deep in her belly?

Was it too long, or was it not long enough…?

Maybe the really disturbing thought was that the memory was more than simply about that physical touch of lips on lips and the unspoken conversation that it had evoked. It was about what had led up to that kiss.

That gruelling case when a young man, the love of someone's life, the father of a child who was too young to understand that his life was about to be changed for ever and another who hadn't even taken a first breath, had been ripped away from the world and, despite the best training, the best equipment and enough experience to know exactly what they needed to do, she and Eddie had been helpless to prevent it happening. Keeping enough of an emotional distance from the heartbreak that went way too close to the bone because it was so personal had been so much harder than usual. She'd had to fight hard and Jodie had even wondered if Eddie might have witnessed that hidden struggle.

Had he seen something she'd thought she had been successful in hiding from anyone for so long she didn't even consider it to be an issue these days? It was the last thing Jodie would have wanted to happen but, at least if he had, he had also made it clear that he wasn't about to pry too far into her personal life. She'd bitten his head off, mind you, when he'd asked why she might not want to join in a happy hour at the local pub, but he hadn't been offended. Quite the opposite? The look he'd given her made her think he might understand far more than she might be comfortable with, but it had also made her begin to feel, deep down in her bones, that she could trust him.

And how powerful had *that* feeling been?

Powerful enough that, when combined with the stress they had both experienced that day and what it was about this newcomer in her life that was so damned attractive, it had probably made that kiss inevitable. On her side, anyway.

That Eddie had responded the way he did—almost as if he'd expected the opportunity to arise and had been looking forward to it—had ignited something that Jodie wasn't ready to acknowledge. Not that there was any point in even thinking about it. No matter how attractive they might find each other, going any further down that track was not going to happen.

You didn't mess around with your crewmates and that was that.

End of story.

Except it was still there.

Nobody else knew it was there, of course. Eddie was so

good at hiding it that Jodie might have wondered if it was actually there herself in the days following that unfortunate lapse of good judgement in the storeroom that night.

But the occasional eye contact that was held for just a heartbeat too long, that gave her an unmistakable frisson of a sensation she preferred not to analyse too deeply, was a dead giveaway. So were those touches of physical contact that was inevitable when you were working so closely with someone—taking a drug ampoule from their hand to double check the name, dosage and expiry date, for example. Or holding a limb so that a splint or dressing could be applied with minimal discomfort.

Maybe Eddie wasn't feeling it as much as she was and that was why it was so easy for him to carry on as though nothing had happened?

As the days passed and Jodie relaxed enough to step back from what had, after all, been no more than a momentary blip in what was becoming a good professional relationship, she could see a gleam in Eddie's gaze occasionally that was definitely an acknowledgment that they had stepped, briefly, into a very different space. One that they both knew was simply not acceptable amongst crew members and could, in fact, get them both into a lot of trouble, but that gleam suggested that Eddie had no regrets. That, perhaps, he liked the fact that it was a secret between them?

Whatever. What had impressed Jodie was that he was so good at keeping that secret. Instinct told her that she could trust him to keep on keeping it, which was strengthening the impression that she could trust him on a personal as well as a professional level. And wasn't that the basis for a friendship that could grow into the kind of bond she had with the other people on this air rescue base that she considered to be her family? And, if she was really honest with herself, that buzz of sensation that she knew perfectly well was all about an unusually strong sexual attraction was not exactly an unpleasant thing to be experiencing occasionally.

It made her feel distinctly more alive—where every sense became heightened to the point that colours were brighter and food tasted better and you could feel things with a much keener awareness. It was kind of similar to the heightened awareness and the ability to think and move faster that came with the rush of adrenaline associated with the more dangerous challenges one could face working on a frontline helicopter rescue crew. Challenges like rescues at sea, which could mean that a medic needed to be lowered to the deck of a moving vessel or dropped into a rough sea to reach a person in the water. The sort of missions that didn't happen often and were more likely to occur in unpredictable conditions, so regular training sessions were vital to keep skills as sharp as needed for when an emergency like that presented itself and there were lives at stake for both the rescuers and those in trouble.

Jodie and her crewmates were gathering in the meeting room upstairs at the base, early on the morning of a day they weren't on duty. Was that why it looked as though Eddie hadn't bothered shaving this morning? Jodie had to stop herself taking another look at the shadow on his jawline so she didn't get distracted by wondering how that faint stubble might feel beneath her fingers.

Or against her skin...?

Dion had an image projected onto a whiteboard at the front of the meeting room and Jodie deliberately focused on the chart of numbers and letters.

'Here's the marine shipping forecast for the Cromarty area,' Dion told them. 'And it looks like we couldn't have ordered up a better day for this training session.' He pointed to a column of figures. 'There's a light breeze with a wind speed of six knots, gusting to nine. Cloud cover of twenty percent with no rain expected and a swell of less than a metre, lasting six to seven seconds.'

'Nice...' Alex was looking happy. 'Is the coastguard rescue team good to go?'

'They've already been out in their all-weather lifeboat doing some training of their own with a couple of new volunteers. They're expecting us on scene in forty minutes, so you'd better get your skates on and get into your wetsuits. You'll do the Hi-Line exercises first with the coastguard rescue team, but they'll stay on scene for the rest of the session when you're doing the person in the water retrieval.' Dion was smiling at them all. 'Stay safe,' he said. 'And have fun...'

Oh...*man*...

Seeing Jodie Sinclair encased in that skin-tight black wetsuit, that didn't leave very much at all to the imagination with regard to every curve of her body, had to be the sexiest thing Eddie had ever seen. He found himself needing to take a deep breath and stop himself taking yet another glance. He followed Alex's example instead, and watched the sea beneath them as they became airborne and headed straight offshore.

It was a brief period of time between their preparations and arriving at the designated area for the training exercise and staring at a relatively smooth patch of the North Sea wasn't enough to stop Eddie's mind from going where it was determined to go.

Back to that kiss…

Yet again…

He knew it wasn't going to be repeated. It shouldn't have happened in the first place, and the last thing Eddie wanted was to even suggest breaking rules that could end up with disciplinary action against Jodie and, worse, him being transferred to another crew or even fired but…but knowing all that didn't seem to be enough to let him just forget about it.

On the contrary, the idea of a secret, *illicit* liaison with Jodie was taking that level of desire to a whole new, unbelievable notch. Which, in a way, was a good thing because Eddie knew that reality could never live up to an expectation like that, except in fantasies. And sexual fantasies would never encroach on his mind during working hours. Ever.

He knew it wouldn't be at all surprising if he found himself thinking about Jodie in that wetsuit when he was alone in his bed in that tiny basement flat later tonight, mind you…

Spotting the bright orange paintwork of the coastguard vessel below them made it easy to flick any personal thoughts from his mind. He raised his hand to point it out to the others but they'd already seen the boat.

'Target sighted,' Alex said. 'One o'clock.'

'Roger that.' Gus was establishing contact with the boat crew as he got the helicopter into a position and speed that would keep them at a steady distance behind the vessel. The boat crew were well trained in this exercise but Gus still went through every step with them again.

'The Hi-Line will be lowered. Take hold of the weighted end and take in the slack, coiling the line onto the deck. Do not attach the Hi-Line to any part of the vessel, is that understood?'

'Loud and clear,' came the response.

Alex was leaning out of the open door of the helicopter, his hand on the line as it was lowered towards the boat, and Eddie was also watching it carefully. This type of boat didn't present as many problems as a yacht with its mast and rigging would but they still had to be sure the 'heaving in' or Hi-Line didn't snag on anything.

They paid the line out again as Gus dropped the helicopter's position further behind the boat and then it was Jodie's turn to be winched down first. The line that the two deck crew on the coastguard boat were holding was still attached to the winch hook and, as she was lowered, Eddie was watching the Hi-Line even more carefully now. The crew on the boat had to haul the line in to keep the correct tension that would stop Jodie being spun by the rotor wash or the lines dropping into the sea or getting caught on anything. He was holding his breath as he watched her getting close enough to get pulled onboard the boat, detach the winch hook and signal to have it raised.

The process was reversed to take Jodie off the boat and lift her back into the helicopter and then crew members both in the air and on board the boat swapped places so that others could get the hands-on experience that exercises like this provided so well. It was Eddie's turn to be winched down and it went as smoothly as he had expected. Too easy. He'd done some pretty hairy rescue missions in the dark, in much bigger seas than this in Australia but it was always good to refresh the skills, especially when working with a new crew.

Gus moved the helicopter a little further away from the

coastguard vessel for the second part of their refresher training. Both Jodie and Eddie needed flippers, masks and snorkels in addition to the lifejackets over their wet-suits for this part of the exercise.

'Who's going to be our victim for the first run?' he asked. 'Jodie?'

'Fine by me.' She pushed her foot into the second, bright orange flipper. 'Could do with a dip.'

The sea conditions might be ideal, with a rescue boat not far away, but there was still something a bit scary about being dropped into the ocean.

Well…not dropped, exactly. Jodie couldn't say anything around the mouthpiece of her snorkel. She couldn't hear anything either, because she couldn't wear her usual helmet with its inbuilt sound technology in the water, but she could see Alex's lips moving and knew exactly what his calm voice would sound like as he went through his own protocol and patter with Gus after being cleared to open the door and then attach the winch hook to Jodie's harness.

'Moving Jodie to door. Clear skids.'

'Clear skids,' Gus would say if he was happy for the winch to proceed in these conditions.

'Clear to winch out?'

'Clear to winch.'

Jodie could see the skids passing her line of sight as she dropped beneath the helicopter. She could see the grey swells of sea water coming rapidly closer.

Alex would let the others know what was happening by counting down the metres as she got closer to enter-ing the water.

Jodie didn't look up but she knew Alex would be leaning out, safely anchored by his own strop, watching her every move. She couldn't look up, anyway, because she was busy opening the carabiner that had kept her attached to the winch hook. She took it off and then held it out and up so that Alex could see it clearly and know that it was safe to retrieve the hook back onboard.

She glanced up to see the hook swinging as it was quickly wound back up. Eddie would be getting ready to be winched down now and he would be carrying an extra harness for her. Jodie's job was simply to float in the water, being the patient. Someone who'd been caught in a rip and swept out to sea, perhaps. Or a survivor from a yacht that had caught fire or been sunk by a collision or bad weather. She always welcomed the opportunity to see what she did for a job from the point of view of the person who was being rescued but, as she rode the swell in the chill of the ocean water around her, she could sense something more this time.

Because it was Eddie that she could see waiting on the skid of the hovering helicopter for the okay to be winched down to rescue her.

Jodie was someone who was firmly anchored in reality and never willingly conjured up any kind of fantasy situation unless it was a patient scenario or some other kind of simulation that could improve her skills—like learning to escape from a helicopter when it had crashed into water, for example, so it was more than a little disconcerting to find herself suddenly imagining what it would be like to be in real danger. To have Edward Grisham swooping in like a knight in shining armour, albeit dressed in a wet-suit and unrecognisable with his head covering, mask and snorkel on. To feel him holding her and keeping her safe as they were both lifted out of that danger.

Oh, my...

Jodie could see that Eddie was entering the water now, not far away from her. She raised both her arms in a signal for help and was ready to get the harness in place and be hooked onto the winch hook still attached to Eddie. He held his arm straight up to let Alex know they were ready to be winched up and Jodie could feel the drag of the water as she was pulled clear.

Now she could really feel what it was like to be this close to this man's body and it was, quite literally, stealing her breath away. Because she already knew what it was like to be kissed by him? Because there was genuinely an element of danger in what they were doing so her senses were already maxed out? Maybe it had something to do with the rush of external air pressure from the helicopter's rotors or it might have been the combination of all those factors. It was no time at all, really, before she was safely back inside the cabin and could breathe again but...something had changed, hadn't it?

Something had escaped from the place it had been so very carefully confined for a very long time.

And Jodie wasn't at all sure what she should do about that.

Everything that had been in touch with, soaked in or splashed by salt water had to be thoroughly cleaned after the training exercises were finished. Gus and Alex took care of helicopter surfaces and winch gear like harnesses and strops but Eddie and Jodie were responsible for all the items they'd used themselves. Rinsing the likes of masks and snorkels was an easy enough task but the most time-consuming chore was getting out of their wetsuits, having a hot shower to warm up properly and then washing the suits.

There was a tub plumbed onto the outside of the hangar near the storeroom and a line to hang the suits on after they were washed. Eddie was opening all the zips on the suits and turning them inside out as Jodie filled the large tub with cool water and added the liquid cleaning product.

Alex appeared around the side of the hangar. 'We're done with the chopper and putting it away. Do you guys need a hand?'

'Nah…we're good, thanks,' Eddie responded. 'Thanks for today, mate. Reckon it's my turn to shout you and Gus a round at the Pig and Thistle this time if you don't mind waiting a wee while so that we can finish our housework here.'

But Alex shook his head. 'Gus is taking his family out to dinner tonight for a birthday celebration and… I've got a date.' The way the young crewman ducked his head suggested that this was both a new relationship and potentially promising.

'Ooh…' Jodie was grinning. 'Bring her along. I'll let you know her suitability rating later.'

'I'm not sure she's ready to meet you lot yet, but if she's brave enough we'll drop in. Not that I'm going to take any notice whatsoever of your suitability score.' Alex might be grinning back at her but he shook his head even more firmly as he turned to walk away. 'You might want to take a look at your own love life before you start offering advice to others, my friend.'

'I'm perfectly happy with my love life exactly the way it is, thank you.' Jodie took the wetsuits from Eddie and plunged them into the water. 'Can you get the masks and snorkels dry and put them away while I do this? And did you find where the flippers ended up?'

'Yeah... Alex had already put them away.' Eddie picked up the masks. 'Do you think he'll bring his date to the pub?'

'Doubt it.' Jodie laughed. 'We're probably far too intimidating.'

'Do you still want to go?'

Jodie seemed to be focused on kneading the wetsuit fabric to make sure the cleaner was doing its job. 'Sure... why not? I think we've earned a bit of down time, don't you? And the Pig and Thistle does some amazing potato skins. Don't know about you, but I'm starving after all that exercise and sea air.'

Jodie's casual question was still hanging in the air as Eddie headed for the cupboard where the wetsuits would hang once dry again. There was a rack for flippers of various sizes and the other accessories needed for sea missions.

Why not, indeed?

Because if nobody else turned up, it might feel like a date?

No. He pushed that unhelpful thought aside. This was, in fact, a perfect opportunity to do what colleagues should be able to do without even blinking—share a drink after a good day of working or training together.

It might even be a step closer to friendship?

Oh, help...what had she been thinking?

She'd had the chance to get out of this when they'd discovered Gus was busy and Alex unlikely to bring his new girlfriend for a drink with his workmates but she'd been the one to say she'd like to go anyway. Because they'd earned it and because she liked the crispy, deep-fried potato skins that arrived too hot to pick up instantly, covered with a generous sprinkling of sea salt crystals and grated Parmesan cheese.

So, here they were with a basket of potato skins in front of them, along with tall glasses of her favourite lager and… Eddie looked gorgeous in his faded old jeans and a ribbed black fisherman's jumper with the sleeves pushed up and his hair all rumpled and even more of a five o'clock shadow than he'd had this morning and…

And it suddenly felt like a *date*…

What was even worse was that that occasional pleasant buzz of sexual attraction had become a steady hum that was increasing in intensity and impossible to ignore. Maybe talking about work would help?

'So…have you ever done a sea rescue for real?'

Eddie nodded. 'Quite a few,' he added, before taking a big bite of the crunchy potato snack. 'I worked on the coast of Australia. There's a lot that happens at sea.'

Jodie picked up a potato skin for herself, which was as delicious as they always were, but she was watching Eddie from the corner of her eye as he finished his and then sucked some grains of salt and cheese fragments from his fingertips. That hum of sensation in her belly was split in half by a spear of what could only be deemed sheer lust.

Thank goodness he started speaking then, because Jodie would have been incapable of saying anything.

'Had three guys in a lifeboat once. Big seas. The mast on their yacht had snapped and it overturned. The swells were big enough for the inflatable lifeboat to disappear between them and it was in the middle of the night and raining. The wind was enough to have me swinging like a pendulum.'

Jodie's jaw was dropping, her food forgotten. 'Sounds terrifying.'

Eddie could have made himself sound like a real hero by denying that but, instead, his face sobered as he held her gaze.

'It was,' he said quietly. 'I was in the water and swam to the boat and the two guys that were still conscious insisted I take their mate first because he was the worst off, but I could see they were all in trouble. I was supposed to swap with my crew partner for the next retrieval but it was going to take too long so I just went down again myself. Twice. Getting them on board ASAP was the best we could do for them. They were dangerously hypothermic.'

'And the first guy?'

'I kind of knew I was winching a body by the time I had him in the harness.' Eddie shook his head. 'But I could have been wrong and, in the end, I was glad we took him home. His family were very grateful to get him back. They came to see me, after the funeral. To tell me how much it meant to them. To thank us.'

Jodie could see the muscles in his jaw and throat moving as he swallowed hard. As if he was holding back tears?

'Sometimes,' he added softly, 'there are moments in this job that make you feel very humble, aren't there?'

There were. But some people never felt like that because it took a level of compassion and humanity that wasn't a given, even in a profession that was all about helping other people. It was also rare to find a man who was okay with not only feeling but sharing something that emotional.

Jodie couldn't look away from Eddie.

He wasn't looking away from her either.

And it was like that moment in the storeroom, before that kiss, only it was ten times more intense.

It was Eddie who broke the bubble of silence they were in, in the middle of a crowded, noisy pub. His words were so quiet Jodie shouldn't have been able to hear them as clearly as she could.

'I think I want to kiss you again,' he murmured.

It was Jodie's turn to swallow hard.

'I think I want you to,' she said.

'We work together. We can't do that.'

'No...' Jodie felt the need to dampen her lips with the tip of her tongue and she could actually feel the intensity go up a big notch as Eddie's gaze dropped from her eyes to watch her mouth. 'But...have you ever...?'

'Yeah...'

'Did anyone find out?'

'No...'

The quirk of Eddie's eyebrow suggested that an encounter could be all the more desirable because it was against the rules. She could believe that. Jodie dragged her gaze away from his face. She could see the basket of potato skins sitting there, getting rapidly colder, but she wasn't hungry any longer. Not for food, anyway.

'I don't do relationships,' she told Eddie without looking at him. She would never lead anyone on, nor allow them to expect something she was not prepared to give.

'Neither do I,' he said.

Aye...she could believe that too. Someone like Eddie would have any number of women throwing themselves at him. Living a life of casual encounters or a series of 'friendships with benefits' certainly fitted the initial impression of him as being a maverick. She might have been wrong about that on a professional basis but it could still well apply to his personal life.

And if there were none of the expectations that came with a relationship, wouldn't that mean the possibility of conflict would also be non-existent? That was why the Mark and Zoe incident had been such an issue, wasn't it? Why it was understandable that Dion had made it so clear it was not to happen again on the Aberdeen Air Ambulance base.

But what she and Eddie were—sort of—discussing was no more than a hook-up. A mutual decision as adults who wouldn't be hurting anyone else by giving in to a sexual chemistry they happened to have discovered with each other.

Jodie released her bottom lip from where it had been caught between her teeth. Somehow, she managed to keep her tone perfectly casual. Matter-of-fact, even.

'It *is* kind of distracting, working with someone that you find attractive,' she said.

'It is.' Eddie cleared his throat. 'Maybe it's something we just need to get out of our systems?'

'You mean…' Jodie couldn't finish her sentence. Her mouth was getting dry. She reached for her glass and took a mouthful of the cool lager. Then she raised her gaze to meet Eddie's. 'Are you saying we should do something about it?'

'I'm saying it's an option. Might let us get past the distraction and be able to move on.'

The thought that Eddie might have been thinking about that kiss as much as she had only added to an intensity that was about to spiral out of control. Jodie knew she was playing with fire because there were things about this man that reminded her of Joel—the love of her life that she had no intention of even trying to replace. Ever.

But, in a way, that was also her safety net. Because it meant that she'd never fall in love with Eddie. Or anyone else. This was purely about sexual attraction and it wasn't as if she'd denied herself the occasional indulgence in what was a basic need, after all. And perhaps once would be enough. To satisfy her curiosity.

To satisfy a level of want that was becoming almost unbearable...

Her word was only a whisper. 'Where?'

'My place is just around the corner.'

Jodie pulled in a slow breath. Her gaze drifted towards the food and drinks they'd ordered. 'You don't want to finish any of this?'

'No.' Eddie's chair scraped on wooden floorboards. He held out his hand to help her to her feet and then leaned closer so that his lips brushed her ear. 'I want *you*, Jodie...'

CHAPTER SIX

His apartment.

His bed.

His…epiphany?

Who knew sex could be like this? This much fun but, at the same time, feel like something so much more than simply *fun*?

Something genuinely funny covered those awkward moments of getting naked with someone for the very first time because, in Eddie's haste to peel Jodie's tee shirt from her body, it somehow rolled itself up and made the armhole too small to let her get her arm out. They were both weak with laughter by the time they had unravelled the fabric and removed the garment.

But then, as Eddie dropped the tee shirt onto the floor and stood there looking down at Jodie wearing nothing more than her bra and knickers, the enormity struck him of doing this—the most intimate of touching—for the very first time with someone new. With an almost reverent movement, he lifted Jodie's chin with a gentle forefinger and bent his head to kiss her.

Softly.

It felt as if he was making a promise to respect this. To respect *her*. And to remind her that she could trust him.

And then sheer need took over and broke any remaining barriers due to awkwardness or possibly guilt that they were doing something that would be so disapproved of in their workplace, and it was at that point that Eddie discovered that passionate sex could also be both demanding and playful. And, oh...*so* satisfying...

It was later, when they slowed down and savoured every moment of doing it all over again, that Eddie realised this was something special.

When he raised his head from the lingering kiss they shared when they'd finally caught their breath again, he had another moment when he imagined he could see past whatever it was that Jodie used so well as a protection for what she didn't want the world to see.

And it almost looked like...a yearning for something?

A wanting of more? More of what they'd just discovered with each other, perhaps?

It was gone so fast it could well have been wishful thinking, replaced by a gleam of what looked a lot more like mischief.

'You're not so bad at that,' Jodie told him.

'I was about to tell you that,' he protested.

They both laughed. But they hadn't broken that eye contact and, when the laughter faded, there it was again. Eddie instinctively let his gaze shift because it felt as if he might be invading Jodie's privacy and he knew she wouldn't like that.

'Are you hungry?' he asked. 'I can offer you some toast. I've even got a jar of Vegemite I brought back from Australia.'

The way Jodie screwed up her nose was the cutest thing Eddie had ever seen. But then she shook her head.

'I should go,' she said.

'You don't have to.'

'Yes, I do.' Jodie was rolling off the side of the bed. Reaching for her tee shirt that was still rolled up into a strange shape. 'Sleeping in my own bed has always been non-negotiable.'

Eddie got out of bed himself and pulled on his jeans as Jodie got dressed. So Jodie had never gone to sleep with someone after having sex? Why not? Had she never felt safe enough with someone to make herself that vulnerable? Or was it the best way to keep something completely casual? To make sex a meaningless hook-up that implied that there was nothing particularly personal involved.

And who was he to judge? Eddie had done that himself on too many occasions in the past. He hadn't had any intention of doing it again, but then he'd never met anyone like Jodie Sinclair, had he? She'd been up for it— as much as he'd ever been and...okay... Mick's accident had been a wakeup call and he wanted something more in his life, but he didn't have to go cold turkey on that new resolution, did he?

One last 'just for fun' encounter had been too tempting to pass up.

Eddie had nothing on but his jeans as he opened the door to let Jodie out into the night. He hadn't even bothered to do up the stud button.

'Want me to walk you to your car?'

'I'm a big girl, Eddie. I can look after myself. And my car's only about two minutes down the road.'

It was the first time she'd called him Eddie, rather than Ed. It made it feel as if something had changed, which was hardly surprising given that they knew each other a hell of a lot better than they had this morning. Her independence was yet another thing he liked about her so he was smiling as he leaned against the door jamb.

'So…' His tone was a question all by itself.

'So what?'

'Do you think it worked?'

'Ah…' Jodie's eyes narrowed a little. 'Did what work, exactly?'

'Did we get it out of our systems?'

He could almost see the lightning-fast progression of her thoughts and the implications of any response she made. In the end, she didn't say anything, but she was trying to hide a smile as she turned away.

''Night, Eddie…'

''Night, Jodie…'

He stood there for a long moment, watching her walk towards her car. She hadn't even given him a hint of an answer to that question, but he realised she hadn't needed to. They both knew the answer, didn't they?

They hadn't got it out of their systems. What they'd done had probably made it even more pervasive. And compelling. But did that matter? If they were both totally on the same page and either of them could call it quits at any time without any hard feelings and simply walk away—the way Jodie was walking away tonight—there was no real reason *not* to do it again.

It was a real shame that Eddie had decided to move on from a casual, friendship with benefits kind of arrangement because he'd never met someone like Jodie who'd been so upfront about not being interested in anything more than sex.

She was, or at least had been, his perfect woman.

It was a week before Jodie decided she could answer Eddie's question that was, effectively, whether indulging once had been enough as far as getting that sexual attraction to each other out of their systems. She could have answered without hesitation at the time he'd asked, but that had been why she'd waited. To make sure that she was in control.

Of course she was. Okay...maybe she'd been tempted, just for a heartbeat, to stay the rest of the night with Eddie, but she hadn't broken that rule and she wasn't about to. Sleeping with someone was a very different thing to having sex with them. Jodie had always thought it was an even more intimate thing to do. A step closer to a space she wasn't going to ever share again.

She was pleased to discover that she wasn't the only one in control at work as well. Like the aftermath of that kiss that was now ancient history, Eddie didn't give the slightest hint that there was anything happening between them that might be breaking a rule that had become an unwritten law on this rescue base.

It was a busy week that had included a full four-day shift for Blue Watch at Triple A. Four days packed with the usual variety of emergency medical situations. They'd attended several car accidents and a truck that had veered off the road and rolled into a ditch.

They went to a cardiac arrest on a picturesque golf course where the victim was lucky enough to be playing a round with a retired doctor who started CPR and a clubhouse that had an automatic defibrillator that had kick-started a perfusing heart rhythm again despite the blocked cardiac arteries. It had been touch and go to get the man into a catheter laboratory with a second arrest mid-flight but they'd heard later that he'd survived and undergone the bypass surgery he needed.

They'd collected a hiker who'd broken her ankle badly slipping on a track deep within the Cairngorms National

Park and there'd been another job the very next day, quite close to that one, where a man who'd been white-water rafting had been thrown into the rapids and hit rocks hard enough to break a few ribs. He'd been in the water for some time before his companions could get him to shore and, by the time the air rescue crew arrived, he was also becoming seriously hypothermic. In an effort to cheer him up, one of his friends had made a joke about nobody wanting to get naked with him to warm him up, like in the movies.

And that joke—or possibly the way Eddie had caught her gaze as they were both smiling—seemed to have been the catalyst for a definitive decision. The wash of relief Jodie felt when their shift was over for the day and she found Eddie, alone, hanging up his flight suit in the locker room was enough to also make her realise how much she had wanted to give him this answer to that question. Relief mixed with the rather heady thought that, in a very short time, she might be able to feel that delicious anticipation again. A feeling that would probably be all the more intense for both knowing what might lie ahead and having waited this long to experience it again.

'You know those potato skins we left behind at the Pig and Thistle the other night?' she asked.

'Not likely to forget them in a hurry.' Eddie's tone was equally casual. 'Shame we didn't get to finish them.'

'Do you think they might have kept them for us? So we could get them heated up?'

Eddie appeared to give it serious thought. 'I'm sure they thought of doing that, but there are probably some health and safety regulations that prevent them keeping food for a week.'

'Hmm…' This conversational foreplay was more fun

than Jodie had expected. 'I suppose we could always buy a fresh basket some time...'

She knew perfectly well that Eddie understood this throwaway suggestion had nothing to do with eating anything at the pub just round the corner from his apartment and she was quite confident that he was about to say he thought it was not a bad idea when the door to the locker room opened and Alex came in.

'So...' Jodie shut the door of her locker with a decisive click as she swallowed her disappointment. 'I'm off to my bouldering session. Fancy a workout, Ed?'

'Is bouldering where you're rock climbing without any safety harnesses or ropes?'

'That's the one.' Jodie grinned at him. 'The risk is minimal when it's inside at the gym and there are nice soft mats on the floor. Alex...do you want to come and give it another go?'

Alex shook his head. 'Once was enough for me, mate. Besides, I'm...busy tonight. Going to a movie.'

'Are you now...?' Eddie gave Alex a direct look. 'It's about time we knew her name, isn't it?'

Alex shrugged. 'Georgia,' he admitted.

'And what does Georgia do?' Jodie also had Alex pinned with her glance.

'She's a nurse at Queen's. In ED.' Alex pulled on his anorak and shut his locker. 'And I'm not answering any more questions. See you guys tomorrow. Have a good night.' He turned as he reached the locker room door. 'You *should* go and try that bouldering,' he told Eddie. 'You might like it a lot more than I did and, even if you don't, you'll discover muscles in the next couple of days that you never knew you had.'

Jodie was looking at Eddie. Alex had just given them

the perfect way to be seen spending time together away from work without anyone suspecting that anything else was going on. 'Are you up for it?'

Eddie held her gaze. 'I was born up for it,' he said.

He didn't have to say he was talking about more than a new physical challenge as a workout. Alex was already out of the door and that message was loud and clear in his eyes.

Jodie smiled. What was even better was that she was still in control and she was going to make this waiting game last a wee bit longer.

'Let's go, then. You can rent some climbing shoes at the gym.'

The relief was almost overwhelming.

It was partly there because Eddie had managed to get himself along an albeit beginner's level series of foot and hand holds on the wall of the gymnasium without making a total idiot of himself.

But it was more the relief of discovering that Jodie wanted to spend some time with him again—that she had initiated it herself—when they both knew exactly how it was going to end up. Would it be in her bed this time or back to his place? Not that it mattered. Eddie might be curious to see where she lived but there was plenty of time for that to happen. Plus, he knew that as soon as they touched each other the rest of the world would fade into insignificance, anyway.

It should have been frustrating that they were spending an hour in this noisy gym with a basketball team practice going on in the background and a group of very keen climbers scrambling along this end wall but, in its own way, it was adding to a tension that Eddie hadn't acknowledged had been building for a whole week. Stretching it out a little further was only going to make the breaking of that tension so much better. Possibly better than anything Eddie had ever been lucky enough to experience in his life.

Okay…if being here doing something as acceptable as a gym session after work with a colleague wasn't the best cover they could have come up with for hiding a secret liaison, Eddie might have been tempted to catch Jodie as soon as she finished her higher level scramble and drag her out of the door. Instead, he stood back, shifting to ease muscles all over his body that he suspected he might well be feeling tomorrow and watching Jodie reach for a handhold on an overhang and then stretch her leg to try and find a foothold that would get her higher on the wall. For a moment, she looked like a very, very sexy human starfish.

Eddie blew out a breath, took a glance over his shoulder as if he was also interested in the basketball game going on, although he'd really only wanted to look at the time on a huge wall clock, and then turned back to keep watching Jodie. The climbing session was due to wrap in another five minutes or so.

And he couldn't wait.

He was going to make sure this was an evening that Jodie wouldn't forget in a hurry. One that, hopefully, she wouldn't want to wait a whole week before doing it again.

'Keeping it a secret only makes it better.'

Eddie had been struggling to find a topic of conversation with Mick that might interest him or at least make him smile. He hadn't seen his brother smile once in the last couple of weeks, so when Mick had asked how things were going at work now that he'd had time to settle in properly, he'd found himself confessing what was going on between himself and Jodie Sinclair.

'It started a few weeks ago. You remember I told you about that water rescue training we did on a day off with some of the coastguard volunteers?'

'Yeah…sounded fun.'

'What was even more fun was that Jodie and I ended up at the pub afterwards. We were starving but we ended up not even eating what we'd ordered. Went back to my place instead and…this'll make you laugh… I was in so much of a rush to get her clothes off, I ended up tying her in knots with her own tee shirt.'

'And she came back for more?'

Eddie could feel the warm glow that started something deep in his gut, spreading right to the tips of his fingers and toes.

'Aye…' The affirmative word was almost a sigh and Eddie could feel his face softening with the sound. It was partly due to gratitude that Jodie had not only come back for more but that neither of them seemed at all inclined to put a stop to it yet. Another part of that sound was simply amazement that he could have found someone so like himself. Someone whose company he was so at ease with. They liked the same kind of food. They laughed at the same jokes. They liked pushing themselves to conquer any new challenge, physical or mental. They were passionate about the same work.

'People must have twigged that something's going on between you.' Mick was staring at Eddie. 'Especially if you go around looking like a love-struck puppy, like you're doing right now.'

Eddie adjusted his expression instantly. 'We might like

each other,' he admitted. 'But neither of us in "in love".
We're friends, that's all.'

Best friends, a small voice at the back of his mind
suggested.

Lovers…

If Eddie had ever believed in such a thing as a soul
mate, then Jodie would have been at the top of the list
of possibilities.

But he didn't believe in the idea of "the one" and,
even if he did, Jodie had made it very clear that it wasn't
going to be her, so he stifled that unwelcome voice that
was coming from nowhere. If the feeling wasn't there on
both sides, or if either one or both of the people involved
had put up an enormous roadblock so it could never get
past a particular point, surely that instantly ruled out the
possibility of being someone's perfect partner?

'People know we're friends,' he told Mick. 'And they
know we spend time together out of work, but that was
Alex's idea.'

'Your crewman?' Mick's jaw dropped. 'He pushed you
two together to start dating and you still think nobody
knows you're breaking the rules? Or does the secret ex-
tend to all your crew members?'

Eddie shook his head. 'Alex suggested Jodie took me to
her bouldering class because he didn't want to go back to
it. They think I fell in love with the sport and they think
it's a great idea. The base operations manager even suggested we both got into some abseiling as well because
they're the sort of skills that could come in handy on a
mission when we can't get anyone from a mountain rescue team on scene quickly. Jodie's keen because that
would mean she could free climb up wild cliffs and then
abseil down and save time before having another go.' He

grinned at Mick. 'So there you go—we have one night every week when we're expected to spend time together. Plus, it's an excuse to get out on our days off—to go hiking and look for some wild rocks to play around on.'

'Play around on is right,' Mick muttered. 'And I don't believe you're going to be able to keep it secret.'

'We're managing so far.'

They were so good at switching off any personal connection at work, in fact, that as far as Gus and Alex were concerned, Eddie and Jodie had just welded themselves into a tight, professional team. The connection between them actually improved their professional relationship—as though there was an element of communication where they could read each other's body language so well, it was almost like telepathy.

'You'd better make the most of it while it lasts.' Mick's tone was a warning.

'I intend to.' Eddie nodded. 'Who wouldn't? Jimmy wasn't wrong—there *are* some girls who just want to play. And man… I've never found a playtime like this before. It's perfect.'

'Lucky you.' Mick shook his head. 'But I hope you're being careful about more than just keeping it a secret. What are you going to do if she gets pregnant?'

'She won't.' Eddie was more than confident on that score. 'She's passionate about her career and she's got no interest in a long-term relationship—with anyone. Having a kid would be the last thing she'd want. Besides, you taught me well. I'm always careful.'

'Should have listened to my own advice, shouldn't I?' There was a smile on Mick's face now but it was too wry to count as something positive. 'And been a bit more careful myself.'

Eddie's heart broke a little more. He hated that his brother was having to go through this and now he felt guilty that he'd been telling him how amazing his sex life currently was. But it wouldn't feel right to be hiding what was going on in his own life from his brother and maybe continuing to treat Mick with kid gloves, saying only supportive things and letting Mick take this journey at his own pace wasn't going to help in the long run.

Mick was cooperating with everything being asked of him in the way of occupational and physiotherapy and his upper body strength was improving to the point where he could wheel his chair. He was close to being able to transfer himself from bed to chair as well, which would be a big step towards independence, but it felt like Mick saw it more as an admission of failure that he would never walk again. He had regained almost normal sensation in his legs some time ago but the hope of that becoming meaningful movement was beginning to fade and nobody would be surprised if Mick had actually lost hope.

Letting him bemoan things that had happened in the past certainly wasn't going to help anything either, but assuming that when Mick had said he should have been more careful he'd been referring to being jilted on his wedding day after believing he was about to become a father was an easier route to take for Eddie. It suddenly felt too daunting to open the can of worms that was how Mick was feeling about his future.

'Oh, come on...' Eddie made his tone amused. 'You were over Juliana by the end of that pity party we all had on your non-wedding day. If I remember correctly, it was you who declared that we would only ever need each other?'

Mick looked away. 'Sorry,' he muttered. 'I know I'm being a wet blanket. I'm glad you're having fun with Jodie.'

'Just trying to emulate your exploits.' Eddie grinned. 'I lost count of how many women there were after Juliana. It was like you were single-handedly trying to prove that you were the overall winner of the "Fearsome Threesome" that Ella used to call us.'

'My ears are burning...' Ella walked into Mick's room as Eddie was speaking. She had the strap of a laptop bag over her shoulder and looked like a woman on a mission. 'Are you talking about me?'

'Not exactly.'

'Did you both get Jimmy's text?'

'My phone battery's dead,' Mick said. 'But Eddie told me it's about the locum position in Aberdeen. He's coming up next month?'

'He is.'

'Does the position come with accommodation? Like you had when you came here?'

'Possibly.' Ella nodded. 'But we've suggested he stays at our place. House-sitting.'

'House-sitting? Where are you and Logan going? You *never* take holidays.'

'Exactly.' Ella perched on the end of the bed. 'We've never even had a honeymoon so we decided that this was an opportunity we couldn't pass up. Jimmy's going to house-sit for us and we're going on honeymoon. To New Zealand.'

'New Zealand?' The surprise had been enough to catch Mick's interest. 'Wow...now there's a place that I've always fancied visiting. I should have done when you were in Australia, Eddie. Missed my chance, didn't I?'

'Funny you should say that...' Ella was unpacking her laptop. 'Because when Logan and I were searching destinations we came across something that I thought might interest you.' She clicked on a link and then put the computer on Mick's lap. 'Don't say anything,' she told him. 'Just have a look. I'll send you the link so you can look at it more thoroughly later, if you've got your own laptop charged.'

'What is it?' Eddie got to his feet to peer over his brother's shoulder. He could see slide show images changing automatically. Gorgeous scenery of mountains and beaches and forests. Happy, smiling people. What looked like a state-of-the-art gymnasium. And...wheelchairs? Yes...there were people wearing what looked like designer uniforms. Including a very gorgeous young woman with long blonde hair and a smile with a wattage that would be enough to power a small town.

'It's a rather exclusive rehab centre.' It sounded like Ella was making an effort to keep her tone casual. 'On the Coromandel Peninsula, which is not far from Auckland in New Zealand and looks like one of the most beautiful parts of an already gorgeous country.'

'I've been there,' Eddie said. 'Just for a couple of days but it was incredible. I'd go back in a heartbeat.'

'Sorry, we're not inviting you.' But Ella was smiling. 'We thought that Mick deserved a bit of a break if he felt like it. We'd like *you* to come with us.'

'To *New Zealand*? To play gooseberry on your *honeymoon*?' Mick gave a huff of laughter. 'You have got to be kidding.'

'Nope.' Ella waved her hand, dismissing his reaction. 'We're not suggesting you come everywhere with us, but we'd travel with you and stay while you got settled in for your own holiday. And then we'll get a camper van and drive all the way down to the South Island and back again. We thought if we were going to go that far, we might as well do it properly. We've both got a ton of leave to use up and cover's been arranged so we're thinking at least a month. You could come back with us, Mick or…if you like the place you could stay for longer. It'll be summer there and it might be good to escape the worst of a Scottish winter. They also have an amazing reputation for what they can do for spinal injury patients. Anyway…'

Ella didn't elaborate on the comment. 'I can't stay,' she told Mick. 'I'm on call for the obstetric emergency response team tonight so I need to get back. I just popped in to tell you about this.'

'You could have just emailed the link.'

'You might have just deleted it.' There was something in Ella's tone that made Eddie think she might also be thinking that some kind of change was needed in the way they were supporting Mick. Letting him just slide further into shutting himself off from the world wasn't an acceptable option.

Mick picked up the laptop to hand back to her and he must have touched the mousepad that stopped the slide show continuing to loop. The image on the screen was that of the blonde woman in her designer scrub suit with the dancing blue eyes and that smile that suggested life couldn't get any better.

Eddie could see Mick staring at it, his eyes narrowed as if the screen—or that smile—was bright enough to be hurting his eyes. He caught Ella's gaze as she took the laptop back and knew that the tiny shake of his head, unseen by Mick, was enough to convey his opinion that this was a great idea but there was very little chance that

Mick was going to agree to visit a new rehab centre, no matter how beautiful the setting was. Or any of the therapists on the staff, for that matter.

It was a fantasy rehab centre.

Too good to be true?

Eddie felt a trickle of sensation run down his spine that felt almost like a premonition. Was what he and Jodie had found with each other too good to be true?

Was it going to crash and burn?

No...

'I need to head off too,' he told Mick. 'I've got a bouldering session at the gym this evening and I'm going to finally get myself off the beginner's level.'

'Don't break anything,' Mick warned. 'I'm the only one in the family who's allowed to be out of action.' He winked at Eddie. 'Get out there and wave the flag for the "Fearsome Threesome".'

'Will do my best.' Eddie gave his brother a fist bump after Mick had tried, and failed, to escape his sister's kiss.

He followed Ella from the room, confident that he wasn't going to break anything in the near future—including the fantasy relationship he was lucky enough to be enjoying with Jodie Sinclair.

CHAPTER SEVEN

ABERDEEN AIR AMBULANCE'S annual fundraiser was an event that was circled on a huge number of local calendars judging by the crowds that gathered every year, especially when the weather was as kind as it was today, which was a huge relief. Like the vast majority of air ambulance helicopters in the UK, Triple A had to be funded by a charity organisation and there was an army of faithful volunteers—often including the patients and families of people whose lives had been saved by the service—who put in a massive amount of work to make this event as successful as possible.

The star of the show—the gleaming black H145 helicopter that Gus and Alex had polished to perfection this morning—was hovering above that crowd, giving them time to finish the important things they were doing, like getting their faces painted, being given the paper cone of hot chips they'd ordered, climbing out of the bouncy castle or just going to the loo. Everybody wanted to get to a good spot around the edges of the football field to see the drama of the close-up winching demonstration that was about to happen, that would give them a taste of what the air ambulance might do when it received an emergency call.

The Blue Watch crew were more than happy to sit

well above the scene for a while and let the anticipation build. There was quite enough to be looking at to keep them entertained.

'This is a much bigger deal than I expected it to be,' Eddie said. 'It looks like a cross between a funfair and some Highland games. Is that a pipe band on that stage?'

'Aye.' Alex was grinning. 'And when you and Jodie are talking to all the wee bairns who want to come and have a look at the helicopter, me and Gus are going to have a go at tossing a caber.'

Jodie laughed. 'No, you won't. You both have to stay with the chopper and help entertain the masses.'

'I'm not going anywhere,' Gus muttered. 'I'll be too busy keeping all those sticky fingers off my paintwork.'

'You'd be lucky to be able to pick one of those logs up with you both holding each end of it,' Jodie said. 'You do realise they can weigh nearly as much as you do, Alex, don't you?'

'I'll use one of the little ones they've got for the kids to try out.' But Alex turned to look at Jodie. 'How do you know how much I weigh, anyway?'

'You know it's one of my splinter skills.' Jodie's smile was smug. 'I like to estimate how much a patient weighs so that I know when to save my back from getting wrecked by calling in lifting assistance from someone else on scene. Like a firie or two.'

'Speaking of firies…' Eddie craned his head to see beneath them. 'I can see a couple of ambulances, which is fair enough given the first aid cover you'd need for an event of this size, but what's the fire engine down there for?'

'We get support from all the emergency services,' Jodie said. 'There'll be a police car somewhere as well, but the fire truck is a favourite for the kiddies. They can buy a ticket and get a ride on it.'

'No pony rides, then?'

'They might get a bit freaked out when we get low enough to do our demo,' Gus put in. 'Don't think any-one wants to cope with ponies bolting through a crowd like that. How's it looking down there? Is our audience in place?'

Eddie eyed the rows of people forming behind the ropes that were keeping them well away from the centre of the football field. 'Looks like half the crowd is there. I'm thinking the rest will be able to see most of it from where they are.'

'Aye…' Alex attached his strop to the safety anchor. 'I wouldn't be giving up my spot in the kebab queue just to watch you and Jodie dangling in mid-air.'

'That's because you get to see it all the time.' Jodie wagged her finger at him. 'You're spoilt, you are.'

Eddie didn't seem to be sharing the joke. 'I hope that bouncy castle's well tied down,' he said.

'I'm sure it is,' Jodie said. 'But that's a good point. Gus, can you radio through to the event management team and get them to make sure nobody's inside the castle—or those big ball things—when we're landing?'

'Roger that.'

Jodie turned her head in time to catch an intensity in Eddie's eyes that made her heart skip a beat.

'You weren't there, were you?' she asked. 'At that ter-rible accident in Tasmania a few years ago?'

'No. But I had a very good friend who was in one of the first helicopters to arrive on scene. She had such bad PTSD afterwards, she ended up walking away from her career. Last I heard, she had no intention of going back.'

She...

A very good friend. Someone he was still in contact with?

The flash of something like jealousy took Jodie completely off-guard and it was strong enough to be…ridiculous…that was what it was. As if she and Eddie were in a deeply significant relationship and she'd just found out he was cheating on her?

Or perhaps it was something else that was messing with her head. That hint of pain in Eddie's voice? That knot in her gut that was an empathy with how profoundly he cared about other people? Both the female paramedic he knew and the children who had been involved in an accident that had hit headlines around the world.

'It was a really freak gust of wind, wasn't it? I read that it might have been a mini tornado.'

'I heard about it too.' Alex nodded. 'The castle got lifted about thirty feet into the air. What was it—five kids that died?'

'Six in the end,' Eddie said quietly. 'One died later in hospital.'

Gus spoke calmly. 'It's all good here,' he said. 'They've already closed the area with the bouncy castle and the human hamster balls. They won't open them until we've landed and shut down and then they'll close them again when we're due to take off.'

'That's hours away,' Alex informed them. 'Isn't it grand that we get to spend our whole day off together?'

'Yeah, right…'

Jodie laughed, happy to see that Eddie was smiling again. As her gaze brushed his, she knew he wasn't complaining about the company. It was easy to see that he wanted to be with her and time outside of a shift when their patients were their first priority was a real bonus. Not quite on the same level as when they had their secret, private times together but it was still a bonus.

For both of them.

'It's two minutes to show time.' Gus sounded focused on what they were really here for—to showcase the equipment and skills they had available to save lives and encourage people to spend their money and buy raffle tickets and rides and make donations that would help the organisation keep running and provide an even better service over the coming year.

'I'll do a circuit around the whole field and then get a bit lower,' he added. 'We'll do the winch demonstration and then land dead centre. You guys all ready?'

The winch demonstration was a rerun of what they'd done on their sea rescue training day. Gus kept the helicopter steady at a low enough level to give their audience the thrill of feeling the wash and not only hearing the beat of the rotors. Jodie got winched down to the grassy field and unhooked herself and then Eddie went down, put her in a nappy harness and Alex winched them both back up to the helicopter.

Jodie knew that someone would be giving an explanation over the loudspeakers to the crowd about what was happening so she hoped they would be able to hear it over the noise of the hovering helicopter. At least Alex knew how to play to the crowd and he made it a slow ascent. So slow that it felt like they were simply hanging in the air without moving at all at one point.

Not that Jodie minded. The harness wasn't the most comfortable thing to be wearing once it was carrying her weight but she didn't mind at all that her hips were between Eddie's legs and the point of contact for her body was against his lower abdomen.

Quite the opposite.

She was loving it. She enjoyed Eddie's company as much as he seemed to enjoy hers. He was an intelligent and funny companion and they had so much in common that they never ran out of things to talk about. Jodie might not have met any of Eddie's family members, of course, with them keeping their private time together such a secret, but she felt as if she knew them now.

She knew how close to his brothers Eddie was and how much he was worried about Mick. She knew that he adored his big half-sister, Ella, who was eight years older than the triplets and had been another mother to them when their shared mother's IVF treatment had been unexpectedly too successful and had instantly doubled the size of their family. She knew how hard it had been on Eddie and his brothers when his mother had lost her battle to cancer when they were only teenagers and that their broken-hearted father had died not long after.

Eddie said that was why the siblings had all ended up with medical careers but Jodie knew there was more to it than personal tragedy, at least in Eddie's case. He had always been destined to do a job that was focused on people because he was a person who genuinely cared about others.

A kind man.

She liked him. A lot. This day together really was a bonus and she intended to enjoy every minute of it. And when it was finished, she knew that Eddie would probably be as keen as she was to spend some more time together because it had been nearly a week since they'd been together in the way that was starting to haunt her nights when she was at home by herself.

Together alone.

In Eddie's apartment.

In Eddie's bed...

And Jodie loved the anticipation of that too. She was loving almost everything about Eddie, to be honest. She loved how casual things were. How astonishingly good the sex was. How surprisingly easy it seemed to be to keep it a secret.

It had been going on a lot longer than she'd expected it to, mind you, but why fix something if it wasn't broken? Jodie had never found someone who seemed to feel exactly the same way she did about long-term relationships or anything that might require commitment of some kind. She liked him enough for a friendship to be more than welcome and, hopefully, that could continue when they'd finally had enough sex to be able to agree that the unusually distracting level of attraction to each other had worn off.

Which would be soon, she was sure of it.

Just...not *quite* yet.

Safely back in the cabin of the helicopter, they kept the door open and waved at the crowd as Gus brought the aircraft down to land on the grass. Event officials were preparing to shift ropes and do some crowd control to let people closer to talk to the crew, look inside the helicopter and ask what Jodie knew from experience would be endless questions from both children and adults as the crew watched to make sure that everyone and everything stayed where they were supposed to be and remained undamaged.

It would be full-on and could be seen as a chore, given

that it was sucking up one of Blue Watch's days off, but it always felt like a privilege to be involved in a public relations exercise like this. To be a face of a service that she was so proud to be a part of.

On top of that, probably for the rest of Jodie's life, doing something extra like this, especially if it involved a winching demonstration, was always going to remind her of when it had all started with Eddie, wasn't it? When being in such close physical contact as he'd winched her up from the sea had made that attraction between them spiral so completely out of control. It seemed ages ago now but, because their 'arrangement' was so casual and it was disguised so well by their apparently mutual interest in bouldering, it was nothing to worry about so there hadn't been any need to pull the plug on it just yet.

It wasn't as if they had even spent a whole night together because Jodie made sure they only went to Eddie's apartment so that she was always in control and could leave whenever she chose, but what would happen when they went away for a weekend together? When they could be sharing a motel unit, for example? Would she break her ironclad rule of not falling asleep in the same bed— let alone the arms—of a sexual partner?

There was just such a weekend coming up soon, with an abseiling course high in the Cairngorms and, ironically, it had been Dion who'd heard about it and persuaded both Eddie and Jodie to enrol. An all-expenses-paid weekend away to enhance skills that would be valuable within the team of rescue medics. It would be a great cover, if they needed one, to spend some time together this evening. If anyone noticed, it would be a perfectly reasonable excuse to want to discuss the upcoming course and go through the list of gear they needed to take. As a local, Jodie could tell Eddie where to go shopping for any outdoor clothing or other essentials he might not have. She might even go with him if they had time before the shopping centres closed.

Given the length of time that Jodie had been working with Eddie now, it shouldn't have come as a surprise that he was so good at interacting with people in this kind of social situation. After all, he could charm little old ladies and reassure frightened people with an ease she'd seen him employ with everybody he came into contact with through his work.

Like he had on his first day at work with Triple A, when he'd crouched beside that young mountain biker, Caitlin, and smiled at her.

Sorry we took so long, sweetheart...

Jodie could still hear that tone in his voice. The one that had almost made her envious of their patient. Now she was enjoying hearing snatches of his voice, when she wasn't talking herself, as they both got on with talking to the eager crowds of children and teenagers pushing in to get a closer look at the helicopter and ask their pressing questions. Some event officials were helping to protect the aircraft and their gear because Gus and Alex had been sent off to wander through the crowd to chat to people and help sell raffle tickets. When they came back, the biggest raffle prizes would be drawn in front of the helicopter and then it would be time for them to take off and head back to base.

Currently, Jodie was sitting at the helicopter's rear cabin opening—between the open clam-shell doors beneath the tail—to keep an eye on their stretcher, which they'd put on the grass to act as a display shelf for some of their equipment. She only had to turn her head to see Eddie sitting in the other open door—the one they would slide open to winch out of.

A proud mother was urging a small boy, with a mop of red curls, who looked about five years old to step forward to talk to Eddie. He'd already been to a face-painting station and he had the blue and white Scottish flag on one cheek and the Triple A logo on the other. He was also clutching a soft toy replica of one of the air rescue's black helicopters.

'Do you like working on the helicopter?' he asked Eddie shyly.

Eddie, sitting in the open cabin doorway, smiled at the boy. 'What's your name, buddy?'

'Connor.'

'Are you old enough to keep a secret, Connor?'

Connor nodded solemnly. 'I'm *five*,' he told Eddie.

'Okay... Don't tell anybody but...' Eddie leaned closer and spoke in a stage whisper that even Jodie could hear. 'It's the very best job in the whole wide world.'

Connor's eyes were huge.

'What do you want to do when you grow up?' Eddie asked.

Connor took a visibly deep breath, stood on tiptoes and whispered something in Eddie's ear that made him grin widely.

'I'll keep the seat warm for you, buddy,' he said.

Something was melting deep within Jodie's chest as she watched the exchange. Maybe it was the hero worship in those big eyes under the shaggy red curls of the child's hair. Or the way Eddie had bent his head so that the secret that was being whispered was something special that was just between the two of them.

Whatever it was, it touched something that felt surprisingly tender. It made Jodie think of how Eddie would be with his own children one day in the future.

And that shouldn't have bothered her because Jodie had made peace long ago with the idea that there weren't going to be children in her own future—either in partnership with their father or as a single mother. She'd smacked the button on her biological clock to silence any alarm and, okay…she was going to miss out on things that other people considered the most important part of their lives, but there were plenty of other people who were happy and fulfilled without having children of their own and she was one of them.

Something else she'd learned about Eddie's family, in fact, was that his sister felt the same way. After spending so many years mothering her much younger brothers, she'd always said she didn't want to have any children of her own. She'd 'been there, done that' according to Eddie and she didn't need to do it again. If things were different, Jodie would have liked to meet Eddie's sister. To get to know his whole family, even.

But things weren't different and Jodie was still damping down the hotspots of an unexpected emotional reaction to the thought of Eddie having a child of his own—with some unknown woman he was going to meet in the future—when she turned her head to see a teenager who was reaching to push a button on the defibrillator that was attached to a frame that would have gone over a patient's feet if someone had been lying on the stretcher.

'Don't touch that.' Jodie's warning came out more

sharply than she had intended. 'That's an expensive bit of kit and we can't afford to have it damaged.'

'I just wanted to see how it worked.'

'Well…' Jodie sucked in a breath. She could see little red-haired Connor walking away with his mother and knew that Eddie was glancing in her direction, perhaps because he'd heard her snap at someone? 'I can tell you anything you want to know.'

'Why's it got so many buttons?'

'Because it can do so many cool things. It can take your blood pressure, tell us how much oxygen you've got in your blood, whether your heart is beating normally and it can give you an electric shock to help restart your heart if it's stopped.'

'Like on telly when you hold those things on top of them and yell at everyone to "Stand Clear"?'

'We don't use paddles any more. We have sticky patches and electrodes that clip onto them. They're much safer.'

The teenager shrugged. 'Not so cool, though.'

'The people that need their hearts started again don't seem to mind. And we do still have to tell people to stand clear.'

'Can it take my blood pressure?'

'I don't see why not.' Jodie found a smile. 'Take your anorak off and then sit down on the stretcher here.' She patted the end. 'Roll up the sleeve of your jumper too. I'll need one of your arms above the elbow.'

She opened a pouch on the side of the defibrillator case and took out the blood pressure cuff, turned the machine on and plugged the cord attached to the cuff into its slot.

A small crowd was gathering as she wrapped the cuff around the teenager's arm.

'This will start getting tighter on your arm as soon as I push the button,' she warned. 'It has to get tight enough to stop the blood getting into your arm, but it's only for a second and then you'll feel it getting loose again. Keep still and you'll see the numbers coming up on the screen. You can see your heart rate already, see? It's only sixty, which tells me you're probably quite fit. Do you play sports?'

'Bit of footie.' But the lad puffed out his chest a bit. 'And I ride my bike.'

'Keep it up. It's good being fit.' Jodie reached into the pouch again for the finger clip. 'Here…we'll put a pulse oximeter on your finger too and see what percentage of oxygen you've got in your blood.'

The teenager grinned at his mates who were watching, delighted to be the centre of attention. As his facial expression exaggerated how uncomfortably tight the cuff was becoming, Jodie noticed that Eddie had joined the spectators and he was enjoying her 'patient's' reaction. He'd be just as good at handling his teenaged son as making them feel special when they were five years old, she thought.

But he had a woman beside him who had a baby in a front pack and Jodie couldn't help imagining Eddie wearing a pack like that or with a baby in his arms and that tender spot in her chest was being touched again. This time, hard enough to hurt. It wasn't simply imagining that faceless woman in his future who would be the mother of his children. It was all too easy to imagine how it would feel to trust this man enough to start thinking about building a future with him.

Building a family.

Having his baby...

But what was a whole lot worse than imagining it as an abstract concept involving that faceless partner, Jodie was doing more than tapping into feeling a part of that picture.

She *wanted* to be a part of it.

It was only the tiniest, embryonic seed of a feeling but it was a yearning that she knew had the capacity to be so potent—and dangerous—that Jodie found herself unable to release the breath she had in her lungs. Dear Lord...she'd never been this close to losing control of her emotions in private, let alone in a public arena. She could almost feel tears prickling at the back of her eyes. Just blinking hard, once, was enough to send them packing, mind you. And focusing on what she was doing dealt with any other wayward thoughts.

'There you go. Your blood pressure is one hundred and ten over seventy, which is perfectly normal for your age group. Your oxygen saturation is a hundred percent too. You get top marks.' The sound of Velcro ripping apart punctuated her sentence as she removed the blood pressure cuff. 'Anyone else want their blood pressure taken?'

The chorus of assent was so enthusiastic Jodie knew she'd be kept very busy for the rest of her time at this event. And that was fine. Exactly what she needed. She might even add to the busyness and offer to do a demonstration of a three-lead ECG or find someone who was brave enough to have a finger prick so that she could test their blood glucose level. This was what they were here for, after all—to make the public aware of what they could do and help support the service with the kind of extra funding that could provide the latest model of a piece of equipment like this defibrillator.

Eddie was just as busy. He was showing someone how to step into a nappy harness that could be used to winch them up from an accident scene if they weren't so badly injured they needed a stretcher. Jodie looked past him to see if she could spot Gus or Alex coming back their way. A bit of extra help would be great, but what would be even better would be to get this gig done and dusted so that she could get home and go for a long, long run.

And do a bit of boxing as well.

Whatever it took to get this new tension out of her body and her head back into a space that she felt comfortable with, because otherwise it had the potential to morph into a sense of panic and Jodie Sinclair would not permit that to happen. The first step of making that process effective was, fortunately, already crystal-clear. She had become too close to Edward Grisham and she had to dial it back before it got any worse.

Way back.

She'd known that the aspects of their relationship that crossed the acceptable boundaries of friendship would have to stop soon, but had it really only been on the way here to this event that she'd been thinking that it didn't have to end quite yet?

How wrong had she been?

It had already gone on far too long. She'd slipped into a forbidden comfort zone and hadn't even noticed that safety barriers were being lowered. Seriously damaged, even? She'd been seduced by the feeling of being able to trust as much as she had by any irresistible physical pull towards Eddie.

She should have ended their illicit liaison long ago.

No. She should never have let it start, but she had. Willingly. Now she had to deal with getting out of it.

Back to safety.

CHAPTER EIGHT

HE HADN'T SEEN it coming.

Well…that wasn't exactly true, was it? Eddie had known right from the start that what was going on between himself and Jodie was never going to be long-term. He just hadn't expected to be blindsided by how suddenly it had been terminated. He certainly hadn't anticipated it being the footnote of what had otherwise been a very enjoyable day of taking part in the annual fundraiser for the air rescue base.

As soon as they'd lifted clear of the football field, in fact, with a cheering crowd waving them off. It was only a few minutes flying time before they'd get back to base, but it was enough time for Jodie to not only drop her bombshell but to make it seem like no more than a casual dismissal.

Eddie had been the one to suggest a drink and perhaps a pub dinner later that evening at the Pig and Thistle.

'It's Saturday night, after all, and I don't know about you guys, but I was a bit disappointed I didn't get the chance to get a kebab or some hot chips from one of those food stalls.'

'I've got plans later but I'd be up for a quick beer first,' Gus said.

'I'm in.' Alex nodded. 'Georgia's on night shift.'

'Count me out this time.' Jodie's tone was oddly off-hand, which Eddie instinctively knew was significant. 'I've got other plans tonight.'

She hadn't even glanced in Eddie's direction but then he was trying not to stare at her. Or to react to what felt like a bit of a slap, to be honest.

But perhaps he was overreacting? Eddie waited a beat but knew he had an easy way to find out. He kept his tone just as casual as Jodie's had been.

'Do you want to pop into that adventure clothing outlet on your way home? I could meet you there.' Gus was already bringing the helicopter down on his approach to land on the platform outside the hangar. 'Doesn't shut for another half an hour and I need some good waterproof gear for that abseiling trip. What was it you wanted? New gloves?'

'There's plenty of time for me to do that next week.' Jodie's smile was perfectly friendly. As teasing as her tone, even. 'You don't need me to hold your hand while you go shopping, Eddie. As long as you don't buy some fluorescent pink over-pants, of course.'

Her gaze only grazed his but it was enough to send the silent message that time together out of work hours was definitely not on Jodie's agenda today. Maybe not tomorrow either. Had she, for no discernible reason, even decided that she no longer wanted it at all?

And…dammit…

It *hurt*…

Maybe he'd known it could never last, but why hadn't she just talked to him about it when they were alone? They could have agreed to stay friends. He would have respected her decision.

Or would he? Maybe Jodie was giving him this message in front of their colleagues as a reminder that they'd been lucky not to get caught out before this. Maybe she knew that if they were alone he would have tried to persuade her that it could continue for just a little longer.

One more night…?

And why not? Maybe what was really bothering Eddie was that he didn't really understand why it was happening like this. It wasn't as if anyone else knew what was going on. Or that he'd given any indication that he wanted something more than Jodie was prepared to give which, in the past, had always been when an alarm had rung loudly enough to prompt Eddie to find the kindest but quickest way to stop things going any further.

Okay…maybe this was karma. He'd done this to so many women he had no right to feel that it was unjustified to have the shoe on the other foot. Jodie had always had the right to back off from the intimate extension to their professional relationship whenever she chose to and he had to respect that, even if it might be the last thing *he* wanted.

Gus was shutting down the engines and the rotors were already slowing. The snap of safety belts being unfastened sounded like a punctuation mark to more than the short flight home.

Eddie reached to slide open the door.

'No worries,' he said. 'But I'm not making any promises about the pink pants.'

Alex was laughing. 'It's not a bad idea, actually. Nice and easy to spot when someone has to come and rescue you out in the wilderness of the Cairngorms.'

With another crew on duty today, there was no reason to leave this helicopter outside and there were chores to do to make sure any equipment that had been on display or used during its time at the fundraising event was clean, tidy or replaced, ready for when it would be used for its normal workload again—which could be any time at all, if a big emergency occurred and every resource the city had needed to be deployed.

Eddie had assumed Jodie would take care of the defibrillator that she'd been using this afternoon. After the popularity of people having a three-lead ECG taken, it was highly likely that the pouch containing the electrodes needed topping up and the batteries would need to be changed for fully charged ones. But Jodie simply got out and walked away and Eddie felt himself frowning.

Something wasn't right.

He unclipped the defibrillator from its shelf. 'Back in a minute,' he told Alex.

'Hey...' He caught up with Jodie before she entered the hangar.

Was it his imagination or did Jodie flinch just a little when she heard his voice?

No... When she automatically flicked her gaze upwards at the same time, Eddie caught a glimpse of something in her eyes that he'd never seen before.

Fear...?

His mouth suddenly felt dry. 'What's up?' he asked quietly. 'Jodie, are you okay?'

Whatever it was he thought he'd seen—or perhaps felt—in her expression had vanished and Eddie felt the tension that was making it hard to breathe start to release its grip on his chest. Maybe whatever was going on had nothing to do with him? With *them*?

'I'm fine.'

Sometimes silence could be more significant than any words that could be found and, sure enough, Jodie filled the gap by the time they were in the middle of the hangar, halfway between the storeroom and the locker room.

'Okay... It's just... I realised that it's become a bit of a habit, Eddie. And the longer habits are there, the harder they can be to break and...if that happens, breaking them is bound to cause a bit of collateral damage.'

He didn't have to ask what she meant. She was talking about them. About the sex. The best sex he'd ever had the privilege of discovering. He wasn't sure whether Jodie was thinking that it becoming a habit would mean they became complacent and their secret would be found out or that she considered the collateral damage would include emotional pain for either of them but, if things got messy, they both knew it could mean they'd never work together again. And if someone had to leave the base completely, it would definitely be Eddie because he'd only been here such a short time.

Eddie didn't want that to happen.

Did that explain what he thought he'd read in her eyes? Or had she been afraid of telling him? Was she worried that he might be hurt? That *she* might be hurt if they took this any further?

Eddie didn't want that to happen either. Even the possibility of Jodie being hurt outweighed any emotional discomfort he might need to deal with himself.

'It's okay, Jodie,' he said. 'It's your call. We both knew it had a "use-by" date.'

Jodie nodded but her gaze dropped. 'I should do the defib,' she said. 'I was the one playing with it all afternoon.'

'I've got this.' Eddie found a smile. 'We're a team, remember?' He waited to catch her gaze lifting so that she would know he was trying to reassure her that he was going to do his best to make the transition from friends with benefits to simply friends as painless as possible. '*We've* got this,' he added quietly. 'And, hey...'

'What?'

'I promise I won't buy any pink pants.'

Jodie was laughing as she turned away to head for the locker room and Eddie's smile was genuine now. He might have just lost something that had become important in his life but he was damned if he was going to let their very real friendship vanish as well.

He'd meant that promise. He was going to make this change in their personal connection easy. Hopefully, they could still work together without any issues. Have social time with the whole crew together. Perhaps they would both even be able to cherish memories of how good it had—briefly—been between them.

The Saturday following the fundraising event was the last working day for Blue Watch's next roster and Jodie was finally starting to feel as if she could relax.

She wasn't needing to keep herself busy between callouts with less than urgent tidying or stocktaking in the storeroom or cleaning and sorting gear that hadn't been used in recent times. She could be in the staffroom, sitting at the table having a coffee with the rest of her crew and other staff members around.

Including Eddie.

In a way, nothing had changed because—as far as she could tell—nobody else had had any idea what had been going on between herself and Eddie. They'd successfully kept both their attraction to each other and what they'd ended up doing to get it 'out of their systems' a secret.

But too much had changed for Jodie because she was

still so aware of his presence. She could still feel that pull towards him that had become such a pleasant frisson of both the emotional and physical history they'd created with each other and the anticipation of building on it even more.

Now there was only the history and Jodie was missing that anticipation.

She was missing being alone with Eddie, but that was only strengthening her resolve to stay well away from him. That odd feeling of panic she'd experienced at the fundraising event had subsided, thank goodness, but it had given her a painful wake-up call. She wasn't as bullet-proof as she'd thought she was, was she?

Since then, however, during the rest of her days off and with even more determination, when she was back at work, Jodie had reminded herself that her career was the only thing she was truly passionate about in her life. She didn't want a meaningful relationship, let alone children—with Eddie or anyone else—and that tiny seed of yearning that had sprouted in such an unwelcome fashion had been firmly rooted out. She'd kept her guard up constantly at work, just to be on the safe side, but now she was realising she didn't need to.

Eddie was keeping that promise he'd made and he was making this easy. Nothing had changed with their ability to work together so well.

He didn't seem upset at all that their fling was over either. He still seemed to be enjoying her company. Wanting to keep their friendship intact.

Jodie wanted that as well. And as soon as she'd filed those memories into a compartment that she could choose whether or not to open, normal life would resume and everything would be good again.

Better than good. She'd never had a colleague that she could trust to the extent she trusted Eddie and that made a huge difference when a call came in that they just knew was going to be a big one.

Just such a call came through late on that Saturday afternoon.

'Car versus truck.' Dion came into the staffroom as their pagers were sounding. 'Multiple casualties. There's an ambulance crew on scene and they've done an initial triage and say they've got one Status Zero and one, possibly two, Status Ones and a Status Two. They can't be sure because they need the fire service to get access to the car.'

Everyone was on their feet already and heading for the door and stairs down to the hangar. A Status Zero meant that there'd been a fatality and Status Ones were serious enough to be in danger of losing their lives without immediate medical intervention. A Status Two patient also needed urgent medical care.

'All available road crews are being diverted,' Dion called after them. 'And a fire crew has just located on scene. If there are any other helicopters available they'll be on standby and I'll alert our backup crew.'

Blue Watch lifted up from the helipad within the next two minutes. The cockpit screens were updating with all the details they needed, including the exact location of the accident, which was on the outskirts of Aberdeen, on a road with a rural speed limit high enough to mean that a collision would be serious. The truck had come in from a side road.

'There's a quarry up there,' Alex said grimly. 'If that truck was carrying a load of rock, it would be heavy enough to have hit anything else on the road like a bomb going off.'

'There's multiple nose-to-tail impacts behind the car too.' Jodie was reading the screen on her tablet. 'There's something that doesn't quite add up here. Why were there so many vehicles on that section of a country road?'

'Maybe the first car was going slowly enough to hold them up,' Eddie suggested. 'That can cause a bit of road rage and it only takes one stupid move to set off a chain reaction that can be catastrophic.'

Gus was on a radio channel with emergency service personnel on the ground. 'They've closed the road to traffic in both directions to give us a landing area on the tarmac,' he reported. 'But we've got power lines on one side and some trees on the other. Second option is a field, but they'll need to cut access through a hedgerow and a fence and there may be some sheep in there. We'll do a circuit and check it out.'

They could all see the line of stalled traffic snaking along a road bordering a tributary of the River Dee. The flashing lights of the emergency services already on scene were visible next and a low, slow circuit gave Gus and the crew the chance to choose their best landing spot.

'It's a limousine,' Eddie pointed out. 'With a side impact from that truck that's rolled.'

Jodie's heart sank. The occupants of a luxury limousine were unlikely to have been wearing safety belts.

'That might explain the convoy of traffic behind them,' Alex said. 'It could be a wedding party. There's an old castle further along the river that's a popular venue for receptions.'

'We'll land on the road,' Gus decided. 'The sooner we get you guys down there, the better.'

The descent of the helicopter felt like an echo of Jodie's heart, which was still sinking as she wondered if the person who had already died was either the bride or groom in that car. She didn't want to do this. It had been hard enough that day when they'd lost the young farmer who had the little boy and a pregnant wife. This was even closer to the bone for Jodie because it involved a couple who had only just married each other. Who were the happiest they'd ever been as they contemplated their new lives together as man and wife. A future built on love and trust and hope.

A future that had just been shattered.

Like it had been for herself and Joel.

Jodie knew she had to pull herself together. There were critically injured patients that might not survive without the help they could get from someone who was absolutely focused on doing what was needed without the distraction that emotion could cause. She knew she could do this. She *had* to do this, but it was going to be the hardest thing she'd ever done.

She caught Eddie's gaze when they were out of the helicopter, their kits on their backs and other equipment in both hands. The scene commander from a major incident police truck was striding towards them and it was only a matter of seconds before this scene would swallow them both for as long as it took.

But Jodie only needed to hold Eddie's gaze for a heartbeat to know that he understood her silent plea.

Stay close. I need you…

Something wasn't right.

Actually, there were so many things that weren't right that Eddie's senses were being overloaded as he tried to process this scene. The driver of the truck laden with tonnes of rock had slammed sideways into the front half of the stretch limousine, killing the driver of the limousine, probably instantly. The truck driver had been thrown clear as his vehicle tipped sideways, but he had been hit by large rocks spilling from the load and, by the time the air rescue crew had landed, he was also Status Zero.

There were dozens of people milling around a scene bordered by too many damaged cars to count, dressed up in the kind of clothes you wore to weddings with the men in smart suits and the women in colourful dresses with hats or flowers in their hair. There were small girls in puffy white dresses and boys in miniature suits who must have been flower girls and pageboys and a cluster of young women dressed in long, matching pale yellow dresses, one of whom was still clutching a bouquet of flowers. It struck Eddie that this should have been such a happy gathering with those bridesmaids looking like a patch of sunshine, but everyone was looking so shocked and the women wearing yellow were all sobbing and hugging each other. Other people were holding onto the children and some were sitting on the ground or walking around in a dazed fashion, clearly injured, with paramedics moving amongst them.

For Eddie, Jodie and Alex, this was the background of their focus. There were plenty of medics—with more arriving in road crews—to assess and treat the minor to moderate injuries. They were heading to the epicentre of this catastrophe—the wedding car. An ambulance crew was doing CPR on a young man who had been lifted from the wreckage of the car to be laid on a blanket covering flat ground and Eddie's first thought was that a miracle would be needed to get him back from a cardiac arrest caused by any major trauma, but he could see that this patient had suffered a severe head injury as well.

'How long have you been going?'

'Twenty minutes,' someone told Eddie. 'We'll keep going for a bit longer. Right...ready to shock. Stand clear...'

'We need you inside the car,' a senior medic, still co-ordinating triage of the dozens of people involved in this scene, told Eddie and Jodie. 'The bride's in a bad way too. She was conscious on arrival but her condition's deteriorating rapidly. Chest injuries, query flail chest and she had a major haemorrhage from lacerations to both arms which is under control. Watch out for the broken glass in there.'

'Thanks.' Eddie stepped into the slightly tilted floor space of the car's interior, slipping off his pack to put to one side as a paramedic stepped back to give him access. He turned back to offer his hand to take Jodie's pack but, to his surprise, she put her hand in his to step up into the crunch of broken glass on metal. This was the woman who was so fiercely independent she automatically refused assistance to even carry a heavy bit of kit but she was gripping his hand for a moment as if it were a lifebelt.

They were both double gloved as protection in an environment with multiple hazards but, for just a heartbeat, it felt to Eddie as though this was skin to skin contact and a part of him felt the ache of missing having Jodie in his life the way she had been only days ago. He'd kept his feelings well hidden over the last few days, though, and he knew that Jodie was grateful that he was making it easier for her, but what was bothering Eddie in this moment was that he had the feeling there was something going on with Jodie that he didn't understand. Something that was linked somehow to her decision that they stopped seeing each other.

Something important?

Yeah…something definitely wasn't right with Jodie. He'd known that ever since they'd got out of the helicopter and he'd got the impression he was seeing something in her eyes that was dark. Something even more secret than their relationship out of work had been. Something that was threatening enough for Jodie to have triggered a surprisingly powerful protective instinct in Eddie, but there was nothing he could do right now other than hope that Jodie could cope with whatever it was that was bothering her.

It was a huge relief to see the absolute focus coming into her eyes as he felt her letting go of his hand. This was the Jodie Sinclair he was used to seeing—the highly qualified paramedic who was in control of any situation she was faced with and poised to act swiftly to do whatever she could to save a life. He listened to her rapid-fire questions to the medics already there and could almost see the plan of initial interventions forming in her brain as she gathered information about her condition and what injuries had already been noted.

'So she was conscious when you arrived?'

'Only just. Incomprehensible speech and groaning. We had to wait for the firies to cut into the side of the car and then get the other passenger out first. She could squeeze a hand on command but didn't open her eyes. We put her GCS at less than ten. We put in an oropharyngeal airway, put her on high flow oxygen and got an IV line in.'

'What's her heart rate now?'

'One twenty.'

'Respirations?'

'Thirty.' The young paramedic was trying hard to keep up with Jodie's speed.

'Blood pressure?'

'Initially one ten over sixty. Now systolic's ninety and we couldn't get a diastolic.'

'Pulse ox?'

'Currently ninety…no, make that eighty-eight…'

'Okay… I'm going to have a listen to her chest. Keep that mask on her and the oxygen on high flow. Can someone find some shears, please, so we can cut her dress clear?'

Eddie had always been impressed with watching Jodie at work like this. But, right now, he was proud of her as well. He might not know what it was that had threatened her enough to be making this so much more of a challenge, but he did know it would have had to have been something huge to rattle one of the most professional and focused paramedics he'd ever worked with.

The bride's beautifully curled and braided hair framed an unmarked face, but her arms were badly cut by the broken champagne glasses and shards of the bottle she had been thrown into. Her chest must have caught the table holding the champagne bucket and the intricate beading on the bodice of her dress was soaked in blood. Jodie knelt amongst the bunched-up fabric of the wedding dress as she cut through the heavily beaded bodice with shears to assess her for the kind of injuries that were putting their patient's airway and breathing at imminent risk of failing and then handed the shears to Eddie, who tackled the skirt of the dress. They would need to do a secondary survey as soon as the breathing and airway was controlled, but finding any open long bone fractures or an injured pelvis were part of the primary survey to check for major haemorrhage.

While Jodie was focused on listening to breath sounds, Eddie asked the medics on scene—apart from one who was crouched at the patient's head with a bag mask, keeping the oxygen flow in place and ready to assist her breathing—to step further back to create space as he opened their kits.

'Multiple fractures,' Jodie confirmed as she lifted her hands and then pulled the earpieces of her stethoscope free. 'Chest is hyper-resonant, she's got neck vein distension, she's tachycardic and hypotensive.'

'Tracheal deviation?'

'Can't see any. Yet.'

Jodie caught Eddie's gaze. There were so many possibilities to think of, but the most important right now were a tension pneumothorax or cardiac tamponade from bleeding around the heart. Blunt chest trauma could interfere with the function of the heart and lead to obstructive shock, it could damage coronary arteries and effectively cause a heart attack, or there could be a time bomb waiting in the form of a tear to the aorta, which was the major vessel taking blood from the heart to the rest of the body.

There was nothing they could do to treat an internal injury like that in the back of a crushed car. What they could do, however, was to intubate their patient to control her airway, keep her oxygenated, decompress her chest if an accumulation of blood or air was preventing her breathing and—above all—get her to a major trauma centre and close to an operating theatre as fast as possible. In order to do that, however, they needed to move her out of the wreckage and into a space where they had clear access all around her. If they ran into difficulty securing her airway they would need more pairs of hands, more equipment and the ability to work from any angle.

There was plenty of help to get her onto the stretcher that Alex had placed as near as possible to the car, but it was Jodie and Eddie who prepared for and carried out the rapid sequence intubation, working together as seamlessly and skilfully as they'd been able to do since they'd first met. The gorgeous wedding dress was no more than a pile of discarded, blood-soaked, beaded and embroidered fabric by the time they had the only survivor from the limousine ready for transport—almost hidden by all the monitors they had in place over and around her body. A portable ventilator was doing her breathing for her, there were blood products being infused and every vital sign was being recorded.

She was still alive but Eddie could feel all eyes on them from the crowd of people watching silently. Or almost silently. He heard the grief-stricken cry from a woman who was in the arms of a man and with paramedics and police officers who would have been keeping her updated on what was happening. She was the right age to be a parent of their patient. Or was she the mother of the groom?

The collective grief from all those people was palpable and Eddie saw the way Jodie's glance swerved as they walked past where the new husband's body had been covered with a sheet and was being protected by a police officer. He could see the lines of tension in her face, which could be due to how critical their patient's condition remained, but Eddie knew, deep down, that it was more than that. He'd never seen Jodie less than in control, no matter how critically ill her patient was. It wasn't that she seemed in danger of losing that control now, but her face was pale and tense enough to worry Eddie and the thought that she might be in some kind of trouble was enough to be squeezing his heart so hard that it hurt.

Not that he could allow head space to even think about it right now. They had their work cut out for them to keep this patient alive long enough to hand over to the trauma team already waiting for them in the resuscitation area of the Queen Mother's Hospital in Aberdeen. By the time they accompanied her right into the department, to allow for all monitoring equipment to be changed over, stayed long enough with their handover to see her being rushed up to Theatre and then got back to base and dealt with all the cleaning and restocking that came in the wake of such a big incident, their shift was well over.

Alex had been helping Eddie as the second person to sign off the use and replacement of restricted drugs so it took time to realise he hadn't seen Jodie since she'd taken the cleaned portable ventilator and the defibrillator out to slot back onto their shelf in the helicopter cabin. He wasn't going to head home until he'd seen her, however.

Because he still had that feeling that something wasn't right.

He went upstairs to file his paperwork, to be met by Dion.

'I've had an update from a mate of mine at Police HQ. They've only just cleared the scene after the investigation by the serious crash squad. He wanted to pass on their thanks for your part in what he said was one of the most traumatic accident scenes he's ever been to.'

Eddie swallowed hard. 'It was a rough one.'

Dion put his hand on Eddie's shoulder but his gaze shifted to look down the staircase.

'Is Jodie okay?'

Eddie followed his station manager's gaze to see Jodie

sitting in the open door of the helicopter that had been rolled back into the hangar for the night.

Just sitting, with her head bowed and her shoulders hunched.

'I'm not sure,' he answered honestly. 'I'm a bit worried about her.'

'Tell her your patient's got through surgery,' Dion said. 'She's in the ICU. You did well. Both of you.' He gave Eddie's shoulder a squeeze as he let it go. 'And take care of her, will you? You'll be able to do that much better than I can. Take her out for a drink maybe? Talk things through for a debrief?'

Eddie went down the stairs, aware of the irony of having just been given permission to spend time with Jodie away from work when it was something she no longer wanted.

But, as a colleague and a friend, he wasn't about to let her be alone right now.

'Hey...' He walked up to where she was sitting so still. 'Dion tells me that our bride is in ICU. She made it through surgery.'

But the news didn't seem to be welcome. To his horror, Eddie could see the sparkle of tears in Jodie's eyes before she dropped her gaze to avoid his and her voice was no more than a whisper.

'Might have been better if she hadn't.'

Eddie had never seen Jodie this close to tears. He'd never heard such a bleak tone in her voice. It didn't matter that he had Dion's permission to spend time alone with his crewmate. He would have done this anyway.

'You're coming with me,' he told Jodie.

She shook her head. 'I'm going home,' she said. 'I might go for a run.'

Eddie put his finger under her chin so that she was forced to meet his gaze. 'It wasn't an invitation,' he said softly. 'Dion reckons we need a debrief and I agree with him, so I'm just telling you what's going to happen.' He held her gaze. 'You're safe, Jodie. And I'm going to make sure you stay that way.' He let his hand slide down her arm until it reached hers and then he pulled her to her feet and then into a hug. It didn't matter that Dion was probably still watching them. His lips were against her ear. 'Maybe I need this as much as you do. So you're coming with me, okay?'

He felt rather than heard Jodie's response as her head moved slowly against his shoulder. Up and down.

Okay...

Eddie glanced up as he led the way out of the hangar and he saw Dion was also nodding as he turned away. The older man probably assumed they'd be heading for the Pig and Thistle—maybe with Alex and Gus for a full crew debrief—but Eddie was quite certain that Jodie needed a far more private space than that.

She needed protection, and that was something he wasn't about to let anyone or anything prevent him providing.

CHAPTER NINE

IT WASN'T THAT cold this evening, but Jodie seemed frozen to the point where it seemed like it was too difficult to even move her facial muscles enough to talk.

So Eddie didn't ask any questions.

He lit the gas fire in the small living room/kitchen area of his apartment and, when that didn't seem enough, he pulled the duvet from his bed and wrapped it around Jodie as she sat, hunched, on his couch.

He made her a mug of hot, sweet tea and, when that didn't seem enough, he added a slug of his favourite whisky. He made one for himself as well and sat beside her as he sipped the drink.

It was Jodie who broke what was actually becoming a rather companionable silence.

'It's Saturday night. Don't you have something better to do than sit at home like this?'

'Nope.' Eddie shook his head. 'I probably would have gone to visit my brother, Mick, but I know my other brother, James, was coming up today so I can catch up with them both tomorrow.'

'How's he doing? Mick, I mean...'

Eddie drained his mug. 'Not great. He's not eating properly and he's losing weight. He goes through the motions of doing his therapy but it's kind of half-hearted and any progress has stalled. It's like he lost a much bigger part of himself in that accident than just the ability to walk. My sister Ella's thinking we might have to think about a family intervention of some kind.'

'Like what?'

'She and her husband have found this idyllic-looking rehab centre in New Zealand. They want to go there for a belated honeymoon and they've got this idea of taking Mick and putting him somewhere different for a month or two. Somewhere gorgeous and warm with forests and a beach that's safe enough to take disabled people swimming in the sea. He says he doesn't want to go because he'd be a burden for all that travelling, but she says maybe they should just take him anyway.'

'Does he have a wife? Or a partner?'

'No.' Eddie let his breath out in a wry huff of sound. 'He fell in love enough to want to marry a rather gorgeous Brazilian woman who told him she was pregnant with his baby a few years back. James and I were right beside him at the altar as his best men on his wedding day—waiting for the bride who never showed up.'

Jodie was silent for a moment and then her voice was very quiet. 'Had *she* had an accident? On the way to the church?'

'The only accident she had was to get pregnant,' Eddie muttered. 'The real father of the baby had turned up and that was that. They were off to live happily ever after together and Mick was thoroughly and very publicly jilted. He vowed he'd never make the mistake of committing himself to any woman after that and he persuaded me and James to join in the pact. We needed to learn from his example and never try to get married. Life was short and we all needed to live hard. Mick took the rules a bit more seriously than we did, mind you. I've never felt the urge to jump off a cliff to go hang-gliding.' Eddie stopped as he remembered the first moment he'd ever set eyes on Jodie, in the staffroom that morning, when she'd been declaring that the best thing ever was to jump off the side of a mountain with just a small parachute to keep you alive. He lifted his mug and then remembered it was empty. 'Want a top-up?' he asked Jodie.

She held out her mug. 'Yes, please...'

Eddie busied himself in the kitchen for a few minutes and when he carried the fresh mugs of spiked tea back to the couch he found Jodie still snuggled into the duvet like a caterpillar in a cocoon, but she didn't have that frozen look to her face any longer. Her lips were a much better colour as well.

He handed her a mug and then held his up to touch it. 'Cheers,' he said.

But Jodie just nodded and then took a long sip of her tea.

'I get it,' she said, a moment later. 'I get what Mick gets out of doing that dangerous stuff.'

'The adrenaline rush?'

'It's bigger than that when you lose something that's really important. For me, it started when I wasn't that bothered about whether or not I was going to survive the jump. It was like throwing myself into the hands of fate. If I got caught, I survived—and maybe that would mean there was a reason to keep going.'

Eddie's breath caught in his chest.

'What did you lose?' he asked quietly.

'The love of my life.'

Wow... There wasn't anything Eddie could think of to say. That was about as important as it got, wasn't it?

No wonder he'd been so certain that Jodie couldn't be 'the one' for him, or rather that he wasn't *her* soul mate. She had already had one. At least he could put his arm around Jodie as her friend, and she seemed to like that because she leaned against him.

'I met Joel when we started high school together,' Jodie continued softly. 'We were friends from the first day and we started dating when we were fourteen. We never even thought about dating anyone else. We took a gap year when we left school because we wanted to travel to as many places as we possibly could before we settled down and went to university and got good jobs and then started having kids.'

Jodie wasn't looking at him, so Eddie tightened his hold on her just a little and made a sound that let her know he was listening to every word she was saying. That he knew this was important and that she had more to say. He wanted to hear that too.

If felt like he *needed* to hear it.

'We got as far as Bali,' Jodie said. 'And it was so beautiful and we were so happy that we decided to get married. On the beach. As soon as we could. I bought a pretty white dress at a market and had my toenails painted with tiny white daisies on them. I think the most expensive thing we bought was a gorgeous bunch of gardenias that I was going to carry. Joel bought a cheap white shirt at the market, but he wore it with his shorts that were bright blue—as blue as the sea and the sky the day we got married. He went swimming in them later that day in the sunset... I just went in as far I could without getting my dress wet while I was holding it up because I didn't want to ruin it. I wanted to keep it for ever and wear it on every anniversary...'

The silence was heavy this time. Jodie had her eyes closed.

'My dress got ruined anyway,' she finally said, in a broken whisper. 'I was kneeling on the beach in the dark, hours later, when they finally found where the rip had taken him and brought him back to put in my arms. I couldn't move, even when the waves broke all around us.'

There were tears rolling down Jodie's cheeks now and Eddie's heart was breaking right around her like those waves on her tragic wedding day. He understood her words that it might have better if the bride they'd gone to today hadn't survived after losing the man she had just married. Jodie knew the agony she had ahead of her.

How hard must it have been for Jodie to have coped with that scene?

It was instinctive to reach for her with his other arm as well. To enfold her and hold her close. To brush away the tears on her face and pull her tight against his chest as she cried. He was crying himself, but part of that emotion was because he knew he was holding the most extraordinary woman he'd ever met. Someone courageous enough to pick up the pieces of her broken life and make something totally awesome out of it.

Someone who had, today, faced up to what must have brought back the worst memories she could have and she had been able to put them aside in order to help someone else.

Someone who deserved every bit of the love and happiness she had dreamed of having in her life.

In her sadness, Jodie felt smaller than he remembered her being in his arms. Vulnerable. Eddie bent his head and pressed a kiss against the tousled waves of her hair. He felt her head move beneath his lips but he hadn't expected the way she raised her face so that *her* lips touched his.

And then they were kissing each other and Eddie could feel Jodie's need that was almost desperation. Was it a need for him? Or did she simply need human contact and an affirmation of life?

It didn't matter.

Jodie needed this and he could give it to her and that was the only thing that mattered. He scooped up the whole bundle of duvet with her inside it and carried it to his bed.

It was the last thing Jodie would have planned to happen after a rough day at work. The last thing she would have thought she wanted.

But it turned out that it was exactly what she needed.

Being held like this. Not being alone under that comforting layer of the warm duvet. Being naked so that she could feel the warmth of Eddie's skin against hers and the touch of his fingertips and hands as they moved over her body, making her skin tingle.

Making her so aware that she was still alive.

Gentle enough to make her feel cared for. Cherished, even.

She was the one who pushed things into a demand. For something harder and faster and challenging enough to be almost a battle.

So that she could be aware of winning? To remind herself that she could still be in control?

To remember that she was a survivor.

That she was lucky enough to be able to appreciate the good things that life had to offer. Like this…the comfort of touch. That sharp pull of desire and the delicious, if brief, dip into ecstasy that made the rest of the world fade for as long as it lasted.

She would continue to survive, Jodie thought as she lay in Eddie's arms with only the sound of his breath in the air around her and the thump of his heart beneath her cheek. She would carry on with what had become her passion in life as well. She might not be able to win every time. Nobody could have saved the young groom today and there was no way anyone could prevent the struggle that his bride was going to face if she won her battle for her life, but Jodie knew she had made a difference and who knew how many other lives she would be able to save in the future?

She propped herself up on her elbow. 'I'm not sure Dion would approve of that debrief,' she said.

One side of Eddie's mouth curled upwards. 'Dion won't know anything about it.'

'No.'

'The only thing he'll want to know is that you're okay.'

Jodie nodded. Thanks to Eddie, she was. But then she caught her bottom lip between her teeth.

'I don't want anyone else to know,' she told him. 'About what I told you? About Joel? I don't want anyone trying to second-guess how well I'm going to cope at a difficult scene. Or keep me from doing my job.'

'I would never betray a confidence,' Eddie said. 'But nobody's ever going to stop you doing your job. You coped as well as anyone could have today. Better than most. I knew something was bothering you, but I could see the moment you shut it down and just got on with it. And…' Eddie touched her face softly '…knowing what I do now makes me realise just how strong a person you are. You're amazing, Jodie.'

Jodie pulled away from his touch. She sat up and then leaned over the side of the bed to pick up some of her clothing.

'I have to go,' she said, pulling her tee shirt over her head without bothering to put her bra back on. She was about to swing her legs out of the bed, but she paused and turned to catch Eddie's gaze.

'I'm glad you know,' she said. 'Because it means you understand why I can't do this again. Why *we* can't do this again. Why I don't do relationships. I… I like you too much, Eddie, but I'm not going to let myself fall in love with you and the easiest way to stop that happening is to stop *this* happening.'

Eddie's gaze softened. 'I get it,' he said quietly. 'You've experienced such a devastating loss that you never want to go through that again.'

Jodie shook her head. 'It's not that I don't *want* to go through it again. You make it sound like a choice. I *can't* go through it again. It was a loss that made my world stop turning and, if it happened again, I'd never be able to get it started a second time.'

This time, she did get out of bed to get the rest of her clothes on.

'You don't do relationships because you made some kind of pact with your brothers when one of you had been burned by a bad relationship that was obviously never genuine on both sides and you'd probably all had far too much to drink.'

Eddie made a face. 'You're not completely off the mark, there.'

'It's not a good enough reason.' Jodie felt her heart break a little as she looked back. 'I *really* like you, Eddie, and you deserve more than just skating through life on a superficial level, having sex that doesn't mean anything.' Her voice wobbled. 'You deserve someone who can give you a hell of a lot more than I could. You deserve to find out what love is really about and…and that's never going to be with me and that's why this is never going to happen again. Okay…?'

It wasn't a question. Any more than Eddie's had been when he was telling her that she was going to go with him so that he could look after her.

Because he cared that much about her.

Jodie didn't even stay in Eddie's room long enough to give him the chance to respond. Maybe she cared too much about him too.

Maybe that was why this was a lot harder than she had expected it to be.

Perhaps it was a good thing that it was never going to happen again.

Because that last time with Jodie was already haunting Eddie. He'd been thinking about her when he'd finally fallen asleep just before dawn and she was his first waking thought when he became conscious again.

Texting her was not pushing any boundaries she might not want him to cross, was it? It was something friends could do?

You okay?

He sent the text before he had time to talk himself out of it.

The response was immediate.

I'm good. Just off for a run. Might go hiking up the Cairngorms tomorrow and get a look at where we're going to that abseiling course.

Oh… The fact that she was okay thinking about time they would have together on that course was enough for Eddie to breathe a sigh of relief. He wanted to suggest he went with her but he knew that would not be a good idea—for either of them.

Instead, he sent:

Keep an eye out for snow. I might need another pair of those pink pants.

He received a 'thumbs-up' emoji back, but the text came in at the same time as another one and, as Eddie read Ella's message, he realised he couldn't have gone out of the city for the day anyway, because it seemed their concerns about Mick had suddenly escalated into a crisis. Their brother had apparently stopped eating altogether and was avoiding talking to anyone by pretending to be asleep.

Even as Eddie drove to the rehab centre as soon as he was up and dressed, he was still thinking about Jodie.

About last night.

Of course it had been different, he told himself. They'd had a really rough day being part of the horror when a joyous wedding party turned into an unthinkable tragedy that was going to impact so many lives. And Jodie, with the echo of her own tragedy, had been through an emotional maelstrom that had made their time together seem far more significant than it really had been. No wonder it had taken the sex to another level.

One that made it feel it was more like touching souls than merely parts of their physical bodies.

Was that the kind of connection that Jodie had had with Joel? The love of her life that she had no intention of even trying to replace? Eddie found himself wondering what it would be like to be loved so hard that the world would stop turning if something happened to him.

The only people he'd ever felt a bond like that with were his siblings, especially the brothers he'd been so close to even before they knew each other existed. There were times when they felt like one being that had been split into three parts and the worry that he was driving towards a real test of whether that bond could ever be broken was finally enough for Eddie to let Jodie go.

From his personal life? For ever?

No. That was never going to happen. Not on a really personal level because he was never going to forget what it was like to be that close to Jodie Sinclair and he knew he was never going to find anyone remotely like her again. She'd said she wasn't going to allow herself to fall in love with him—as if it was something that was possible to control? Eddie wasn't so sure about that.

Because he was starting to wonder if he had already fallen in love with *her*.

What he could do, however, was to stop himself thinking about her this much. For now, anyway. He knew she was okay and coping in her own way with her passion for physical activities. And Eddie had more urgent matters to focus on that could well fill all the days off before he would be anywhere near Jodie again.

* * *

As a family, the Grishams—and Logan—gathered around Mick, spending time with him individually and together, with and without the support of the rehabilitation centre's psychologists and therapists. It was another emotional rollercoaster for Eddie, but it did make it easier to have something so important to deal with that it was actually possible to stop thinking about Jodie during his days and he was so exhausted by the time he fell into bed at night that he was asleep almost instantly.

This crisis with Mick was important—and personal enough—to stop him feeling weirdly envious of a ghost.

Envious of anyone, even, who had a partner in life who loved them that much. He watched his sister being wrapped in her husband's arms in a moment when they thought they were unobserved and the strength of their love for each other was enough to bring a lump to his throat.

He wanted that for himself one day.

And while he could understand why, he still felt sad for Jodie that she would never allow herself to feel like that again about anyone else.

Okay...he felt sad for himself too. That he couldn't be the one who could fill that gap in her life, but that was going to have to be a secret. Even more of a secret than the stolen hours he and Jodie had spent together because that had been a shared secret.

How he was feeling now was entirely his own.

When Mick responded to the deep concern of the people who loved *him* the most and agreed to go along with the plan his family had suggested, Eddie's days suddenly became far too busy to think about anything or anyone else. Ella and Logan had already booked their honeymoon. James was already planning to start his locum position in Aberdeen's Queen Mother's hospital. With Mick agreeing to try a visit to the exclusive treatment centre in New Zealand, and extensive online interviews with the medical teams involved on both sides of the world before the New Zealand centre agreed to take him, there were suddenly what felt like a million things to get organised and chaos was lurking around every corner.

Airlines had to be contacted in person to plead for last-minute seats and the special assistance that would be needed. Ella and Logan took care of the medical side of caring for Mick on such a long journey, taking supplies for any contingency they could think of. A new wheelchair had to be sourced that was suitable for travelling and patient records copied and filed. James was due to move so he had to pack his flat up in Edinburgh so he could sublet it and he had too much to shift up to Ella and Logan's place with only a motorbike for transport so Eddie made a couple of trips south with his SUV to help.

On his last day off he helped with taking everybody and their huge amount of luggage to the airport and stood side by side with James as they watched Mick being taken onto his flight that would connect with the long-haul journey to New Zealand. Eddie had helped bring one of his brothers even closer to where he was building his new life but he was sending the other to the far side of the planet at exactly the same time and...

And it felt weird. As if the fabric of his life was being pulled apart all over again. Not with the painful rip that Mick's accident had created but in a sense that puzzle pieces were being juggled because they didn't fit where they'd been placed so it was time to try something new.

For all of them.

Thank goodness it didn't feel weird to be back at work. If anything, the potential awkwardness of being crewed with someone he'd had an off-limits sexual relationship with seemed to have been burnt off by the emotional overload both he and Jodie had been through in the last few days.

A time that had been intense enough to have generated thoughts and feelings that were over the top. Like thinking that he'd fallen in love with Jodie? Eddie was grateful for the filter of emotional exhaustion that allowed him to find a reality that would be much easier to live with than the secret angst of a very immature unrequited love.

This felt like a genuine friendship between himself and Jodie now. One with a foundation that was rock solid because they shared a secret that only the two of them knew.

Two secrets, in fact.

Eddie would never dream of breaking Jodie's trust by sharing the very private information of the tragedy she'd had to deal with in her past. And he knew that Jodie was not about to confess to anyone how close she and Eddie had become while they'd sorted out that small issue of how attracted they'd been to each other.

That was in the past too.

Hopefully, Jodie felt the same way he did and didn't regret any of it. Because it had generated a personal level of trust that could have taken decades to build in an ordinary kind of friendship. Add that to the professional level of trust they had been building on since they'd first worked together and it was something very special indeed. While he might not have fallen *in* love with her, Eddie cared about Jodie very much and that was a more than acceptable form of love between good friends.

Hey…it would probably last a lot longer than any other kind, wouldn't it?

Good news arrived a couple of days later, that Mick was safely at his new rehab centre in New Zealand after the long journey had been completed without any complications. Ella had sent Eddie a photograph of him meeting his personal therapist, Riley, who was none other than the blonde woman with the beautiful smile who'd featured on the rehab centre's webpage.

Eddie smiled and forwarded the photo to James. 'Lucky man' he added as a caption.

He was even luckier, though, wasn't he?

Eddie was fit and healthy. He had a job he loved and a crew to work with that was absolutely the best. He had a friendship that was going to last a lifetime if he had any say in the matter and, as a bonus, he was going to get out into the mountains and spend a couple of days with that friend doing something new and exciting. He couldn't wait.

CHAPTER TEN

WAS THIS WHAT real happiness felt like?

Being out in nature in a place so beautiful it was a constant reminder of how lucky she was to be alive?

Floor-to-ceiling windows in this unexpectedly gorgeous lodge afforded stunning mountain views against a clear blue sky and even included a glimpse of a waterfall above the forests surrounding the river and this outdoor recreation centre. Declan—one of the instructors for the abseiling course both Jodie and Eddie were attending this weekend—told them in the meet and greet that, if they were confident enough, they could be doing their more advanced outside sessions tomorrow close to the dramatic curtains of water that the falls created in the cliffs. Today, however, along with some real beginners to abseiling, they would be playing on some smaller crags that were less intimidating.

Eddie caught Jodie's glance and grinned. Then he leaned closer so that only she could hear him. 'Dream come true for me,' he whispered. 'I've always wanted to get up close and personal with a waterfall.'

The first session was indoors and covered information that was already more than familiar for both Jodie and Eddie with the knowledge and experience they'd gained, both through their rescue winch training and their now

shared hobby of bouldering, but their attendance here
was partly a box-ticking exercise that would allow them
to get accreditation with the organisation that provided
International Rope Access qualifications and then move
on to more advanced levels. If nothing else, it promised
to be a fun weekend out in the kind of environment they
both loved.

Who wouldn't be happy?

'Putting aside our personal protective equipment like
helmets and gloves,' Declan said, 'these are the two vital
elements that you could not abseil without. A rope and a
harness. We'll get into the carabiners and belay devices
that are the interfaces between the two very soon but let's
start with this.' He picked up an item from the top of one
of the closest piles on the floor of this lounge.

'This is a basic harness. Sorry, Eddie and Jodie—
they're not up to the standard you guys will be used to,
with all the bells and whistles for attachments, but they're
all we need for what we're going to be doing.' He held the
harness up by the largest loop. 'This loop goes around
your waist and the two loops underneath go around your
legs and there's a loop on the front which is where your
belay device will be attached. We want to get you all into
one that's fitting well and is comfortable. We'll come
around and help. Maybe Jodie and Eddie can give you a
hand as well, when they've got their own harnesses on.'

Jodie saw Eddie from the corner of her eye a minute
or two later, adjusting the buckles on the leg loops of a
harness a young woman was wearing and Jodie actually fumbled with one of the buckles she was working
with herself to help someone else. It was as if she could
feel the brush of Eddie's fingers against the top of her
own legs. She could certainly feel the tingle of sensa-

tion that pooled low in her body, but it wasn't desire, she reminded herself. It was a memory and Jodie was finding that she could not only deal with it but perhaps even learn to embrace it.

Okay…if she was honest, she was really missing the intimate part of what they'd had together but, if that was the price for keeping her world under control and safe, then she was prepared to pay it. No. As she'd told Eddie on that last, poignant night they'd had alone together, it wasn't a choice at all. It was simply something she had to do in order to survive.

That spiral of sensation was another reminder that she was alive and could experience pleasure from her body as well as her environment and the anticipation of a challenge—as long as she could keep within the safety barriers she was busy rebuilding. And, if she was honest, it had to be adding a bit of spice to the way she was feeling.

Eddie, bless him, was still making this transition easy so it was beginning to seem like they might be lucky enough that they could end up being friends with none of the awkwardness that usually came when people took a friendship too far and then tried to dial it back.

So yeah…

This felt like a level of happiness that was the most Jodie could ever expect—or allow—if she was going to keep herself safe, so she was going to make the most of this weekend.

She couldn't help another glance in Eddie's direction, though, and, as if he'd felt it, he looked across the room, one eyebrow raised just enough to make it a question.

You okay? You enjoying this?

Jodie smiled back. Holding his gaze felt so natural. Weirdly, being able to feel that dimension to their friendship that should have made it harder to be around Eddie was making her feel even safer. Because she trusted him completely and she knew he cared enough about her to want her to be safe. And happy.

She could feel her smile widen into a message that Eddie wouldn't be able to miss.

I'm loving it...

She looked...happy.

Being in Jodie's company and sharing a good time that was making her this happy was...well...it was the best that Eddie could hope for, wasn't it?

Exactly what he had always wanted to be able to have with any woman he'd been attracted to enough to get closer than simply a friend or colleague, after the need to step back from expectations of it becoming something more. He was getting a masterclass in how to be the perfect playboy, in fact, which would have been very useful a decade or more ago. Given that he'd known what he was signing up for right from the get-go, he should be just as happy as Jodie was with the way things were going. And he would be, he told himself firmly, as soon as he got used to this new normal.

They moved onto ropes after everyone was wearing a secure harness.

'These are at the thicker end for the size of climbing ropes,' Declan told them. 'That makes them run slower through the belay device and gives you better control over your speed. We're going to practise tying some knots now and top of that list is the Prusik friction knot. It's this knot that will be your safety mechanism and stop you falling, so it's important. When we've mastered that, we can head outside and you can have some fun on some real rocks.'

It took a while, because most people were struggling to assimilate the information and techniques about unfamiliar knots but, with a smile here and a quick glance there, Eddie and Jodie were soon quietly having a bit of a race to see who could do the fastest and neatest coiling and tying of the practice lengths of rope. And it was fun.

Was this his own safety mechanism for being with Jodie? Doing something challenging enough to need focus? Eddie already knew that professional boundaries kept things safe at work, but how good would it be to enjoy time together out of work like this without being blindsided by the occasional flash of the kind of pain— or was it sadness?—that came from thinking something huge had been lost for ever?

Yeah…the challenge and fun of the hours spent outside for the rest of the day made Eddie confident that this new normal could work. It helped that Declan divided the group early on that afternoon so that he and Jodie could do some more intensive training.

'We'll sort out a programme for completing all levels of the accreditation course tomorrow and maybe you can book in to come and stay here again.'

'Sounds like a plan.' Jodie nodded. 'I'd be up for that. What about you, Eddie?'

There was almost a plea in the glance Eddie received. Could they do this? Together? Have a real friendship and maybe stay in each other's lives for ever? Eddie had a strong misgiving that trying to do that might hold him back from ever moving on from being with Jodie but he made sure he sounded enthusiastic. Fake it till you make it, right?

'Count me in,' he agreed.

* * *

Maybe it was because he was physically tired by the end of the afternoon sessions that it got more difficult to be near Jodie. Maybe the echo of that misgiving was doing its best to put down roots. Or perhaps it was the thought, as evening fell, that they were both going to be sleeping under the same roof but in different beds that tipped the balance.

Whatever the cause, by the time dinner was over, Eddie wasn't feeling nearly as happy as he had been. Cell phone coverage was dismal in this mountainous area so he couldn't distract himself by messaging his family to catch up on how Mick was, whether Ella and Logan had rented a camper van yet or if James had had any interesting cases coming through his new emergency department at Queen's. He didn't want to go and join Jodie where she was helping other members of the group who wanted to practise their knots again because that certainly wasn't going to silence that niggling thought at the back of his mind that he was only making things worse by trying to convince himself that a friendship with Jodie was going to be enough.

That the sensible thing to do would be to create some distance. Not just tonight but back at work as well. It might even help if he had a quiet word with Dion and got himself shifted to a different crew? In the past, in a situation like this, Eddie would have simply packed up and moved to another job. Another country. He would have found a fresh start and, he was a bit ashamed to admit it but it was the truth—he would have found a new friendship with the kind of benefits that would have been more than enough of a distraction. But he couldn't do that this time. And it wasn't just because of that wakeup call that had made him want a more meaningful relationship and commitment in his life.

He was in this difficult space in his head because of the same reason he was in this new city and new job. There were things in life that were too important not to commit to. Discovering that coming back to his home-land of Scotland had made Eddie feel like he was where he truly belonged in the world was a bonus, but he had come back for his family. He was living in the same city as his brother James for the first time in years and Mick's absence was temporary. He'd come back, hopefully ready to make his own commitment to embrace life again, and Eddie needed to be here to support him.

So he couldn't leave Aberdeen. He couldn't leave his job. Relationships with family—and hopefully a part-ner—might be at the top of his list of important things in life but his career wasn't just a job, it was a major part of who he was. Stepping away from air rescue to work on a road crew felt like it would be a step too far, but cre-ating a bit of distance by being in a different crew and working opposing shifts on the air rescue base seemed like an option that could work.

But what could he say to Dion? That he was sorry he'd broken the rules? That he'd been stupid to think that it would be no problem to have one last superficial, just-for-fun hook-up with a gorgeous woman but it was never going to happen again? And no harm had been done. The attraction had been mutual but it was over and done with? End of story—for both of them?

No. He couldn't do that because it would get Jodie into a whole heap of trouble. He probably couldn't even make it sound convincing when he wasn't sure he be-lieved it himself.

And what about that misgiving that had the real potential to start growing like a weed?

How on earth was he supposed to find the person he wanted to be with for the rest of his life when he was still this close to Jodie? When, deep down, he knew it would be impossible to find anyone he wanted to be with as much as he still wanted to be with Jodie Sinclair.

Oh, man… He needed to clear his head.

He picked up his anorak and walked over to where Declan was having a coffee with the other instructors.

'I'm just going to get a bit of fresh air,' he told them.

'Got a torch? The moon might be out now but it could disappear any time.'

'Yeah…' Eddie put the band of the forehead torch over his head.

'Stick to the tracks,' Declan advised. 'And don't go too far, okay? You'll want a good night's sleep so you're ready for tomorrow's challenges.'

Eddie smiled and nodded, but he lengthened his stride as soon as he got outside the lodge.

If he was going to get any sleep at all tonight he would have to deal with the conflict going on in his head and that was clearly going to take more than just a bit of a stroll.

Jodie could feel Eddie's absence before she could see that he wasn't in the lounge or dining area of the lodge any longer.

'Did Eddie go to bed?' she asked Declan when he joined the group to offer to put a documentary about abseiling on the wide screen television.

'No. He went outside for some fresh air. He should be back any time now—I told him not to go too far.'

There was no real reason for Jodie to wander outside to see if she could see him returning. There was probably every reason why she shouldn't, but it was impossible to focus on the documentary, despite its amazing scenery and photography.

Something didn't feel right and…and it was something important enough to feel urgent.

She slipped out of the room, found her warm jacket and torch and went outside, following the main track they had used earlier today that led uphill from the lodge. She kept expecting to see Eddie coming downhill around the next corner but she began wondering if he'd even taken this track at all, until she cleared the main band of forest that gave way to areas of bare rock at the base of cliffs. She could see a flicker of light above her that had to be Eddie's head torch.

She could also hear how much louder the background sound of the river was and that was when she remembered what Eddie had whispered in her ear this morning.

'I've always wanted to get up close and personal with a waterfall…'

He had to know that going alone at this time of night was far from sensible. It was out of character for Eddie to be taking a risk like this, no matter how confident in his abilities he might have felt. Jodie was going to tell him exactly how stupid he'd been, in no uncertain terms, as soon as she caught up with him.

Rehearsing what she was going to say only made her feel increasingly worried and she pushed herself to go faster. The next time she saw the light it was a lot closer.

'Eddie…' She had to yell to get heard above the sound of water crashing onto rock. *'Stop…* Wait for me…'

The light got brighter as if he'd turned his head at the

sound of her voice. Then she heard his voice. It was faint but she could tell it wasn't calling her name. He wasn't saying any words.

It sounded like a cry of astonishment.

Or fear...?

And then the light was snuffed out as if a switch had been flicked.

He'd fallen.

Jodie knew that.

She just didn't know how bad it was. Maybe she would hear him calling for help, or better yet—see his light again any second as he got to his feet and kept coming down the track.

But that wasn't stopping a fear that was turning her blood to ice in her veins.

Eddie could have fallen too close to the edge of the waterfall and been swept away. He could have been smashed against rocks and knocked unconscious. Or he might be trapped below the surface by the force of the water pounding into a deep pool.

Oh, dear Lord...he might be *drowning*...

A broken sob broke from Jodie's throat. No...that sound and pain was really coming from a very different place.

Her heart...

Her soul...

All those safety barriers she'd built up so very carefully over the years were totally useless, weren't they? They'd been swept away as easily as if that waterfall had picked them up and made them vanish into nothing more solid than a fine spray of liquid. She'd been lulled into a false sense of security over the years simply because she'd met the person who could change everything.

She hadn't seen it coming or recognised it at the time but she'd never actually been safe from the first moment she'd met Edward Grisham.

She loved him. Just as much as she'd ever loved Joel. More, perhaps, because this was strong enough to have annihilated those protective barriers. She might have denied it so effectively she hadn't realised it was happening, but that day at the fundraising event when she'd felt that yearning to be a part of Eddie's future—to be holding his baby in her arms, even—had been a sure sign that she'd lost any protection she'd thought she had. No wonder she'd panicked and backed off. But how had she believed she was back in control? That she'd never be in this particular space ever again, with her world in danger of slamming to a halt so devastatingly she'd never be able to start it turning again.

'*Dammit*, Eddie…' Jodie's words were choked. By unbearable emotion and the fact that she was so out of breath it felt as if her body was on fire. She was forced to stop and bend over, her hands on her knees as she struggled to get enough oxygen to take the pain from her muscles and allow her lungs to function adequately again.

She was close enough to the river for the rushing water to be a constant background sound. Straightening, Jodie pushed closer, to find a dark, deep pool, surrounded by enormous boulders with a small waterfall that was catching the moonlight enough to make it shimmer as it foamed down the vertical drop from the ledge of rock about five metres above Jodie. This wasn't the waterfall they could see from the lodge windows because that one had to be over a thirty-metre drop and the big one would have been what Eddie was heading towards, wouldn't it?

He didn't do anything by halves.

Except...

Jodie was still looking up at the lip of the ledge the water was flowing over so smoothly and she saw something in the trees to one side of it. A glowing spot that was too bright to be swallowed by the moonlight. A shape that had to be manmade.

'*Eddie...*' Jodie had to clear the lump from her throat and try again. '*Eddie...?* Can you hear me?'

'*Jodie?*'

The spot of light moved. Disappeared and then appeared again, right beside where the water started its drop. It was too dark to see Eddie's face beneath the bright bulb of the torch but Jodie could sense every one of his features. Those dark eyes, that strong nose...those lips that could curve into the most delicious smile in the entire world...

The relief that he was not only alive but conscious and moving was enough for tears to be streaming down Jodie's face and her voice was raw.

'Oh, my God, Eddie... Are you hurt?'

'I don't think so... Maybe a bit. I tripped and went into a slide and bumped a few rocks on the way. I landed in the water but managed to catch a tree branch before I went over the top. I can't get close enough to see... Can I climb down to where you are?'

Jodie scanned the rock face on either side of the waterfall. It was almost sheer but, with her practised eye, she could pick out the variations in contour and texture that could provide grip or support for hands and feet, although that would still be risky with how wet the wall was from the waterfall's spray.

'No way,' she called. 'Even going up would be a challenge. If you fell and didn't land in the pool, you'd kill yourself. I'd kind of prefer that you didn't do that.'

What an understatement. But Jodie was still grappling with the realisation that she was head over heels, heart and soul in love with Eddie and that was too huge to even think about putting into words. She pulled out her phone but had to watch helplessly as two bars on her phone went to one and then reception cut out completely before she could even try calling for help.

'I'll try climbing back up to the track, then...' Eddie shouted. The torchlight swerved and hit the trees again. And then, to Jodie's horror, it faded, flickered and went out.

She heard Eddie's groan of frustration. 'I think my batteries are dead. But maybe I can... I could...'

The sudden short silence from above turned into another groan that made Jodie catch her breath.

'What's wrong?'

'I... I'm a bit dizzy, that's all.'

'Did you bump your head in that fall?'

'I don't know. I don't remember...'

Jodie saw the dark shape that was Eddie's head disappear. Was he lying down? Losing consciousness? Confused enough to think it might be a good idea to try climbing back to the track without even torchlight to guide him?

'*Eddie?*'

There was no response.

'Don't move,' Jodie yelled. 'I'm coming up.'

She had no choice. Yes, she knew it was dangerous, but

she couldn't stay here and not know whether Eddie was okay. She knew she should go for help but she couldn't go in the opposite direction to where Eddie was. The need to be close to him—to be able to *touch* him—was the only thing filling her mind.

It wasn't as if she didn't know what she was doing and the first few metres were easy. The faults in the rock were almost like steps and there were plenty of hand grips. But then her fingers started getting colder and it was harder to see whether it was safe to stretch towards a new hold or if the light from her torch was creating shadows that were illusions of a protrusion or gap that wouldn't actually be able to take her weight. The darkness outside the circle of light from her torch made things so much worse. She couldn't see how far she'd come up but it felt like a yawning chasm beneath her that would swallow her instantly if she fell. She couldn't see how far it was to the top either and, at one point, she froze—glued to the wall like a spider, unable to see how to get higher but knowing it would be impossible to turn back. There was only one direction she could go, despite her feet aching so badly and her fingers beginning to go numb.

She could only ever go towards Eddie...

And, unexpectedly, as she reached up to skim her hand against the rock to try and locate a handhold, she felt herself caught by a strong grip around her wrist. Eddie was leaning over the edge. He scrunched his eyes closed as she tilted her head up and blinded him with her torchlight but his voice was as strong as his grip.

'I've got you, sweetheart. You can do this...'

Sweetheart...

He'd called her sweetheart for the first time—the first person to ever call her that—and the endearment filled her heart and then wrapped itself around her entire body like a hug as she used the safety of his grip as a hold and pushed herself up towards him.

And then she was in his arms and she could hear him telling her that she was safe and that everything was going to be okay, but Jodie was sobbing. And…angry…

She was *so* angry.

She pushed herself back and didn't care that he had to shade his eyes from the glare of the beam of light on her head.

'This is all your fault,' she shouted through her tears. 'It shouldn't have happened.'

'I know, I'm sorry…' Eddie tried to wrap his arms around her but she was pushing back hard with her fists. 'But it'll be okay. I promise. I'm not hurt. *You're* not hurt. Declan knows I'm out here, and they're probably already on their way to find us, and—'

But Jodie was shaking her head. 'I'm not talking about *this*. I'm talking about falling in love with you. I told you I couldn't do this again…that I couldn't ever let myself love someone enough to make losing them the end of the world and…and now it's happened and…and I'm scared because I have no idea what to do about it…'

All the fight suddenly drained out of Jodie and she closed her eyes, feeling her body go completely limp—surrendering to being folded into Eddie's arms and held against his chest.

He was still making reassuring sounds and his voice was so clear because it was right beside her ear, so close she could feel the warmth of his breath.

'It's not a problem,' he was telling her. 'I promise… Because I *do* know exactly what to do about it.'

She looked up. 'How? What…?'

Eddie pressed the button that turned off her torch. For a heartbeat or two Jodie couldn't see anything at all due to the sudden change in light, but then she found she could see Eddie's face in the moonlight. She could see his eyes. And his smile.

'Because I love you that much too,' he told her. 'And I know how scary it is. If I lost you it would feel like way too much of my world was ending as well. That's why I had to try and be happy to just be your friend, even though I knew it would never be enough.'

'So what are we supposed to do? I thought I could protect myself from it ever happening again, but that didn't work out so well, did it?'

'We're going to protect each other,' Eddie said, simply.

'How can we do that?'

'We can love each other. For as long as we're lucky enough to have together.'

'You make it sound so easy.'

'Maybe it is when you don't have a choice. When, you know...you kind of want the world to keep turning.'

Jodie's last coherent thought, as Eddie's lips covered hers in the most amazing kiss that had ever been bestowed, was that maybe he was right.

Didn't someone even say that once? That love made the world go round?

The kiss couldn't last, of course, but that didn't matter because Jodie knew there would be an infinite number of kisses to come. And hearing the calls of people coming to find them was the first step back to safety. Back to where her life was going to start all over again.

With Eddie.

He turned on her head torch and they heard the shout of delight from the searchers.

'There you are, Eddie. Are you hurt?'

'No,' he called back. 'I'm a bit stuck but I'm not hurt.' He lowered his voice so that only Jodie could hear him. 'I've never felt better, to be honest.'

He smiled down at Jodie and she smiled back.

She'd never felt better either. Her eyes were filling with tears again, but this time they were such happy tears they felt like liquid joy.

'I love you, Eddie…'

'I love you too, sweetheart.'

The sound of voices and the beams of torchlight were getting closer but…there was time for one more kiss before anyone broke this bubble, wasn't there?

Eddie answered her unspoken question instantly without saying a word.

Of course there was…

EPILOGUE

Three days later...

THE DAILY TEAM briefing of the Aberdeen Air Ambulance base had just finished and everybody had all the information they needed about weather conditions, levels of staffing and resources and potential disruptions to the shift. The last administrative team member was following Red Watch out of the meeting room and Dion was picking up his laptop computer when he noticed that Blue Watch wasn't moving.

'You guys on strike or something?'

'Jodie told us to hang around for a minute,' Gus said. 'I think she wants to say something.'

'I do.' Jodie nodded.

'Me too,' Eddie added.

Dion caught the look between the two paramedics and groaned. 'I hope it's not what I think it is,' he growled. 'I made myself very clear before you started work here, didn't I, Eddie?'

'You did,' Eddie acknowledged. 'Sorry, Dion...'

'What?' Alex was staring at Eddie. 'What have you got to be sorry about?'

Gus was staring at Eddie as well, but he wasn't looking bewildered like Alex.

'No way...' He was grinning. 'Are we talking shenanigans?'

'That's all it was supposed to be,' Eddie admitted. 'In which case we wouldn't have needed to confess anything. But...' He glanced at Jodie and clearly couldn't stop a smile spreading over his own face. 'Turns out it's a thing. The *real* thing.'

Jodie was smiling back at him. 'It is,' she confirmed. 'Definitely not shenanigans.'

'I don't believe it,' Gus said. 'And there I was thinking Jodie's job was more important to her than any relationship could ever be. What was it you said to me? "Been there, done that and never doing it again"?'

Jodie was trying—and failing—to stifle her grin. 'Things happen...' she murmured.

Dion was shaking his head. 'I don't believe it either. What's next? You're both going to go on holiday together and jump off the top of mountains? It was bad enough worrying whether Jodie would come home in one piece.'

'You don't have to worry about me,' Jodie told him.

'That's my job now,' Eddie added. 'I'm going to keep this amazing woman safe. Or die trying...'

'That's what I'm talking about,' Dion growled. 'Now I have to worry about losing my two best paramedics in one go.'

'Not if we're working on different watches,' Eddie pointed out. 'That's why we thought we'd better come clean and stop breaking the rules.'

Dion shaded his eyes with his hand. 'This is my fault, isn't it? I might have said it wasn't allowed but then I pushed you into each other's arms, didn't I? After that horrific job with the wedding accident. I told you to take Jodie out for a drink. To talk to her. To make her feel better...'

'He did.' Jodie's nod was solemn. 'He made me feel a lot better.'

'But that wasn't where it started,' Eddie assured him. 'It was actually where it was supposed to finish.'

'I had no idea,' Alex said. 'I just thought you guys liked working with each other.'

'We do,' they both said at the same time.

Jodie gave Dion a direct glance. 'I guess it kind of is your fault, though,' she said. 'It was you that talked us into doing that abseiling course last weekend and if it wasn't for that little whoopsie that Eddie had by the waterfall we might have just ignored how we really felt about each other.'

'A *whoopsie*...?' Dion could feel himself going a little pale. 'Do I want to know about what that entailed?'

'You really don't,' Eddie said firmly. 'And we've got more important things to talk about. We're due to start our shift in a few minutes and we can't keep working together, can we? Not when you made the rules so clear.'

'Well...it's not *exactly* a rule...' Dion's heart was sinking. The last thing he wanted to hear was that either Jodie or Eddie was planning to resign and work somewhere else.

'We're living together now,' Jodie put in. 'It's not as if we really need to spend every minute of every day together by working together as well.'

The look that passed between Eddie and Jodie suggested something very different, however. It was a look that brought a lump to Dion's throat, in fact. They loved each other, these two. At a level that most people could only dream about.

'You've moved in with Eddie?' Alex asked Jodie. 'That's going to be a bit of a squeeze in that wee basement apartment.'

'No. I've moved in with Jodie,' Eddie said. 'We came back from being together up in the mountains and decided that we were going to start the way we intend to spend the rest of our lives. Together…'

Both Alex and Gus were looking delighted.

'It's brilliant news,' Alex said. 'And I might know someone who can take over the apartment for you.'

'No need,' Eddie told him. 'My brother James is house-sitting for my sister Ella but they'll be back well before his locum at Queen's is due to finish. He's going to need a place of his own, especially if he decides to hang around a while longer after Mick gets back.'

'Sounds like things are falling into place nicely, then.' Gus nodded. 'It was meant to be.'

'It's all right for some,' Dion muttered. 'How am I supposed to deal with this? Swap one of you for someone on Red Watch?'

'You did say it wasn't exactly a rule,' Gus reminded him. 'And it's not as though any of us even noticed anything was going on. As far as we knew, they're the perfect team at work. The best… I don't want it to change.'

'Neither do I,' Alex said.

Neither did Dion, to be honest. Maybe he should just trust his instincts here.

'Fine,' he snapped. 'We'll leave things as they are, then. It's probably going to create more of an issue trying to separate you two than it would be letting you carry on working together.'

Man…just the glow from that glance that was passing between Eddie and Jodie now was like sunshine getting into the darkest corners ever.

They *were* the perfect team.

And he couldn't be happier for them.

'That's sorted, then,' he said gruffly. 'Let's get on with it, shall we?'

* * * * *

REBEL DOCTOR'S
BABY SURPRISE

ALISON ROBERTS

MILLS & BOON

CHAPTER ONE

'THERE'S NO ONE HOME.'

Sarah Harrison climbed back into her car, closing the door very quietly so as not to wake the passenger in the back seat. She also kept her voice low enough to be little more than a whisper.

'I don't know why I'm surprised. He's probably on a full night shift in the emergency department he's working in now.' Sarah made a tiny but disparaging sound with the puff of breath she released. 'And if he's not, he'll be out on a date. He might have only moved here a couple of weeks ago but I'm quite sure he's not spending his nights alone. Leopards never change their spots, do they?'

This was the correct forwarding address, according to the friend who had bent a rule or two to obtain the information for her at a hospital in Edinburgh where he'd been working at, but this ancient, converted barn with stone walls and a slate roof, down a private country lane well outside the city limits of Aberdeen looked like something from the pages of a country house and garden magazine. Sarah had imagined him living in a modern inner-city apartment. A penthouse, perhaps, with a swimming pool or at least a jacuzzi—like any good-looking playboy in a B-grade movie would be housed in?

Sarah leaned her head back and closed her eyes.

She had never been this tired in her entire life and, for a nurse who'd spent over a decade working long shifts in emergency departments that were often stretched to breaking point, that was saying something. Did all new parents feel like this? So exhausted they actually felt unwell?

She caught her bottom lip between her teeth. It didn't matter how hard this was because it was simply what she had to do. What she'd promised to do. And Sarah Harrison had never broken a promise in her life.

But he wasn't home, despite the huge black motorbike parked outside the barn that fitted the image of the man she had come to find far more than the house did. Was he taking a bath, perhaps, and had decided he didn't want to get out to answer the door? No. There weren't enough lights on to make it look like someone was at home. Unless he was in bed? It was a bit early to expect him to be asleep, but maybe he wasn't alone…?

'I'm not sure what to do,' she admitted aloud. 'We've got plenty of time but it'll take us thirty minutes to drive back to the other side of the city and we've got to get home to the B&B before midnight or we'll be locked out.'

It was more than tempting to start the car and drive away. She could come back tomorrow. Or should she go to the Queen Mother's Hospital in Aberdeen instead, and ask for one of their locum consultants to get paged to the reception area? No…she couldn't do that. This had to be kept private because there was the potential for something—or should that be some*one*—to prevent her keeping a promise that was far bigger than the one that had made her drive all the way from Leeds to be parked in front of this seemingly empty house.

If she started the car and drove away she might find an excuse to never come back. She might convince herself that she'd been right all along and this was a very bad idea, despite any perceived rights of another person who didn't realise they were involved. She'd done her best, after all, driving what felt like the length of the whole country to get here. It wasn't her fault he wasn't home.

Starting the car would have another benefit as well. She could turn the heater on and crank it up. Even though it was warmer than she'd expected driving this far north into Scotland, Sarah felt a chill around her that was cold enough to suggest it was heading straight for her bones. It was also sudden enough to send a shiver down her spine and make her open her eyes and sit up. Sitting here being indecisive wasn't going to help anything, was it?

She reached for her anorak that was neatly folded on the passenger seat and tugged it on. She was about to turn the key in the ignition of her SUV but a sound from the back seat made her freeze.

A small sound. Not much more than a whimper but Sarah felt her heart sink when she twisted her head to see a tiny hand coming over the side of the rear-facing baby capsule. It was a tense hand with spiky fingers, like an angry little starfish.

She checked her watch. 'You're not due for a feed for another forty-three minutes,' she said. 'And I changed your nappy not that long ago...'

But the whimper was turning into a warble. Sarah had to climb out of the car, open the back door and climb in again, because the car seat was anchored in the middle of the back seat.

'Are you cold too, darling? No, you're all wrapped up like a bug in a rug and your hands are lovely and warm… What's the matter, Button?'

The warble was being punctuated by hiccups and Sarah knew what that meant. Strength was being gathered for some serious screaming to commence.

She undid the safety harness holding the baby in the capsule and scooped her out, picking up the soft, fuzzy blanket to wrap around her. Then Sarah wriggled out of the car carefully. Walking for a few minutes was the best option here, for both of them. That bouncy, rocking walk that could sometimes settle her even when she was really miserable, and a sleeping baby would be preferable to having one that was creating a major distraction in the car when she was driving on unfamiliar rural roads.

A comforting, bouncy walk would help Sarah as well. It had been a lifesaver during the dark days of the last couple of weeks since this baby's mother—and the person Sarah had loved most in the world—had died.

She found herself looking up at the stars as she heard a whisper of Karly's voice.

'I want you to take her, Sass… To look after her…'

'I will… I am already. Ever since you got sick…'

'I know… But I want you to adopt her properly and not just be her appointed guardian Make it legal. Be her real mum…'

'I will…'

'Do you promise…?'

'I promise…'

'Cross your heart and hope to die…?'

Oh, God…the memory of the oath they'd used to cement promises from when they'd sworn eternal friendship on their first day of school together was too poignant now. Sad enough to make the stars overhead nothing more than a blurred streak of light in the inky sky.

Sarah fought back. This so wasn't the time or place to tap back into her grief. She couldn't break down. Not in the middle of nowhere. When she was totally alone.

Except she wasn't totally alone, was she?

They weren't alone.

There were headlights coming towards them down the lane and the shape of the vehicle became very familiar to someone who'd been living in London for so long. Aberdeen clearly had black cabs as well. The driver didn't turn off his lights as he pulled to a stop even though Sarah was standing directly in front of the taxi.

She felt another shiver run down her spine.

She was, quite literally, standing in the spotlight and any second now she would have to explain why she was here. The chance to run away and avoid this confronting situation was rapidly evaporating.

'What the *hell*…?' James Grisham could see the woman with a baby in her arms standing in the glare of the headlights.

The woman sitting beside him in the back of the cab craned her neck so that she could also see what he was staring at. Her suspicious tone was a good match for her scowl. 'Who's that?'

'Never seen her before in my life,' James declared.

'Maybe she's lost,' the cab driver suggested. 'Or having car trouble. Want me to stick around?'

'Aye… Thanks…' James glanced at his companion as he reached for the door. 'You stay here for a minute too, Janine. Just till I see what's going on.'

He got out of the car.

'Are you Dr Grisham?' the stranger asked over the sound of the baby's howling. 'Dr James Grisham?'

'I am.' It was a little disturbing that this woman knew his name. 'And you are…?'

'Sarah Harrison.' She was jiggling the baby she was holding, turning it away from the glare of the headlights. 'And this is Ivy. Ivy Peters.'

'Ivy doesn't sound very happy.' James was frowning. 'It's rather late to be out and about at this time of night with a wee bairn, isn't it?'

She nodded. 'I've driven up from Leeds to see you. I found a place to stay in the city, but then I thought it might be better to get this over and done with as quickly as possible.'

'I have no idea what you're talking about.'

James narrowed his eyes to take a better look at this woman. Probably in her thirties, he guessed, with a no-fuss hairstyle, parted in the middle and hanging straight down to almost touch her shoulders. Fine features. She looked a bit like a…librarian?

'Do I know you?'

She shook her head this time. 'But you have met a friend of mine. Karly Peters?'

James was echoing her head shake. 'Doesn't ring any bells.'

He heard the taxi door slide open behind him. He caught a whiff of Janine's slightly cloying perfume as she came to stand beside him.

Janine flicked a long tress of blonde hair over her shoulder. 'What's going on?'

'I have no idea,' James said slowly. Whatever it was, however, needed to be over and done with as far as this stranger was concerned and that made it a strong possibility that he wasn't going to like it either.

'It might be better if you take the taxi back into the city, Janine,' he said.

'Oh, Jimmy…' Janine's head tilted as she smiled up at him. 'But you were going to show me your sister's gorgeous house. I adore barn conversions…'

'This is your sister's house?' Sarah was staring at Janine with an expression that was unreadable but definitely not very friendly. Or impressed. 'I was told it was *your* forwarding address.'

'Who told you that?'

'Someone from the general infirmary in Edinburgh. You obviously don't remember meeting Karly, but you did tell her that was where you were working at the time. At that Emergency Medicine and Disaster Management conference in Paris last year?'

Her last words were almost drowned by an increase in the volume of the baby's howls but it didn't stop James from joining the dots with surprising speed. The name Karly was most definitely ringing a bell that was rapidly getting louder. That conference had been about ten months ago. And the baby this woman was holding was an infant that was probably only a few weeks old and had the same surname as Karly. But this had to be a mistake, surely? James couldn't deny he had no complaints about his sex life but he'd always, always been so careful.

No protection was entirely infallible, however. He

knew that. Had he really been so confident that he'd never be one of the tiny percentage of failures?

The distraction of the baby crying didn't diminish the triggering of an adrenaline spike that advertised a primitive 'fight or flight' response to the information those dots were hurling in his direction either. If anything, it made it sharper. James could feel his heart skip a beat and speed up. A knot formed in his gut. He could almost feel the prickle of hairs trying to stand up on the back of his neck and down his arms.

Thank goodness his years of working in emergency medicine had taught him how to take control of a potentially catastrophic situation and the first thing to do was to step back from a personal response and look at what needed to happen first.

'Are you sure you've never seen her before?' Janine sounded suspicious now. 'It's more likely you've just forgotten. We all know what you're like…'

'Quite sure,' James said firmly. He put his hands on Janine's shoulders and turned her back to face the taxi. 'But there is obviously something I need to talk to this person about. Thanks for calling me, Janine. I really enjoyed catching up but we'll have to call it a night.'

'But…' Janine was resisting the gentle pressure that was encouraging her towards the open back door of the cab. Her body language was telling James that she was not happy at all. 'I can't believe you're doing this…'

'You did say you'd come up to Aberdeen to visit your grandma,' he reminded her. 'I'm sure she'll be waiting up for you to get home.' He pulled out his wallet and peeled off a bunch of notes to thrust through the front window of the cab.

'I'll get her home safe, don't you worry,' the driver assured him as Janine climbed into the back and slammed the door shut behind her. Then he tapped the side of his nose. 'Never rains but it pours...' He grinned at James. 'Best of luck, mate.'

Good grief... James watched the taillights of the car disappear as it turned into the lane. Had this random taxi driver been joining the same dots?

A shiver got added to the other physical reactions he was collecting.

'You'd better come inside,' he said reluctantly to his surprise visitor. 'It's far too cold out here for a baby. Do you need anything from your car?'

It wasn't cold inside the barn, despite it being a very large and mostly open-plan space.

A very impressive space with the massive, ancient beams and trusses overhead and the glow of richly polished wooden boards on the floor. The space was broken into distinct areas by the positioning of furniture and what had to be an original interior stone wall that how housed an open fireplace and had a staircase on one side that led to a mezzanine floor. The warm colours in the Persian-style rugs and shelving that was overflowing with books were contributing to the homely feel of this beautiful renovation. So was the heat from the big open fireplace that still had glowing coals in its grate.

It was too warm, actually. Sarah felt a prickle of perspiration on her forehead and realised she needed to get her warm jacket off as soon as possible. She carried Ivy inside and James followed with the baby seat from the car and the big bag of essential baby items that she'd said she might need, even though they wouldn't be staying very long.

'Make yourself comfortable.' James walked past her and put the bag down beside a couch positioned in front of the fire. He shifted the fire screen to put another log onto the coals. 'Can I get you something to drink?'

She *was* thirsty, Sarah realised, but the last thing she wanted was to be sitting here having a cosy cup of tea as if this was a social occasion.

'No, thanks.' She put the still distressed baby on the couch cushions for a moment so that she could peel off her anorak, leaving her with just a light jumper over her shirt. The long boots her jeans were tucked into would have to stay on for now. 'But if you could heat up Ivy's bottle I'd be grateful. It's in the cool pack inside that bag. It's freshly made formula but it'll need heating in a microwave for about thirty seconds. She's not due for a feed for another twenty-five minutes but it's worth a try to see if that's what's bothering her.'

She stared back at the startled glance she got from James. Was he impressed with her well-rehearsed preparations and schedule for Ivy or was he unfamiliar with the best advice on how to care for babies with a predictable routine?

Not that it mattered, but it was probably a good thing that Ivy was making it very obvious that looking after an infant wasn't all cuddles and smiles.

Perhaps the expression on this man's face was more like a shade of shock, in fact. Was it wishful thinking that he was looking rather pale—as if his worst nightmare had just walked up and smacked him in the face?

That might be a good thing too. Sarah had the power

to make it go away. To rescue him completely. She only needed his agreement. If Karly hadn't decided to get her solicitor to witness a statement about who Ivy's father was which could be kept with the birth certificate, Sarah wouldn't have needed to be here at all.

'You never know, Sass... Ivy might need a bone marrow transplant one day. Or a kidney. Or she might want to know who her father is when she's old enough to understand.'

'You want her to know that he didn't want anything to do with her? That he offered to help pay to make the whole "problem" go away?'

'You'll think of something nicer to say. You could tell her I didn't know how to find him so he didn't know about her.'

'What happens when she turns up on his doorstep and hears the truth?'

But Karly had been slipping back into a deep, drug-enhanced sleep by then. It wasn't going to be her problem, was it?

Ivy's howling had subsided into a tired sobbing that was heartbreaking. She was also rubbing her nose against Sarah's arm, which meant she was hungry.

'It's coming, darling.' Sarah cuddled her closer and kissed the dark hair that was wispy fine but had been rather distinctively long and lush and inclined to stick up in random spikes from the moment she'd entered the world.

Her father's hair…?

Sarah glanced up as James returned with the bottle of milk. He didn't just hand it her. He sprinkled a few drops of the liquid onto the inside of his wrist, as if he knew about testing it to make sure it wasn't too hot, and he was nodding as he hunkered down in front of the couch so that his head was at the same level as Ivy's and the bottle was within easy reach of Sarah's hand.

She took it but tested the temperature again herself before offering the teat to Ivy. Her little mouth opened instantly and within a few seconds Ivy was making soft grunting sounds with the effort of sucking so hard.

'She sounds like a wee piglet.'

Sarah could hear the smile in James's voice and looked up to find he was looking directly at her. He *was* smiling and there were little crinkles at the corners of his eyes. Dark, dark eyes.

And heaven help her but Sarah could suddenly understand completely why Karly had been mad enough to have a one-night stand with a random stranger when she'd gone to that conference.

James Grisham was undeniably gorgeous-looking.

Fortunately, it wasn't hard to drag her gaze away before she could reveal what she was thinking. Sarah had to adjust her grip on Ivy so she could tuck an annoying strand of her shoulder-length hair behind her ear. Oddly, it felt damp. It wasn't that she was feeling overheated now, though. If anything, she was feeling cold again. Shivery…

'Are you okay?'

'I'm fine.' The response was an automatic reaction to a question like that but the tone of Sarah's voice was much sharper than she'd intended it to be because the concern in James's voice was so unexpected it was shocking. Or maybe it was the feeling that it was so sincere?

Oh, yeah…any woman would fall under this man's spell in record time, wouldn't they?

Sarah could almost feel herself falling, which was ridiculous because men like James Grisham never made it onto her radar of desirable colleagues or potential friends, let alone anything more significant.

Bad boys.

Playboys.

Men who couldn't be trusted with your heart, that was for sure.

Men who couldn't be trusted with caring for a vulnerable infant or raising a precious child either.

'So...' Sarah cleared her throat. 'As you've probably realised, Karly was Ivy's mother.'

'*Was?*' James sounded shocked. 'Past tense?'

'She died last week. Pancreatic cancer. She knew it was a possibility but she put off getting a diagnosis or starting any treatment because she was pregnant and, as I'm sure you know, sometimes it's not even found until it's far too late.'

Sarah was fighting back a wave of grief again. And the 'if only...' accusations.

If only she'd spotted something earlier. If only Karly hadn't been so obsessed with her appearance, which made it normal to notice she was not eating well and/or losing weight again.

James was standing up again. 'That's tragic. I'm so sorry to hear that.' He was rubbing his forehead with his fingers and then Sarah heard him take a deep breath. 'And Karly told you that I'm Ivy's father?'

'She made a formal will after Ivy was born and named me as her testamentary guardian, but she also made a signed and witnessed statement declaring you to be the father. Not that she would tell me anything about you when she discovered she was pregnant.' She could feel frown lines forming on her forehead. 'I could understand why she didn't want you involved.' She scowled at James. 'Did you really think that Karly would go through with a termination just because you offered to pay for it?'

'*Excuse* me…? What on earth makes you think I *knew* that Karly was pregnant?'

Okay…it was very definitely a shocked expression on his face now, but it seemed to be morphing into something far more like anger. Disgust, even…? Sarah hadn't expected this. She'd thought he would simply dismiss the accusation as merely a fact. Nothing to be proud of, perhaps, but also nothing to be particularly ashamed of.

But the expression on James's face was anything but dismissive. 'You think the only involvement I would have wanted was to offer *money*?'

He sounded deeply offended and Sarah's gut instinct was that his reaction was genuine. Come to think of it, if Karly *had* spoken to James or written to him, why hadn't she given Sarah his email address and phone number instead of just telling her where he'd been working? But… this was confusing. She and Karly had never kept secrets from each other.

All her preconceived expectations of what this man would be like were being twisted and turned upside down and that could only make the outcome of this meeting more uncertain. And Sarah didn't like uncertainty in any form.

Anxiety, in addition to the heat in this room, was making Sarah feel slightly dizzy, as if she couldn't catch a coherent thought. To make it even more difficult to think, Ivy jerked her head back from the teat of the bottle, scrunching her face into an outraged glare that suggested Sarah was responsible for whatever had stopped her enjoying her food. Maybe she'd felt the tension escalating in her body?

James was saying something but she couldn't make any sense of his words. Or maybe she wasn't hearing them clearly enough due to Ivy's renewed howling, along with a weird roaring sound in her head.

Oh…*no*…

Sarah knew what was happening now, but it was too late to do anything to prevent it. Her only thought was that she needed to put Ivy somewhere safe, but she couldn't move. She was vaguely aware of James looming over her and taking the baby from her arms.

And then she slipped into the blackness.

The bottle of milk bounced off the couch and onto the floor as James plucked the baby from arms that had gone limp enough for her to be in danger of landing on the floor herself.

He could only watch in dismay as Sarah crumpled and fell back against the cushions, having clearly lost consciousness completely.

Even more disturbingly, James's ability to take calm control of a potentially catastrophic situation seemed to have suddenly deserted him.

It felt as if someone had just pulled the plug on his life and he was in danger of getting washed down the hole in the dangerous current that had come from nowhere to crash into his life like a tsunami.

He was looking at a complete stranger who could possibly be dying right in front of him.

And he was holding a shrieking baby that was, apparently, his own child.

CHAPTER TWO

IT TOOK A HEARTBEAT.

Maybe two. But then, thank goodness, James rediscovered his ability to deal with this new twist in what already felt like a crisis.

Somehow, he managed to step back from any personal connection. An emotional reaction to the bomb that had just been detonated in his life was inevitable, but it would have to be switched off until further notice. It was Sarah, who was lying there so still and silent, that needed the attention. He tucked the baby into the cushioned interior of her car capsule and covered her with the fuzzy pink blanket that she had been wrapped in.

Within seconds, he'd lifted Sarah's legs up so that she was lying on the couch, removed a cushion and tilted her head back to ensure that her airway was open. He then put the fingers of one hand on her neck to feel for a carotid pulse and the other resting on the bottom of her ribcage to feel for any movement of her diaphragm that would confirm she was breathing even if it was too shallow to be seen beneath her clothing.

Her heartbeat was rapid but strong and regular enough to be reassuring and she was breathing so at least he knew that she hadn't suffered a sudden cardiac or respiratory arrest that might have been challenging to manage this far away from a clinical facility. Her skin felt damp but hot rather than clammy and it was so pale she looked like a ghost. Not that James knew what was normal for her, of course, having never seen her before in his life. He checked her neck and wrists for a medical alert bracelet or pendant that would warn him of any serious underlying conditions like asthma, epilepsy, heart problems or diabetes but found nothing.

'Sarah? Can you hear me? Open your eyes...' James rubbed his knuckles on her sternum when his voice and shoulder shake failed to get a response, but even a painful stimulus wasn't felt. His mind was automatically flicking through the possible causes for unconsciousness.

She hadn't given any sign of being injured or critically unwell in the few minutes he'd been talking to her so he could rule out a significant head injury or something like blood loss or sepsis for the moment. He would have expected some warning signs, such as a sudden onset severe headache, for an imminent CVA like a ruptured aneurysm as well. He couldn't smell any alcohol fumes and the thought of a drug overdose was just as improbable in someone who took her responsibilities seriously enough to have a baby's routine planned down to the exact minute the next feed was due.

The *baby*...

James turned swiftly as he suddenly realised that the only sounds he could hear were the crackle of the log burning in the fireplace and Sarah's slightly noisy breathing. It was kind of disturbing to find two dark eyes fixed on him. Did the baby somehow realise how serious this situation was and that he was the only person who could do anything to help?

'I'll be right back,' James told Ivy. 'I need to get my first aid kit. Don't move, okay?'

Despite running, leaving the front door open as he went to grab the kit that pretty much filled the boot space of the car in the garage, Ivy was protesting his absence by the time he got back to the couch less than sixty seconds later.

'You're okay,' James told her firmly as he unzipped the pack and opened it on the floor. 'I need to look after your mum.'

Except she wasn't her mum. She was only this baby's mother's friend, who had come to find the man who had been identified as the father and she had something to do that she needed to get over and done with as quickly as possible.

Like leaving the baby with its other biological parent because she'd discovered she didn't really want the responsibility of being this child's guardian for at least the next two decades?

James shook the terrifying thought off, despite the realisation that his protective barriers against having dependents in his life might well have suffered a catastrophic breach. There was something far more urgent he needed to think about. He opened a small case, peeled open the foil covering for a lancet and held Sarah's middle finger to prick it. He fitted a test strip to the blood glucose monitor and then held the other end to the drop of blood that had appeared on her fingertip. It took only seconds for the monitor to beep and confirm his suspicion. The level was too low to record.

Sarah was hypoglycaemic. She was unconscious so he couldn't give her anything oral like food or even a glucose gel. He could give her an injection of glucagon but that was intramuscular and the effects would take too long. Luckily, he carried bags of IV dextrose, so he grabbed everything he needed and arranged it on the floor beside him. If Sarah was diabetic this could be a time-critical situation. If she wasn't, giving her blood sugar a rapid boost wasn't going to do her any harm.

Ivy was still crying but it was a miserable, hiccupping sort of sound that suggested she was too tired to make too much of a fuss.

'I'll be there in a minute,' James told her. 'I have a bit to do here first. See? I'm putting a tourniquet on the arm here and that will make it easy to find a nice big vein. What do you think, Ivy? Shall we go for the antecubital vein in the elbow? Yeah… I agree. And a sixteen-gauge needle? Yes…we want this dextrose to work nice and fast, don't we?'

James swabbed the skin, inserted the cannula and secured it as he was speaking. By the time he was priming the tubing and attaching it to the small bag of solution, he noticed that the baby had fallen silent. Was she listening to him?

No…it seemed that his commentary had been boring enough to send Ivy to sleep. James positioned the IV fluid bag higher on the back of the couch and spent a few minutes taking a full set of vital signs on Sarah. Her blood pressure was higher than he'd expected and her pulse still rapid. She was also running a fever. Had she been feeling so unwell that she hadn't eaten in a long time?

It was more likely that she was a diabetic—possibly

a brittle one—and an infection was interfering with her control. If she took insulin or drugs to lower her blood sugar that could well be enough to have tipped her into a dangerously low level. James was debating whether to go out to her vehicle and see if he could find a handbag that might contain clues when Sarah suddenly moved her head from side to side and groaned.

'Oh…no…'

'You're okay.' James put his hand on her arm to stop her bending it and potentially dislodging the cannula, even though the small infusion bag was nearly empty now. 'You've had a hypo. Are you diabetic?'

'Yes…'

Sarah's eyes opened. Quite smartly for someone who was just emerging from a hypoglycaemic episode but everyone was different. Some people would be groggy and confused for up to thirty minutes in a post-ictal phase, but for others it was as if a fully conscious switch had been flicked off and then back on. Sarah Harrison clearly fell into the latter group of patients.

'Where's Ivy?' she demanded.

'Right here beside the couch, in her car seat. Next to your feet. She's safe. And asleep.'

'How long have I been out?' Sarah was trying to sit up.

'Stay still for a minute,' James ordered. 'Your dextrose infusion hasn't quite finished. I'll get you a cushion so you can sit up enough to see Ivy.'

He propped her up with the cushions he'd removed earlier and he could see the wash of relief that went over her face as she spotted the peacefully sleeping infant.

'You've been out for about ten minutes,' he told her. 'I had to get my kit to test your blood glucose level and then get an IV line in. You're going to need something to eat or it could drop again fast, and that's not exactly safe when you're looking after a baby, is it?'

Not *a* baby.

His baby.

'This has never happened before. I use a continuous blood glucose monitor. My phone would have sent an alert if it lost contact with the sensor.' Sarah reached for the pocket of the anorak draped over the arm of the couch but let her breath out in a sound of frustration. 'I must have left my phone in the car.' She pushed up the sleeve of her jumper on her other arm. A small round disc fell onto the couch.

'It's come out.' Sarah sounded shocked. 'Maybe I knocked it when I was putting my jacket on in a hurry in the car.'

'Or maybe your skin has been so damp the cover lost its stickiness.' James picked up the small electronic device with a tiny filament that would have been inserted just under the skin so it could sense and transmit the levels of glucose in the wearer's blood. 'Did you realise you're running a fever? Your temperature's thirty-eight point six.'

Sarah shook her head. 'That might explain why my BGL had gone high enough to need an increase in my insulin dose. I knew I wasn't feeling great today but I thought I was just tired. It was a long drive and I haven't had much sleep and it's been…a pretty rough time…'

Of course it had. She'd lost a friend who was close enough for her to have taken legal responsibility for her baby. James had no right to criticise any of her choices or actions.

'I've had all my vaccinations,' she told him. 'Covid, flu and whooping cough. Even the meningococcal vaccine because diabetes can affect the immune system. I looked up everything and got them all before Ivy was even born because I knew I'd be the one looking after her.'

Already, that level of research, planning and following through on the results wasn't at all surprising about this woman he'd only just met, but James knew the kind of focus needed to keep tight control in type one diabetes. Under normal circumstances, Sarah was probably the perfect patient.

An upward glance showed James that the dextrose infusion was complete. It had done its job well. He disconnected the tubing but didn't want to pull the cannula out until he was sure that the levels were stable.

'I'll do another finger prick,' he said. 'And I'll go and get your phone for you. Have you got another sensor you can put on?'

'Yes. There should be a zip-up cooler pouch on the front passenger seat. That's where I keep my insulin and other supplies.' Sarah held out her hand so that James could extract a drop of blood from her finger.

'You don't use an insulin pump?'

'No. I've tried them on more than one occasion but I prefer the control I get by managing it myself.'

That statement summed up his own impression of this woman so well it almost made him smile. If you wanted something done well, then Sarah Harrison was just the type of person you'd want in charge of it.

'You don't wear a medic alert bracelet either,' he commented. 'I'm sure you know how helpful they can be in an emergency.'

'They can also be very *un*helpful,' Sarah said quietly. 'I don't like people making assumptions that there's something wrong with me or judgements about how I choose to live my life and what I'm capable of achieving. In a medical emergency, checking someone's blood sugar level should be an automatic vital sign to take. It was for you, wasn't it?'

James couldn't argue with that. He could also respect Sarah's right to privacy.

'Back up to four millimoles per litre,' he said as the monitor beeped. 'But I'd be happier if it was higher and we need to make sure it stays there. The dextrose in that infusion will wear off fast. When I've got your phone I'll make you a sandwich so you've got some complex carbohydrates on board. And is there someone I can call for you? A friend or family member that could help?'

'No.' Sarah met his gaze. 'It's just me and Ivy.'

It sounded so final. So…lonely?

'Do you like cheese?'

'Sounds great.' It looked like it was a bit of a struggle to stay awake. 'Thank you.'

It was the first time James had actually noticed her eyes. They were a shade of hazel brown that was the same colour as her hair. They looked darker than they probably were, due to how pale her face still was. And the look in them was… Well, it gave James more than a bit of a squeeze around his heart, to be honest.

Anyone would feel sorry for her. She wasn't remotely hungry, was she? She'd gone through hell in the last goodness knows how long and she was probably feeling ghastly with whatever bug she'd picked up on top of being exhausted, but she was going to do whatever it took to get through this unexpected life obstacle.

Including eating a sandwich that was going to be an ordeal to get through and might not even stay where it was supposed to.

He had to admire that...

There was no point in rousing a soundly sleeping Ivy to give her the rest of her milk and, besides, Sarah was still feeling fragile enough to want to lie back on this comfortable couch and close her eyes for a few minutes while that sandwich was being made. James had given her a good dose of paracetamol to help bring her temperature down so she might start feeling a bit better very soon.

She was horrified that she'd lost consciousness. What would have happened if she hadn't been lucky enough to have been with a doctor who had a well-equipped first aid kit on hand? What if he hadn't come home when he had and she'd gone into a coma parked outside an isolated house miles from anywhere? He hadn't needed to point out how unsafe people might consider her to be as a primary caregiver to a helpless baby. Sarah could feel a growing fear that she might be in trouble here.

That her whole future might be in the hands of this man.

A man who Karly had spent one—apparently spectacular—night with.

A man who, quite possibly, had just saved her life.

With an effort, she managed to swallow a tiny bite of the sandwich she was holding. And then she smiled at James, who was now sitting on the couch on the other side of the fireplace.

'It's a great sandwich,' she said.

There was a gleam in his eyes that told her he knew perfectly well that she was only trying to be polite. 'You're doing well,' he said. 'You'll be halfway through it if you take another bite. Just as well I cut the crusts off, isn't it?'

Sarah could feel her smile widen enough to feel genuine. 'Thank you,' she said quietly. 'And... I'm sorry I ruined date night for you and your girlfriend. I couldn't give you any warning I was coming because I only had an address. I didn't want to find you at work because I thought you'd prefer to keep it private when you found out that...that...'

'That I have a child I knew nothing about?' The tone of James's voice was dry. 'Aye... I should thank *you* for that. Especially when you might have given the hospital grapevine some juicy gossip if someone had overheard you announcing that I'd offered to pay for a termination.'

Sarah ducked her head under the pretext of taking another nibble of her sandwich. It wasn't just a fever that was making her cheeks feel too warm.

'Sorry,' she muttered, giving up on taking that bite of bread that tasted like cardboard and cheese that seemed vaguely soapy. 'But I did believe her at the time, which was why I never tried to persuade Karly to let you know what was going on when she got sick. I was convinced that you were some irresponsible playboy or possibly a sex addict. Either way, it seemed like you were someone who didn't give a damn about any repercussions of failed contraception or broken-hearted women.'

James gave a huff of sound. 'That's a bit harsh,' he murmured. 'And I can assure you that protection was used on my part even after Karly assured me she was on the Pill.'

Oh… Sarah so didn't want to go anywhere near the mental images that were trying to surface here, so she focused on what seemed like another lie Karly had told.

'She wasn't on the Pill,' she said aloud.

'Are you sure about that?'

'We didn't keep secrets from each other.' But Sarah let her breath out in a sigh. 'At least, I didn't think we did. But she did have a thing about avoiding doctors or drugs if she could find an alternative and she'd been adamant that the risk of taking the Pill was too high for her because she had a history of getting migraine headaches.'

'Why would she have said that she was taking it, then?'

'I have no idea. Maybe there's a lot of stuff I didn't know about her.' And she never would now. Sarah had to fight a renewed threat of tears.

James broke the silence that fell. 'How long had you known each other?'

'Since our first day at primary school. We were both five years old. Karly was in a foster home. I was being brought up by my grandmother. Neither of us had any siblings so we decided that day that we would be sisters. For ever.'

James was silent again for a long moment. 'I'm really sorry for your loss,' he said quietly, then. 'I came close to losing one of my brothers not so long ago and that was devastating enough. That's why I've moved up to Aberdeen. Why I'm looking after my sister's house for a while. To be closer to my family—the people that really matter…' He blew out a breath. 'And, just for the record, Janine isn't my girlfriend. She was someone I worked with in Edinburgh and she turned up at work today and wanted to catch up over dinner.'

'She didn't look too happy about being sent home.'

'Possibly. But I can assure you she has absolutely no reason to be broken-hearted.'

The implication was that neither had Karly, and his words felt like a reprimand for the opinion of him that Sarah had unleashed. And fair play. For heaven's sake… She'd had no right to judge him like that. So what if her best friend and some gorgeous guy happened to have been attracted enough to each other to have had a one-night stand when they were a long way away from their normal lives and never likely to see each other again? She would have done the same thing herself, wouldn't she?

Um…no…

But she might have wished she *could* have been more like Karly and made the most of an opportunity like that. She might have discovered that sex didn't have to be so predictable and kind of boring…

Sarah managed another small bite of the sandwich. Maybe the paracetamol was kicking in or her body was happier with its levels of blood sugar because she wasn't feeling quite so awful. Just tired. So tired that all she wanted to do was curl up in front of this fire and sleep for a week.

With Ivy's father watching her and making a judge-ment call about whether she was competent to be an adop-tive parent?

Sarah sat up straighter. 'I should go,' she said. 'I'm feeling much better, thanks to you, and my BGL is high enough for me to be safe to drive. I'm booked in at a B&B

in town and I need to be back there before midnight or we'll be locked out.'

James just looked at her. And smiled.

A smile that gave him those crinkles around his eyes again. One that was kind enough to give Sarah such a lump in her throat it felt like a bit of that horrible sandwich. She could feel a tear that had appeared so fast she had no chance to catch it before it rolled down the side of her nose. This wasn't like her at all. How sick and weak was she, to feel this helpless?

Lost, even?

So grateful that some stranger was kind enough to be prepared to look after her?

'The only place you're going, sweetheart,' James said firmly, 'is straight to bed.'

CHAPTER THREE

'HEY, EDDIE...SORRY—did I wake you up?'

'You woke us both up. It's...' The pause suggested that his brother was checking his watch. Or maybe that muffled sound was him apologising to his partner, Jodie, before he rolled out of bed and let her go back to sleep. There might have also been an unmistakable kissing sound. 'It's six-thirty a.m.,' Eddie said clearly, a few seconds later. 'On a day off. What's going on?'

'I just wanted to let you know I'm not going to make that hike we were planning on doing up in the Cairngorms today.'

'Hang on a tick.' James could hear that Eddie was moving. He heard the sound of running water and then a clunk of crockery. 'I need coffee,' Eddie muttered. He'd activated the camera on his phone now but it was propped up on the kitchen bench so all James could see were Eddie's hands spooning coffee into a mug.

James could do with another cup of coffee himself but he couldn't move right now. He was sitting on the couch with a sleeping baby in his arms. An empty milk bottle sat on the arm of the couch and his free hand was now occupied with holding his phone as he spoke to his brother.

'Is the weather forecast bad?' Eddie asked. 'Is that

why you're wimping out of the hike? Jodie and I will still go, you know. Even if it's snowing. We like a bit of a challenge.'

'I have no idea what the weather forecast is,' James said. 'I can't go because I've got someone here.'

'Ah...' The sound was drawn out. Amused. 'Overnight visitor, huh? Lucky you. Who is she?'

'Her name's Ivy.'

'And I'm guessing she's still asleep? Worn out?' Eddie face came into view and he was grinning broadly. 'Good to know that you haven't lost your mojo. And that you're settling into your new job so well.'

James felt suddenly weary. He could hear an echo of Janine's accusation last night.

'We all know what you're like...'

Even a complete stranger who lived in a city he'd never been anywhere near had heard about him.

'It seemed like you were someone who didn't give a damn about any repercussions of failed contraception or broken-hearted women...'

He wasn't that bad, was he? Okay, it might take a while to do a head count of women whose company he'd enjoyed over the years but he'd only been playing a game that hadn't hurt anyone, as far as he knew. He worked hard. He played hard. He was making the most of his life.

A life that had just had a frighteningly huge bomb hurled into it.

James held the phone further away and tilted it, watching Eddie's face as he saw what he was holding.

'*That's* Ivy...?'

'Aye...'

'Where's Ivy's mother?'

'Not here.'

'Why not?'

'She's dead.'

Eddie nearly choked on the sip of coffee he'd just taken. James listened to his brother swearing, watched the screen image bouncing as a dishcloth was found to wipe the splatters off his phone and then saw the shocked expression as Eddie sank into a chair at his kitchen table.

'Are you telling me you've got a dead person in your house?'

'Good grief, no…it was Ivy's mother's friend who turned up late last night. Her legal guardian, apparently. She'd decided to let me know that I'm Ivy's father, even though Ivy's mum chose not to tell me she was pregnant for some reason.'

Several seconds of shocked silence from Eddie gave James plenty of time for a small voice at the back of his mind to put the knife in.

He knew the reason perfectly well, didn't he? He might have believed that his 'mojo' included being completely honest with women about his status as a committed bachelor but he was more than happy to give them a night they would never forget, Karly—like Janine and God only knew how many others—thought they knew what he was *really* like. She'd convinced her friend that he was an irresponsible playboy and/or a sex addict.

The thought that he might have left women feeling used instead of appreciated was…well, it was shocking, that was what it was.

Almost as shocking as being presented with a small human he might well have contributed to creating.

He'd had a whole night with Ivy now and the shock

still hadn't worn off. He wasn't feeling any kind of connection to this baby. It felt like someone else's baby.

Someone else's problem that had just been handed to him.

He'd known for hours that he needed help and he'd waited as long as he could to ring the first available member of his support network, but he couldn't blame his brother Eddie for not being happy about being contacted at this hour of the morning.

He did his best to summon a smile. 'Anyway… I thought I'd share the joy and let you know that you might be an uncle. Not that I've done a DNA test or anything, but I have to admit I had a rather memorable night with Ivy's mother in Paris last year and the timeline fits…'

'Show me again?'

Eddie stared at the sleeping baby for a long, long moment. 'Don't think you need a DNA test,' he said quietly. 'Have you seen that hair?'

'Hard to miss,' James agreed.

'Don't you recognise it?'

'What do you mean?'

'You know that bookshelf under the picture of zebras that Ella's got on the wall? The one that's got photos in gaps between the books?'

'I'm looking at it right now.'

'Can you see the one she's got of us when we were babies?'

'It's too small to see from here.'

'Go and have a look.'

James tucked the phone against his ear with his shoulder and got up, carefully adjusting the hold he had on the sleeping baby. He walked towards the bookshelf. He knew the picture Eddie was talking about, he just hadn't looked at it for a long time. The photo had been taken in Dundee, where the three Grisham boys and their big sister Ella had grown up. The triplets were about four or five months old at that point, lying in a row on the floor, grinning up at the camera. And each of the triplets had spikes of dark hair going in every direction.

If Ivy had been transported back in time to lie on the floor with the three boys, she would have been a perfect match.

The thought was enough to give James a very strange sensation deep inside his chest. A sensation he couldn't identify exactly, but it felt familiar—like an echo of how he felt when he spoke to or saw one of his brothers when they'd been out of touch for a while?

A feeling of *connection*?

No… James didn't want to feel like this. He needed to keep his doctor's hat on and view this situation from a distance that wasn't going to be influenced by emotion. Lives could be at stake, otherwise.

His life—as he knew it?

Eddie's voice broke the silence and his tone was sombre. 'Did she get left on your doorstep? With a note on the basket?'

'Nothing that dramatic.' James was watching the way Ivy was scrunching up her face. Was she about to wake up and start crying again? He'd been up with her for hours now, trying to let Sarah get as much sleep as possible. 'Well…actually, it was kind of that dramatic. The woman who brought her here collapsed with a hypoglycaemic episode. I had to give her a dextrose infusion.'

'She's diabetic?'

'Type one.'

'And she's driving around with a baby?'

'It's not her fault.' James wasn't sure why he felt such a strong desire to defend Sarah, but there it was. 'She normally has very good control. She's got a viral infection. Probably flu. That's why I can't come for that hike today. I need to make sure she's okay and look after Ivy.'

'And what then…?'

James could feel how damp Ivy's bottom was against his arm. He could also feel her whole body starting to move. He let his breath out in a sigh. 'I don't know. I hadn't been thinking any further than getting through the night, to be fair. And talking to you, seeing as you're the only family member currently on this side of the planet.'

'Do you need us to come over?'

Us… Eddie was part of a couple now. He and Jodie were as much in love as it was possible to be and James was very happy for his brother. Thrilled even, but he wasn't sure that their company would make this any easier.

'I think I need to talk to Sarah properly, first. She hasn't explained exactly why she's here, other than to tell me that she's the baby's guardian and I'm the father. It could be that there are relatives—grandparents, maybe—that are planning to get involved and raise the kid. Or she might be planning to put her up for adoption or something and needs my consent?'

'How would you feel about that?'

'I don't know.'

Okay…that wasn't entirely honest. He'd probably feel relieved, wouldn't he? Not about adoption to unknown strangers, but a stable family unit of grandparents and possibly extended family was a very different proposition. Even having someone here who wasn't related but had been prepared to take on legal responsibility for Ivy was a relief.

'Hmm.' Eddie didn't sound convinced either. 'We're here if you need us.'

'I know. Thanks...'

'Are you going to tell Ella next?'

'No. I don't even know where she and Logan are right now.' The reason James was here, housesitting for his sister, was because she and her husband were taking a long overdue honeymoon, exploring New Zealand in a camper van.

'They're in the South Island, I believe. Around Queenstown. Last I heard, they were going to do some Lord of the Rings tour. They're having a ball.'

'Good for them. Maybe don't tell her about this yet. Or Mick.'

'He's not having a ball.' Eddie was shaking his head.

'It's not another UTI, is it? Or something worse?'

James's heart was sinking. The third triplet, Mick, had been injured badly enough in a hang-gliding accident a few months ago to be facing the rest of his life in a wheelchair. The reason that New Zealand had been chosen as a honeymoon destination by Ella and Logan had been partly because it had enabled them to travel with Mick and take him to a world-renowned rehabilitation centre there.

'No, nothing like that,' Eddie reassured him. 'But you know that cute blonde who got assigned as his physiotherapist?'

'I think her name's Riley.'

'Yeah...well, he had a row with her yesterday. She told

him if he wasn't going to stop feeling so sorry for himself she wasn't going to be able to keep working with him.'

'Really? Doesn't sound very professional. She must be used to people who find it hard to come to terms with a spinal injury after leading such an active life.'

Ivy let out a whimper that made it sound like she also disapproved of this Riley's approach.

'Sounds like she gave him chapter and verse about some of the tetraplegic patients she's worked with and how thankful they would be to have the potential Mick's got to have an amazing quality of life. How the only thing that's holding him back right now is his attitude.'

'How do you know all this?'

'Spoke to him last night. He wanted to know if I agreed with her.'

'You didn't say yes, did you?'

'I kind of did. I said we'd all been worried about his state of mind since the accident. That was why we'd come up with the plan to send him to a rehab centre that looked as if it might help.'

'What did he say?'

'He's obviously thinking hard about it all. He said he was sorry for everything he's put us through. I told him to apologise to Riley. We'll have to wait and see what happens next, I guess.'

'I've got to go,' James warned. 'Things are going to get noisy around here any second now. They don't smell so great either. I think I've got a pair of pants that need changing.'

'I'll bet you have.' Eddie was grinning again. 'And you might want to change Ivy's too. Talk to you later, bro. Good luck!'

* * *

Feathers…

Was that the secret?

Maybe it was some other natural fibre, like wool, that was making this bed so comfortable it felt like a nest that Sarah never wanted to crawl out of. The duvet was fluffy and light and there seemed to be a soft topper on the mattress. The fat, squashy pillows had moulded themselves so well around her head that she couldn't quite tell where her face ended and the pillow began.

But something had not only woken her up but was nagging her to move.

Oh, yeah…that quiet but insistent ringtone on her mobile phone was an alarm that her blood sugar levels needed attention.

The air felt cold on her bare arm as she reached for the device on the bedside table and her shoulder hurt. So did her elbow. Even the joints in her hand were aching and it was quite hard to open her eyes far enough to peer at the screen of her phone.

She had expected to see that her blood glucose levels had gone up higher than an acceptable level, given that she felt as if she'd been asleep for days but, weirdly, it was a low level that had triggered this alarm. The level wasn't low enough for her to be in danger of losing consciousness, however. Or to explain the kind of brain fog that was bordering on major confusion. Had she not eaten enough yesterday? Or given herself an incorrect dose of insulin?

The small tube of fast-acting, chewy glucose tablets she could see directly in her line of vision was familiar enough but Sarah couldn't remember putting them on this table. Or pouring the glass of fruit juice that was beside them, along with a small blister pack of paracetamol capsules.

She'd never actually *seen* this particular table before, in fact.

Sarah realised how much her head was aching as she tried to make sense of odd impressions that were the last things she could remember.

Being helped up a set of stairs by a man with strong hands and a reassuring voice. A man who looked like every woman's tall, dark and handsome fantasy. Sarah could almost hear an echo of his voice as she pushed herself up onto one elbow to reach for the glass of juice. She needed sugar and this liquid form would work fast and disperse the remnants of what could be a confusing dream. A couple of those anti-inflammatories seemed like a good idea too, with so much of her body aching.

It was as she swallowed the capsules that Sarah realised it wasn't simply an echo she was hearing of that voice. Snatches of words were floating upstairs.

'...we'd all been worried...since the accident...'

What accident?

Her brain was clearing. Sarah could remember the long car drive. She could also hear something other than the soft tones of this man's voice. A sound that cut straight into her heart.

Ivy...

And she was crying.

Sarah pushed back the fluffy duvet. Her legs were as bare as her arms but her jeans were draped over the end of the bed, along with the woollen jumper she'd been wearing over her tee shirt yesterday. She wasn't about to waste any brain power trying to remember getting undressed, even though the sight of her abandoned bra was a little concerning. She didn't bother putting it back on and just pulled her jumper over the tee shirt she'd been sleeping in. She pulled on her jeans but left her boots and socks on the floor, only grabbing her phone as she made her way out of the room.

This was urgent.

The stone steps felt cold beneath her bare feet but there was a fire blazing in the living area below and, suddenly, Sarah could remember everything. This man—James Grisham. Having a hypo that had been serious enough to be dangerous, not only to herself but to the precious baby she had promised to protect and cherish.

Worst of all, Sarah realised that it had been James who had helped her up to that bed last night.

Had he taken her bra off…?

Oh…dear Lord. Sarah had to pause at the foot of the stairs, still clutching the banister rail. Her cheeks felt as if they were on fire.

'Hey…' James looked up from where he was kneeling on the floor, grappling with changing Ivy's nappy. 'I'm not sure you should be out of bed. You look like you're still running a bit of a fever.'

'I'm fine.' The warmth of the fire was welcome as Sarah went closer. 'You've got that nappy on back to front,' she told him. 'It's a lot easier to make the sticky tabs work if they're the other way round.'

'Oh… Maybe that's what Ivy was trying to tell me.'

The look that might have been relief on Ivy's face was enough to bring a lump to Sarah's throat. The bond she had formed with this tiny person in just a matter of weeks was astonishingly powerful. Ivy had even stopped crying, having spotted the face she was most familiar with.

'Here…let me.' Sarah crouched beside James, lifted Ivy's bottom by holding both her feet in one hand and turned the disposable nappy. Then she fastened it and poked the baby's feet into the legs of her onesie. Ivy was protesting again by the time she was snapping the stud buttons shut and the sound made Sarah feel appallingly guilty about having left her in someone else's care.

'Has she had some formula?' Her tone came out more sharply than she had expected. 'Has she had any sleep?' She reached to pick Ivy up. 'Do you even know anything about looking after babies?'

'She's still alive,' James pointed out calmly. 'So I think I know enough. Yes, she's had some sleep. More than me. And yes, she's also had some formula. I found the can in your bag. Luckily, I know how to read so it wasn't too difficult to follow the instructions on the label.'

Sarah winced, cuddling Ivy a little closer. 'Sorry…' She looked up, expecting to find an angry man looking back but, if anything, James was looking as if he was on the verge of smiling at her. 'Thank you for looking after her. And me…'

'How are you feeling?'

'A bit rubbish. Kind of achy.'

'How's your BGL?'

'My alarm went off to let me know it was low. Did I give myself any insulin last night?'

'No. I've been on the couch all night. I would have noticed if you'd gone past me in the direction of the fridge, which is where I've put your insulin. Your levels were good after the dextrose infusion and that sandwich you finally finished. You looked like you fell asleep as soon as your head hit the pillow but I knew you'd applied a new continuous monitor so I didn't think I needed to disturb you to poke your finger overnight.'

'But you left the supplies there, like the juice and glucose tabs?'

James nodded. 'You'll need some food too, if you're low. We also need to talk, but we're not going to do that until I'm satisfied that you're feeling well enough.'

'I've got some muesli bars in my bag.'

'I was thinking more along the lines of some hot, buttered toast.'

Oh…comfort food… Perhaps she wasn't feeling quite so bad, after all.

'I'd like that,' Sarah admitted. 'But I can make it if you tell me where the kitchen is.'

James only lifted a single eyebrow but she could imagine what he was looking at. A flushed and probably totally dishevelled woman with bed hair and only half her clothes on, sitting on the floor like a deflated balloon with a still grizzly baby in her arms. Talk about seeing someone at their worst—or had that been when she'd keeled over in front of him last night? Maybe he could even read her mind right now and see that she was wondering how she was going to get to her feet without her knees giving way or dropping Ivy as she tried to keep her balance, let alone making it as far as a kitchen?

'Let's see if you can make it to the couch first,' was all he said. He put a hand under her elbow to help her up, and when she gratefully sank onto the corner of the couch closest to the fire he draped a soft mohair blanket over her legs. 'Don't move,' he ordered. 'I'll be back with some toast and a cup of tea. Did you take any of that paracetamol I left upstairs?'

'Yes.'

'Good. It should bring your temperature down and make you feel better soon. What would you like on your toast? Jam?' A corner of his mouth twitched. 'Cheese?'

'Um...would you have any peanut butter?'

'I'm sure there'll be some somewhere. Stand by...'

Sarah watched him disappear through the gap on the other side of the fireplace and found herself struggling to swallow past the lump that had reappeared in her throat.

Looking the way he did was more than enough to explain why Karly had been attracted enough to James to have that fateful one-night stand.

Did he have to be so damned *nice* as well?

Sarah had thought the man she'd been coming to confront would be only too happy to sign away an inconvenient problem that his playboy lifestyle had produced. Now, she was beginning to wonder if she should have followed her instincts and stayed as far away from him as possible. She could have had, ooh...maybe fifteen years before Ivy got curious enough about her biological father to want to do anything about it.

But, for Sarah, it would have been difficult to ignore that black cloud in the distance. Giving both herself and Ivy the security of certainty had been the driving force to come here when the risk that the outcome wouldn't be what she wanted had seemed extremely small. Like that blonde woman hanging off his arm last night, Sarah had been sure she knew exactly what James Grisham was like and she'd been so confident that even the idea of fatherhood would have him running for the hills.

But then she'd met him.

She was almost certain that Karly hadn't told her the whole truth.

And that black cloud of uncertainty felt even more threatening now. Hovering right over her head, in fact. Ivy's father might be a lot nicer than she'd imagined but that was actually ringing alarm bells. Of course he was charming—that was the modus operandi for playboys, wasn't it? And men who were driven by their sex lives were at the completely opposite end of the spectrum to the kind of men Sarah admired. They were totally unsuitable, not only as life partners but very likely as an ideal father figure.

But she had to face facts. And obey rules, for that matter. Like promises, they were something else that Sarah had never broken in her life. James—in conjunction with the UK's legal system—had the power to interfere with the future Sarah had promised Karly she would provide for Ivy.

Destroy it, even?

No. She wasn't going to let that happen.

She might not be firing on all cylinders, physically or emotionally, but she knew her rights as Ivy's legal guardian and she was more than ready to fight for them, if that was what it was going to take. Because this was for Karly. And Ivy. And for herself. Sarah might be at the bottom of that list but that didn't make it any less imperative.

She had a promise to keep.

CHAPTER FOUR

JAMES WAS WATCHING her like a hawk.

The plate of peanut butter toast and the mug of tea was waiting on the coffee table in front of the couch while Sarah took a finger prick blood glucose reading to confirm the information she was receiving from her device, calculated the carbs in the breakfast she was planning to eat and dialled up the amount of the rapid-acting insulin she needed to take.

She didn't mind that he was watching her. It was making her feel a little self-conscious, but it wasn't as if it was male attention on her body due to any sexual interest. James was a doctor. He'd already had to pull her back from a hypoglycaemic episode so he had a professional interest in what was going on, that was all. He confirmed that when he spoke.

'Just out of interest, why do you go to all the trouble of the calculations you need to make and having to do multiple injections during the day instead of using an automatic insulin pump?'

'It's not like I have anything against technology,' Sarah told him. 'I love my continuous glucose monitor. Total game-changer. I've got an app to work out the insulin to carb ratio if it's food I'm not familiar with, but something like toast is easy.'

'Does managing it yourself give better control?'

'For me, yes. And I don't have the stress of pump failures, skin reactions or working around things like having a shower. I've given pumps a good go over the years too, but I always go back to this.'

It had become even more important to know that she had an almost foolproof system when she'd had the stress of learning how to care for a newborn baby. Sarah pulled up her jumper and tee shirt just enough to expose a small patch of her abdomen, pressed the tiny needle against the skin she pinched together and then pushed the button to deliver the dose.

'I get the impression you like having complete control in your life.' James was nodding. 'You seem to plan ahead and be very organised. It was very easy to find anything I needed for Ivy—and you—in that bag. The luggage pods are even labelled.'

Was he criticising her? Not everybody had the luxury of letting life flow around them and choosing any pleasurable distractions that they had the time and inclination to pursue. It was no wonder her tone was a little defensive as she responded.

'I got diagnosed with type one diabetes when I was only twelve.' She put the cap back onto her insulin pen with a decisive click. 'My grandma was really nervous about anything to do with needles so I had to learn how to manage it myself from day one. I use a long-acting insulin for background control and a rapid-acting one to cope with meals or exercise.' She lifted her chin. 'I've had twenty-two years of practice, so it's something I'm really good at, but I'll be even more careful now after last night's wake-up call.'

They both glanced towards Ivy. Sarah had tucked her into her car seat cocoon when she'd fallen asleep while James was making breakfast and she could expect her to sleep for at least ninety minutes at this time of day.

Time enough to enjoy the warmth of her own cocoon on this couch. And the toast. Sarah was surprised how good it tasted.

'I'm feeling a lot better,' she announced, between bites. 'It was probably just some twenty-four-hour bug.'

'Good to hear,' James said, but his tone held a note of caution. 'But you should rest up today. You could go back to bed. Or stay on the couch. I can help with Ivy— I've got a day off today.'

There was something else in his tone that felt like a warning. Did he want to keep watching her to make sure she was capable of looking after a defenceless infant? Yeah…his next words made her realise her instinct was correct.

'When was the last time you had a hypo that caused you to lose consciousness? Does it always come on without any warning like that? I'm used to people being aggro or confused or getting dizzy or nauseated and so on.'

'It hasn't happened for years. And it won't happen again. I've never left my phone behind before. It was just a combination of the long drive and being sick and…and I was kind of stressed because Ivy was crying and then you arrived back suddenly. It wasn't part of the plan that you wouldn't be at home when I got here.'

James lifted an eyebrow. 'Do your plans generally work out perfectly?'

Sarah just looked at him. 'If I could control life that well, I wouldn't be here, would I? Ivy would still have her mother. And I would still have my best friend who was the closest thing I'll ever have to a sister. The only family I had left, actually.'

James got up to put a log on the fire. 'Sorry... I don't know why I said that. Maybe because I had the feeling that you can get everything else in your life under rather impressive control.'

Sarah had lost her appetite for the toast now but she needed to keep eating to make sure her blood sugar didn't drop too far. She chased the bite down with a mouthful of tea. She wasn't offended by the idea that she gave people that impression.

'Karly used to call me a control freak,' she conceded. 'I was the organised one. I stuck to the rules. That might have been why she didn't even tell me she was pregnant until she was into her second trimester. And why she told me what she did about your reaction. She knew it would be enough to...' Her words trailed into silence.

'Enough to what?' James prompted.

'To put you right out of the picture as far as I was concerned,' Sarah admitted. 'Karly knew that I don't have time for men who aren't completely reliable. Dependable *and* careful. And kind...'

'How's that working out for you?' James sounded curious rather than nosy. 'I seem to remember you saying that it's just you and Ivy?'

Fair call. Sarah forced a smile. 'I'm single,' she agreed, tightly. 'But, on the plus side, that means there's nothing to stop me caring for Ivy. There are no other relatives on Karly's side.' She could feel James staring at her and avoided meeting his gaze. 'I've also taken six months off work. Karly and I both thought it was the best idea.'

'And Karly has legally appointed you to be Ivy's guardian, yes?'

'Yes. It's called a testamentary guardianship. It confers parental responsibility and grants the ability to have a say in any important decisions in Ivy's long-term care and upbringing.'

It didn't mean that she had an automatic entitlement to have Ivy living with her if there was a dispute, but there was no need to tell James that yet, was there?

'What Karly really wanted was for me to formally adopt Ivy.' Sarah took a deep breath. 'So that I can be her *real* mum.'

'And that's what you want to do?'

'Yes…' Sarah not only caught James's gaze this time, she held it. 'Oh…*yes*…'

He didn't break the eye contact. 'But if I'm her biological father and you're not even genetically related to Ivy, how does that work?'

'All you have to do is sign the consent papers Karly's solicitor gave me.'

He still hadn't looked away. And Sarah couldn't. She might have rehearsed what she intended to say to Ivy's father when she found him but she hadn't bargained on someone looking at her like this.

As if what she was doing was somehow very, very wrong?

Wow…

He'd been presented with an unexpected baby and now it was going to be whisked out of his life?

No…not 'it'. Ivy was a 'she'.

A real person.

He watched Sarah, who was eating the rest of her piece of toast with an expression that suggested it was purely medicinal. James allowed himself several deep breaths before he said anything else and even then he had to be careful to keep his tone neutral.

'So…' he said, finally. 'I sign your papers and what then? I know I have a daughter but I never see her again? She grows up thinking that her father wasn't even interested in her?'

Sarah was biting her lip, looking uncomfortable.

'Why did Karly even make a witnessed statement about me being Ivy's father?'

'She said it was kind of an insurance policy. In case Ivy needed something like a bone marrow transplant or a kidney donation.'

A shiver ran down his spine. 'Have they picked up a health issue with Ivy?'

'No…she's fine. I think she was just imagining things that might go wrong in the future.' Sarah shook her head, as if dismissing his concern. 'And she'll know who you are. We can stay in contact with photos and video calls and things. You can visit any time you want to. I can bring her up to Scotland to visit you.' She was offering him a tentative smile. 'I know the way, now.'

Even a small smile changed Sarah's face from being one that he wouldn't have noticed particularly if she'd walked past him in the street, but James stamped on the thought that she was more attractive than he'd realised.

'Where is it that you live?' he asked.

'Leeds.'

'And do you work?'

'Yes. I'm a nurse. So was Karly. We did our training together and then looked for jobs at the same hospital so we could share a flat. We ended up in the same department in the end because we both loved Emergency so much. We both graduated as Emergency nurse practitioners about a year ago.'

James blinked. A nurse practitioner qualification was the highest rank for nurses. It gave them the scope of practice to diagnose and treat minor injuries and discharge patients without them having to wait to be seen by a doctor.

'To be honest, though,' Sarah continued, 'I prefer to be part of a team and the Resus room is my absolute favourite place to work. After we did a MIMMS course I even wondered if I should switch to being a paramedic.'

'You've done MIMMS—Major Incident Medical Management and Support?' James was impressed. 'So did I, when I was working with a HEMS unit for a couple of years.'

'I'm part of a group. We meet once a month to do a tabletop exercise in planning and management as a refresher and take turns inventing the simulated emergency situations. It's my favourite night out.' Sarah's smile was wry. 'Or it used to be, anyway.' It looked as though she was consigning that part of her life to the past. 'I was supposed to have gone to that conference in Paris where you met Karly,' she added. 'The only reason I didn't was because my grandmother was dying. She'd been sick for a long time.'

James had been drawn to that conference because of its focus on disaster management. Emergency medicine was his own passion and the drama of working in a re-suscitation area made it his favourite place to be as well. Right now, he was feeling a connection that he wasn't sure he wanted to have with Sarah Harrison.

'But you've taken time off work.'

She nodded. 'With my savings I can cover at least six months.'

'And after that?'

'I've got a great job I can go back to. There's also a good creche near the hospital that I can get Ivy into.'

'You've got it all planned, then.'

'Karly and I spent the last weeks of her life talking about it so…yeah…'

It felt as if Sarah was avoiding meeting his gaze now. Shutting him out?

'What would happen if I didn't sign those papers?'

Her gaze flicked up. Her face tightened. 'I'd still be Ivy's guardian. I'll still look after her. And protect her.'

'What if I want to look after her?' James wasn't sure if he was playing devil's advocate or whether he needed to hear the words aloud to see if they might be true. 'What if I want her to live with me? The hospital where I work—The Queen Mother's—has an excellent creche on site, I believe.'

He couldn't miss the unmistakable flash of fear in Sarah's eyes and James felt an urge to tell her every-thing was going to be okay, because there was some-thing about those wide eyes in that pale face underneath hair that looked as if it hadn't seen a hairbrush in a very long time that was pulling at his heartstrings. Pushing buttons in a part of him that he'd finally gained much better control of as an adult. The part that made it impossible not to care more about the feelings of the people he loved than his own.

But he couldn't afford to let anything emotional run rampant right now. And he couldn't assure Sarah that this was all going to have a happy ending, could he? His world had been turned so abruptly upside down that James wasn't sure what was going to happen in the next five minutes, let alone the next five years.

'It would have to go to court,' Sarah said quietly. 'A judge would make a decision about what should happen in Ivy's best interests.'

She was staring at him.

He was staring back at her.

And then a small squeak from the direction of the car seat made them both turn their head sharply. Ivy was awake again.

Not crying, though. She was moving her arms. Holding them up as if she wanted Sarah to pick her up. Or did she want to check that her hands were still attached to the end of them? James found himself smiling at the notion as he looked at those tiny hands and all those perfect little fingers.

Ivy seemed to be looking straight up at Sarah but James had a very clear view of her face so he could see the moment the baby's lips began to curve.

He could hear Sarah's gasp. 'Oh…are you smiling, Ivy?' Sarah was blinking as if she was close to shedding a tear as she slid a graze of eye contact in James's direction to see if he could see what she was seeing. 'It's her first smile…'

Ivy was getting the hang of it quite fast in that case, James thought. Both sides of that miniature mouth were curving up and there were even little crinkles around her eyes. And when she opened her mouth she looked like she was the happiest baby on earth. She even made a sound—a delicious little gurgle—and it was then that James could feel something melting inside him.

His heart, perhaps?

'I can't do it,' he heard himself saying.

'Do what?' Sarah's head swerved towards him.

'I can't sign those papers. I can't let you just take Ivy away from me.'

If this was a chess game, James had just fired the warning shot of announcing 'check'.

It was not as final as a 'checkmate' where Sarah would have no choice but to concede total defeat but it was still an undeniable shock that she tried to hide by sliding off the couch and kneeling in front of the car seat to smile back at Ivy.

She couldn't deny, however, that she could feel a smidge of what could only be relief.

Because James was, unless proved otherwise, Ivy's father and it hadn't felt right suggesting that he sign away his responsibilities as a parent. It wasn't simply that he had the right to be a part of Ivy's life. It was because Sarah had seen the look on his face when Ivy had bestowed her first ever smile on the world and…

…and it meant something.

Something huge enough to have made her heart hurt. Because Sarah—and Karly, for that matter—had known what it was like to grow up without having a mum or dad. Sarah had been so much luckier than Karly, having a doting grandmother whom she adored, who had been only too willing to step into the gap left when her parents had both been killed in a dreadful car crash. But, even though she'd been too young to really remember them, she'd still felt the hole in her life from not having what she'd always thought of as a 'real' family.

That had been the connection that had bound her and Karly together so tightly. That was the reason why Sarah hadn't hesitated in her promise to look after Ivy for the rest of her life. Now it was the reason that, no matter how difficult this might become, she had to accept that James was also going to be part of her life. *Their* lives? That was possibly the best-case scenario Sarah could hope for, here. If it went to court, who was to say that a judge wouldn't decide that Ivy would be better off living with her father than simply with a friend of her mother's?

Sarah swallowed hard. Her voice was no more than a whisper as she looked up at James. 'I'm not going to walk away from the promise I made to Karly. I *can't*… I was there when Ivy was born. I was the first person to hold her. I didn't just promise Karly, I promised Ivy—even if I didn't say it out loud in those first minutes. I'm her guardian.' She managed to not let a wobble creep into her voice. 'Or are you planning to fight that?'

She couldn't stop the tears that were sneaking into her eyes. This renewed threat of tears was very different to the joyful reaction to Ivy's first smile she had just blinked back. Because this meant so much and because she was still feeling unwell enough that the prospect of having to fight for it was almost overwhelming.

Because part of her believed James could win that battle and another part wanted him to, so that Ivy would have a father who loved her enough to be prepared to fight for her.

Like she'd never had…?

Oh…*no*…

Tears were something that had the ability to leak past any protective barriers James might have developed over so many years of dealing with people in situations that were terrifying or painful or tragic.

Women's tears were always that much harder.

Especially from strong, courageous women who were determined to protect any children in their care.

Like Sarah.

Like his mother had been…

The whole family had been devastated when the struggle to survive a terminal diagnosis began for Colleen Grisham, but for James it was as if he could feel the weight of everyone else's fear and grief on top of his own. Ella had been away at university already, training to become a nurse, but she'd come home as often as she could because the triplets were only teenagers and their father was barely coping with the practicalities, let alone the emotions of such a difficult time. It was James who'd learned to appear strong enough to offer comfort to his mum, his dad and his brothers. Who'd learned to bottle up his own tears and be so aware of the first sign of them in anyone else.

Who'd known that the best way to protect himself in the future was not to add anyone else into that close circle he had around him—the people he loved as much as life itself.

Sarah might be safely miles away from that circle but

it still tore his heart a little to see the way her eyes were sparkling with the extra moisture that was gathering in them. Any moment now, a drop would roll down her face and he'd want to put his arms around her and hold her close.

He had to try and get control of this—for both their sakes.

'*No*,' he said emphatically. 'That's not what I mean at all.'

Ivy was squeaking again and Sarah reached to pick her up but James saw the way she hesitated for a heartbeat, closing her eyes as if she needed to gather strength.

'Here…' He moved to crouch on the floor beside her. 'Let me…'

He didn't wait for a response, sliding his hands underneath the baby to support her head and her body as he lifted her and then got to his feet. 'I meant it when I said you needed to rest today, Sarah. If you don't, you're not going to get better quickly and…and Ivy needs you.'

Her eyes were wide and the tears seemed to have magically evaporated. There was something that looked like hope in them as he said that and it made James feel good.

As good as it might have felt to comfort Sarah with a hug?

She was pushing herself upright and went back to sit on the couch. She looked like she would much prefer to lie down but she wasn't going to. Not yet.

'What *did* you mean, then?' she asked. 'You're hardly in a position to raise Ivy by yourself, are you?'

'I wouldn't be by myself.' Ivy seemed to be enjoying being held and was quietly gazing up at the man holding her, so James walked over to the bookshelf and picked up the photo Eddie had reminded him about. He handed it to Sarah by way of underlining his statement.

Her jaw dropped. 'Is one of those babies you?'

'Aye.'

'But there's three of you.'

He smiled at her. 'There generally is with triplets.'

Sarah didn't see the smile because her gaze was still fixed on the photo, but Ivy did and she smiled right back at him.

'Your *hair*...' Sarah whispered.

'I know, right?' James had no right to feel this proud of something he had no control over. 'The Grisham genes are clearly strong.

'We've got an older sister too. Ella. Well, she's a half-sister because our dad came along years after her own dad died. Mum and Dad really wanted a baby but it wasn't working so they used IVF and, as they always told people, it worked a bit too well. We're not identical triplets but we may as well be. We're a tight unit and, thanks to Mick's accident and Eddie falling in love with Jodie, it looks like we're all going to be living close to each other.' He took a deep breath. 'Bottom line is that I've got a pretty good support network.'

'A whole family,' Sarah agreed quietly, putting the photo down on the coffee table.

James nodded. 'One that you could also be a part of. You're involved too and nobody's going to shut you out. I can promise you that.'

'But I don't live here.'

'I didn't either until there was something important enough to make it the best option.' James wasn't going to say anything more. There were too many threads to untangle to get distracted by logistics.

'What if Ivy was *your* baby?' he asked quietly. 'You would want her to know her father, wouldn't you?'

'Yes…'

'You'd want to share the parenthood if it could work, wouldn't you? To share the costs? The decisions? The worry…?'

He just let those threads float in the air too.

'What I'm saying is that we're both involved and we need to make a plan around that. But we also need to get to know each other. You, me *and* Ivy.'

Ivy started whimpering as if she knew she was being talked about.

'Is it time for her to have another feed?' James asked. 'I can make up some formula.'

'When did you last feed her?'

'I'm not sure. Maybe five-thirty a.m.? Ish…?'

'And she had a nappy change about an hour later but she didn't sleep as long as usual…' Sarah was frowning as she looked at her watch. 'Her schedule is all over the place. She should have slept for a few hours. I hope she hasn't caught whatever bug I've got.'

'She's not running a temperature. I think she needs a sleep—like you do. Why don't I take her out for a while? There's some paperwork I'd like to pick up from my office at the hospital, seeing as I'm going to have a day at home, and I'm sure there are a few supplies we're going to need for Ivy.'

'But…we need to talk.'

'There's plenty of time for that. You can stay here.

Get over this bug. There's no need for you to rush back to Leeds, is there?'

'I've got a GP appointment booked for Ivy to have her eight-week vaccinations but that's not till next week so I guess there's nothing urgent...' But Sarah sounded hesitant.

'Have a sleep. A shower, if you feel like it. There's a stack of clean towels in the bathroom upstairs and plenty of shampoo and so on. Help yourself to anything you want to eat or drink too. I'll take the bag with the formula and nappies and everything and I'll be back in a few hours.'

Her jaw had dropped. 'On a motorbike? Are you *kidding*?'

'My sister's car is in the garage. I'm using it sometimes to keep the battery charged.'

'Does it have safety belts in the back? Ivy's car seat has to be in the back. Rear-facing. In the centre seat because, statistically, that's the safest place—furthest away from any potential impact.'

'I could always drive your car.'

James gave her his best smile. Not that it was a conscious decision, like giving someone a *Trust me, I'm a doctor* smile or an *It'll be worth it, I promise* kind of smile. This was a *real* smile. One of genuine appreciation. An offer of friendship?

'I feel like I know you already,' he added. 'And I'm willing to bet you've chosen the safest model out there. You know you can trust me to keep Ivy safe.' James was serious now. 'And I know you're perfectly capable of looking after yourself, Sarah, but I'll do whatever I can to keep you safe as well. You're the closest thing Ivy has to a mother and she needs you. Don't you, Ivy?'

He was rocking the baby as he looked down to include her in the conversation, partly because he wanted to give Sarah a moment to think about what he was offering. Would she trust him enough to give herself the chance to close her eyes and escape for a while from what could very well be an impossible emotional overload.

And then James looked up and caught her gaze. '*I* need you,' he added softly. 'We're in this together, okay?'

Sarah didn't say anything.

But when she finally nodded slowly it felt like a win. As if they had taken the first steps in the right direction, even though neither of them had a map for this journey they were both on.

Oh…that *smile*…

The one she'd felt all the way down to her toes.

She was feeling it again when she was standing under the hot rain of an excellent shower hours later. Or was she just feeling so much better? And grateful for the chance to rest? Sarah hadn't had such a deep sleep in weeks. Months, even, because she had been poised for any change in Karly's condition and then to attend to any needs of a newborn baby.

The thought that she'd trusted a total stranger enough to let him take Ivy away to allow herself to get the kind of rest her body was desperate for was unbelievable but, weirdly, Sarah only had to remember that smile to keep her anxiety at bay. Or perhaps she was remembering that he had not only saved her life, he hadn't judged her to be an unfit mother for Ivy in the wake of that incident.

He'd even said that she was the closest thing to an actual mother that Ivy had and that she was needed, and that had been the most affirming thing anybody had said to her in these last, traumatic weeks when her life had altered beyond recognition.

He'd said *he* needed her too, and somehow, while she'd been sleeping, she'd begun to process it. Despite the opinion of this man that had been so firmly embedded in her head before she'd met him and was still lingering at the back of her mind, everything James had said was resonating on a level that was undeniably attractive. His words were creating thoughts that had the potential to slip into any gaps in the plans she'd been making for her own and Ivy's future.

They could smooth the rough patches of how hard Sarah knew it was going to be sometimes as a single parent, like the worries about money or choosing the right school or being terrified of a sudden high fever. How much better would it be to have someone else to share the weight of responsibility of raising a child—like she and Karly had been planning to do before they knew how sick Karly was.

There was a much more positive side to this coin too. It wasn't simply the relief of being able to discuss the pros and cons of big decisions or sharing any struggles. It would mean having someone else who was just as invested in celebrating the special things like first steps or words or delighted to stick a crayon scribble that was supposed to be a person onto the fridge with a magnet.

And there was something so much bigger than any of this that was on offer. James Grisham had a whole family. Confirmation by way of a DNA test would be needed, of course, to make everything certain and legal but it did appear that Ivy was genetically linked to the Grishams and that meant that even in the innermost circle there were aunts and uncles, along with her father, available to offer love and care and the anchor of home for the rest of her life.

James was even suggesting that Sarah could be a part of it because of her connection to Ivy.

Sarah's tears were mingling with the water from the shower as she tilted her head back. She wasn't going to rush into anything unless she knew it could be trusted a thousand percent but...but wasn't this exactly what Karly would have dreamed of for her baby?

To have an entire family just appear out of nowhere?

For Ivy, it was like winning a lottery that you couldn't even buy a ticket for.

CHAPTER FIVE

IT HAD BEEN beyond busy all day.

The Accident and Emergency department in Aberdeen's Queen Mother's Hospital had been unusually hectic during this weekend shift that James Grisham had been rostered on for. He'd been thrown into the deep end as soon as he'd changed into his scrubs, draped his lanyard and stethoscope around his neck and clipped his pager to his pocket—walking into the department at the same moment a middle-aged patient under CPR was being brought in from the ambulance bay.

That the resuscitation attempt was successful made it one of those great days to be fighting life or death battles but there'd be no time for anyone to do anything more than smile at each other and say something like 'Well done', or 'Good job, wasn't it?' James had barely stopped moving since that first case, with his duties including triaging the patients coming in by ambulance so that he could choose the appropriate areas for them to go to. Resuscitation was for the most critically ill patients, Majors for serious cases and Minors for anything that could wait for a while if necessary.

The ones coming in by ambulance tended to be the time critical injuries and medical emergencies, like the man whose heart had stopped, apparently due to an arrhythmia. James had later dealt with two people with chest pain and evolving heart attacks, a major stroke, trauma from a cyclist being hit by a car, a bowel obstruction, three people with abdominal pain, one of whom had appendicitis and another with acute biliary colic from gallstones, respiratory infections, a couple of broken bones and—even though he was due to go off duty in about ten minutes, he was on his way to meet an ambulance which was coming in with someone who might have a chicken bone lodged in his throat.

'I can take this one.' A consultant who was covering the department until midnight caught up with James as he headed for the automatic doors that led out to the ambulance bay. 'Isn't it about time you went home?'

'I'm happy.' James waved him off. 'But I'll leave the next one for you. There's an ambulance with an ETA of two minutes with a Status One from a motorway pile-up on board, and there's more to come. You're going to be busy for a while.'

'True.' His colleague grinned at him. 'Just the way we like it.'

James threw a smile over his shoulder. A great emergency department—like this one at Queen's—could provide everything you could hope for in the huge variety of cases and severity, great facilities and colleagues to both work with and refer patients to and, for the most part today, he'd been treating people who were more than grateful for the help and reassurance they needed so badly when they were having a seriously bad day.

But how ironic was it that the chaos and challenges of this job were suddenly the familiar constants in a life that had changed irrevocably in a matter of only days? The eye of the hurricane happening in his personal life, in fact? James had known he was destined to work in emergency medicine ever since he'd been at medical school and he'd always loved his job, but over the last week, having a day like this where there was barely a moment to think about anything else, in a department he now felt completely at home in, had become even more of a happy place—a respite from the shock of having his world not just tipped upside down but shaken hard at the same time.

Not that it was an ordeal to have Sarah and Ivy still staying with him at the barn. He hadn't given her any choice but to stay that first night, and the next night she'd still felt unwell enough for it to have been the only sensible thing to do, but her decision might have also been influenced by the bit of shopping he'd done on the way home from picking up that paperwork from his office. It was just as well he had taken Sarah's roomy SUV because it had required two of the baby emporium's staff members to pack in all the supplies he'd managed to gather in a very short space of time, like a bassinet and linen, a baby bath, nappies, extra clothes and tins of formula. Oh, aye…there'd been that square of the softest fabric he'd ever felt that had a small and super cute, fluffy little lamb on one corner so that the rest of the square looked like a dress it was wearing.

Who knew that there were things like this and that they were, adorably, called 'loveys'?

Sarah obviously knew and James had a feeling that it was that smallest purchase that had sealed the deal and stopped her heading off to find somewhere else to stay with Ivy until she was well enough to head home.

She had recovered more each day and James realised that his first impressions of her determination to overcome any obstacles in her life by a mix of courage and rigid organisational skills hadn't given him the full picture by any means. She was devoted to Ivy to a degree that made James envy the friendship she must have had with Karly. She was so good at managing her diabetes that it was easy to imagine that, under normal circumstances, nobody would know about it unless she chose to tell them. She was also highly intelligent and…and great company. She and Jodie had hit it off instantly when Eddie had insisted they brought dinner round for them both the other day, and Ella and Logan had clearly liked her when they met her via the video call they'd made the day the DNA results came through and confirmed what James had already been quite sure of in his own heart.

Ivy was his daughter.

And that knowledge, along with the huge responsibility to protect this infant and the chaos of considering the future, came with a sense of wonder and pride that he'd contributed to creating this small human with the most amazing hair and smile in the entire world. Thoughts of Ivy and, by default, of Sarah were always in the back of his mind and could be tapped into at any time, but James had been an emergency physician for many years now and it was easy to shut any mental doors that kept him from being distracted from his job.

Which was why it was such a respite to be here, especially when it was hectic, and why he wasn't rushing to leave on time today. Thanks to that video call with his older sister and her husband, the clock was ticking more loudly for their return to Scotland, with Mick, in just a couple of weeks. That was on top of the already ticking clock that was counting down the days until Sarah decided it was time she went home. Depending on Ivy's cooperation, during the dinner that Sarah was cooking tonight and however long it took into the evening, it was imperative that they talked about the immediate future and how much James would be able to be present in his daughter's life.

In the meantime, however, James was going to see a young man who had been eating fried chicken for his dinner and had come straight from the fast-food restaurant to ED, convinced that he had a bone lodged in his throat. One last case for the busy shift and, more than likely, one more story he could entertain Sarah with if he wasn't quite ready to dive into the heavy conversation regarding what was going to happen next in their lives.

The beautiful barn conversion that was the home of Ella Grisham and her husband, Logan, was a joy to be staying in.

The kitchen and well-stocked pantry seemed to have been designed to cater for large family gatherings so it had been child's play to create a small dinner for two that would be forgiving if James was late getting away from the hospital. A potato gratin was in the oven, a couple of steaks were bathing in some marinade and Sarah was adding some mustard and garlic to the vinaigrette dressing she was making for a colourful, fresh salad.

And she couldn't remember the last time she had felt this good.

It was probably because she'd shaken off the last remnants of that viral illness.

Or maybe it was because it had been such a lovely day and she had gone shopping with Ivy for the groceries, explored a little bit of Aberdeen and then spent some time outside in the afternoon sunshine when they got back, watching the ducks on the pond that provided the most picturesque part of this serene rural setting.

But that didn't quite explain the fact that her sense of wellbeing had increased so noticeably since James had arrived home, and that was despite the somewhat disturbing prospect of the overdue discussion they had to have this evening about Ivy's immediate future. Sarah was finding it remarkably easy to push it out of her mind, in fact. James was clearly in no hurry to broach a serious topic, probably because he had Ivy in his arms and was holding her last bottle of milk before her bedtime. On top of that, he was busy telling her a story about his shift.

'So he's sitting there, having enough trouble swallowing to be drooling and complaining of a pain on the left side of this throat that was severe enough to prevent him turning his head to that side. No palpable mass in his neck and his lungs were clear.'

'Could you see anything?'

'No. I used a laryngoscope torch and a mouth mirror but couldn't see any trauma or swelling or even a hint of a foreign object embedded anywhere.' James leaned over the top of Ivy to put an almost empty bottle onto the kitchen table. 'I think she's full. She's almost asleep.'

'If you burp her, I'll check her nappy and then put her to bed.'

James nodded, and carefully changed the baby's position so that she was upright and well supported with one arm while he rubbed her back in circles with his other hand.

'Is this okay?' he asked.

'It's great. You can do some gentle pats as well.' Sarah wanted to hear the end of the story. 'So how did you find the chicken bone? Did you get a CT done?'

'Soft tissue, lateral neck X-ray did the trick. It was hiding in the left tonsillar crypt, just above the hyoid bone.'

'Did you get a consult with ENT?'

'Nobody was available to do an immediate endoscopy. He was uncomfortable but it wasn't an emergency so it was suggested he could wait for an outpatient appointment tomorrow, but I didn't want to leave him like that.' James was patting Ivy's back now. 'And he didn't want to go home like that, so I suggested that I had a go myself and he was more than up for it.'

Sarah blinked. James might be new at handling babies but he wasn't lacking in confidence in other areas, was he? 'What did you do?'

'Anaesthetised his throat with Benzocaine spray, gave him some conscious sedation with Midazolam and Fentanyl and I used a video laryngoscope and then some alligator forceps to get the splinter out. Worked a treat.'

Ivy chose that moment to release an impressive burp by way of punctuation and both James and Sarah laughed aloud.

The grin that remained on James's face as he caught Sarah's gaze made it look as if he considered the burp a personal triumph.

And Sarah grinned right back at him. What woman wouldn't respond to a gorgeous man smiling at her like that? Nobody would dispute how attractive he was with that tousled dark hair, those eyes and that killer smile that held more than a smidge of mischief. His delight in the achievement of feeding and burping a baby was contagious too, especially in the wake of that rather charming doubt in his own abilities that made it clear he had none of the arrogance that such good-looking men often did have.

This was the kind of moment that all new parents must take delight in as they learned the new skills required to keep their babies happy, Sarah thought, but there were so many other layers in play here, it quickly spiralled from pleasure into trepidation. This was anything but a normal situation for new parents. She couldn't forget that James was the actual parent. That they were in the kitchen of his sister's home. That big decisions needed to be made and that, if compromise was necessary, it would very likely be Sarah who would be the one who had to concede.

And maybe she also needed to remember that James Grisham was an expert in charming women and getting what he wanted from them. She couldn't afford to fall under his spell. For Ivy's sake as much as her own.

Sarah's smile faded as she turned away to screw the lid on the jar and shake it hard to mix the olive oil and balsamic vinegar with the other ingredients.

'I'll get Ivy sorted for bed,' she said. 'It'll only take a minute to cook the steak and we'll enjoy our dinner more if she's asleep. Unless you're starving? It is getting late.'

James stood up as she walked towards him and took a now very sleepy Ivy from his arms. There was a slightly awkward moment in being this close to each other. Was James as aware as she was of the way their arms were touching? That their fingers brushed, skin to skin, as she took the weight of Ivy's head? Was that what made him clear his throat so abruptly as he stepped back?

'I know my way round a barbecue,' he said. 'Why don't I go and fire it up?'

'That would be great.'

'How do you like your steak done?'

'Just on the well-done side of medium, please.'

'I might have guessed you'd have an exact response.' James was laughing again. 'I'll do my best.'

The sound of his laughter followed Sarah as she climbed the stairs. Oddly, it didn't offend her that James thought she was as much of a control freak as Karly always had, and that was partly because it was true but also because it almost sounded as if he admired the trait rather than disapproving of it.

Or maybe it was the sound of his laughter that felt like it was seeping into her body through her ears and trickling down to curl around her heart. She found she was smiling again herself as she took care of the baby's pre-bedtime routine.

She couldn't help herself, could she?

She liked Ivy's father.

More than she'd expected to. Way more than she should. But that was the problem with bad boys, wasn't it? They charmed you into thinking the rules didn't matter.

But they did. As much as being in control mattered. Especially for Sarah. She'd learned that long ago.

The meal was so good it seemed a shame to spoil it by opening a discussion that could rapidly become difficult, so James told her stories about growing up as one of triplet brothers.

'It was like we were a single unit. The Grisham boys. Ella called us the "Fearsome Threesome". If one of us did something, we all did it—good or bad. We never told on each other either. Ella swears it was me that stole our mother's nail scissors one time and started the haircutting incident but I'm pretty sure it was Mick.'

'Oh, no… How old were you?'

'About three. Probably old enough to know better.'

Sarah was smiling but James wanted to make her laugh again—the way she had when Ivy had produced that magnificent belch. He wanted to see that sparkle in her eyes and feel that, just for a moment, she had forgotten the serious side of life.

Had he really thought there was nothing particularly special about her when he'd first seen her standing in his driveway that night? That she was ordinary enough to disappear into the background of some quiet place like a library or a laboratory? Maybe it was true he wouldn't have noticed her if she'd crossed his path but that would have been his loss, wouldn't it?

There was something about her that was very special indeed.

Sarah suddenly glanced up, a last mouthful on her fork poised halfway to her mouth, as if she'd somehow caught the gist of his thoughts. There was a hint more colour in her cheeks as she seemed to try and focus on what he'd just said.

'I'll bet you were a real handful as you grew up. Were you all daredevils like Mick? Are you into extreme sports like hang-gliding as well?'

'I've given it a go but I'm not as adventurous as Eddie.' James was only too happy to be redirected from wherever his thoughts had been trying to take him. 'I work in a nice, safe emergency department instead of flying into dangerous situations like he does with the air ambulance. And Mick was the one who started taking things a bit too far. I think it was a knee-jerk reaction to getting jilted but it became a habit.'

'Getting jilted?' Sarah's eyes were wide. 'You left that bit out when you were telling me about Mick's accident the other day.'

'It's years ago now. He thought he was going to become a father so he proposed to his Brazilian girlfriend, Juliana. We were all dressed up in tuxedoes, waiting at the front of the church for a bride that never turned up.'

'Why not?'

'The real father of the baby had come to find her. She was already at the airport to head back to Brazil with him by the time we'd lined up in front of the altar.'

'That's awful…'

'We did get very drunk that night,' James admitted. 'And we made a vow that none of us would go looking to get married or even caught in a permanent relationship. That we were going to live in the 'now' and make the most of our lives and our careers and the only people we needed around for ever were each other. We would celebrate the good stuff and be there for each other for any bad stuff.' He let his breath out in a sigh. 'Eddie's well and truly broken that vow now. And my wings have certainly been clipped.'

Sarah put her fork down on her plate so carefully it didn't make a sound.

'They don't have to be,' she said. 'I'm quite prepared

to be Ivy's primary caregiver. It's not as if you're even in a position to be a full-time father.'

And, just like that, here they were.

About to make plans that were going to affect the rest of his life.

'Finding out I'm a father has changed my life dramatically,' James said slowly. 'But it had already changed—the moment Mick had his accident—and we all got the wake-up call that life could be a lot shorter than we might want. It's probably taken a lot longer than it should have but my brothers and I are finally growing up and settling down. Eddie's with Jodie. It sounds like Mick's turned a corner in his recovery and I won't be surprised if he gets back to a brilliant medical career—or competes in the Paralympics in the future or something. And me? I'm here for my family because that's the most important thing I have in my life other than *my* career.' James took a deep breath. 'And my family now includes my daughter. Right now, Ivy is the most important person in the world as far as I'm concerned. I'm going to find out what bureaucratic hoops I might need to jump through with the registry office to get my name officially recorded on her birth certificate and…and I really don't want you to take her back to Leeds.'

Sarah's face was completely still as she absorbed his words. 'But that's my home,' she said in a whisper. 'It's where my job is and my friends are. It's where I grew up. Where I *live*…' She shook her head. 'I can't stay here—this isn't even your house.'

'I know. I was planning to move into the apartment that Eddie's moved out of, but that's a basement flat that's not at all suitable for having a baby there even part time.

I've decided I'm going to find somewhere else to rent.' James swallowed hard. 'It's too soon to think about buying anything because there are too many things still up in the air. I don't know how Mick's going to be when he gets back and my job here is just a locum position. It could be that I don't have to stay in Aberdeen for ever. I might even be up for moving to Leeds if that's what it takes to be a part of Ivy's life—who knows?'

Sarah seemed to be listening carefully. James tried not to sound as if he was pushing her. He certainly had no intention of threatening her with legalities or moral obligations to him as the biological parent. This wasn't going to work at all if they became enemies, but even if Ivy didn't exist he wouldn't want to hurt Sarah.

Because she was special.

Because he really admired her.

He really liked her. A lot…

'What I'm wondering is…if I find a big enough house, maybe you could stay longer. A few more weeks. A month? Maybe two, if it's working? We could share caring for Ivy in the same way we're doing it here? If we could take our time making the really big decisions, then isn't it more likely that they might be the best ones? For Ivy *and* for us? You don't have to give me an answer right now but would you think about it? Please…?'

He might not be pushing her but he knew that Sarah could see how important this was to him because her face—and especially her eyes—were expressive enough to reveal exactly what she was thinking. This woman might be in complete control of her life but that didn't mean she didn't feel things very deeply. He could see flashes of all sorts of emotions she was experiencing.

Fear, surprise, doubt. Hope, perhaps? And something else, as her gaze finally softened, that looked like…empathy.

For him?

She was thinking this through from his point of view as well as her own and Ivy's?

Of course she was. That didn't surprise him either. On top of everything he admired about Sarah Harrison, he'd known she was compassionate and caring.

What he hadn't known was what it felt like to have her looking at *him* like this. As if she really cared. As if… they might be able to have the kind of friendship that he'd envied Karly having with Sarah so much?

Sarah was nodding slowly. 'I'll think about it,' she promised.

As she got to her feet and picked up her empty plate, James felt himself take a step closer to that friendship he'd glimpsed and…it felt surprisingly good.

Very, very different to how he'd ever felt about wanting to be close to a woman, in fact.

He was also aware of a wash of relief that Ivy wasn't going to be whisked out of his life and back to Leeds immediately. He wanted to hug Sarah. He stood up and reached for his plate but what he really wanted to do was reach for Sarah and dance around the kitchen with her.

To kiss her…?

Good grief…where the hell had that thought come from? Maybe this new feeling for the guardian of his child wasn't so different to all the other women who'd come—and gone—from his life and James felt oddly disturbed by what had to be just an automatic reaction thanks to old habits. Deplorable habits, as far as Sarah was concerned. Irresponsible playboys could be dismissed. Sex addicts should clearly be avoided at all costs.

Thank goodness he had the errant impulse under control within a heartbeat. His connection with Sarah Harrison had absolutely nothing to do with physical attraction and never would because it was based on something far more important for both of them.

Being Ivy's parents.

It was just as well Sarah had turned towards the kitchen sink.

She hadn't seen a thing.

CHAPTER SIX

'WE'LL JUST POP in for a minute.' Sarah unclipped the safety belt holding Ivy's car seat. She already had the strap of the bag, containing all the baby essentials that were now a priority in her life, over her shoulder. 'You'd like to see where your daddy works, wouldn't you, darling?'

She turned to look at the solid, square shape of Aberdeen's Queen Mother's Hospital that was modern enough for the wall of glass windows to be the most prominent feature. There were signs making it easy to find the way to Reception or Accident & Emergency, but Sarah felt as if she could see past those first main signs and through some of those countless windows to the inner workings of the hospital with its imaging departments of X-ray, MRI and Ultrasound, the operating theatres, wards and Intensive Care Units, Outpatients, Pathology—even the locker rooms, gift shops and cafeterias.

Every hospital was a world of its own but the atmosphere they had in common was always familiar and, for Sarah, it felt like home. Being a nurse was such a big part of her life. Of who she was. And she hadn't realised how much she was missing it until she walked into the reception area of Queen's and headed for the main desk to ask if they could call Emergency and see if Dr Grisham might be free for a minute or two. She was quite happy to wait.

More than happy, in fact, because it meant she could sit out here and soak in the feeling of being where she belonged. Of remembering that, while she wouldn't want to be doing anything else at this point in her life, she was more than the primary caregiver of a precious baby who had lost her real mother. One day, especially if she had support in raising Ivy, it would be possible for her to return to the job she loved so much.

Not that she got more than about sixty seconds to enjoy the bustle of a busy hospital entranceway. Wearing scrubs and an expression that didn't disguise his concern, James came striding though the opening to one of the corridors that led from the reception area.

'Sarah…what's wrong? Is it Ivy?' He crouched down in front of the car seat and tugged one of the brightly coloured toys hanging on elastic from the handle to make it dance. 'Hey… Piglet. How're you doing?'

Sarah could hear the way his breath huffed out in relief as Ivy grinned up at him.

James was smiling back at his daughter. 'She doesn't look like there's much wrong with her.'

'There isn't. Sorry… I didn't mean to get you worried by arriving unannounced. I hope we haven't interrupted something.'

'Only coffee. It's weirdly quiet in ED at the moment.' James looked up at Sarah. 'You know that "calm before the storm" kind of feeling?'

'All too well. I won't keep you. I just wanted to show you some photos of a house in Ferryhill that we went past when we drove near Duthie Park this morning. It's got a sign outside saying it's available to rent so I checked it out on the agent's website. Look…'

Sarah opened the link on her phone. 'I have no idea if it's the sort of thing you like but I noticed it because it reminds me a bit of my grandma's house where I grew up.' She showed James a picture of the lovely stone-built terraced house to rent in a leafy street, close to the lovely green park and walkways along the river. 'It's even got the same kind of wooden floors and plaster cornices.'

Sarah was looking at the image but she could feel the shift of James's glance and the way he was focusing on her. As if he'd realised instantly that this was her way of telling him that she had not only processed his suggestion and decided that she was happy to stay in Aberdeen longer but that being involved in the choice of where they would live would help her feel as if she was still, at least partly, in control of her own life.

'Come and have a coffee,' he said. 'I might even be able to take my lunch break and I'd like to see some more photos. Maybe we can call the agent and make an appointment to go and see the house.'

'Okay… I'm not in any huge hurry to get home.' Sarah turned her head. 'Which way is the cafeteria?'

'I was thinking of our staffroom,' James said. 'It'll be a lot less crowded. Would you like a quick tour of our ED on the way? It's one of the best I've worked in so I'm sure you'd appreciate the setup.'

Oh…if being in Reception had made Sarah feel at home, walking into an emergency department would be like being surrounded by family. Losing her job *and* Karly had taken away an overwhelmingly large part of her life, hadn't it?

'Yes, *please*... I'd love that.' She bent to pick up the car seat and almost bumped heads with James, who was already holding the handle. They grinned at each other and then James led the way towards his department. She certainly did appreciate what looked like a very sleek setup, from resuscitation areas close to the ambulance bay entrance to one side to cubicles for less urgent patients on the other side of a well set up central area with multiple computer stations to access records and test results and a huge digital whiteboard that had all the information on every patient in the department, what the provisional diagnosis was, where they were and who was looking after them. A man with a white coat over his scrubs was standing in front of the board as a nurse in navy blue scrubs was pointing to something.

'That's Cameron Brown, our HoD,' James said. 'And that's our nurse manager, Jenny, he's talking to.' He greeted his colleagues as they got closer. 'This is Sarah,' he told them. 'I'm going to let her see whether the coffee here's any better than what she's used to in Leeds. She's a nurse practitioner in the ED there.'

'Ooh...' Jenny's smile was welcoming. 'I hope you're thinking of coming to work here. We're currently a wee bit short of nurses with your kind of qualifications.' But her attention shifted to the car seat before Sarah had the chance to respond. 'Who's this little angel?'

'This is Ivy.' Sarah could see the deep breath James was taking. Was he about to out himself as a father for the first time in public?

Yes...and there was a note of pride in his voice as he added to the introduction.

'Ivy's my daughter,' he said.

Cameron's eyebrows rose but his phone started ringing as he opened his mouth to say something and he took the call instead.

'Ah…have you come to check out the day care facilities?' Jenny was nodding as she smiled at Sarah, clearly assuming that she was Ivy's mother and James's partner.

Sarah couldn't help a sidelong glance. Would James put her straight? With a look that might give the impression that the idea was ludicrous?

'It's a fabulous creche,' Jenny said. 'I had both my kids in there since they were about this age until they started school and they absolutely thrived.' Her voice trailed into silence as she heard the tone in Cameron's voice and the rapid-fire questions he was asking.

'How far away? How many? Right…keep me posted. We'll be on standby.'

He ended his call. 'Major incident activation,' he said. 'A viewing platform in the Cairngorms somewhere near the path up to Ben Macdui has apparently collapsed and possibly more than twenty people have fallen about thirty metres into a gully. Police and Mountain Rescue are already on the way to the scene but we're the nearest trauma centre so we've been put on standby to receive any serious cases.' He eyed James. 'You've done disaster management training, haven't you?'

'I have. I'm qualified as a Medical Incident Officer and I've been involved with situations in both London and Europe. I've also had some HEMS training.'

'Perfect.' Cameron's nod was brisk. 'There's a helicopter being diverted from an Aberdeen Air Ambulance call and they'll be touching down on the roof in around ten minutes to pick up someone qualified to act as the MIO as part of the initial response and triage. Would you be prepared to go? We're the closest major trauma centre and I've got to put our plan into action, clear space in the department and get all relevant specialties on standby.'

'Of course.' But James was turning away from his HoD to nod in Sarah's direction. 'Sarah's got a MIMMS certification. I think she should come with me.'

Sarah's eyes widened. She could feel her heart rate pick up as adrenaline began to flood her body. The reason she'd come into the hospital in the first place was completely forgotten but the feeling of being where she belonged and wanting to be part of what was going on around her had just become a whole lot stronger. A pull that was almost impossible to ignore. All she'd need to do was provide her Personal Identification Number and they could quickly confirm her qualifications on the Nursing and Midwifery Council register.

But she shook her head without hesitating. 'I can't leave Ivy.'

'I'll take her up to the creche myself,' Jenny said. 'She'll be safe, I promise you. I'll take personal responsibility for that if the response goes on after creche hours.' The older nurse met Sarah's gaze and there was understanding there. And a plea. 'There are people out there in trouble and they need all the expert assistance we can provide. You've got more expertise than any other nurses I could send.'

'We need to get our kits and overalls and get up to the helipad, stat. Come with me…' It was James who was holding Sarah's gaze now. 'Please…?'

Sarah couldn't shake her head again. She could feel the beat of her heart in her throat as she stared back at

James and thoughts flew past so rapidly they could only coalesce into a feeling rather than words. Whatever she'd thought of this man before she'd made the road trip from Leeds to find him in the first place was forgotten as convincingly as the reason she'd come to find him at his place of work today.

He had no reason to trust that she was good at her job, other than what he'd learned about her as a person since she'd turned up on his doorstep, and yet she could see that he genuinely wanted to work with her.

That he trusted her...?

Wow...

That trust went both ways, didn't it?

This man might not have intended to become a father but the way he'd not only accepted Ivy into his life but was stepping up to meet both moral and practical responsibilities made him just the rock Sarah needed as she got to grips with the unknowns of her own new life. Someone she could trust to protect and care for Ivy as much as she intended to do.

Someone who had saved her own life and was asking her to help him do the same for others.

Okay... There was no way she could say no. Sarah grabbed her phone, handed the bag of baby supplies to Jenny, used a scrap of paper to scribble her full name and PIN for someone to check the nursing register and went after James, who had already turned away and seemed to know exactly where he was going.

'Wait...' she called. 'Wait for me...'

There was a wide walkway, with automatic doors at either end, that connected the emergency department to the ambulance bay. To one side of this corridor was a locked storage room beside a decontamination area but James had learned the code for this lock as part of his familiarisation with a new location.

'Here…' James lifted a small-sized pair of bright orange overalls from a hook and handed them to Sarah. 'Get these on.'

He pulled on a larger size himself, over his scrubs, zipped up the front and pulled on a fluorescent yellow vest with MEDICAL INCIDENT OFFICER emblazoned on a silver back panel.

'Here's a vest for you.' He handed Sarah one with NURSE on the back as she was slipping something into a pocket of her overalls. 'What are those?' he asked.

'Muesli bars. And glucose tablets. I always carry them.'

The glance Sarah slid in his direction looked wary. Did she think he might regret his decision to take her with him if she reminded him of her diabetes and the disaster of their first meeting? If anything, he was impressed by her attention to risk factors. They were heading into what would undoubtedly be a high-stress situation for an unknown length of time and possibly considerable physical exertion required. All these factors would affect Sarah's control of her blood glucose level but she was clearly in control, which meant it was one less thing he had to think about.

'I'll get the advanced care and drug kits. We'll both need one of those red rucksacks as well.'

'Are they standard issue first response kits?'

'Yes. I had a quick look when I checked this room out. They've got triage labels and pods colour-coded for "airway", "breathing" and "circulation". There are extensive dressing packs and there's saline and IV giving sets.'

All the basic requirements to keep someone's airway open, help them breathe if necessary and control major external haemorrhage. Other equipment and supplies would be available on ambulances and rescue aircraft. He worked rapidly along a shelf, handing Sarah a stethoscope that she slung around her neck, a radio that she clipped on and a logbook and water-resistant pen that went into a pocket. She grabbed a handful of disposable gloves from a box on the wall herself and shoved them into another pocket as they ran for the lifts.

The helicopter was landing as they reached the hospital roof. The sliding door on the side opened and a paramedic jumped out to make sure they could climb on board safely while the rotors were still running. It wasn't until he got close enough to hand them helmets that James recognised him.

'Eddie…'

He received a flash of a grin as well as a helmet. 'I thought it was about time we worked together, bro.' But Eddie was looking as surprised as James had been when he saw who was with him.

'Sarah…? You're working here now?'

'Just in the right place at the right time.' James could hear Eddie clearly over the noise of the rotors as he pulled on the helmet with its inbuilt audio equipment. 'She's got qualifications in major incident management as well as her nurse practitioner skills.'

The reminder of what had brought them all to this place at this time was enough to make anything personal irrelevant and James could see how focused Sarah was as she fastened the strap of her helmet and bent to pick up the rucksack beside her. She certainly looked the part with her hair tucked away under the helmet and wearing those overalls and vest, but it was more than simply a uniform. He could see that she understood exactly what they could be heading towards and there was a determination in her face that he was feeling himself.

It was a privilege to be allowed anywhere near a disaster scene, let alone become a part of an attempt to find and help any survivors. James knew, in that moment, that Sarah would push herself to do whatever it took to help those people and...

And he felt proud of her.

Jodie was part of the air ambulance crew and James and Sarah were introduced to the others as they sat down and buckled themselves in.

'This is Alex, who's our crewman, and Gus is our pilot.' Eddie gave a thumbs-up to Gus, who was watching to see the moment he was clear to lift off again. He pulled out a tablet as the helicopter took off. 'What's the latest sitrep, Alex?' he asked.

James turned away from watching the roof of the Queen Mother's Hospital fall away beneath them. He also wanted to hear what the most recent situation report was.

'The police have officially declared this a major incident.' Alex was holding another tablet. 'And we have an exact location.' He turned the tablet so that James and Sarah could see a map on the screen and he zoomed in by stretching it with his fingers. 'There's no road into the gully but there is a rough track that allows access by foot, which will probably take a good twenty minutes. We'll put you and Sarah down at the Casualty Clearing

Station that's being set up on the nearest road and someone will take you in.'

'Unless I can find a place to put you down a bit closer
to the scene,' Gus put in. 'We'll be winching Eddie and
Jodie down, but if there's a flat spot close enough I can
touch down and let you all out.'

'Fingers crossed.' Eddie nodded. 'That would save a
lot of time. We want to get to anyone with critical injuries as soon as possible and we can expect anyone that's
survived a fall like that to have some major trauma.'

James found himself meeting Sarah's gaze in the beat
of silence that followed. How many survivors could be
expected after such a catastrophic fall? How horrific
would their injuries be?

She was scared.

Of course she was. James could feel a beat of the same
kind of fear of the unknown himself.

But he also got a glimpse of the kind of courage this
woman had. The ability to take on something, no matter
how daunting it might seem, because…she could. Because it was the right thing to do.

Like raising a child who was, as far as she knew at
the time, devoid of any biological family that might care
about her.

That determination he already knew she had was being
mixed with that courage now. He could even hear the
way she pulled in a new breath and left any shadow of
that fear behind.

'Has the type of incident been confirmed?' Sarah
asked.

'Yes. It's a structure collapse and fall. It's a large group
of outdoor education students—ages about eighteen to

twenty-one. One of the tutors witnessed the incident and sounded the alarm. Apparently, they were all crowding onto the lookout because someone had a selfie stick and they wanted a photo of the whole group with the view in the background.'

There was another silent moment as they all imagined the horror as that platform gave way under too much weight.

'There are survivors,' Alex added. 'No estimate of numbers, though. Nobody's got to the scene yet but the tutor could hear shouts for help.'

'Hazards?' Sarah was obviously using the METHANE acronym to gather whatever information was available. They already knew it was officially a major incident and the exact location and type of disaster it was.

'Mostly the terrain. Like the rough ground, the river and potential fall of debris from above. We won't know whether there's any risk of secondary collapse of the platform until the fire service experts have had a look. Check with them re stability if they're on scene when you get there. Be very careful if they're not, okay?'

'We've already covered access,' Jodie added. 'Number of casualties is still unknown but there are twenty-three course attendees and a tutor that are currently unaccounted for.'

'Emergency services are getting every resource available mobilised. Police, fire, mountain rescue. Even the Red Cross. There are road ambulances on the way from as far away as Aberdeen but it'll take a while for them to arrive.'

'There are at least two other helicopters on the way,' Gus added. 'From Glasgow and Inverness. And a local pilot is going in to see what he can report. He's going to look for any possible landing spots along the river going in from Braemar.'

'Jodie will be the ambulance incident officer until someone more senior arrives,' Eddie said. 'But the longer she can actually treat patients rather than get caught up in admin, the better.'

James caught the gaze shared between his brother and the woman who was his partner both professionally and personally and he felt a squeeze in his chest that was tight enough to be painful.

The *respect* in that glance was palpable.

So was the love...

And, just for a split second, Eddie had a flash of realisation that took him back to the night of Mick's jilting and the vow the three brothers had made to stay uncommitted to one person in order to avoid heartache and get the most out of life. In this brief moment of time, however, as he caught the power of that glance James could not only understand why Eddie had broken that vow, he was deeply envious.

He wanted to know what it would feel like to be *that* close to someone.

Because he had the feeling that Eddie might have been the first to realise that they had got it wrong that night. That staying unattached to anyone other than each other could be what was *preventing* them getting the most out of life.

The thought evaporated as Gus spoke over other radio traffic.

'We'll be over Balmoral estate in a couple of minutes. When you see that you'll know we're nearly there.'

* * *

Sarah listened to the bleeps, occasional static and voices of incoming updates as they got closer to the mountains in the Cairngorms National Park. She saw small villages below, following the line of the winding river, and the unmistakable turrets and spires of Balmoral Castle, but the sounds and sights were no more than a background as the tension rose. She actually jumped when she heard a new note in Gus's voice.

'Here we go. That's the track we're after at three o'clock. It's running alongside and sometimes through that stream that feeds into the River Dee.'

The crew in the cabin all leaned to see down to the right side of the helicopter.

The roadside at the start of the track was a mass of blinking lights from all the emergency vehicles already on site. Police cars were blocking the road to any normal traffic and Sarah could see two fire trucks and an ambulance. A jeep with a flashing orange light and a roof rack laden with gear looked as though it would belong to a mountain rescue crew. She could see that the chain of command, headed by the police, was already working to accepted protocols. The inner cordon would be the start of that track to begin with, with the casualty clearing station in front of an ambulance loading station and then a space before the outer cordon where road cones were being placed to define lanes and control the vehicles moving in and out.

'The local guy reckons there's enough flat space where the track meets the edge of that stream to get you down on the outskirts of the scene,' Gus told them as they left the cordons behind and followed the walking track into the gully. 'And…there it is…' he said only moments later, slowing to a hover. 'Looks like you've got a welcoming committee.'

A group of uniformed people were moving back onto the track to get out of the way but it was still a tight space and they had to follow directions fast to get out of and away from the aircraft safely. James was out before Sarah and she was grateful that he turned and held out his hand to take hers. This was more than a bit scary.

'Keep your head down,' he reminded her. 'Here we go.'

The grip on her hand was tight enough to be reassuring and Sarah wasn't about to let it go as she bent double to run under the spinning rotors. Alex was going to unload their gear and they could pick it up when the helicopter had lifted again.

She went to let go of his hand when they caught up with Eddie and Jodie and the rescue personnel waiting on the track but it seemed as if he wanted to keep holding it for a heartbeat longer. Raising her gaze as she pulled in a deep breath, she found James looking down at her. She wanted to look away so that he wouldn't see that fear that was trying to bubble up again. What were they about to face?

Was she even capable of dealing with something this huge?

But it was already too late to shift her gaze. It felt as if James had already seen everything.

He didn't say anything aloud but he didn't need to. That look said it all.

You're not alone, Sarah… We can do this…

CHAPTER SEVEN

THE SCENE WAS like something out of a disaster movie.

High above them, at the top of a steep, rugged cliff, they could see the poles that had held the viewing platform, their jagged, broken ends like smashed teeth pointing into the void where people had been thrown. Some people had been thrown clear of the solid, flat wooden structure to fall onto boulders in and beside this fast-flowing section of the mountain stream. It was possible there could be people who had fallen—or jumped—onto the cliff further up but the suddenness and speed with which this catastrophe had unfolded meant that the majority of the group packed onto the wooden floor, against the rails that should have kept them safe, had stayed together and it might have only been in the last few seconds that the platform—the size of a small room—had tipped and then landed on top of both people and boulders.

The first responders to this scene, which probably included the people who had alerted emergency services and the first local volunteers and police who could get to this remote location quickly, had already tried to help and it looked as though they had stayed to try and comfort survivors. James could see someone kneeling beside a person lying on the ground near the stream and another who had an arm around someone who was sitting, their head bent enough to touch their chest.

His heart sank as James flicked his glance back to where the platform had landed. Parts of the structure had broken and were heavy enough to be pinning the still figures that could be seen at the edges. One section was clearly teetering on top of the largest boulders.

'It's not stable.' The fire officer, wearing a vest that designated him the officer in charge, broke the quiet moment as the medics took in their first impression of the scene and the hazards it might contain. 'Don't get close enough to touch it. We've got USAR trained firies who are on the track already, carting in the gear we need to keep you medics safe while you're working.' He glanced up. 'We've also got someone watching for any further debris falling, like those poles and the concrete blocks that will have anchored them. If you hear a long, unbroken blast on a whistle, move back fast, okay?'

James gave a single nod. He could feel the tension around him that was sharp enough to cut yourself on. He could hear the sounds of people in pain. He could almost smell the blood and fear. As a member of the medical team who could do something to help people who were suffering, he was desperate to get started. The so-called 'golden hour' for treating major trauma patients had already ticked well past so they couldn't afford to lose any more time, but that didn't mean they could rush towards the first victims they could see. There was a good reason why the protocol they needed to follow had what seemed like a slow start.

He took a pack of labels from his pocket and saw that Jodie also had one in her hands.

'Sieve and sort?'

James nodded again. 'You and Eddie start at the stream and move in. Sarah and I will start from the cliff.' James spoke over his shoulder to the fire officer as he began moving. 'Has anyone been seen further up?'

'Search and Rescue have sent a team up to abseil down when we give them the all-clear. We don't want any debris being dislodged until we're working here.'

The first tool of managing a scene like this was called the 'sieve'. It was a rapid walk-through the whole scene to assign priority for medical attention. The only reason they would do anything to a victim at this stage was to reposition them to make sure their airway was open before checking that they were breathing or apply a tourniquet to obvious external haemorrhage. James walked towards the cliff to where he'd seen the person sitting with one of the first responders providing comfort and reassurance to someone who looked to be only in her late teens.

'I could have walked out with her, but I thought it would be safer to keep her still until someone who knew what they were doing had checked her.'

James handed Sarah a green label with an elastic loop to attach to the girl's wrist. If a victim was walking or capable of walking, they received this label that gave them a delayed priority three.

'You're doing a great job,' James told the first responder. 'Keep her here for a bit longer. We're doing a rapid triage right now but a team will be assigned to come back and do a more thorough check on everybody very soon and they'll decide the best way to get everyone out.'

It was only a matter of a few steps to the crumpled figure of someone who was lying on their back, not moving and making no sound.

Sarah was slightly ahead of James and she crouched, tilting the man's head to ensure the airway was open. Then she put her hand on the man's diaphragm and her face close enough to be able to feel a breath on her skin.

'Breathing?' James asked.

'No.'

James handed her a black label. There was no time to get caught by the emotion of finding a young person who had tragically lost their life. They had to keep moving.

The next person they came to was also lying very still, unconscious, but she was breathing. James watched the slow rate at which her chest was rising and falling. It took only a few seconds to estimate how many breaths she would be taking in a minute.

'Respiratory rate of less than ten,' he said.

He handed Sarah a red label, which was the highest priority for receiving immediate medical attention, and she slipped the elastic band around the girl's wrist.

After assigning two more black cards they were getting closer to the platform and there was a person who was lying on their side with their eyes open. She gave what sounded like a stifled sob when she saw James and Sarah approaching.

James crouched beside her. 'What's your name, sweetheart?'

'Catherine…'

Her voice was quiet and her face was too pale, but they couldn't yet take the time to do a thorough primary survey and find out what her injuries might be. James could already tell that her respiratory rate was within acceptable levels. He took her hand and pressed against a fingernail for a rough check of her circulation by watching for capillary refill. It took less than two seconds, which meant that while this patient still needed urgent medical attention, she could go into the second priority for the moment.

'Yellow card, Sarah,' he said. He knew that Catherine's condition could deteriorate at any time and make her a red card priority but he made sure his tone was reassuring. 'We're going to be back very soon to look after you, Catherine,' he said. 'I promise.'

By the time they met up with Eddie and Jodie at the central point of this disaster, where people lay trapped beneath the platform, more and more rescue personnel were arriving. Fire service members were carrying the heavy gear that was going to be needed to stabilise the platform and then cut it up to remove it, which would give medics access to a lot more victims—if any had survived. In his peripheral vision, James could see Eddie attaching a black label to the ankle of someone whose upper body was under the edge of the platform. He lay down to try and see beneath the obstruction.

'Can anyone hear me?' he called loudly.

There was only silence after his call. Could anyone have survived not only the fall but being crushed beneath something this solid? Eddie called again, however.

'If you can make any noise at all, calling or tapping will let us know where you are. We're not going anywhere until we get everybody out, okay?'

James could see several ambulance officers standing, with packs on their backs and other gear like oxygen tanks and defibrillators in their hands, where the track

was at its closest to this section of the creek. Two more
arrived who had their gear in a Stokes rescue basket and
he could see how eager they were to be told who they
could attend to first and who would need to be packaged
for winching out by helicopter or carried out in the basket stretcher to where their ambulances would have been
parked at the casualty clearing station.

It was the job of the medical incident officer to make
those decisions. James could hear a helicopter approaching now and he knew that, if the resources were available, it would be preferable for anybody who'd been red
or yellow carded to be stabilised and then winched from
the scene. Chances of survival would be greatly increased
by being flown to definitive care in an emergency department rather than delaying that journey by being carried for too long over a rough mountain track and then
possibly have an ambulance transfer to get somewhere
a helicopter could land. With the influx of rescuers and
equipment now, it would be impossible to clear this area
enough for someone to land where Gus had delivered
his crew.

He turned back from his sweeping gaze of the scene
to find Sarah watching him.

'You okay?' he asked quietly.

She nodded. James had already known that she would
be fine but he'd needed to check. 'Stay here and work
with Eddie,' he told her. 'Jodie and I need to step back
and manage the resources we're getting, here. Jodie?'

Sarah watched James and Jodie walking to where the
entrance point at the track was getting crowded with so
many people and so much equipment. It was overwhelm-

ing to try and look down on this as a big picture and decide what needed to be done and who needed to be treated
first and she was grateful she didn't need to be the one
making those decisions.

How amazing was it that Ivy's father *was* the person
who was capable of doing just that? Even the way James
was holding himself as he walked—his shoulders back,
walking as if he knew exactly where he was going and
why—was enough to inspire confidence.

And deep, deep respect…

'Sarah…?' Eddie's voice was deceptively calm. He'd
moved a piece of timber to get to someone further around
the platform. 'Can you find a tourniquet in my kit, please?
I've got a femoral bleed here and I don't want to take the
pressure off.'

Unzipping the pack made a sound that Sarah would
later remember marked what felt like the real start to this
mission. When things got so busy that, looking back, it
became a blur. There was a base layer of all the physical
tasks she was completing, assisting paramedic teams as
they assessed, treated and packaged patients for transport, but every one of her senses was overloaded with
the enormity of the whole scene.

The volume and complexity of sounds was extraordinary. There were people near her asking for equipment
or drugs to be found or something to be done, like keeping pressure on a bleeding wound or checking vital signs
by taking a pulse or blood pressure. There were people
shouting instructions further away, like the rescue crews
who were trying to stabilise the platform by placing sloping metal struts that had a flat base and could telescope
out with a rachet mechanism to fix themselves to what-

ever needed to be made secure. Occasionally there was
the roar of a chainsaw or the deafening beat of helicopter rotors as an aircraft hovered to lower a stretcher and
then winch a patient onboard and sometimes there was
the heartrending cry of someone in terrible pain.

And those sounds, along with the dreadful injuries
Sarah was seeing, added a layer of emotion to this experience that she knew she couldn't afford to even begin
to process until this was over.

Jodie left the scene with one of the most critical red
card patients they winched up to a helicopter. At one
stage Sarah was helping Eddie as he assessed Catherine, who was still conscious but only just. She was confused about where she was and what had happened and
her blood pressure was low enough to suggest she had
some major internal bleeding going on. Eddie upgraded
her priority to red and got her on the next helicopter that
became available.

Sarah had seen James on more than one occasion but
not to speak to. He was in one place and then another,
checking on patients and directing new medical teams
to where they were needed. He was talking to firemen
and Search and Rescue people and at one point she saw
him speaking to a team that then began the grim task
of taking the fatalities away by stretcher, presumably to
a temporary morgue until they could be identified and
relatives informed.

James was much closer to Sarah when he came to
watch a section of the platform being lifted clear, but she
stayed where she was for a moment because she already
knew that the first victim they would access was the person that Eddie had long ago attached a black label to. She

watched James in the hope of catching his gaze. Perhaps he would tell her where she should go next, given that the number of medics on scene were now outnumbering the number of people needing their attention. Sarah had even found time and space to check her own blood glucose level, which was, amazingly, still within an acceptable range despite all the stress, but she made herself eat something anyway.

She was still watching James as the fire officers stepped back and she saw his face as he took in what he could see, which was, presumably, a tangle of bodies. The sombre moment seemed contagious enough for the general noise level to suddenly drop and it was in that quiet beat that Sarah heard what sounded like a cry.

A man revved the chainsaw, stepping in to tackle the next section of the platform, but Sarah waved at him.

'Stop,' she yelled. 'I think I heard something.'

James walked towards her. 'I was told this whole area had been checked several times for any survivors.'

'I'm not sure,' Sarah admitted. 'But…it felt like someone was calling. From somewhere under the middle.'

James held up his arms. 'Can everyone be quiet, please? We need to be able to hear.'

The chainsaw was switched off. People stopped talking. Thankfully, there were no helicopters approaching or hovering right now.

Sarah knelt beside the smashed edge of the platform and peered beneath it to the narrow gap made by the boulders it was resting on. The torch on her helmet lit up the darkness and she gasped, lifting her head to find James right beside her.

'Oh, my God…there's someone here,' she told him.

'And she's alive…' She dropped flat again. 'Hey…' she called. 'I'm Sarah… What's your name?'

'Mika…'

Sarah had been doing so well keeping her own emotions under control, but this—finding someone alive when it seemed like all hope had been lost—brought tears to her eyes and a catch to her voice.

'We're going to get you out, Mika, okay?'

'Okay…'

Sarah shifted as she felt James squeeze closer to be able to see what she could see, but there was a sound of distress from Mika.

'Don't go away…' she said. 'Sarah…?'

'I'm here, darling. I've got James with me. He's a doctor…'

'Mika?' There was a gentle tone in James's voice. 'Are you having any trouble breathing?'

'I…don't think so…'

'Does anything hurt?'

'My legs… There's something on top of them. Something really heavy…' Mika's voice broke in a sob. 'Please…help me… Get me out…'

There were people crowded behind where Sarah and James were lying on the ground.

'We could lift that section of the platform and give you access right now,' a fire officer said. He started to call instructions to his team, but James cut him off.

'No…wait…' James disappeared as he scrambled back to his feet.

Eddie was there as well and Sarah could just hear him explaining to the fireman why they had to wait to free this victim.

'She could have an extremely heavy weight on top of her legs. She's been under there for hours now.'

'If the weight gets lifted before we've treated her, she'll get the effects of something called crush syndrome,' James added.

He must have turned away or lowered his voice so that there was no chance of Mika hearing, but Sarah knew what he would be saying—that lifting a heavy weight from where it had been crushing a significant part of a human body could release toxins that could cause dysrhythmias and cardiac arrest. They needed to protect Mika from that danger by giving her intravenous fluids and drugs that would counteract the acid, myoglobin and potassium leaking out of dying muscle cells. Putting tourniquets on between the crushed area and the rest of the body could also help, but how were they going to be able to do any of that in this horribly limited space? Even someone Sarah's size would have difficulty getting close enough to touch Mika.

Or would they?

Sarah wriggled forward a few inches. And then a few more. Her helmet was scraping against wood but she had enough room to move her arms quite freely. She stretched out her hand. Mika stretched out hers and their fingers touched. A heartbeat later and Sarah was holding Mika's hand and there was no holding back emotion in this instant. Sarah hadn't felt like this since she'd held Ivy, moments after the baby had taken her first breath. Or when she'd held Karly, moments after *she* had taken her last.

'It's okay,' Sarah said, her voice raw. 'We're going to take care of you, Mika. We're going to get you out of here…'

* * *

James had seen the top of Sarah's body disappear beneath the edge of the platform and the sudden bolt of what felt like fear took him by surprise. She was putting herself in danger.

He didn't want anything to happen to her.

For Ivy's sake...

The fire officer was watching too. 'It's stable enough,' he said. 'If you can reach her to do what you need to do, that's all good. I'll get our guys in position to lift things off as soon as you give the go-ahead.'

James lay down again and tried to join Sarah in the space beneath the planks of wood but it took only seconds to realise he wouldn't be able to get anywhere near Mika. He could, however, talk to Sarah and reach far enough to pass her things. He had Eddie outside, who could deliver whatever he asked for. In this almost underground space it felt like they were cut off from the outside world, but there was strength to be found in not being alone here with someone who desperately needed their help.

He could do this. With Sarah.

They could do this.

'Can you get any vital signs?' he asked. 'A heart and respiration rate? What's her radial pulse like?'

'She's breathing well,' Sarah told him. 'Heart rate's a hundred and ten but she's got a good radial pulse and steady rhythm. Mika? If no pain was zero and ten was the worst you could imagine, how would you score the pain in your legs?'

'Ten...'

'We'll give you something for that right now,' James

promised. 'Sarah, can you get close enough to be able to administer some intranasal fentanyl as a starting point?'

'Yes… I think so.'

Eddie found a syringe and drew up the drug. James reached to put it in Sarah's hand.

'There's an atomiser on the end of the syringe. Get Mika to turn her head to one side if she can. Aim for the centre of the nasal cavity before pushing the plunger.'

Her fingers brushed his as she took the syringe. 'Okay.'

James could see how awkward it was for Sarah to move but she somehow made it look easy. 'What about getting IV access?' he asked. 'We need to get some fluids running. Intraosseous if we can't get a vein.'

'I've got good access to the elbow and hopefully Mika's blood pressure is enough for it not to be too hard to find a vein. Pass me a tourniquet?'

James handed her the tourniquet and then an alcohol wipe and a cannula. He held his own gaze steady to help give Sarah more light, so he saw the moment she got access to a vein and the skill with which she eased the cannula into place and then managed to secure it, all the while keeping up a steady stream of communication with Mika to let her know what she was doing.

'Keep your arm nice and still for me… Good girl… that's perfect. Sharp scratch now… There…all done. I'm just going to tape it on so it won't get pulled out. We'll be able to give you more medicine for that pain soon…'

She sounded so calm, James thought. As if she knew exactly what she was doing and had every confidence that it would work. If he was Mika, he would find it very reassuring. He would believe every word she said. He'd also seen the skill she'd already displayed in the work she

was doing. He would believe she was capable of whatever she set her mind to achieving.

Eddie had a giving set primed and ready for James to
give to Sarah to attach to the cannula plug.

'Find a pressure cuff to put on the bag of saline,' James
reminded Eddie. 'We need to get several litres of fluid
infused before we lift that weight so we'd better get on
with it.'

There were drugs to be drawn up and administered
as well. Sodium bicarbonate, calcium gluconate, nebu-
lised salbutamol. There was pain control to keep on top
of and James wanted Sarah to try and get ECG electrodes
in place so they could monitor Mika's heart rhythm before, during and after the release of the weight.

It took time, but it was no surprise that Sarah was able
to get the electrodes for a basic three-lead ECG in place
on Mika's wrists and the sides of her abdomen and when
the static subsided James was happy with what he could
see on the screen. There were no warning signs of a dangerous level of acidosis or electrolyte imbalance like flat
or missing P waves or peaked T waves.

'Sinus rhythm,' he told Sarah. 'Looking good.'

Something Sarah couldn't manage, however, was to get
combat army tourniquets around the top of Mika's legs.

'There's a broken beam just over the iliac crest level. I
can't reach past it far enough to be able to do anything.'

He could hear the effort in her voice. Pain, even.

'Don't keep trying,' he told her. 'We can be ready to
put tourniquets on the moment we get clear access. We've
got people positioned to take the weight and lift any time
now. I'll give you a countdown…'

'Sarah?' There was an urgent tone in Mika's voice. 'I'm scared… What's going to happen?'

'They're almost ready to lift the bit that's trapping your legs. It'll be bright light that might hurt your eyes and it's noisy, with lots of people around. I think I can hear a helicopter that's not far away too, and that might be coming to take you to hospital, but don't be scared. I'm right here. I won't leave you.'

'Sarah can stay with you,' James promised. 'She can come with us when we take you to hospital.'

Mika was sobbing. 'Can she hold my hand?'

'Of course I can, hon,' Sarah said. 'Here it is… You hold mine too. As tight as you need to.'

James could almost feel that hold himself as Mika's distress lessened. A short time later, he took a deep breath. They were as ready as they could be.

'On the count of three,' he called a few minutes later. 'One…two…*three*…'

The tension ramped up the instant the weight came off Mika's legs and rescuers were able to get to her. Sarah stayed lying beside her patient, amongst the rocks and broken timber, so she didn't have to let Mika's hand go as other medics moved in to take over her care and get her ready to be winched clear of the scene of this terrible incident. The monitors that would set off alarms if there were any signs that her condition was suddenly deteriorating after the removal of the weight were reassuringly quiet.

James let out the breath he hadn't realised he was holding and looked away from the screen back to Sarah. Did she realise that all the work she had done to help prepare Mika for this next phase of her rescue had paid off?

That she might have played the biggest part in saving a life, here?

Sarah had streaks of dirt and blood and possibly tears on her face and she was squinting in the glare of daylight but, as she looked up to catch his gaze, there was a hint of a smile there as well.

A nanosecond of private communication just between them before the controlled chaos of continuing and extending Mika's treatment began.

We did it...

And in that same moment that was no more than a passing flash, James remembered again that he'd once thought he would never have noticed Sarah Harrison if their paths had crossed on a busy street. That she wasn't remotely like the gorgeous women he'd always chosen to get closer to.

This time, however, despite the way she was looking right now, James knew exactly how wrong he had been. Sarah wasn't simply special, or skilled, or impressive in the things she could do or her attitude to life.

She was absolutely stunning.

With that amazing ability the brain had to register emotions that covered so much detail in such a tiny fragment of time, James was also aware of something else.

Relief?

That Sarah Harrison would never appreciate, let alone reciprocate, any kind of attraction. Ivy was the person who mattered above all else in any relationship he was going to have with Sarah and life was complicated enough already, wasn't it? He was a father now, for heaven's sake, and he had to learn to juggle new responsibilities with the work that he had devoted his adult life to so far. He had a brother coming home very soon who would need considerable support for the foreseeable future. His social—and sex—life felt no more important than a distant memory.

Priorities had changed so much that major parts of his life were unrecognisable. Thank goodness some things hadn't changed. Like the focus needed to get a critically ill patient into an emergency department and, most likely, into Theatre in order to save her life.

Sarah was still holding Mika's hand as the paramedic crew worked to splint and dress her badly crushed legs so that she could be transferred to a stretcher. One that was being lowered from the Aberdeen Air Ambulance helicopter that was hovering directly overhead, so that had to be Jodie who was bringing it down. Eddie would want to travel back with the last patient he was treating who needed to be evacuated and there was no reason for James to stay on scene any longer either.

He could end an experience he was going to remember every detail of for the rest of his life in the same way he'd started it.

With Sarah…

CHAPTER EIGHT

THE BEEPING OF her phone to announce the arrival of a new text message was becoming a welcome sound.

The first message had arrived almost as soon as Sarah had carried Ivy inside after getting her home from the hospital as darkness fell.

Is Ivy okay?

Sarah had texted back.

All good. People in the creche awesome. They stayed late when they knew we were on our way back. How's Mika doing?

In CT. Theatre on standby.

Keep me posted.

A 'thumbs-up' emoji appeared on her screen.

Sarah got the fire going, carried a now grizzly Ivy into the kitchen and managed to make herself a slice of toast and prepare a bottle for the baby virtually one-handed.

'We both need to eat,' she explained. 'And sleep. I don't think I've ever been this tired in my life.'

But she wouldn't have missed any of it, Sarah thought as she settled herself on the couch, smiling at Ivy's contented snuffling as she attached herself to the bottle and got stuck into her dinner.

'Your daddy wasn't wrong,' she murmured. 'You are a wee piglet.' She took a large bite of the peanut butter toast and then reached for her phone as it beeped again.

CT scan suggests one leg can't be salvaged. Maybe both.

Oh, no. Poor Mika.

She's still alive. Cardiac and renal function okay.

I feel bad I didn't stay. I promised I would.

She was intubated by the time you left. She didn't notice, I promise.

James had added a smiley face emoji.

I'm going to come home soon myself. Surgery might take hours.

Good thinking. You must be exhausted.

There was a short silence then, and Sarah put the phone down to shift Ivy's weight and tilt the bottle to a better angle. The new beeping was a surprise because she thought the conversation had finished.

You were amazing today, Sarah. I'll bet Mika will never forget the person who was brave enough to be under there with her and do what it took to save her life.

Sarah found herself blinking back tears as she responded.

You were there too, you know.

Not likely to ever forget...

This time the silence was longer and Sarah used it to scroll a news feed which linked her to a broadcast about the tragedy in the Scottish mountains today.

'There are six people in hospital,' a newsreader announced. 'The number of fatalities has risen to twelve, but that may go up. Three of the young victims are in serious or critical condition in the Queen Mother's Hospital in Aberdeen.'

Sarah hadn't noticed anyone with cameras at the scene today but she was seeing footage of the crowd of rescue workers and a helicopter in the distance overhead. And then she saw a large section of that platform being lifted and there *she* was...lying on her stomach, holding Mika's hand.

Good grief...she was barely recognisable as she turned to blink at the brighter light but Sarah could remember that moment so vividly. She could remember seeing James and the wash of emotion that had to be the peak of what had been an overwhelming experience that they had been through together. She'd known that they had forged a bond in the last few hours that would link them for the rest of their lives—even if they weren't already linked, thanks to Ivy.

This was a much more personal bond that was just between the two of them. One that had underscored that trust she already had in James, but this was more than knowing he would protect and care for Ivy.

It almost felt as if she was under that umbrella of protection. Not just because he'd pulled her through that hypoglycaemic crisis the first night they'd met—any doctor would have done that.

No... Feeling like this was part of a new bond too. Because Sarah would never forget the way he'd looked at her after they'd walked around as they began the triage on that horrific scene together and the first thing he'd asked was whether *she* was okay.

Oh, help... Emotions were threatening to do her head in right now. Sarah swiped her screen to end the images that were taking her back to the scene. Ivy's lips were slack around the teat of the bottle so she put it down beside her half-eaten toast and moved Ivy upright onto her shoulder to rub her back.

The baby's burp made her remember the first time James had done this. His laughter and that grin on his face.

The tears that were escaping now felt like happy ones, but it was a warning that Sarah needed to keep an eye on herself. She should probably check her blood glucose levels and have more to eat.

Oddly, it was right at that moment that her phone beeped again.

Have you eaten? I could pick up some Thai food or a pizza on the way home.

Sarah sent back the emoji of lip-licking.

Pizza please. Calzone is my favourite.

It felt as if he was going home.

To be with the most important people in his life, even. How weird was that?

He'd had no idea that Sarah Harrison even existed such a short time ago and he certainly hadn't dreamed that he had a child of his own.

It all felt a bit too emotional as James pulled into the driveway of what was, he reminded himself, his sister's home, not *his*.

His head was all over the place, to be honest. He'd seen too much, done too much and felt way too much over too many hours and he was totally exhausted, physically, mentally and emotionally.

He was also starving and the smell of the wood-fired pizzas on the passenger seat of his sister's car was driving him nuts, although they were nowhere near as hot as they had been when he'd collected the takeaway order. It would be very easy to heat them up again in the oven, however, and James was feeling good about being able to do something for Sarah, who had to be just as wrung-out as he was. Providing a meal was a basic but always welcome gesture of caring for someone.

It was even better to offer a favourite meal.

'These guys apparently make the most authentic pizzas in Aberdeen,' he told her as he carried the boxes inside. 'And I have some red wine. Because you can't eat Italian without some red wine, right?'

Sarah was smiling. 'I do believe I've heard that rule somewhere.'

'Did you get my text about putting the oven on?'

'I did. It's hot.'

'Let's get these pizzas warming up, then. And find some wine glasses.'

It was Sarah who found the cupboard where the wine glasses were stored. She was standing on tiptoe to reach them as James closed the oven door, after putting the pizzas on a baking tray. He straightened up to find he was suddenly standing far closer to Sarah than he had expected. Bumping her arm, in fact.

'Oops…sorry.' James could see what she was doing now. 'Let me get those glasses for you.' He reached up but Sarah still had her arm there and he bumped her again. And then they did a version of those awkward, impromptu dance moves that happened when you were in the street trying to avoid a stranger's path but you both moved in the same direction.

Sarah laughed and stopped moving.

So did James.

And then, for what felt like a very long moment, they simply looked at each other. Sarah looked as tired as he felt. And…

'Did you realise you still have mud on your face?'

'What? I washed it.'

'Well, it is kind of hiding, I guess.' James touched the

streak on the angle of Sarah's jaw, just below her ear, that ran into her hair.

He knew instantly that he shouldn't have done that. But how could someone's skin generate a sensation that felt like actual electricity? James had never felt anything quite like that in his life. It seemed like Sarah might have also been aware of the sensation. She had already stopped moving but now it felt as if she had just frozen. As if she was totally shocked by his touch.

James dropped his hand, but not quite fast enough. Or perhaps it was the fact that he'd made eye contact with Sarah that was making this suddenly so intense? Under this light it looked as if that rich hazel colour had flecks of gold in it. Like stars, or fragments of sunshine. Her lips were slightly parted and...

And all James could think of for one heartbeat, and then another, was touching those lips with his own so that he could find out if they were as soft and delicious as they looked.

Good grief... He needed to get a grip. He also needed to break that eye contact before Sarah could have any idea what was running through his overtired brain.

'Sorry,' he murmured again. Then he took a breath. 'Right. Glasses. Wine. Let's go and sit by the fire for a few minutes until our dinner's warm enough.'

'Yes, let's.' Sarah was turning away.

She touched her face herself as she did so, her fingers finding the patch that marred the softness of her skin. Astonishingly, James could feel a faint aftershock of that jolting sensation, as if he was touching her skin again himself.

'I had no idea I'd missed that bit of dirt.' Sarah shook

her head. 'I was waiting to have a proper shower and wash my hair after Ivy was settled.'

She was speaking quickly, as if she needed a distraction. Or perhaps she was determined to ignore the possibility that an irresponsible playboy and/or a sex addict might have just made some kind of move on her?

And that was just what James needed to flick off the unacceptable switch of feeling physically attracted to Sarah. He didn't want to prove her right.

'You never got a chance to show me those pictures of the house you looked at this morning. Can you send me the link to the website?'

'I've probably still got it open on my browser.' Sarah picked up her phone. 'Yes…it's right here. Look…'

They sipped the excellent red wine he'd opened as James scrolled through images on a website and then they ate the delicious calzone pizzas with their crisp, egg-washed and parmesan-dusted dough encasing pepperoni and fresh mozzarella, onion, spinach and mushrooms.

'This is *so* good.' Sarah sighed.

'This house is so good.' James was having another look at the images. 'It's not far at all from where Eddie and Jodie are living.'

'Really? I'd like that,' Sarah said. 'It would be good to be in the city as well. I mean, I love being out in the country but when you're on your own with a baby it can get a bit…lonely…sometimes.'

Of course it could. Especially when you were grieving the loss of a friend who was as close as a sister. Maybe grieving the loss of a chosen lifestyle as well. Having worked so closely with Sarah today, James knew how good she was at her job and that she had the same kind of passion for her work as he did himself.

'The house is close to Queen's. That's a bonus too.'

After today, it was obvious that Sarah could easily fit in with his new department. Was it possible that Sarah might consider a move to Aberdeen, even? No…he was getting ahead of himself. James didn't even have a permanent job at Queen's himself. They needed to take this journey one step at a time.

'Three bedrooms,' he added. 'And two of them have ensuite bathrooms…' He found a smile as he glanced sideways in time to catch Sarah eating the last bite of her pizza. 'That's one each for you and me and Ivy could have the one without the bathroom.'

'It's quite expensive…' Sarah chased down her bite of food with some wine. 'But I do have someone I used to work with in Leeds who's keen to take over Karly's room in the apartment we shared. She's going to pack up some more clothes and things and send them up to me by courier so I don't have to do that drive again just yet.'

'That's helpful. It's a long drive.'

'It wouldn't work long-term because I'll need that room for Ivy, but it will give her the time to find somewhere else. And she'll pay for the room, which means I could help with the rent of this place for as long as I'm here.'

James shook his head. 'You're not going to pay any rent,' he said firmly. 'The house I move into is going to be my home for the foreseeable future.' He waited for Sarah to lift her gaze and meet his and he spoke carefully. 'I want you—and Ivy—to feel as if it's your home as well. For now,' he added, to dilute any pressure his words might imply. 'And for whenever you visit later maybe, until we decide what we're going to do long-term.'

He broke the eye contact to check his watch. 'I don't think it's too late to call the agent.' He tapped the phone's screen. 'If it's still available, let's find out just how fast we could make this happen. We need to find somewhere before Ella and Logan get back home.'

He ended the call a short time later as Sarah came back from carrying their dirty dishes into the kitchen. 'The house is currently empty and the lease could be taken over as soon as the paperwork is signed and the fees paid. I've asked for an option to be held for me until to-morrow afternoon. The agent's going to be there at mid-day to get the meter read and I said I'd come and have a quick look on my way to work and make a decision then. It's good timing. There's a departmental meeting first thing, which is a debrief for today's major incident response so I need to be there, but I'm not starting my shift until two o'clock.'

'I'll be in town then too. I've got an appointment for Ivy's vaccinations at a medical centre at eleven o'clock. Could I come and have a look with you? I'd love to see inside the house.'

'Of course… I wouldn't want to take the house if you found you hated it.'

'I won't hate it.' Sarah sounded quite sure. 'I think I love it already.'

James could feel some of the emotional overload of the day lifting at the prospect of something positive on the horizon. 'Sarah…?'

Her glance was curious. 'Yeah…?'

'Thank you…'

Did she realise that he was thanking her for more than finding a house they could share for the next little while? That her willingness to give him time to adjust to being a father and redefine his life was... Well, it was a gift, that was what it was.

Sarah's smile was shy, as if she was embarrassed by his appreciation.

'I'm going to go and have a shower,' she told him, scrambling to her feet. 'Apparently I have dirt on my face...'

The hot water was rinsing away any visible remnants of the day, along with the shampoo bubbles that were streaming down Sarah's body, making her skin feel slippery as she brushed them away. She closed her eyes and let it rain directly on her face to simply enjoy the sensation of the warmth and water for a moment longer.

Except it wasn't really the water she was thinking about, was it?

It was the memory of James touching that soft skin on her neck, just below her ear. That spear of sensation that had shot straight into the core of her body that probably had a lot to do with the look he was giving her. As if he wanted to *kiss* her...?

A look he'd probably given women a thousand times over the years so it was no wonder he was so good at it.

It was no wonder Karly had succumbed to it either. She wouldn't have had the slightest hesitation in grabbing that moment in the kitchen and letting James kiss her. She could almost hear her friend's voice as a whisper in her ear.

'You need to live a little, Sass. We both know how short life can be...'

Sarah shifted just enough for the needles of hot water to be hitting her breasts instead of straight onto her face. What would it be like, she wondered, to be more like Karly and embrace moments in life like that?

To let someone, who was in no way a candidate for a meaningful relationship of any kind, kiss her senseless? Make love to her, even...?

Would she discover what other people seemed to find so compelling about sex that had, so far, totally passed her by?

Oh, my... Sarah shut the water supply off in the hope of shutting off that particular line of thought. She'd never broken the rules she'd made for herself regarding men. They were as iron-clad as the rules she had developed for managing her blood glucose levels and healthy eating regime.

Pizza and wine had been a bit of a treat but that was okay.

Sex with James Grisham would not be okay. He was Ivy's father and this whole situation was quite complicated enough. Sarah wrapped a towel around her body as she realised she hadn't brought the soft leggings and oversized tee shirt she wore as sleepwear into the bathroom. She picked up another towel to squeeze some of the dampness out of her hair as she left the bathroom.

And then she realised she'd left her phone downstairs because James had been using it to call the estate agent about the house. Without thinking, she opened her door, planning to dash downstairs and retrieve her phone so she could make sure she hadn't missed an alert about her glucose levels.

The last thing she expected to see was James standing right in front of her, with only a towel wrapped around his waist, his skin still glistening with moisture. He'd washed *his* hair too, and it was sleek against his head in dark tousled curls. He hadn't shaved so his jaw was shadowed and…and so damn *sexy*…

Sarah dropped her gaze so that she could make contact with his eyes because she knew he would be able to tell exactly what she was thinking, but now she could see the definition of muscles in those bare arms and the gorgeous olive colour of his skin. And…

And she could see her phone in his hand.

'I thought you might need this,' James said. 'My bad. I just remembered I'd been using your phone to call the agent, not mine.'

Oh, man…

Had this been the biggest mistake James had ever made?

He could see way too much of Sarah's skin. He could feel the soft heat of it. Worse, he could *smell* it and it was the most compelling aroma ever…

He heard a tiny sound which might have been Sarah trying—and failing—to say something. Or was it Ivy, stirring in her bassinet in the far corner of this large bedroom?

The thought that this might be a very good time for Ivy to wake up and demand attention slid through the back of his mind so fast it simply evaporated. Because it was at that moment that Sarah looked up at him and the heat between them was enough to be melting something.

Common sense, perhaps?

That thought didn't gain any traction either. Because James knew that Sarah was feeling this heat just as much as he was. The way her pupils had dilated so much it made her eyes look black suggested that she was perfectly well aware of what was hanging so palpably in the air between them. He remembered that moment in the kitchen when he'd first thought of kissing her and the desire to do so had been like nothing he was familiar with. Had that astonishing intensity been there because of what Sarah was thinking—and feeling? That she had wanted to kiss *him*? Despite her opinion of his past history with women? Or was it because of it?

Because she knew that this didn't have to be a big deal. That they were two people who were seriously attracted to each other. Two people who'd shared an extraordinary—and exhausting—experience today and were both too tired to worry about a bigger picture. Maybe they needed the escape. Or the joy of something so life-affirming?

But still, James hesitated.

Until he saw a big droplet of water from her wet hair escape and trickle down her forehead to catch on her eyebrow. It was a purely instinctive action to lift his hand and use his thumb to brush the drip away before it could get any closer to her eyes. His gaze never left hers and, beneath that tiny skin-to-skin contact, James could actually feel Sarah leaning into his touch as she let her eyelids begin to drift shut.

He slid his hand into the warmth of her damp hair to

cradle the back of her head and watched her lips part as she tilted her head in invitation for the kiss that was as inevitable as taking his next breath.

But still, James held back. He bent his head enough to touch his forehead to Sarah's. He turned it so that his cheek could feel the side of her head without actually touching it. He let his nose brush hers as softly as a feather and he would have done it all over again except for the whisper of a sigh from Sarah that sounded like surrender.

Or maybe it was the sound of some kind of key being turned. A lock being opened.

An invitation for both of them to step into a totally private place?

He brushed his lips against hers. Once…twice…

The third time he let them settle, his whole body tuned to the tiniest nuances in Sarah's response that would tell him, far better than any words, whether this was something she really wanted as much as he did.

It was a long, long moment before James broke that contact in order to take a breath.

And this time he was the one to let it out in a sigh that was, most definitely, complete surrender…

CHAPTER NINE

IT MUST BE TRUE.

Practice really did make perfect, didn't it?

How else could James be so good at making something so world-rocking as far as Sarah was concerned seem like nothing particularly out of the ordinary?

It probably helped a lot, mind you, when the sound of his phone ringing floated up the stairs in that space of time where they were both beginning to catch their breath after the most intense sexual experience Sarah had ever had in her life.

'I'd better get that.' He dropped a quick kiss on Sarah's forehead. 'I asked them to let me know when Mika got out of Theatre.'

James had his towel wrapped around his waist again when he returned to sit on the side of Sarah's bed a short time later.

'She's in Recovery,' he told her.

'How is she?'

'Stable. They're ready to transfer her to the intensive care unit.' But there was a catch in his voice. 'She's lost one leg. Transfemoral amputation. She's going to need more surgery on the other leg, including a full knee replacement, but the surgeons are cautiously hopeful they can save it.'

Sarah could feel them both being sucked back onto the rollercoaster of this extraordinary day and the crash from the high point she was falling from, after James had just physically taken her somewhere she had never quite believed really existed, felt like it could be devastating. But James caught—and held—her gaze.

'You okay?'

Two tiny words. The same words he'd used at the scene today, after those awful first minutes when they had begun their daunting task of dealing with death and disaster. When he'd made her feel as though he cared about how she was feeling. There was time, now, to feel the squeeze on her heart with the thought that there was still someone in the world who really cared about her. It was enough to change the angle of that rollercoaster and put the brakes on that fall.

'She's alive,' Sarah said quietly. 'And that's a bit of a miracle so…yeah… I'm okay.'

But James was still holding her gaze and Sarah could sense the undertone to his query. Was he checking in to make sure she wasn't upset about the dramatic change that had just occurred in how well they knew each other?

She wasn't. Sarah had willingly taken the risk of breaking her own rules and wondering if she could be more like Karly and it was fair to say it had been a very successful experiment. All she needed now was to channel a bit more of Karly to be able to handle the aftermath so it didn't create any issues that might affect them being able to share the parenting of Ivy in any way.

This wasn't a situation Sarah had ever been in before

but instinct told her to keep it light. To give James—or perhaps both of them—the chance to escape by making it clear that it had been a one-off?

So she made a face as she blew out a sigh. 'It's been quite a day, hasn't it?'

'Sure has.'

'Are *you* okay?'

'Never better.' There was something in his eyes that was definitely a compliment but Sarah pretended not to notice.

'You must be as tired as I am.' Her lips curled into just more than a hint of a smile. 'We were exhausted already but then we threw some wine and sex into the mix.' Her smile widened a little. 'What were we thinking?' The smile was fading now. 'But…thank you,' she whispered.

He didn't ask what she was thanking him for. Maybe he thought it was for simply asking if she was okay after the news about Mika. Or for his support during the gruelling hours of being part of that disaster scene today.

Or might he have guessed it was for making love to her as if she was the most beautiful, *desirable*, woman in the entire world? As if the feel and taste of her body was all he could ever want. As if everything she'd been brave enough to do back to him had been better than anything he'd expected?

It didn't matter. She had let him know she appreciated any or all of those things. And she'd offered him a way out. She'd let him know that she could be like Karly and not make their sexual encounter any more significant than it was intended to be. That it had been a combination of factors that had led to something that neither of them had planned and she had no expectations that it was going to happen again.

James seemed to have got the message because he smiled back at her. 'I should be thanking you...' Then he leaned in and cupped her head with his hand, tilting it so he could press a kiss onto Sarah's hair. 'Sleep well...'

'What's her name?'

'Ivy.' James was carrying the car seat after helping Sarah get it out of her car.

'She's so *cute*.' The estate agent, Maureen, unlocked the front door of the stone house in Ferryhill. 'I absolutely adore that hair. How old is she?'

'Eight weeks.' It was Sarah who answered this time. She cast an anxious glance at Ivy and reached to make a tiny adjustment to the fuzzy pink blanket tucked around her. Taking her for all those vaccinations had been more stressful than she had anticipated, but Ivy seemed to be coping remarkably well now that the poking with needles and having to swallow nasty-tasting liquid was over with.

'This is the perfect family home,' Maureen said happily. 'I can't wait for you to see the garden.'

The hallway was wide enough for a bicycle to be propped against a wall.

'No problem to fit a pram in here,' Maureen pointed out. 'And so many lovely walks to go on with the river tracks not far away and Duthie Park just down the road. Imagine how good it will be, having picnics there in the summer—or maybe a birthday party for wee Ivy in the playground in years to come? They've got magic fairy houses there.'

James shared a glance with Sarah that took a moment

to interpret. Was he apologetic or slightly horrified that Maureen was assuming they were a couple with the baby they shared?

Had she been mistaken in thinking that James, thanks to all that practice of being the perfect playboy, had been able to make it remarkably easy to smooth over any awkwardness of some rather large personal boundaries having been crossed? That perhaps the thought of being seen as a couple was enough of a shock for such a committed bachelor to make James regret what had happened last night?

She hadn't had that impression first thing this morning. James had certainly been in a bit of a hurry this morning to get into work for that departmental meeting, but he'd come into the kitchen to grab a coffee while Sarah was feeding Ivy and it had felt—almost—as if nothing had changed.

Ivy had even unleashed one of her loud burps having finished her breakfast and it had become an automatic trigger to make eye contact with James and share a smile. And yes…there might have been a deeper level to that eye contact and smile, but Ivy was grinning at them both and Sarah had definitely felt a wash of something like pure relief.

She was okay.

They were okay…

She didn't want James to start regretting what had happened between them.

Sarah certainly wasn't going to regret it.

Hopefully, her casual shrug would reassure him that she wasn't bothered by Maureen's assumption. It would have been odd if she hadn't thought they were Ivy's parents and were interested in renting this house as a family home. And Sarah wasn't about to tell a complete stranger what the unusual relationship was between herself and James.

She wasn't exactly sure she knew precisely what it was herself now.

She tried to seem engrossed, taking in all the features of the lovely sitting room they entered, with the polished wooden floor, high ceilings and the old register grate with the brightly coloured, flower-patterned tiles set into the cast-iron frame. What she was really thinking about, however, was the most amazing night of her entire life.

Who knew that sex could be *that* good?

That there didn't need to be any awkwardness or embarrassment or disappointment that lingered long after that particular milestone in a relationship was reached?

Okay... Sarah gave her head a tiny shake as she followed Maureen and James out of the sitting room and through a dining area that led into a large kitchen, making the ground floor of this house a very attractive, light-filled open-plan living space. She looked down at the beautiful flagstone floor but she was actually giving herself a firm reminder that, even in her imagination, she needed to correct her terminology.

She wasn't in any kind of romantic relationship with James. Even if that phone call hadn't interrupted the afterglow last night, she couldn't imagine that there would have been any romantic cuddling going on. It had only been about the sex.

And even if they ended up having sex every night for as long as she was in Aberdeen—the thought of which sent a rather delicious thrill down the length of Sarah's spine—any new dimension to the partnership they'd been thrown into was…

Temporary, that was what it was.

Sarah was still tired today, but she made an attempt to focus on this house tour in case James wanted to discuss it later. Upstairs, there were two charming bedrooms with sloping walls and dormer windows, one of which looked out over a private back garden. There was a wooden bench to sit on, against a background of hydrangea bushes with bright blue flowers, and a tree in front of it with a branch that curved over the grass and…

'There's a swing,' she said in delight.

'Isn't it perfect?' Maureen beamed. 'I knew you'd love it.'

It *was* perfect. Sarah could see herself sitting on that bench with James sitting beside her. They were both watching Ivy—who was big enough to be bending her little legs and pushing them out to make herself swing. Sarah could almost catch a glimpse of a dog lying close to the trunk of the tree.

The bubble of the idyllic family scenario popped a heartbeat later as Maureen ushered them towards the master bedroom suite. It wasn't going to happen, was it? At some point, Sarah was going to return to her own life and the job she had in Leeds. And yes, maybe James had suggested that he might be up for moving to Leeds, but that would depend entirely on where he was able to find a permanent job. And with all his family here in Aberdeen it seemed very unlikely that he'd want to move right out of Scotland.

James seemed to be standing very still as he stood and looked at a very pretty bedroom that boasted a chandelier and built-in wardrobes. Was he thinking of how much room there was for sharing that bed? Was he wondering whether life would return to normal once Sarah and Ivy had returned to Leeds and would only be visiting? It was quite possible James was looking forward to having that kind of distance between them.

It didn't matter how good the sex had been, did it? Or that Sarah would be quite prepared to trust James with her life. He was not the kind of man who would ever be content to be confined in a traditional monogamous relationship and nuclear family and he was most certainly not the kind of man that Sarah had been looking to share *her* life with. Like those reliable, predictable men she had dated in the past and, for a chosen few, had gone to bed with.

Not one of them had ever taken her to paradise and back again, like James had done with such apparent ease last night.

As if he caught the gist of her thoughts, James threw a glance over his shoulder and Sarah suddenly knew that he'd actually been thinking about her as he'd been looking at that bed. What was even more disconcerting was that the look in his eyes also told her that he was more than up for doing it all over again. If she was...

Oh, help... Sarah could feel herself blushing. Just as well Maureen was looking down at Ivy again.

'Look at those red wee cheeks,' she said. 'Is it too warm for you in here, my love?'

It was too warm for Sarah, that was for sure. She stepped out of the main bedroom and a few steps took her to the top of the staircase. Something made her turn her head sharply—as if she'd seen something at the bottom of the stairs.

Or some*one*? It was clearly her imagination that was playing tricks on her.

Making her think that Karly had been standing at the foot of these stairs. Giving her a thumbs-up signal, even? Showing her approval of how Sarah had broken the rules and taken a leaf out of her own book, anyway.

Giving her permission to enjoy it as long as it lasted, perhaps?

'Live a little more, Sass... You know you want to.'

Ivy started to cry before they left the house.

'Call or text me,' Maureen said outside, handing her card to James. 'As soon as you've had a chance to talk with each other and make a decision. I've got another appointment to get to.'

She probably wanted to get away from the now shrieking baby. The sound was just what Sarah needed to jolt her out of dreaming of a future that included this family house with its swing in the garden and to stop her thinking about last night and any repercussions, including the temptation to repeat the experience. Nothing other than the present was of any importance right now. She had an unhappy baby to look after.

One who did, indeed, have very red cheeks even though they were outside in much cooler air.

'She feels a bit hot.' Sarah took the blanket off Ivy as James put the cocoon into the middle of her back seat.

'It's probably just a reaction to the vaccinations. Have you given her some paracetamol?'

'No... I was planning to give her some as soon as we got home.'

'Come past Queen's. We've got buckets of liquid paracetamol. I'm sure you'd rather have her settled before you drive home? It'll be a lot more effective if we give it to her before she gets any more miserable.'

'That's true. I could give her a feed too. That might help settle her.'

'We could feed ourselves too, if you like? I've got plenty of time before I need to start work and I've discovered the cafeteria does the best mac and cheese ever, with extra crispy breadcrumbs on the top.'

He licked his lips and Sarah felt a spear of sensation that went straight into the core of her body with enough force to be actually painful.

'Might have to see what Ivy thinks about that idea.'

James nodded. 'I'll meet you in the car park. I'll give Maureen a call on the way. I'm thinking I should take a short-term lease, at least. What do you think? It's perfect, isn't it?'

'I do love it,' Sarah admitted.

'So do I.'

Oh...

Something in his eyes was suggesting that James was thinking about that master bedroom again. The kick deep in her belly wasn't painful this time but Sarah hastily turned back to fastening the seatbelt attachments to Ivy's car seat before James could see any reflection of that desire in her own eyes.

'It's going to be your house,' she reminded him, keeping her tone deliberately light. 'It really only matters what *you* think.'

If his period of living in Aberdeen had followed the plans James had originally made, he would have been about to take over Eddie's basement apartment with Ella and Logan due to arrive home within days. He hadn't dreamed he would be agreeing over the phone to sign up for at least a six-month lease on what was a very grown-up sort of house in a very nice suburb in the city.

A family sort of house.

With three bedrooms, one of which had a very big bed.

A house that he was intending to share with Sarah Harrison for as long as she was prepared to stay on in Aberdeen herself. How much of her six-month maternity leave had she already used up? Two months, probably, if she'd started when Ivy was born but before Karly had died. That left four months.

Four months was a long time.

James pushed his hair back with his fingers as he paused at a red traffic light. Four months was way longer than James had ever dated anybody—even the ones that he could totally trust not to expect anything more than a 'friends with benefits' arrangement. If he was honest, he preferred the sort of night he'd had with Karly. Great fun but only ever going to be for a night or two.

He would never have picked Sarah as someone who was okay with casual sex.

But then he would never have guessed that she could be such an intoxicating mix of innocence and red-hot passion. Vulnerability mixed with a determination to hold nothing back in either giving or receiving pleasure.

Oh, *man*…

James needed a distraction or he'd end up reliving parts of last night's rather memorable encounter and he'd already done that—more than once—this morning.

Every time he'd seen Sarah moving around the barn

as she got herself and Ivy ready for their trip into the medical centre.

For pretty much every minute of the long drive into work. Perhaps he should have taken his motorbike instead of Ella's car and that way he would have been forced to focus even more intently on the winding country road.

It had unexpectedly intruded on his thoughts once or twice in the debrief meeting that he would have normally been totally focused on, but that was because her name had been mentioned by others, including Cameron, who had come up to James at the end of the meeting to tell him he'd been very impressed with what he'd heard about Sarah. He'd asked him to pass on the message that if she was after a job in Aberdeen, they'd be more than happy to talk to her.

And it had taken his mind—and body—hostage when he'd stood at that bedroom door and realised that they could continue playing the game that Maureen had inadvertently started and pretend that they were Ivy's parents and in a relationship. That they were a couple who would be sharing the same bed...every single night...

The thought should have been enough to have James breaking out in a cold sweat but, instead, he was finding reassurance. The timeframe might be longer than he'd ever played with before but it still had a use-by date. Sarah had a home, friends and a job to go back to in Leeds. At some point in the not-too-distant future she would choose to return to her own life and everything would change again.

Rules could be rewritten. Or reinstated?

Okay, he'd made the suggestion that he could consider moving to Leeds in order to be part of Ivy's life, but it

would be years before he could move that far away from
his family. For heaven's sake, Mick would be arriving
back very soon and helping to provide the support for his
brother was the reason he had come here at all.

James pushed a speed dial button on his Bluetooth
phone menu.

'Hey, bro. You haven't lost your telepathic abilities,'
Eddie said. 'I was about to call you. Yesterday was a bit
of a one-off, wasn't it?'

'Let's hope so.'

'How's that girl doing, do you know? Mika? The one
with the crush injury. You stayed with her after we got
her to Queen's, didn't you?'

'Until she went into Theatre, anyway. I've been up to
visit her today. She's in an induced coma in ICU at the
moment.'

'What's her renal function like?'

'Improving.'

'Potassium levels?'

'Under control.'

'She's lucky to have survived,' Eddie said. 'And that
was only because Sarah was brave enough to crawl in
there and start treating her. We would have had to lift
the weight to get near her, and that could well have been
fatal. She's quite something, isn't she?'

'Aye…' And not just professionally. Eddie had no
idea…

'Mind you, she could only do what she was doing because you were handing her everything and calibrating
the drugs and so on,' Eddie added. 'You made a good
team.'

'We did…'

'I like her.' Eddie's statement was sincere.

'So do I.'

'She's not only brave, she's smart. And she's not bad-looking either.'

James made a noncommittal sound. He wasn't about to confess to his brother that he had got rather a lot closer to Sarah Harrison in the wake of their working together. In fact, he needed to change the subject.

'I've found a place to rent in town. Ferryhill. Not far from you and Jodie, in fact. I can move in before Ella and Logan get back. Possibly tomorrow if I can organise getting the lease agreement signed and utilities sorted.'

'That's great. Maybe we could combine a housewarming for you and a welcome home party for them. It would save us all trekking out to the countryside and it's much closer to the rehab centre for Mick. Did he tell you that he's going to be moved into one of the independent units when he gets back from New Zealand? He reckons he's going to be ready to find his own place soon. He's built up his upper body strength and is managing his own transfers really well now.'

'He told me that too. He sounds a lot happier, doesn't he?'

'Just as well. I was seriously worried about him for a while back there. I didn't think he was going to climb out of that hole.'

'I got the feeling that his physiotherapist had something to do with that. Have you noticed how often he talks about Riley?'

Eddie laughed. 'I asked him if he had some extra physical therapy going on there.'

'What did he say?'

'He was offended that I would cast aspersions on her professionalism. He's her patient, after all.'

James was laughing now. 'I seem to remember we didn't think she was overly professional telling him she wouldn't work with him if he didn't stop feeling sorry for himself.'

'I do think he fancies her. Maybe he's even fallen head over heels in love and he's just embarrassed that he wants to follow my example and try a grown-up relationship that involves serious commitment for a change.'

The idea was more than a little disturbing. Would that mean the vow the brothers had made years ago about living life to the full and never risking the kind of heartache that too often came with a long-term commitment or, worse, marriage was no longer even partially intact? That an excuse for the protective barrier James had always relied on no longer existed?

But this was about Mick, not himself.

'I almost hope he has,' he admitted quietly. 'I'd give anything to see him properly happy again.'

'He did sound a lot more positive.' Eddie's tone was thoughtful. 'He said he's got a surprise for us too, but he wouldn't tell me what it was. Do you think he might be bringing Riley back with him?'

James was pulling into the hospital car park. 'I don't think she'd be coming to the other side of the world after knowing someone for just a few weeks. Nobody falls in love that quickly, do they?' He didn't give Eddie a chance to respond. 'Gotta go, but I'll call you later. We'll plan that party.'

'Onto it. Oh, hey…?'

'What?'

'Sarah's not planning to go back to Leeds before we have a chance to have the party, is she? I know Ella's desperate to meet Ivy as soon as possible.'

'She'll be here. That's why I'm renting a house and not moving into your old apartment. There's room for all of us.'

'You're moving in together?' Eddie sounded astonished. 'That's fast work, even for you, mate.'

'Not like that,' James said. He could hear the offended tone in his own voice. 'It just made sense for Sarah to stay in Aberdeen a bit longer so we can work things out.'

'And you do seem to be managing to be in the same house without it being a problem.'

'Mmm.' The sound James made was a little strangled. Because he was remembering that master bedroom in the house they were about to move into?

Remembering how he'd looked at that bed and imagined being in there with Sarah?

Remembering the look in Sarah's eyes when, for some reason, he'd felt compelled to turn his head and catch her gaze?

She was just as interested in it happening again as he was, wasn't she?

Whether or not it *should* happen again, however, was a very different matter.

CHAPTER TEN

IT FELT DIFFERENT.

It might only be for a limited period of time but they were about to deliberately start living together. Up until now, they had simply been thrown together by fate and had both been guests in someone else's house.

They had chosen this house. Together.

It almost felt like…they were a couple…?

As if they hadn't stepped out of the pretence they'd gone along with when Maureen, the estate agent, had made that assumption about them.

Except there was more to it than that.

This was also about what had happened the night before they had been shown around this house. The sex.

That closeness that had hung in the air between them ever since, even though the sex hadn't happened again.

Had that been because James had had two afternoon shifts in a row that hadn't finished until midnight and Sarah wasn't going to stay up and make it look like she was waiting for him to come home?

Waiting for it to happen again when he might be perfectly justified in assuming it was the kind of one-off casual encounter that he was used to in his playboy lifestyle? The lifestyle that Sarah had informed him, in no uncertain terms during that first meeting, that she disapproved of so much? Okay…maybe he *had* been thinking about it when he'd given her that look in the master bedroom of this new house they would be sharing, but that didn't mean he had any intention of repeating it. And Sarah wasn't about to risk a polite rejection—or, worse, humiliation—by being the first to suggest that they should.

Sarah wasn't even sure she wanted it to happen again. Why ruin a memory that she could appreciate for the rest of her life when a second time couldn't possibly be as good? Added to that was a nagging wariness that she couldn't afford to ignore. There was a risk in doing something that could undermine a relationship between herself and James that was only just forming but needed to be rock solid as soon as possible. Not for herself so much, but for Ivy.

Thankfully, it had been such a busy couple of days it was surprisingly easy to not think about it much, as Sarah tackled housework and shopping and laundry in any spare moments that Ivy wasn't needing her attention. She wanted Ella and Logan to come home to find everything sparkling, the pantry restocked and fresh linen on the beds.

There was far more to sort and pack than she'd stuffed into her car for the journey up here to find Ivy's father and it took two trips into the city after the boxes of extra clothing and personal items sent up from Leeds arrived. How on earth had they managed to collect so much baby paraphernalia in such a short space of time?

It was a continuing process as well, it seemed.

A delivery truck pulled up in front of the house as she

walked outside to put the last flattened box into the re-
cycle bin after Ivy had gone down for her first afternoon
nap in her new bedroom. When she turned back, she saw
a top-of-the-range pram that must have cost a small for-
tune being wheeled towards her.

James appeared in the doorway and reached to sign for
the delivery. 'I went shopping yesterday morning before
work,' he explained. 'I thought it would be useful for all
the walking that Maureen was talking about. In the park
and along the river.'

Sarah discovered another item inside the pram when
she parked it in the hallway under the coat rack that had
James's leather bike jacket hanging from one of the hooks.

'It's called a baby bubble.' James held up the small,
caterpillar-shaped padded sleeping bag with a hood. 'It's
wind and rain proof. Because…you know…this is Scotland…'

The baby bubble had faux fur edging on the hood
and fluffy ears on the top and it was so cute that Sarah
felt strangely close to tears. She blinked hard but one of
them escaped.

'Hey…what's up?' James dropped the baby bubble
back into the pram and stepped close enough to catch
that tear with his thumb. 'You don't like the baby bubble?'

'I love it,' Sarah said. 'And… I love that you chose
this for Ivy.'

'She's my daughter.' The statement was matter-of-fact.
'I'll always do whatever I can to support her. And you…'
James was still touching Sarah's face. 'If it wasn't for
you, I wouldn't have known Ivy existed. And don't forget that I need you…'

He was talking about needing her to stay here to give

him time to get used to having fatherhood thrown at him from nowhere. About Sarah being prepared to care for Ivy so that he could keep working while he was coming to terms with this huge change in his life.

But…it felt as if he could be saying that he needed Sarah in a very different way…

And maybe he was? His fingers were threading themselves through her hair. Moving to cup her head the way they had the first time he had kissed her? She could feel a tension that was almost reluctance, though.

'We shouldn't be making this any more complicated than it already is,' James said quietly.

Sarah was losing her own battle to keep her eyes open and not let herself sink into this cloud of desire. She was trying to think of what Karly would say, which wasn't easy when something deep inside her body was melting and in this moment she wanted this man's touch more than anything on earth.

'It doesn't have to be complicated,' she whispered. 'It's just…'

The word for exactly what it was escaped her. She couldn't say it was just sex. Because this was James and he was Ivy's father and he had earned her respect despite anything she'd judged him on before she'd met him and… and she liked him. A lot.

James was staring at her and…she couldn't look away.

'Nice…' she finally said—in the heartbeat before James kissed her.

'Aye…nice,' he echoed when the kiss was finally broken. 'But…'

Again, Sarah could sense what wasn't being said. Was he thinking about a worst-case scenario with her falling madly in love with him and expecting something he would never be able to give her and it would end like an acrimonious divorce—complete with a child custody battle?

That his wings would be clipped even more than the weight of the responsibilities he felt to both Ivy and his brother Mick had already achieved? What was the other part of that vow he'd made with his brothers about never getting trapped in something as confining as a marriage? Ah, yes…

'This is just about where we are right now,' she reminded him. 'About living life. It won't change anything. Ivy comes first, for both of us. She always will. I promise…'

He knew she'd made a promise to Karly that she would never break. And one to Ivy that was going to last a lifetime. Sarah knew that he would trust this promise being made to him now. And why wouldn't he? She believed it herself.

She could feel that trust as he kissed her again. As the heat got dialled up to a cell-scorching level.

This time, if Ivy's nap continued for just a little bit longer, there would be no turning back, for either of them.

'Nice' wasn't exactly the word James would have chosen to describe the intoxicating delights of snatching some very intimate time with Sarah, along with the solid friendship they seemed to be building, but it was definitely a good word for some of the changes he was currently getting used to.

It was nice to feel more in control of his own life, having signed the lease on this house with an option to renew in six months' time if he still had a job in Aberdeen and the owner of the house didn't decide to put it on the market.

It was nice to be living close to Eddie and Jodie and for it to be so easy to get to and from work. He could walk there and save parking hassles when he got around to selling his motorbike and purchasing a far more baby-friendly vehicle.

And this garden might not be as spectacular as the flowing lawns and duck pond at the barn conversion but it was still very…nice.

The swing wasn't the only bonus out here. There was a barbecue and pizza oven built out of bricks just outside the French doors that opened out from the kitchen. It made the whole ground floor, from the living room on the street side to the end of the private garden at the rear, an ideal entertainment area.

With a bit of furniture rearrangement and a portable, folding metal ramp that took care of the steps to the front door, it was also suitable for someone in a wheelchair to visit and the whole Grisham family had gathered to celebrate the end of Ella and Logan's very belated honeymoon, Mick's homecoming, Eddie and Jodie moving in together and, most of all, to introduce Ivy to the other half of her father's family.

Eddie was in charge of steaks and sausages on the barbecue. James was about to start reheating pizzas in the wood-fired oven. Ella had finally given up cuddling the niece she had instantly fallen in love with to allow Uncle Mick to have a turn holding Ivy and Jodie and Sarah were clearly enjoying talking to each other. Logan was making it his mission to keep glasses topped up and look after the background music selection. There was laughter along with the music, the smell of good food and the warmth of being amongst family and it felt so *nice* that it was bringing a bit of a lump to James's throat, to be honest.

Because there had been so little to celebrate in what had brought the Grisham siblings together in recent times that James had felt more than a bit broken himself. It had been almost as bad as that dreadful period when they'd lost their mother to cancer when the triplets had only been teenagers. The worst time had been that awful period in Mick's early rehabilitation after his serious spinal injury when he'd become so depressed he'd completely stopped eating and was avoiding talking to anyone by pretending to be asleep when they visited.

Ella and Eddie—who'd already changed his entire life to move back to Scotland to support his brother—had thrown themselves into working with the rehabilitation centre's psychologists and therapists to support Mick and James had travelled up and down from Edinburgh too many times to count to spend as much time with his brother as he could. It was Ella and Logan who had dis-covered the rehabilitation centre in New Zealand that was gaining worldwide recognition in their successful treat-ment of spinal patients and they had hatched the plan of taking a belated honeymoon so that they could take Mick to spend some time at the centre.

It had clearly been the best idea they could have come up with.

Being needed for housesitting for Ella and Logan had brought James back into the heart of his family. And Mick was looking so much happier. Healthier. He sounded so positive as he talked about plans for his immediate future.

'I'm going to start driving lessons and I'll order an adapted car as soon as I get the hang of the hand controls for braking and accelerating. I can already transfer myself in and out of a car to my chair.'

The surprise Mick had been saving to show them was the movement he now had in his feet.

'I'm getting sensation back in my legs too. They're warning me that it might not be enough to get me walking again, but they have no idea how hard I'm going to work on it. One day—soon, I hope—I intend to walk back into that centre in New Zealand and show Riley just how far I've come. And how proud she can be of the job *she* does.'

James and Eddie had shared a glance. Not that they were counting, but it did seem like Riley's name was being dropped into the conversation at very frequent intervals.

'I'm going to start looking for a place of my own too. It's time I got out of rehab. And I'm taking up swimming. It was Riley that got me started. She even got me out in the ocean before I left. How awesome is that? I never thought I'd feel waves on my skin again.'

James swallowed the lump in his throat that had grown to the point of being painful. 'How 'bout handing my daughter back to her mum so she can put her down to sleep? Dinner's ready...'

Her mum...

It sounded as if James really thought of her as Ivy's mother, which made the bond between them as her parents seem more real, somehow. Deeper.

It made Sarah a part of this amazing family as well.

She'd already met Eddie and Jodie and knew that a true friendship with them both was going to be easy, but the triplets' big sister Ella was irresistible.

'I adore babies,' she'd told Sarah. 'I'm going to be the perfect auntie for this precious wee dot. You just tell me whatever I can do to help…' She pressed a hand to her heart. 'That *hair*… It brings back so many memories.'

'I've seen the photo of the triplets when they were babies. I've heard the story about the haircutting incident too.'

'Oh, there are plenty more stories, believe me…' Ella was laughing. 'I thought I would be put off having a baby of my own for ever after helping raise the "Fearsome Threesome", but after a cuddle with wee Ivy…' She looked up, her gaze going straight to her husband, whose head turned as if he had felt a touch. 'You never know, do you? Even at my age…'

Mick was reluctant to give Ivy back to Sarah.

'I think she likes me,' he said with a grin. 'And I think I like being an uncle. I've never been one before. I need to practise.'

Oh, these Grisham brothers certainly knew how to charm women. Even the tiniest of them had succumbed, judging by that half smile on Ivy's face as she trustingly drifted towards sleep.

'You're not hungry?'

'It'll take James and Eddie a while to get that food on the table. Look—they're arguing about how well those sausages are cooked now.'

Sure enough, Sarah could see James shaking his head sadly as he pointed to a sausage, but both he and Eddie were laughing and even Mick, too far away to be a part of whatever the joke was, was chuckling.

It was strange to be in a room with all the triplets. The three brothers weren't identical but they were similar enough in their looks to all be extremely attractive men with their height and build and that matching dark hair and eyes. There was an edge to Mick that suggested he might well have been the ringleader in their mischief as children and Sarah suspected James was correct in his memory that it had been Mick who'd stolen the nail scissors and initiated that famous haircutting incident.

Ivy stirred and made a sound. It looked as though she was trying to find a more comfortable position in Mick's arms.

'I should put her into her bassinet for a nap,' Sarah said. 'Otherwise, she could get grumpy and you might get put off being an uncle.'

'Swap you for my phone then,' Mick said. 'I left it on the table over there.'

When Sarah handed Mick his phone she must have touched a side button enough for the screen to light up and reveal the image that had been saved as the locked screen wallpaper. Mick must have taken it as a selfie, but he wasn't alone. A woman with bouncy blonde hair and the happiest smile ever was tilting her head far enough sideways to touch his and be in the centre of the photo.

Sarah caught her bottom lip between her teeth. 'Is that Riley?'

He didn't need to respond. She could see it in his eyes—along with so much more—as she handed him the phone and lifted Ivy from the crook of his elbow. She could sense just how much Mick was in love with this woman who was now on the other side of the world to where he was. Instinct also told Sarah that she could well be the only other person who knew and that Mick would prefer it to stay a secret between them. Was that because of that vow the brothers had made years ago— on his behalf, in fact—to not risk the kind of heartbreak Mick had already experienced when he got jilted?

But her heart still ached for Mick as she carried Ivy upstairs, because it was quite possible that his feelings had been secret all along and he hadn't been able to get anywhere near as close to Riley as he'd wanted to be. How easy would it be to fall in love with someone who had been supporting him and encouraging him to believe in himself as he battled such a huge physical challenge? But how impossible would it have been for Riley to allow anything too personal to develop between herself and her patient? It must have felt like a hopeless crush as far as Mick was concerned.

When she came back downstairs, James and Eddie had sorted the meat and pizzas and the dining room table was covered with platters of hot food, fresh bread and salads. Mick was making a joke about the bonus of being in a wheelchair at a buffet because he didn't have to find anywhere to sit down and eat.

Sarah found herself quietly watching all the interactions within this family, with the buzz of animated conversation and plates of food being topped up and enjoyed. If Sarah's stumbling on the secret of what Mick might be feeling about Riley had made things more difficult for him, he wasn't showing it, but both Eddie and James were right beside him and they wanted to hear more about his stay in one of the most beautiful places in New Zealand. They also wanted to hear about all the places Ella and Logan had gone on their camper van tour. There was a lot of teasing and bursts of laughter and just the way everybody looked at each other or offered a touch or quick hug made the unbreakable bonds between these people very obvious, and it was particularly powerful between these triplet brothers.

There was so much love in this room.

This was Ivy's family. And Sarah was being welcomed as part of it.

As Ivy's mum.

This was so much bigger than the feeling of being a co-parent with James. Or the other half of a couple, even. This was the kind of love Sarah had dreamed of finding and it was filling her heart to the point it felt like she didn't have room to take a breath. Her gaze drifted to where James was deep in conversation with Mick and she could feel her whole body softening as she looked at him.

The feeling of that love was still there, but suddenly it had a much sharper focus. A spear of sensation that was threatening to crack her heart open.

Oh…dear *Lord*…

So much for pretending she could be like Karly and be able to have a casual sexual relationship with an impossibly gorgeous playboy and then walk away from it, unscathed, to carry on with her own life. She was in very real danger of falling in love with James Grisham, wasn't she?

She had broken her promise.

No… Sarah managed to drag her gaze away from James. What she had promised was that Ivy would always come first and nothing would be allowed to change that. She put her plate down on the table and headed towards the hallway and the stairs—as if she'd heard a whimper from Ivy's direction.

She could control this. Nip it in the bud before it went any further because she was only just aware of the possibility of falling. If Mick had been able to keep how he felt about Riley a secret when he had already fallen, she could do the same with James even more easily because it hadn't happened yet. She could step back from the brink. If he didn't know, nothing needed to change.

And Sarah didn't want anything to change.

Because she didn't want to lose this glimpse of a life that was everything she could have wished. This was the ultimate dream of family that she and Karly had both missed out on but had tried to create for each other. And this was about putting Ivy first.

The sudden overwhelmingly strong realisation that hit Sarah in that moment made her turn back to let her gaze sweep over the whole group of people that had gathered in this room this evening.

This was where Ivy belonged.

With her father and extended family, who already loved her.

There was no way Sarah could justify taking her back to Leeds.

But there was also no way she could stay unless she could keep how she felt about James a complete and utter secret.

And not go even a single step closer to that brink.

CHAPTER ELEVEN

A WEEK LATER and counting and Sarah was pretty sure she was winning.

She'd just needed to recognise what was needed for her own health and wellbeing and put plans of action and any necessary barriers into place.

Routines had been a part of Sarah's life for as long as she could remember, after all. Eating the right food at the right time. Checking her blood glucose levels and calculating the amount of insulin she needed to inject. Exercising regularly and keeping herself as healthy as possible. The predictability of her routines represented both an insurance policy and a safety net and allowed her to feel like she had control, despite the curve balls life had a habit of throwing.

Even the unexpected and rather large balls that had just come in Sarah's direction, of moving to a new house, realising that she might never return to the place she'd grown up in and—almost—falling in love with someone who had told her that he'd actually made a vow with his brothers that he would never marry. Or get 'caught' in a permanent relationship.

These last months—since Karly had confessed she was pregnant, in fact—had seen the biggest challenges Sarah had ever faced to hang onto her old routines when she had to build new ones around them. She'd come scarily close to failing, when she was struggling with the grief of Karly dying and that night she'd had the hypoglycaemic crisis in front of James. But, looking back, Sarah could already see that she had learned to adapt and there was a new confidence to be found in having coped with such major changes in her life. A confidence that she'd already been able to use to good effect on the day of that disaster scene response.

She had needed some more of that confidence since the move into this lovely old house in Ferryhill too. Or, rather, since she'd recognised the danger she was in, of getting her heart broken by letting herself fall in love with James Grisham. The change in lifestyle was not proving difficult at all. Right from that night when they'd hosted the family gathering, new routines were emerging and...

And Sarah was loving them.

Early mornings were almost the same, except that Ivy now had her own room between Sarah's and the master bedroom that she'd insisted James used because, after all, this was *his* house. The kitchen, which caught the earliest rays of sunlight, was the perfect place to sit and feed Ivy and Sarah could enjoy the peanut butter toast and a mug of tea that had been her favourite breakfast since she was twelve years old.

Later in the mornings, Sarah would put Ivy into the pram James had surprised her with the day they'd moved in and she would walk—through the park and along the river, sometimes taking a sandwich and some fruit to sit and have a picnic lunch somewhere. The local shops were within easy walking distance to get fresh vegetables and other ingredients for dinner and she'd seen notices on a community board advertising local playgroups and events.

The lifestyle was almost as much of a fantasy as real life could deliver, in fact. Sarah was living in what could be a perfect place to bring up a child. In a perfect house. And the element that was straight out of a fantasy she had never even considered playing with, living with a man who seemed only too happy to make her nights as perfect as everything else.

And, yes, of course she knew life wasn't going to last quite like this for ever but, because she knew that, it was okay to make the most of it while it did last, wasn't it? Because it was making it so much easier to make the big decisions about what came next.

The thought that she couldn't take Ivy too far away from her biological family had not changed. If anything, it had embedded itself firmly enough for her to broach the subject with James during dinner one night when they were well and truly settled in to the new house.

'Is there any chance of your locum position here becoming permanent?'

James gave her a startled glance. 'Were you talking to someone when you came in to visit Mika today? Someone like Cameron?'

'I did see Cameron in ICU but we weren't talking about you. Why? Has he said something?'

James shook his head. 'Maybe you're telepathic. He asked me the same question this morning. Said it seems likely that the person I'm covering isn't coming back.' He raised an eyebrow. 'What *were* you talking about?'

'Mika. He'd come up to see how she was doing after her latest surgery yesterday.'

They had both been closely following the progress of the outdoor education student they'd been so involved in rescuing on the day of the viewing platform collapse and the mention of Mika's name had distracted James from the question she'd asked.

'How *is* she?'

'Amazingly positive, even though it's still not certain she's going to keep that leg.'

'I'm keeping my fingers crossed that she won't end up being a double amputee.'

'I think she'd still do well. She's a remarkable young woman,' Sarah said. 'She's got a long road ahead of her but she's got an amazing level of courage and determination and she's lucky enough to have a close family around her. Like Mick is to have all of you. He's doing astonishingly well, isn't he?'

'He sure is. I've never seen him quite this determined. But he's got a way to go yet.'

'That's why I asked about your job. You'd want to stay here if you could, wouldn't you? To support Mick?'

James put down his fork as if his appetite had just vanished. 'I'd want to be as close as possible,' he said quietly. 'Of course I would. But I don't want to be too far away from Ivy either. It's very important to me that I'm a meaningful part of her life.'

'I know...' Sarah took a deep breath. 'That's why I'm thinking that maybe I should move here. To Aberdeen. I don't want Ivy to miss out on having a family like yours around her. It's something I never had and I always knew there was something huge missing from my life.'

James was staring at her. 'You'd do that? What about your friends? And your job?'

'Didn't you tell me that Cameron said he'd be happy to talk to me about applying for a job at Queen's if I ever wanted one?'

'After that major incident? Aye…he did say that but… you'd be starting a whole new life here and…that's a big deal. Are you really considering it?'

Sarah could feel her lips curving a little. 'I started a whole new life the moment Ivy was born. No…it was more like the moment Karly told me she was pregnant. And it's not as if I'd be moving somewhere I didn't know anyone. I'm already making new friends. Jodie, for instance. And your sister, Ella.'

She could see that James was still trying to take in her suggestion. As if something about it was troubling him?

Oh…of course…

'I'd find my own place,' she assured him. 'I wouldn't expect to keep living with *you*.' Sarah's smile widened. She even gave a huff of laughter. 'It would cramp your style a bit, wouldn't it? You'd never be able to bring a date home.' She picked up her plate to carry to the kitchen bench because she'd lost her appetite as well. 'We both need our own lives,' she said as she stood up. 'But Ivy can grow up knowing how important she is to both of us. To all of us. I promised Karly I'd do everything I could to look after Ivy, and giving her a whole family to help protect and raise her is…' Sarah had to swallow hard. 'It's so much more than I could ever give her by myself so it's a no-brainer. It's the right thing to do.'

James was standing up as well. He looked as if he might have a bit of a lump in his own throat. He didn't say anything but he didn't need to. Because he came and took the plate out of Sarah's hands and put it down on the table again. And then he wrapped his arms around her and hugged her.

So tightly it was hard to breathe, but Sarah didn't mind.

Because this was telling her how much of a gift this would be for James, as well as his beloved family.

And…it felt like love…

It had just been a throwaway sort of comment about needing to find her own place so that she didn't cramp James's style.

A joke, even?

But it came back to bite Sarah. Hard.

While the kitchen end of the house caught the first rays of sun, it was the living room that got any late afternoon warmth and it was particularly welcome after a day of caring for a baby who seemed a little off-colour. Ivy hadn't settled for her usual sleep periods, which was unlike her enough to have already increased Sarah's anxiety levels.

'What's the matter, Button?' The bottle of milk was less than half empty but Ivy had lost interest and looked like she might fall asleep at any moment. 'Are you just tired because you haven't had a proper nap yet today?' She dropped a kiss onto the soft spikes of Ivy's hair. 'Let's put you to bed and see if that helps.'

Ivy seemed happy enough to be put into her bassinet and Sarah came back downstairs, turning to glance out of the bay window at the front of the house as she went into the living room on her way to the kitchen. It had become a habit to enjoy a glimpse of the bricked path to the gate and the street beyond with its lovely leafy trees.

She noticed she had left Ivy's cute fluffy lamb lovey on the window seat so she picked it up along with the half empty bottle of milk, looking out of the window again as she straightened. Sometimes she stood here with Ivy in her arms, watching for James to arrive home on his motorbike. Stealing a moment to watch him take off his helmet and unfasten the leather jacket that he would hang on the coat rack as he came through the front door. Letting delicious tendrils of a physical attraction, that was showing no signs of wearing off, weave their way through her entire body.

She hadn't expected him to arrive home this early today, however. And, even more strangely, to be in a taxi that was pulling to a stop right in front of the gate? With remarkable clarity, Sarah found herself stepping back in time to when she'd first laid eyes on James Grisham as he'd stepped out of a taxi. But he didn't walk straight towards her this time. He didn't even know she was watching and she knew he wasn't even thinking about her. He was turning back to the taxi, clearly waiting for someone else to emerge.

Sarah couldn't help remembering who else had been in that taxi that night now. Janine—with her long blonde hair—hanging on his arm. Calling him 'Jimmy'. Pouting with disappointment because she wasn't going to be invited to go inside his sister's house.

Was she in *this* taxi?

About to be invited into *this* house?

It was a woman getting out. And she was blonde, but Sarah knew instantly that it wasn't Janine. It wasn't someone that James was dating either. To her amazement, Sarah recognised Riley—the gorgeous physiotherapist whose photo she'd seen on Mick's phone.

It should have been a relief.

A joyous moment, even, because the only reason that Riley might have to turn up in Aberdeen would be to see Mick, and surely she wouldn't have travelled right across the globe to do that unless she was missing him?

As much as he was missing her?

James was smiling as if he knew he was helping to deliver a fairy tale ending for his brother, but all Sarah could think of was how she'd felt when she'd expected to see Janine getting out of that taxi.

As if the bottom of her world was about to fall out.

As if her heart was about to break into a million pieces.

Had she really believed she had halted the process of falling in love with James Grisham? That she could even joke about him dating women in the future and be okay about it?

She couldn't have been more wrong.

About everything.

Well, not about the dating. Of course he would go back to a lifestyle that was a big part of who he was. He had a vow to keep, didn't he? To live life to the full. To never get 'caught'. Seeing him with other women was going to be a part of her future if she was a part of his life. Possibly a never-ending stream of women and his intimate time with her would be nothing more than a pleasant, but distant, memory. Or perhaps he might even include her occasionally on a strictly 'friends with benefits' kind of arrangement?

She couldn't do that.

Because what she *had* been wrong about was thinking she had only been in danger of falling in love with James. It had already happened by the time the thought had even occurred to her, hadn't it? Maybe the crash landing had been disguised by the emotional overload of working with him during that rescue mission. Or buried under the astonishing revelation of how amazing it had been to go to bed with him. To have him make love to her…

Oh, help…

If she couldn't live with James being a significant part of her life but she also couldn't live with taking Ivy away from her real family, what was left?

Going back to Leeds alone…?

No…

That was unthinkable.

Sarah turned away from the window before Riley came through the gate and James followed with the large suitcase he had pulled out of the taxi. She rather wished she hadn't put Ivy to bed because she could really do with a cuddle right now.

She was in trouble. Part of her was desperately trying to wrap something tightly enough around her heart to stop it breaking apart.

Pressing the lamb lovey over the top of her heart felt like it was helping to hold it together just a little. Sarah could even catch a waft of that gorgeous smell of baby. But it still felt like she was in trouble.

Big trouble…

CHAPTER TWELVE

'THIS IS RILEY, SARAH.' James put the suitcase down beside Ivy's pram. 'She was Mick's physio in New Zealand. I'm sure you've heard him talking about her. Riley, this is Sarah. Ivy's mum.'

'I recognise you from your photo on Mick's phone,' Sarah said. 'I'm so happy to meet you, Riley.'

Sarah was smiling but James could feel that something wasn't quite right.

'Sorry not to give you any warning,' he apologised. 'But it's been a bit full-on. I had no idea myself that Riley was coming here.'

'I'd only been talking to Ella,' Riley admitted, 'because I'd met her and Logan in New Zealand. I needed to try and find out how Mick might feel if I turned up.'

'I could have told you.' Sarah's smile still looked oddly forced. 'He's going to be *so* happy.'

Riley was smiling back. 'That's what Ella thought but…oh… I was so nervous about taking a risk this big. And then I thought…what the heck? It might end up being a disaster or I might end up with the love of my life but, either way, I had to come.' Her smile turned into a grimace, though. 'And then Ella wasn't there to meet me at the airport and, next thing I know, I hear my name being called—asking me to go urgently to the information desk.'

'Ella had a bit of a vagal turn and fainted,' James put in. 'She was being looked after by the airport medic. She was okay but she very sensibly got Riley to drive her back and called Logan, who insisted that she came into the ED to get checked.'

Sarah was looking quite pale herself now. 'Oh, my God... Is she okay?'

James nodded. 'Better than okay, if you ask me. Turns out she got pregnant while she was on her honeymoon and hadn't realised, what with everything else going on.' He grinned at Sarah. 'Piglet's going to get a wee cousin,' he said. 'How cool is that? Logan's still with her and they're getting an ultrasound. He said they'd call in on their way home and let us know the results.'

'I'd better put the kettle on.'

'Eddie and Jodie have gone to pick up Mick and bring him here as well.'

James was watching Sarah's face carefully and her expression reminded him of the first time he'd ever seen her, standing in the headlights of that taxi. Frozen.

Frightened...?

Lost...?

He needed to touch her. To try and let her know that she had nothing to worry about. Not if he was by her side.

'Sorry...' James stepped close enough to Sarah for their arms to touch. 'It comes with triplet territory. You know— If something happens to one of us, it kind of happens to all of us—good or bad. With Riley here and Ella's news, this is definitely one of the good life-changing days that need celebrating.'

'It is…' Was it his imagination or was Sarah shrinking away from his touch? 'It's not a problem. It's what families do. It's a good thing…'

She was avoiding eye contact with him. Moving so that there was a physical space between them as well. For some reason, Riley's arrival seemed to have rattled Sarah, and James had no idea why. Or perhaps it was the idea of his whole family arriving en masse, without any of the planning that had gone into the last family party? She'd been rather quiet later on during that evening, come to think of it, although nobody else would have noticed. But then, nobody knew Sarah as well as James did…

He knew that something had changed.

Something big.

He just didn't know what until about an hour later, when the whole clan had gathered. Ella and Logan had arrived first, radiating the joy of their news, and they'd hatched a plan for Riley to be sitting on the window seat in the living area and Eddie and Jodie would bring Mick in and then keep walking to the other end of the house and out into the garden to where the rest of the family would be, so that Mick and Riley's reunion would be as private as possible.

James texted the plan to Eddie. 'Let's hope Ivy doesn't wake up and spoil the moment.'

'I think she'll be sleeping for a while,' Sarah said. 'She's been a bit unsettled today.'

Ivy did stay asleep. Eddie and Jodie played their part of the plan and when, some time later, Mick wheeled himself into the kitchen with Riley on his lap, her arms around his neck and tears of happiness streaking her cheeks, it was very obvious that this was a happy ending happening right in front of them. The way they were looking at each other had the kind of emotional kick that was there in every glance between Ella and Logan, especially after the surprise they'd had today. Between Eddie and Jodie as well, now that he was so aware of it.

It was the look of love.

The kind of passionate love that James would never experience for himself but was all he wanted for the people he already loved so much so it was kind of contagious. His smile felt misty and he wanted to share his own happiness so he sought out Sarah's gaze.

And then it hit him, like a ton of bricks.

Because Sarah was looking at him the way all his siblings were looking at their partners.

With that level of love that went so far beyond friendship it... Well, it felt as if the axis of James's world was suddenly tilted. It was blindsiding because this wasn't supposed to have happened. Sarah had promised that getting as close as they had wasn't going to change anything. That it wouldn't be a problem to give in to their attraction to each other because it wasn't a big deal. She knew he didn't do significant relationships. She knew it was only temporary.

But it had clearly already gone on too long and it had to stop before it went any further.

Before Sarah got badly hurt.

Or Ivy...

It was hard, being in this group of people who were all *so* happy.

But it was even worse when they all left far too soon because they all wanted to be alone with each other.

That left Sarah alone with James as the door closed after Eddie and Jodie had driven away, after juggling a suitcase and wheelchair into their vehicle, to take Riley back to Mick's unit.

And a silence that was deep enough to drown in suddenly filled the space between them in the hallway.

Somehow, James knew that this pretence of playing happy families themselves was over just as much as Sarah did, didn't he?

All it needed was for someone to say something and Sarah found she was brave enough to be the one to do that.

For Ivy's sake.

'I can't live here with you any longer, James,' she said, very quietly.

'I know.'

There was a catch in James's voice that told Sarah he knew why she couldn't stay, and that was…heartbreaking, because he wasn't going to try and stop her, was he? The longer they kept living in the same house, the more of a problem this was going to become and that wouldn't be fair on any of them. Including Ivy.

Especially Ivy…

'Where will you go?'

'I don't know.' Sarah couldn't meet his gaze.

'You don't need to go anywhere just yet,' James said. 'Eddie hasn't found anyone to take over his old apartment. I could stay there and give you a bit of time to look for something?'

'I should probably go back to Leeds.' Sarah forced the words out. 'There are things that need sorting there so that I can make new decisions. Like my flat.'

And her job.

And the rest of her life?

James was nodding but he didn't say anything for a long moment. A moment that was long enough for them both to feel that silence again. For them both to feel the horror of the sound that suddenly came from the top of the stairs. A cry like no other that Ivy had ever made in her life so far.

It was a scream of pain. So shrill and heartrending it cut through Sarah like a knife. She saw her own shock reflected in James's eyes for the split second before they both turned to get up the stairs as fast as humanly possible.

Ivy was still making that strange cry as they went into her bedroom.

'It's abdo pain.' James was standing back, as if he was in front of a tiny patient who'd been brought into his emergency department and was trying to gather all the information he could, as quickly as he could. 'Look at the way she's drawing her legs up like that. And she's very pale.'

Sarah couldn't stand back. She was reaching to pick Ivy up and comfort her. She held Ivy close, making soothing sounds and rocking her gently as if she might be able to suck some of that pain into her own body and make things better. And maybe it did, because the high-pitched crying stopped almost as suddenly as it had started.

James still sounded like a doctor. 'You said she was unsettled today?'

'She just wasn't herself. And she wasn't very hungry.' Sarah pressed her cheek against Ivy's. 'I don't think she's running a temperature. Is it colic?'

'I don't know,' James said. 'Can you put her down on the bed for a minute? I'd like to check her tummy. And her nappy.'

Ivy screamed again when she felt even gentle pressure on her abdomen. It was Sarah who discovered the blood in her nappy and it was then that she realised they had both stepped into a nightmare that wasn't going to end any time soon because it was just beginning. She wanted to grab Ivy into her arms again and start running. To find safety. Somewhere…somehow… Panic was clawing at her until she felt James touch her, his hand on her arm, his gaze waiting to meet hers.

'It's okay, Sarah,' he said softly. 'We've got this. We're going to take Ivy into the hospital.'

It wasn't simply so much easier to be able to pull the cloak of professionalism around him to deal with every parent's nightmare.

It was the only way James could deal with this without falling apart.

Sarah was absolutely focused on Ivy. Holding her whenever she was allowed to. Glued to the side of the bed, stroking the baby's head and talking to her at other times, like when they had to get a cannula in to get a blood sample and start giving Ivy some antibiotics. She stayed right where she was and wore a lead apron when X-rays had to be taken.

James focused just as intently on the medical side of what was happening and what was being done and said around him.

'Heart rate's one-sixty. She's got a respiratory rate of thirty-six.'

That was okay. Normal.

'White cell count and CRP are normal. No signs of sepsis.'

'Lung fields are clear on X-ray, but look at this abdominal view... Looks like a soft tissue mass in the right iliac fossa...'

That wasn't okay. But James had suspected it would be the case.

'Let's get an ultrasound and get a paediatric surgical consult down here. Call Radiology too. It's looking far more like an intussusception than gastro or sepsis.'

The ultrasound confirmed a diagnosis of an obstruction caused by one part of Ivy's bowel telescoping in on itself.

'We'll make up to three attempts of three minutes each to reduce the intussusception by air pressure under fluoroscopy,' the radiologist told James and Sarah. 'I should warn you that, in perhaps one in a hundred children, this procedure could cause or reveal a perforation that might get rapidly larger and, in that case, she'll need surgery to repair the hole. I'll get the consent forms for you to sign.'

Sarah was holding Ivy, who was, thankfully, now asleep thanks to the pain relief she had been given. Sarah was looking so pale James hoped she was keeping a very careful eye on her blood glucose levels but she didn't sound as if her level of alertness was diminished enough to be another symptom of hypoglycaemia. If anything, she was hyper-focused.

'Can I stay with her?' she asked quietly.

'I'll stay with her,' James said quickly, because he knew that Sarah's request would be denied but, as a medic here himself, he was confident his colleagues wouldn't prevent him being present. 'But you won't have to wait alone.' He tilted his head and Sarah turned swiftly to see Mick wheeling his chair towards where they were standing in the corridor. Eddie was walking beside him.

Sarah blinked. 'How did they know…?'

James shrugged. This sort of thing had happened more than once in their lifetimes. 'Eddie texted when Ivy was having the ultrasound to ask if everything was okay. I had to tell him what was going on.'

And now his brothers were here to support him and they could do that by supporting Sarah while she had to wait. He held out his arms but avoided meeting Sarah's gaze directly because he didn't want to see the fear he knew would be there.

'I'll take Ivy now,' he said.

The baby woke up as she was moved and began crying again but James didn't falter. He simply turned and walked away.

Sarah could still hear Ivy's cries even when she was well out of earshot, in a comfortable family room with Mick and Eddie.

She was way too close to crying herself. Maybe distraction would help?

'Has the jet lag hit Riley yet?'

'Sure has. I made her a cup of tea and by the time I took it to her she was out like a light on the couch. I just covered her up with a blanket when Eddie came to get me. Jodie said she'd stay there so we didn't have to wake her up.'

'I still don't get how you knew something was wrong.'

'It just happens,' Mick said. 'It's a multiple sibling thing, I think. Like twins often have.'

Sarah bit her lip. Distraction wasn't helping.

'It's going to be all right,' Eddie added. 'These guys do this kind of thing all the time and they're good. Jimmy won't let anything happen to Ivy.'

Those tears were closer as Sarah remembered the rigid lines of James's back as he'd walked away carrying Ivy.

'He just walked away,' she whispered. 'With Ivy in her arms. He didn't even look back.'

Eddie and Mick exchanged a glance. Eddie shook his head and Mick swivelled his wheelchair so that he was right beside where Sarah was perched on the edge of a small sofa. Close enough to put his hand on her arm.

'That's just James,' he said. 'Sometimes the way he copes is by putting up a wall and hiding behind it. It's not because of anything you did.'

But Sarah couldn't accept the comfort. James hadn't even looked at her when he'd taken Ivy from her arms. It was hard to breathe past the tightness in her chest and she could feel her eyes beginning to fill. 'I told him tonight that I couldn't live with him any longer,' she confessed. 'I think he already knew why.'

Eddie crouched in front of her. 'What are you talking about?' he asked. 'What did he know?'

'That I broke the rules…' There was no stopping the tears now. 'I fell in love with him.'

It was Mick who got the box of tissues from the table and handed handfuls to Sarah. It was Eddie who rubbed her back.

'It's not that he doesn't care,' he said. 'It's probably because he cares too much.'

Sarah looked up. 'What do you mean?'

It was Mick who answered her. 'I don't know if he told you, but we lost our mum to cancer when we were still at high school. Ella was away at university by then and, while she came home as often as possible, she wasn't there all the time. Jimmy was the hardest hit of all of us and that was partly because he was always the sensitive one out of the three of us. He had to try and make us feel better. It didn't matter how bad he was feeling himself.'

Eddie was nodding. 'Losing Mum—and then Dad, not long after that—was devastating for him. That was when he started building that wall. And he used it a lot, especially when we started dating. He always made sure he didn't get in too deep. He had us. We had him. We didn't need anyone else.'

'Until we did,' Mick said ruefully. 'But then there was Juliana and I said I was never getting anywhere near getting married again.'

'And we all made that stupid pact.' Eddie shook his head. 'All I can say is that I couldn't be happier that I've broken it.'

'I reckon you all know I've broken it now too…' Mick was touching Sarah's arm again. 'And I think Jimmy knows what he's been lucky enough to find. It might just take him a bit of time to come out from behind that damn wall.'

'We've seen you together,' Eddie added. 'You and James and Ivy. You're already a family…'

Thank goodness his family was there to keep Sarah company.

James had felt that distance increasing with every step

he had taken away from Sarah with Ivy in his arms. He knew how hard the waiting would be for her when she had no idea what was actually happening or how long it might take.

But it wasn't easy being in this room either. Far from it.

He'd been allowed in because he was a part of the medical community in this hospital and this patient was his daughter, but maybe that would have been a good reason to have kept him out?

He knew too much, didn't he?

He was standing to one side of this room, trying to focus on what everybody could see on the fluoroscopy screens as the air pressure was gradually increased, but it was nothing more than a blur as his thoughts spiralled.

What if the radiologist's warning had been well founded and there *was* already a perforation in her bowel that had been missed? Or the pressure was enough to create one?

What if they rushed her into emergency surgery but it was already too late to stop the infection and it developed into peritonitis and then septic shock as her tiny body summoned an overwhelming immune system response to the infection?

What if her blood pressure dropped so low it could lead to a dramatic failure of vital organs like her lungs and kidneys and liver and it would be impossible to fight hard enough to save Ivy's life?

However tiny that risk was, it was enough for James to find himself confronting the unthinkable possibility that he could lose Ivy.

It was creating a pain that felt as if his heart was cracking wide open.

And James knew exactly what created that particular pain.

Love…

He loved Ivy. This wasn't just about parental responsibility or the connection of shared DNA or how proud he was of his daughter. It wasn't even anything to do with how adorable this particular baby was and how good it could make him feel to cuddle her or see her smile.

This was true love. As big as the love James had for the brothers who were such a part of who he was himself. For his adored big sister who'd been another mum. And, of course, for his beloved mother he still missed every day.

Those cracks in his heart were getting so wide he could fall into them. If he lost Ivy, he'd lose Sarah as well.

But he was going to lose her anyway, wasn't he?

'I can't live here with you any longer, James…'

And now he could see that look in her eyes. The look that told him how much she loved him. He wanted that love.

He needed it.

As much as he needed the oxygen he was pulling into his lungs through the mask he was wearing.

Because he felt the same way.

'James?' The radiologist sounded as if he was repeating his name. 'Can you see that? We just need to finish up but it's a total success, first go. We'll have to keep an eye on her overnight to make sure it doesn't revert but we're all done.'

No…

Ivy might be fine and would be ready to be taken to the

paediatric observation ward very soon, but they weren't all done. Not by a long shot.

'I'll be right back,' he said.

'Sarah? Can you come out here for a sec?'

'What is it, Mick?' Sarah got to her feet in a hurry.

'Maybe the vending machine down the hall isn't working.' Eddie followed Sarah out of the relatives' room.

But this had nothing to do with the vending machine Mick had gone to investigate. They could all see James walking towards them. Eddie and Mick shared a glance and then a smile and simply melted away into the background so Sarah was standing by herself as James got closer.

He wasn't avoiding her gaze this time. He was holding on to it. Or was it Sarah who was clinging to his?

'Is she…? Is Ivy…?'

'She's fine.'

Oh, *my*… Were those *tears* in his eyes? From relief? Had he been as scared as Sarah had been about losing Ivy?

Except… James was smiling at the same time. At her. And it looked exactly like that hug had felt that day. When she'd said she would stay in Aberdeen so that Ivy could be with her whole family. When he'd hugged her so tightly it had been too hard to breathe but it didn't matter.

Because it felt like love…

And James was holding out his hand to her.

'Come with me,' he said softly. 'Ivy needs her mum.' He took hold her of her hand and she could feel that love through his skin, rushing into her body to find her heart.

He gave it a little squeeze as if he wanted to emphasise his words.

'She loves you so much,' he added softly. 'And so do I.'

'I love you too.'

Nothing more needed to be said in this moment. There would be plenty of time to say it all later. To share how astonishing it was to have fallen in love with both a baby and her father. For now, Sarah just held the hand of this man she loved with all her heart and they walked away together.

To be with their daughter...

EPILOGUE

Four years later...

THEY STOOD, shoulder to shoulder, in matching tuxedos at the front of the church.

Three men.

Three brothers.

James, Edward and Michael Grisham.

There'd never been any doubt that they would be together in such a significant moment in all their lives when Mick was finally going to marry the love of his life in this beautiful old stone church on the outskirts of Aberdeen, Scotland.

The brothers were smiling at each other.

'Déjà vu,' James murmured. 'It's not the first time we all stood in front of an altar like this.'

Mick raised an eyebrow. 'It might not be the first, but it will definitely be the last. And if either of you had waited a bit longer I might have been out of that wheelchair in time to be standing for your weddings.'

'I couldn't wait,' James admitted. 'Not when I realised how wrong we'd all been about that stupid pact to stay single for ever.'

Nobody was going to bother mentioning that the pact

had been made in the wake of standing here with Mick like this that first time—when the bride had failed to arrive—but James made sure they weren't going to have time to even think about it.

'Plus,' he added swiftly, 'I didn't want Sarah to change her mind.'

'As if…' Mick scoffed. 'I hope you know how lucky you are, mate.'

'Oh, I do.' James nodded. He let his breath out in a contented sigh. 'I so do.'

His brothers might not agree, but he certainly did consider himself to be the luckiest man on earth. A husband, a father and a lover who also had his best friend to share the rest of his life with. Ivy had a little sister now called Holly—a name that had amused the rest of the family. Eddie had joked that they'd better not have another daughter or they'd be obliged to call her Mistletoe.

'Who would've thought you'd be the one to take the plunge first?' Eddie shook his head. 'It would have been polite to wait until after Jodie and I got round to it. I *was* the first one to break that pact, you know.'

'It's a long time ago,' James said calmly. 'Let it go.' He caught Mick's glance and held it for a heartbeat. 'I do agree that some things are worth waiting for, though.'

Riley had asked Mick to marry her within days of arriving in Aberdeen and he'd apparently said he never wanted to have a day apart from her for the rest of his life but he wouldn't marry until he could walk down the aisle with her afterwards.

And here he was…albeit with a brother standing very close on each side of him…but it was their emotional support Mick wanted today, not anything physical. With

Riley by his side for the long and hard journey, his recovery from his spinal injury had been inspirational.

The minister appeared and smiled at the Grisham brothers as she took her place. The music being played on the church organ changed to the traditional wedding march and all three brothers straightened and then turned as one, along with all the friends and family gathered, to watch the wedding party coming down the aisle.

Ella was the first, as the matron of honour. She had her gaze firmly on Mick and even from this distance James could see that she was about to lose the battle of keeping happy tears at bay.

The bridesmaids followed. Jodie was glowing in the late stages of her first pregnancy and she smiled at Mick, but then her gaze slid towards Eddie as she arrived to take her place at the front of the church. James could feel the love in the way Eddie was looking back at his wife.

And now Sarah was almost within touching distance.

Looking *so* beautiful in her lovely dress.

His wife.

His love.

Sarah wasn't looking back at him, however. She had turned to see why the three flower girls—four-year-old Ivy, Ella's daughter Maggie, who was her best friend in the world, and her two-year-old sister, Holly, were no longer right behind her.

The three little cousins, who were wearing pretty matching dresses, were carrying small baskets full of rose petals that they were supposed to be sprinkling in front of the bride. Holly, however, had decided to sit down with her basket and play with her petals. Maggie was pointing at her as she tried to alert the adults to the issue but Ivy, who tended to be a bit bossy, was already trying to pull Holly back to her feet.

Behind them, Riley was coming down the aisle on the arm of Ella's husband, Logan. She was looking absolutely stunning in her white gown, holding a simple bunch of white flowers and…she was laughing at the obstacle in her way.

A ripple of laughter from everyone echoed from the walls of this ancient church. Riley held out a hand and Holly decided to allow her aunt to help her scatter a handful of petals. Sarah caught James's glance and he could see relief in her smile.

And pride.

And so much joy…

The minister was smiling just as broadly as everyone else as the wedding party settled into position to begin the exchange of solemn vows.

'Dearly beloved…' she began.

Sarah had Holly in her arms now and Ivy pressed against her leg. James could feel the presence of his brothers and the rest of his family surrounding him and…

And life didn't get any better than this, did it?

Dearly beloved, indeed…

He caught Sarah's glance. He didn't make a sound. He didn't even move his lips but he could still send the most important message.

Love you…

And it came straight back.

Love you too…

* * * * *

COMING SOON!

We really hope you enjoyed reading this book.
If you're looking for more romance
be sure to head to the shops when
new books are available on

Thursday 25th
April

To see which titles are coming soon, please visit

millsandboon.co.uk/nextmonth

MILLS & BOON®

Coming next month

DATING HIS IRRESISTIBLE RIVAL
Juliette Hyland

The mood around the table was far too tight.

Leaning across, he made a silly face. 'I read one self-help book. It was all about keeping lists and staying organised. I mostly remember the raised lettering on the cover. It felt nice.' Knox shook his head, horror at the memory of trying to read it returning. It had been recommended by one of his teachers, a way to focus his tasks.

She'd meant well. One of the few adults in his young life who saw through the mad-at-the-world kid to the well of potential beneath it. *If* he turned in his assignments.

If it was surgery or medical knowledge, he kept everything locked in. If it was something else, there was a good chance that he'd forget. Thank goodness for auto bill pay and a monthly subscription for Post-it notes.

'I take it from the sour look on your face you were not a fan.' Miranda tapped his knee.

Knox looked down. Her fingers had already disappeared but part of him still felt her touch. 'I prefer fantasy. Wizards, dragons, magic.'

'Wizards and dragons?'

Her smile made his heart leap. 'Yep. The more fire magic the wizard uses, the better!' He made a few motions with his hands and she giggled.

He finished his coffee, hating the sign that their outing was nearing an end. 'I can't listen while running, though. For that, I have to have a beat. I tried listening to podcasts that I enjoy since there never seems to be enough time for all the ones I love, but I couldn't make myself actually run at a good clip.'

'Why do you have to run at a good clip?' Miranda raised her eyebrow as she used her straw to pull the last of the whipped topping from the bottom of the cup.

'I—' Knox sat there, trying to figure out the answer. 'I—'

'You already said that.' Miranda laid her hand on his knee and this time she didn't pull it away. 'Just something to think about.'

'Want to get dinner Sunday?' The question popped out, and he placed his hand over hers on his knee. He had no idea what this was, but he wanted to spend it with Miranda.

She looked at his hand then back at him. Her dark eyes holding his. 'Like a date?'

'Yeah. Exactly like a date.' He watched the wheels turn in her eyes. Saw the heat dance across her cheeks.

Say yes.

'All right.'

The urge to pump his fist was nearly overwhelming but he kept it in check. 'I'm looking forward to it.'

Continue reading
DATING HIS IRRESISTIBLE RIVAL
Juliette Hyland

Available next month
millsandboon.co.uk

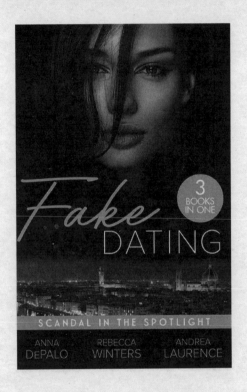

OUT NOW!

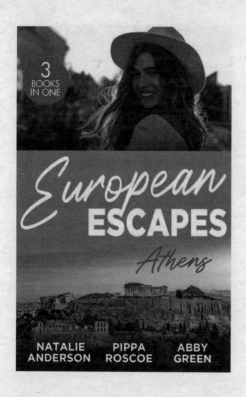

3 BOOKS IN ONE

European **ESCAPES** *Athens*

NATALIE ANDERSON   PIPPA ROSCOE   ABBY GREEN

Available at
millsandboon.co.uk

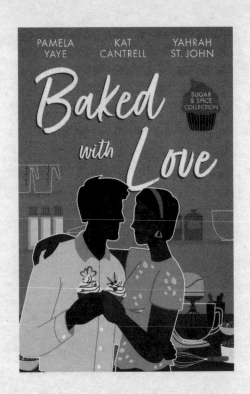

LET'S TALK

Romance

For exclusive extracts, competitions and special offers, find us online:

- **MillsandBoon**
- **@MillsandBoon**
- **@MillsandBoonUK**
- **@MillsandBoonUK**

Get in touch on 01413 063 232

GET YOUR ROMANCE FIX

Get the latest romance news, exclusive author interviews, story extracts and much more!

blog.millsandboon.co.uk